Royal Magpie's
OATH

V. L. LANIUS

ISBN: 979-8-9994572-0-2

Developmental Editor: Story Spellcraft
Copy Editor: Liv Betz
Cover, Interior, and Map Design: V.L. Lanius

Royal Magpie's
OATH

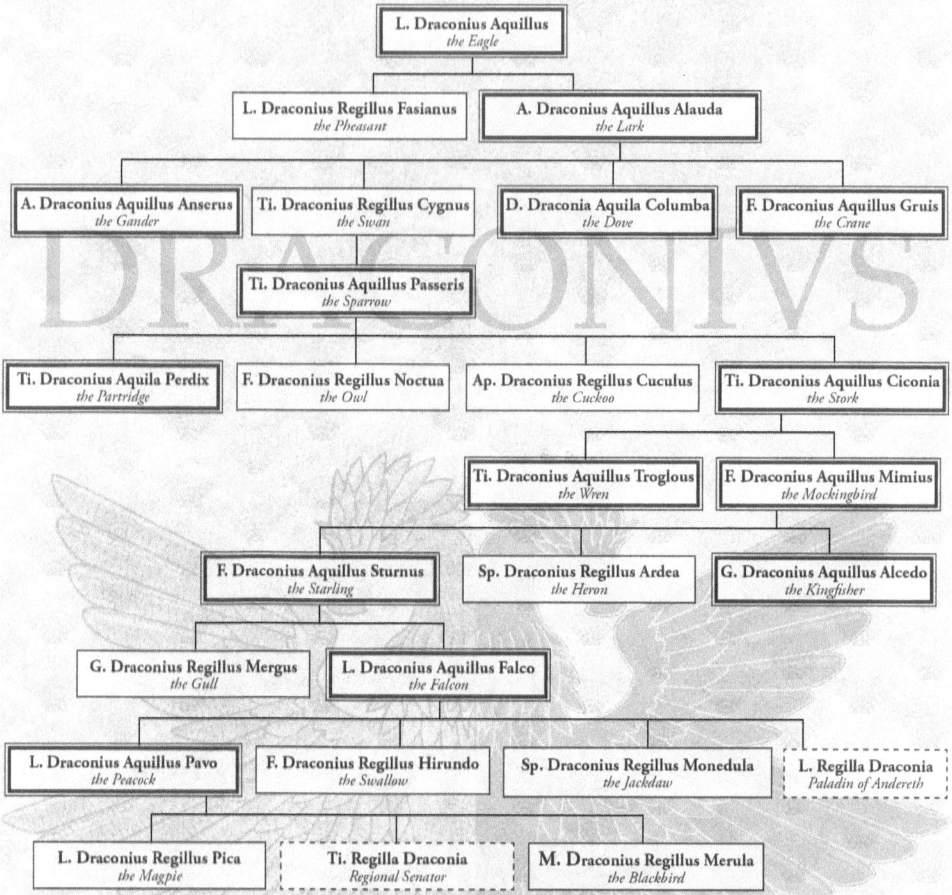
DRACONIVS
L. Draconius Aquillus
the Eagle
L. Draconius Regillus Fasianus
the Pheasant
A. Draconius Aquillus Alauda
the Lark
A. Draconius Aquillus Anserus
the Gander
Ti. Draconius Regillus Cygnus
the Swan
D. Draconia Aquila Columba
the Dove
F. Draconius Aquillus Gruis
the Crane
Ti. Draconius Aquillus Passeris
the Sparrow
Ti. Draconius Aquila Perdix
the Partridge
F. Draconius Regillus Noctua
the Owl
Ap. Draconius Regillus Cuculus
the Cuckoo
Ti. Draconius Aquillus Ciconia
the Stork
Ti. Draconius Aquillus Troglous
the Wren
F. Draconius Aquillus Mimius
the Mockingbird
F. Draconius Aquillus Sturnus
the Starling
Sp. Draconius Regillus Ardea
the Heron
G. Draconius Aquillus Alcedo
the Kingfisher
G. Draconius Regillus Mergus
the Gull
L. Draconius Aquillus Falco
the Falcon
L. Draconius Aquillus Pavo
the Peacock
F. Draconius Regillus Hirundo
the Swallow
Sp. Draconius Regillus Monedula
the Jackdaw
L. Regilla Draconia
Paladin of Andereth
L. Draconius Regillus Pica
the Magpie
Ti. Regilla Draconia
Regional Senator
M. Draconius Regillus Merula
the Blackbird

Aquillus - Emperor

To date, only one Empress has sat on the dragon throne. In this, she was allowed to adopt the royal cognomen and is represented the same as all other emperors.

Regillus - Notable Prince

The royal offspring, especially of branch families, are too numerous to name, therefore only the famous (and infamous) are listed here.

Regilla - Notable Princess

It is impossible to know the full roster of names for princesses born with the dragon's power. Lucia and Tiberia are easily accounted for, but starting with Aquillus Falco's numerous sisters, we cannot be certain of any specific individuals.

Personal Names

Noble Gethki families generally select personal, or first, names from a limited list. It is for this reason that you will find such names abbreviated.

Abr.	*Masculine*	*Feminine*
C.	Gaius	Gaia
L.	Lucius	Lucia
M.	Marcus	Marca
P.	Publius	Publia
Q.	Quintus	Quinta
T.	Titus	Tita
Ti.	Tiberius	Tiberia
Sex.	Sextus	Sexta
A.	Aulus	Aula
D.	Decimus	Decima
Cn.	Gnaeus	Gnaea
Sp.	Spurius	Spuria
M'.	Manius	Mania
Ser.	Servius	Servia
Ap.	Appius	Appia
N.	Numerius	Numeria
F.	Faustus	Faustia
No.	Nonus	Nonia
Tu.	Tullus	Tullia
S.	Septimus	Septima

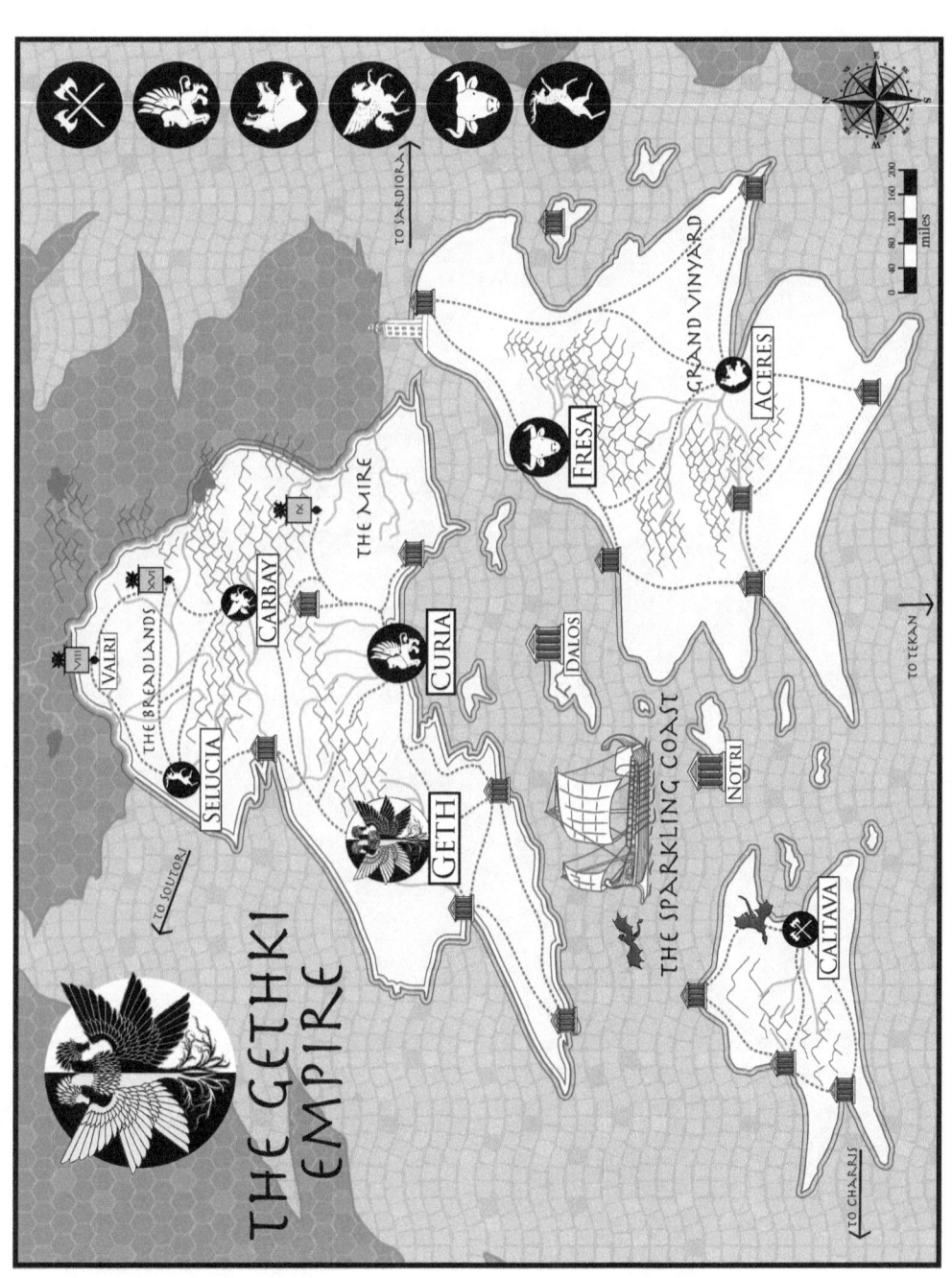

THE GETHKI EMPIRE

TO SARDIORA →

← TO SOUTOR

THE BREADLANDS

VALRI

SELUCIA

CARBAY

THE MIRE

CURIA

GETH

DALOS

NOTRI

THE SPARKLING COAST

CALTAVA

FRESA

GRAND VINYARD

ACERES

TO TEKAN →

← TO CHARIS

miles
0 40 80 120 160 200

PART ONE

POISON

PROLOGUE

A dragon lies dying on a sandy shore. Her sides heave as she struggles to breathe, and poison courses through her veins. She should not have fought that other dragon, but what choice did she have?

Her vision swims. The trees on the island are a brown and green blur, whipping in a cold breeze. Dead leaves swirl in front of her nose. Crows cry out overhead, black specks flitting across her fading vision. Her lips pull back from her teeth as she weakly defies them. She is not dead yet.

The cloud of them only thickens. Sharks thrash in the water behind her, drawn in by the blood spilling from the gashes marring her flanks. No, not sharks. Too big. She tries to focus on the sound. The rhythm. Oars? She tries to bellow, to call out to the sound, but it only escapes as a weak moan. A ship. Will they land for the night?

The splashing grows closer; a distant drumbeat audible now. It floats over the sound of the waves. She thrashes her tail and weakly moves her wings, trying to stand. No use—her strength is gone.

Oh, Aea.

Save me. I do not want to die.

I

CONNECTION

Paladin

Until the sun falls and the moon crumbles to dust, I will be vigilant.
Until the stars dim and my sword turns to rust, I will be strong.
Until the earth heaves and the seas rise, I will be a bulwark.
Until my last breath and death closes my eyes, I will be a protector.
While I live, I am Andereth's shield.
Oath of the Celestial Shield

Pica stands on the deck of *Raven's Flight,* squinting in the last rays of the setting sun. The sleek black trireme leaps through winter waves, sending cold spray into the rapidly cooling air. The steady splash of oars nearly drowns out the rowing song below deck. Pica mouths the bawdy lyrics and taps his foot to the pulsing drums beneath his feet. The tunes are just as vulgar as a legion's marching songs, a bittersweet familiarity. But his attention is elsewhere—on the overgrown island filling the horizon. Crows circle over the shoreline, their raspy calls haunting in the fading light. Pica recognizes their flight pattern—something is dying, or already dead, on the shore ahead. Judging from the number of them, it's big.

The ship crests a wave, then crashes down, sending a splash of salty water into his face. He flips his hair back and rubs his eyes, trying to brush away the burning elemental magic that accompanied the splash. He leans over the railing and peers at the water below the churning oars. The chop froths with metallic silver, catching the fading light and leading toward the shore. Not only big, but magical, too.

He sends magic out to the blood-streaked water. A coiling heat wells inside him, flushing his wind-chapped skin.

"Oh. No wonder I'm so cold," a voice says beside him.

He glances down at his Aunt Lucia, now standing at his elbow. Her black hair, shot through with gray, is tightly braided and gathered at the base of her neck. Calloused hands hold her cloak tightly around her as she stares at the island.

Lucia's eyes are a deep azure, like polished sapphires. The magic of their bloodline seethes deep within her irises, illuminating them with a soft inner light. A patch of dragon scales peeks from under her cloak, royal blue and gold. With each movement, they catch the evening sun.

Pica gestures at the bloody water. "Dragon."

She nods, lips pursed. "Big one, with that much blood. Think it's alive?"

"If it is, it won't be for long."

His magic writhes in his chest as he stares at the circling crows. They haven't descended yet. He still has time. The boards creak beneath him as he shifts from foot to foot, torn. The rational part of him says to leave it be. Dragons can be dangerous.

His body and magic are so much louder. Here's a chance for action, to feel a thrill in his chest again. The urge is overpowering, overwhelming.

Lucia turns to face him. "Don't tell me you're going to—"

He spins on his heel and runs the ship's length toward the stern, shedding his cloak. As he approaches the railing, his feet pound out of sync with the drums below.

"Wait!"

Lucia's lighter steps ring behind him. He reaches the stern and dives overboard as the crewmen shout. The cold water is a shock, but he grits his teeth against it and surfaces, getting his bearings. The metallic blood spreads out, solidifying and sinking in glittering drops.

Pica's skin flushes hotter where it contacts the bloody water. His bloodline magic—the coiling heat resting within him—always reacts to dragons, though the reason has never been clear. When the dragon is hostile, a keen rage consumes him. *This* blood elicits a comforting warmth, like a roaring campfire at the end of a cold march.

He swims as fast as he can toward the shore. The heat draws him forward, like a moth to flame. An enormous form looms on the shore, the unmistakable shape of a dragon, her sides heaving with labored breath.

The blood in the water grows thicker, coating the sand in a metallic slick. He stumbles out of the surf, his limbs moving him forward, ever forward, toward the source. The wind bites at him, but his skin burns with the intensity of his magic, sending steam rippling off his bare arms. Air fills his lungs, cold and wet. His heart thuds in his chest, sending his singing blood through his veins. He's sharp, like an unsheathed sword, sharper than he has been in months.

The last rays of the sunset reflect bronze from the dragon's metal scales. A Greater Dragon. Big one, too—at least 50 feet long.

The dragon lies on her side, her enormous wings limp on the sand. Her head, as long as Pica is tall, rests on the ground, eyes rolled back, and a swollen tongue protrudes between her teeth. Silver foam speckles her lips. Enormous clawed feet open and close spasmodically, gouging lines in the wet sand. Pica's stomach twists at the sight of her struggle. No one deserves such a death. And this time, he can do something about it.

Pica reaches the dragon and presses his hands to her chest. His power surges at the contact. The amulet on his chest burns hot as he pours healing magic into the dragon as fast as possible. He knits her skin together, closes the gashes, and then goes after the poison in her blood. The dragon groans and thrashes, nearly knocking him off his feet. Her head whips toward him and teeth snap closed inches from Pica's outstretched arms. His auric flames blaze to life as his heart rate surges and his vision goes white.

Golden fire, divine fire. Screaming, twisting forms crumble to black bones.

A familiar voice. Burn them, it says. Make an example.

Please no. Don't make me.

The dragon's scream of pain snaps him back. Bronze scales dribble away to reveal scorched metallic flesh. Bile burns his throat, and that familiar twisting of his stomach nearly doubles him over. It happened again. All he can do is destroy the things around him.

She snaps again. This time, he sidesteps. A low buzz fills the air as pale blue lightning flickers between her metal scales. The hair on Pica's arms stands on end.

She's just in pain. She doesn't mean to hurt him. So why does the need to fight sing in his veins? His temples pulse with the thundering of his heart.

Fight.

Save her.

You're nothing but a beast.

Her heart stutters.

"Shit!" he shouts. "No!"

He reaches deeper, trying to pull out every scrap of that raging inferno inside him, weaving it into his healing. He nearly passes out but redirects the energy into the dragon's blood.

Her heartbeat stutters again and stops.

He has to do *something*. He pulls his dagger and slashes first across his forearm, then the dragon's. Silver pours from the new wound. He lurches forward and jams the cut on his arm against the gash.

Oh. Gods.

Pain and pleasure consume him. With his last shred of focus, he finds the dragon's heart through the bloodline connection. Her heart thuds once, then nothing. He screams and hammers his fist against the dragon's chest in time with his own heartbeat, maintaining the magical onslaught. Her heart stutters to life and weakly pumps, mingling their blood further. Pica barely holds his concentration as the edges of his vision grow dark. With one more stutter, her heartbeat speeds, becoming rhythmic. His skin cools as his magic runs dry.

He slumps over the dragon's arm. Distantly, shapes move up the shore—too late. Time blurs. The stronger the dragon's heart beats, the weaker his becomes. Pica closes his eyes as his skin turns cold.

It's for the best.

His heart stops. A hand slams on his chest as his aunt screams his name.

He dreams of fire—a village burning with bright flames licking the sky. A roar, a crash, and the roof falls in. Mud beneath his hobnailed soles. The clank of steel and human forms, like metal wraiths through the smoke.

The village had a name. They all had names—the people being led away in chains, the bodies lying face down in the spring grass. Even the cattle his men now butcher had names.

A scream from behind a wall draws him through the charred remains of a gate. A legionnaire stands over a woman with a bloodied club. She pulls herself away, dragging her mangled legs, painting the ash crimson. The man grabs her arm, leaving a red smear on her pale skin. Pica's eyes narrow.

"Recruit," he snaps.

He doesn't raise his voice. He doesn't need to. The man flinches and releases her, standing quickly to attention.

"Regillus, sir, I—"

"Go."

The recruit cringes at the venom in his tone, salutes, and runs into the smoke. Pica crouches next to the woman.

"Don't touch me, dog," she hisses in accented Gethki.

Her blue eyes are like gemstones in her bruised face. She raises her chin in defiance, then blanches as her gaze meets his. A mix of awe and disgust colors her features as her eyes track to the scales on his neck.

"You're—!"

"Shhh," he says, struggling to keep his voice even. "You don't have long. Choose."

"Kill me."

"What is your name?"

She spits on his sandal. "Do it, Gethki scum."

The dream blurs. The fires die, and the legion marches—beef for dinner, wine for dessert. He cleans the blood from his sword. Another day, another village. Fresh cheese this time, and beer. The screams echo in his head. Twisted bodies, the sobs of the living. The stench of death mingles with the scent of fresh bread.

Pica jerks awake with a strangled cry. His stomach churns as he grabs for the pot next to his bed, retching and gagging. Nothing comes up but bile. The dried tears are replenished by fresh ones as he buries his face into his pillow, waiting for his heart to calm. Sweat soaks the bed, the blankets, his bare skin. He pushes the guilt back methodically, slowly counting to ten. To twenty. He recites the words of his oath, turning it into a chant, a prayer, drawing the curtain on his pain—closing it off until he dreams again.

The entire exercise has become depressingly routine.

The smell of campfires hits his nose first, then the low rumble of two hundred voices buzzing with evening merriment. He slowly sits up, rinses his mouth with water, then spits it into the pot. With a light tap on his magic, he casts a quick cleaning spell and returns the spotless vessel to its place. He'll need it again tomorrow.

An inquiring chirp makes him turn his head to the porthole. An avian shadow blocks the glow of campfires as a bird slightly smaller than a crow taps on the wooden slats.

"I'm up," Pica rasps. After a pause, he adds, "I'm fine."

The bird squawks, his voice equally raspy. He departs in a rush of wings.

Pica rises out of bed in the near-darkness of his cabin, stretching as best he can under the low ceiling. He lights the candles on the small table next to his bedside. The spell takes more effort than usual, and no wonder—he almost drained himself dry. If Lucia hadn't been there...

Black curls fall onto his face as he bends to pick up a crumpled tunic off the floor. He wrinkles his nose at the smell of stale seawater as he searches for the rest of his clothing. He rubs his face, pondering the stubble he finds there. Normally clean-shaven, he has at least a day's worth of growth. A bath, a shave, and a meal. How did the dragon fare? She was alive when he went under. Did they leave her on that beach?

Pica pulls a pair of knee-length breeches from his bag and a set of woolen socks. Some conservative Gethki senators would be appalled at the barbarism of such a choice, but Pica prefers that his legs be warm.

The door to his cabin opens, creaking on its hinges. His half-sister ducks through the doorway as she enters the room. Her curly white hair catches the candlelight, pulled back into a waist-length ponytail. His sister's head is framed with white frills and horns instead of ears, arching backward from her elegant face. Below the pale blue fabric of her short chiton, draconic feet covered with opalescent white scales step gingerly across the floorboards. She holds a tray in her hands. The smell of stew makes Pica's stomach growl.

On her shoulder sits a black-and-white bird with a long, tapered tail. Blue iridescence flashes on his wings as he bobs his head, chattering in a staccato *chak-chak-chak* call.

"Kisara, have I told you I love you lately?" he greets her.

The half-dragon's sky-blue eyes meet his own, her slit pupils dilating slightly in the dim light. They contrast her brown skin and glow with her magic.

"Krakli came to get me," she says. Her voice is soft and lilting, barely audible. "I figured you'd be hungry. Sit. Eat."

"Thanks," Pica says. He sits on the bed and takes the tray from her.

Alongside the stew is a chunk of brown bread, a small bowl of fermented cabbage, and a wooden goblet of *posca*. The scent of the sour wine reminds him of the better parts of military life—camaraderie, brotherhood—points of light in the grinding darkness of war. It's been two months since he left it, but his body and mind linger there like a ghost, ready for the action and danger he no longer faces.

Pica shovels the food into his mouth. Krakli—his magpie familiar —flies over and pecks at the food. Pica waves him off. "Hey, shoo. I know you already ate."

Kisara settles into the chair, resting her hands on her knees. Her tail drapes over the side of it, tip twitching. She watches him for a long moment, her face stoic—her usual expression.

"The dragon is alright," she says, finally. "I thought you'd want to know."

"Oh. That's good."

"Everyone's been worried sick about you," she continues. "Especially Lucia."

"I suppose I should go see her," he says, finishing his food. He drains his *posca*. "I imagine I'm going to be scolded again."

"*Scolded?* You almost *died.* You deserve whatever lecture she gives you."

He's almost died half a hundred times by now—the novelty of such a thing has worn off. Then again, nearly dying in front of his family was new. He can't fault them for being upset about it.

Kisara sighs and puts her hand on his shoulder. "Can I ask you a question?"

"Yeah, sure."

"Why did you do it?"

He shrugs, smiling at the half-dragon. "A more important question is, why wouldn't I?"

She snorts. "You never change."

Pica lays his hand over hers. "Serious answer, I don't know. I didn't think about it. It felt like something I had to do. Not a compulsion, but a strong impulse, a drive, I guess."

"None of the other paladins dove overboard to risk their lives for a dying dragon."

He stands, handing her the tray. "Look, I followed my heart and instincts, and both told me to save that dragon. It was the right thing to do."

Kisara rises, too. "Your cause is noble, sure. You choose the things you want to protect." She follows him into the hallway. "The rest of us do, too. One of them is you, idiot. Try not to forget that."

Lucia greets Pica with a slap to the face. "*Blood magic?* Are you *insane?* Where did you even learn such a thing?"

Pica flinches and rubs his cheek. Her slaps don't hurt anymore, but he finds it better to act like they do. "Auxiliary mage in the 8th saved a man that we thought too far gone," he explains. "I asked him to teach me."

Lucia glares at him. "And you thought it appropriate to use on a *dragon?*"

"It was the only thing that worked. I couldn't let her die."

"Idiot! Have you ever considered the consequences if *you* were to die?"

All the time. "I—"

"What would you have done if I hadn't saved you?" she continues, her voice rising in pitch. "Perished on the beach like the reckless child you are. Did you learn *nothing?*"

Pica rankles at the scolding but keeps it from his face. At twenty-five, he could hardly be considered a child, but he doesn't argue. His aunt steps closer. Despite the height difference, her presence is as imposing as when he was truly a child. He clenches his teeth over his pride, because she's right. Mostly.

"I don't regret saving her, but I'm sorry I was reckless in doing so." He flexes his fingers. "You saved my life, Lucia. Thank you."

Lucia watches him for a few more seconds before she sighs. "Don't do it again." She steps back and crosses her arms. "We've kept the dragon stable, but she requires further healing. You're going to do it."

"You brought her with us?"

"We couldn't leave her on the beach, could we?" His aunt turns, dismissing him. "She was on the deck last I saw. Go."

A few minutes later, Pica steps out into the evening air. The sunset shines off the polished black planks of the deck. Shimmering blue water stretches past the beach to the horizon, shining like thousands of diamonds in the sunlight. The Sparkling Coast, indeed.

The ship rests on shore, pulled in by its crew. *Raven's Flight* is sleek, built more like a chariot horse than a warhorse. The fact that she's a trireme intrigues him—generally, those are solely used for combat and military purposes. Pica wonders, not for the first time, where the Grandmaster hired it. The ship's captain, a burly, blond Caltavian named Ralex, was not forthcoming about her usual purpose. "Do not concern yourself with such things," the man boomed at him with a hearty slap on the back. "She is well suited for someone like you. You will find her most comfortable to travel in."

The ship *is* comfortable, the enchanted bath a seemingly impossible construction, and the private cabins a rare addition. *Raven's Flight* also has several cooks and stewards—employed, not enslaved, a fact that Pica made sure of before boarding. He can't abide slavers and their foul trade.

Banners flap from her main mast; the black ox's head of Fresa on a field of orange; the black crossed axes of Caltava on crimson; the azure and gold six-winged dragon of Geth.

Pica stares at the flags, so like the banners of a legion, yet so different. Two months ago, he was in the thick of an active campaign in the empire's northern territories. Now, he's in the south on a mission ordered by the Emperor himself. There's no war here—no violence, no daily drills, no tents, no long marches in the rain and snow. Pica would assume it was all a dream if his mind didn't return to the violence in his sleep.

Not that they don't have a goal—they do. Several ships have gone missing in the waters to the west, along the trade route with an island called Charris. None of the warships sent to investigate returned, so

Pica's paladin order, the Celestial Shield, was given the directive to investigate.

Pirates on the boundaries of the empire could be the cause. Generally, the Gethki patrol ships take care of such bandits. Perhaps it's a series of storms or a bad year for sea serpents. Any could be true, so they must investigate.

But why was *he* ordered to go? Not that he's complaining. He was ready to take any excuse to escape the living nightmare of war.

A squawk from the railing breaks Pica from his reverie. Krakli watches him with a tilted head. Through their mental bond, Pica senses the spirit's concern. "I'm fine," he lies.

Krakli chatters, turns, and flies away.

Right, he came out here for a reason. Pica scans the deck, confused. No dragon lies there. The expanse of wood is mostly empty, the crew gathered around their myriad of campfires for the evening. Then, it dawns on him. Dragons are shapechangers. He spots the portable hammock on the ship's bow and approaches it with a pounding heart.

She's asleep. He pauses a few feet away, studying her. Her human form is tall but slim, much too delicate for the enormous form he saw on the beach. Long bronze hair, tipped with turquoise and shimmering like metal, spills over the pillow and frames her narrow face. Her skin is nearly as dark as his, a rich brown too shiny to be entirely human. Gold and gems decorate her softly-tapered ears.

He wavers for a moment before kneeling next to the hammock. Her complexion is pallid beneath the shimmer of her skin, her eyes ringed with dark circles. Lucia was right—she needs more healing, sooner rather than later.

Pica places his palm on her forearm and focuses on his spell. The routine of training takes over as his heart rate slows and steadies. He works his way through the mechanics of it, sending his magic into her through their skin contact. Basic checks, then deeper. Though she's a dragon, her body feels human. Fascinating.

He's been near dragons before, albeit younger ones. He always reacted to them—it was almost a magnetic sensation, pulling his attention toward them and making it hard to focus on anything else.

Dragons aren't merely large, intelligent creatures but a force of elemental power, potent personality, and immense strength. This one has been considerably weakened, but being near her is like standing beside a white-hot forge.

Ten minutes later, Calvus approaches with a limp, leaning on his cane. The Grandmaster of their paladin order is well into his sixties, the lines in his dark brown skin etched over a lifetime of laughter and pain. The top of his head shines in the fading sunlight, shaved to the skin. His owlish brown eyes squint as he regards Pica and his patient.

The older man's frail appearance is an illusion. Publius Laberius Calvus is the deadliest, most experienced paladin he knows. While Pica has the advantage in size, strength, and raw magical power, he has never won a sparring match against the old Grandmaster. Aunt Lucia beats him every time, too.

"Good evening, Pica," Calvus greets him in a resonant voice. "You are attending to the dragon, good. How is her condition?"

Pica stands to meet him. The man barely reaches his chest. Pica bows at the waist. "Well met, Grandmaster Laberius. She is improving."

"Should the crown prince of Geth be bowing so formally to an old man?"

Pica snorts. "Right. Changing your tune now?" He clears his throat and places his hand on his chest. "'Even a highborn prince must show proper manners,'" he says, imitating his teacher's solemn tone. "Besides, this is Order business. You're the boss."

"Just so," Calvus sighs. "You get a break from your duties, while mine only increase." He glances past Pica at the dragon sleeping in the hammock. "Her color is much better. Your healing skills have significantly improved since you left us."

Pica frowns. "I've had too much practice."

Calvus regards him with a somber expression. "War grinds down even the greatest of men. Perhaps it is good we took you away from it."

"Will we ever truly be away from it, Grandmaster?" Pica stares at the curl of the bow. "Everywhere I go, there's only more violence, more pain and suffering. Death." He indicates the form in the hammock. "Even dragons can't escape it."

"Such a jaded worldview from one so young," Calvus says. "However, you're correct. We can be such beasts for such 'civilized' people."

"Beasts fight to survive. We fight to dominate and subjugate. It isn't the same."

Calvus sighs. "Just so." He glances at the dragon. "Perhaps it's best if we take her to your cabin. The night air will be upon us soon."

"*My* cabin?" he blurts, then ponders the idea. Out of their group of seven, he is the only one not sharing. They could put her in a tent, but that requires moving her at least twice daily. He's unsure how susceptible she is to cold, but it *is* winter. The enchanted cabins of the ship will provide a stable temperature. It makes sense. Too much sense. He'll give her the bed, and he can sleep on the floor. It wouldn't be the first time.

Pica lifts her out of the hammock and then follows Calvus down the ladder to the room he so recently recovered in himself. She is lighter than he expected, her thin frame resting easily in his arms. Her head lies against his chest as Calvus opens the door for him.

Pica stands in the small room, the last scraps of sunlight illuminating the far wall. The dragon's rhythmic breathing warms his skin through his tunic. Something within him pulses with that breath. He savors the warm heat gently radiating from her.

He ponders it briefly before setting her on the bed. The blankets and linens are fresh, turned down for the evening. He arranges them over her. Her eyes snap open, inches from his face. Lighting courses over her skin, sparks in her turquoise eyes. He reels back, raising his hands to show he has no weapons. The gesture is futile—he *is* the weapon. She snarls at him, pale human teeth bright in her bronze face.

"Sorry, sorry!" he says, retreating, putting his back against the cabin wall.

"Where have you taken me?" she demands. Her voice is low, threaded with a growl.

"You're in my cabin," he says. Quickly, he adds, "It's better for your healing than out in the cold, I mean." Her eyes narrow, and Pica mentally curses. "I'm not going to hurt you. Please don't...transform or anything. It'll be bad for the ship."

The lightning fizzles. Her eyes quickly dart around the cabin before settling on him again. He knows that look in her eyes. He's seen it countless times.

Even a dragon views him as a monster.

Slowly, he moves, keeping his back to the wall, then settles into the chair, wincing when it groans under his weight. She tracks his movement with the intensity of a cornered predator—wary, suspicious, ready to fight. Instinctively, he tries to make himself small and nonthreatening—another futility.

He drops his eyes from hers. She relaxes further, glancing around the cabin again. The sunlight shines on a discolored spot on her neck.

"What's your name?" he asks, keeping his voice calm.

Pica's fingers twitch. He suppresses the urge to get up and pace the small room. The anxiety returns, tightening around his guts like chains. The stench of melting metal and seared skin lingers in his nose. Even when saving someone, he can't help but hurt them.

Is that why she views him with suspicion?

"Levnys, of the Chauvnuth line," she replies. The way she speaks is archaic, though her Gethki is flawless, with the accent typical of the southern seas. Her eyes pass over him, lingering on his neck, then his face. "Scales. Golden eyes. You are a prince, as well as a paladin." After a pause she asks, "What is your name?"

"Lucius Draconius Regillus Pica, if we're being proper."

"Do you wish to be proper?"

"Gods no, call me Lucius."

The dragon's hostile mask slips for the first time. "A prince wishing to be called by his first name. How interesting. Lucius then." She seems to catch herself, and her expression closes again "How did you find me?" she asks.

"Crows over the island," he replies. "Metallic blood in the water. I could sense you through it."

"Sense me." Her voice drops and gains an edge. "With your paladin magic, like I was prey?"

Pica almost laughs at the absurdity of that statement. "What? Paladins can't do that."

"Then explain."

The hostility in her tone pains him. "My family's bloodline. Certain members of the royal family have an affinity for dragons. Aunt Lucia knew you were there, too."

He slowly reaches for the waterskin sitting on the small table. Levnys' eyes follow the movement. The magic-imbued water cools his throat, but does nothing for the heat in his belly. Shadows creep across the room in the fading light. Levnys' face is half-shrouded in the darkness.

Pica should be upset at her suspicion. Didn't he almost die to save her life? All he can muster is exhausted apathy.

"How does it manifest?" she asks. "This...affinity."

"If a dragon is near, I feel hot. Lucia feels cold." Pica takes another swallow of water. He mulls over his next words carefully. "There's an instinct of intentions, although..." Pica's fingers twitch. "I think that's only me. If a dragon means me harm, I get...um. Angry. Fiery rage, all that. Like something—" He closes his teeth over the words.

Like something is alive in his guts. He's never been able to shake the feeling there's something different about his magic, something he can't quite put into words.

It's too dark in the room.

The candles blaze to life with a flash of golden light. Levnys flinches away, closing her eyes at the sudden brightness. Pica curses and quickly dims the fire. "Sorry." He drains the rest of the water. The taste of bile and guilt linger. The walls feel too close, the room too stifling. "If you don't have more questions, I—I should get some air."

Levnys touches the discolored spot on her neck. "One," she says. When she turns back to look at him, her expression is softer, less wary. "Why did you save me?"

"Why wouldn't I?"

"That does not answer my question. You risked your life to save mine. Why do so?"

"Because it was the right thing to do. I was—" His mouth goes completely dry. He fights past the heaviness in his chest. If she's to trust him, he needs to be honest. He can't stand seeing that look in her eyes. In *anyone's* eyes. "I was *driven* to. Something in me—all I know is I did what I had to do the second I sensed you dying on that beach. It felt good. It felt *right*."

Levnys studies him for a long moment before turning her head away. "I see." Her eyes trace the black wood above her, gleaming like gems in the firelight. Her expression morphs from suspicious to contemplative. "You are an unusual man, Lucius."

Pica coughs, unsure what to make of that statement. He rises from the chair with the water skin tucked under an arm. "Thanks," he says. He turns his back to the injured dragon. "Be back soon."

II
ESCAPE

Bard

Folmon leans on the railing of a dirty trading vessel, his weakened legs trembling. He watches the harbor approach as the oars splash rhythmically beneath him. He composes a tune to that rhythm, ever-present in his conscious thoughts and dreams. He'll write a thousand ballads before he gets this one out of his head.

The island of Notri glitters like a jewel, the lamplight of the docks shimmering in the southern winter evening. The weather is chilly, a brisk breeze blowing across the bow as he shivers in his threadbare clothes. The ship's crew has taken everything from him except for a prism on a chain he's managed to keep hidden.

Folmon spreads his hands at his side, his fingers picking an imaginary tune on his mental lute. He bathes in the aura of this place as it swirls and writhes around him. It plucks at his senses like a basso note, reverberating deep within him. Something divine resides here—he's sure of it. He almost dares to hope his luck will change and that there will be a place to escape his torment.

It wasn't supposed to be like this. The captain lied to him, telling him it was a trade ship heading to Caltava. He was going to begin a new life there, free from the turmoils of the capital. Instead, they took him captive, turning him into a thrall. A tool to be used as they saw fit.

"Get your skinny ass below *now*, elf," the quartermaster snarls as if on cue, grabbing Folmon roughly by his slim arm. "I ain't letting you off this ship unless you perform real good for me."

The insinuation threads through the air like a foul odor. Not that the quartermaster would let him go anywhere near the port. Folmon could resist and has in the past, but that earns him worse pain than if he submits. He keeps his head bowed as he shuffles below, barely containing nausea at the stale wine scent of the disgusting man. The quartermaster, a huge, ugly Fresian with lank brown hair and a scraggly beard, has taken a liking to him, to his intense chagrin. He has paid the price of it with no outward complaints since he was beaten nearly to death the one time he did so. Notri is the first port where the ship will be put ashore. This may be his best opportunity for vengeance, should he dare to take it.

Emotions—not his—press against his senses, all greed and lust and a pathetic sense of power. He's been able to sense the emotions of others through touch and magic since he was ten, much to his detriment. Disappointment, disgust, fear, and worse—all scrape against him like scratchy wool. He wishes he could carve that part out of him, leave it rotting in an alley somewhere.

The quartermaster drags him into his cabin, slamming the door and grabbing Folmon by his chin. Folmon submits, responding with the barest amount of interest to keep him satisfied that he will not resist. He keeps his senses open and distances himself as the man forcefully undresses him, his greasy, rough hands bruising his skin.

The man is nearly finished with Folmon when he senses his moment. Folmon has no blade, shield, or armor against his enemy. He has no strength or energy reserves, having been starved since he foolishly caught passage on this accursed ship.

His magic, however, has only grown stronger, building inside him in concert with his resolve to escape this nightmare. He's hidden it and his other ability from the crew for an agonizing four months, suffering helplessly as he searched for a moment—*any* moment—to ensure he can get away.

The moment is now. It rings in his head like a bell, a sweet clarion note at the climax of a finely crafted bardic masterpiece. Folmon's magic surges as he pours it into the vile man. At the same time, his teeth sharpen, and his jaw lengthens.

He opens his newly formed canine jaws and sinks them deep into the soft throat above him. The body jerks as he cuts off the windpipe, and the greed in the man's aura quickly turns to panicked confusion. Folmon bites deeper, finding the big arteries through his magic.

It doesn't take long for the quartermaster to die. Folmon opens his jaws and wriggles out from under the dead man. A quick spell and the man's blood disappears from Folmon's dark skin. He glares at the bed for a few more seconds, his ragged gasps echoing loudly in the tiny cabin. He spits on the corpse, turns, and strides toward the trunk that holds the quartermaster's clothing. His form shifts again, his face sagging as he duplicates the jowls of the dead quartermaster, a round gut forming on top of big legs. Lank hair frames his sallow face. He quickly dresses and sets his expression in a scowl as he opens the door to the hallway. No one greets him as he strides forward, squaring the drooping shoulders of his borrowed form in imitated confidence.

He finds where he stashed his prism, then mutters thanks to his *pater*, the enigmatic demigod from which he receives some of his power. He raises his chin as he walks back down the hallway, riding the wave of adrenaline and giddiness from finally disposing of that vile man.

Barking orders at any crew member he sees, he relies on audacity to carry him onto the deck, down the gangplank, and onto the docks of Notri. Dockmen move around him, too engrossed in their duties to pay him any mind.

The wind is cold now, whipping off the water of the harbor. The quartermaster's clothes are warmer than the thin rags he was forced to wear, but he must seek shelter before night falls.

It can't be anywhere nearby. The stench of this place burns his nose—animal and human excrement mix with rotting fish and cheap wine, and even cheaper perfume. All compliments of the seedy taverns and brothels. There are so many of them that they almost crowd into the dry docks. He pushes past a pair of topless whores attempting to get the attention of the now-milling crew. Stone platforms smeared with blood and worse stretch along the entire length of this section of harbor. He steers well clear of them, avoiding the pleas of the displayed slaves. He glances down the docks. Grand ships are moored there, with clean sails and bright flags. Warships bristling with oars form a loose half-circle, allowing access to only a few opulent ships.

Had he been on one of those ships, perhaps he wouldn't be as hungry or broken. Not that he could ever afford such a thing. His lot in life is in the dirt, fighting for every scrap of food and coin he can.

The harbor gives way to crumbling buildings with peeling frescoes and vulgar graffiti. He moves through the dark alleyways until he's sure he won't be seen before leaning against a damp wall. He shifts again into a plain-faced, black-haired man with a bored expression. He taps into the magic threaded through his enchanted prism, changing the appearance of his clothes. Unlike his flesh and blood, the new clothes are an illusion, a deception weaved over the late quartermaster's uniform, now appearing as a plain tunic cinched with a rough leather belt and long woolen socks. *My name is Attius*, he thinks, plucking a name from his memory. One more Gethki man searching for a place to lay his weary head for the evening.

He *is* weary, his body weak from malnutrition. The quartermaster used food as a weapon against him, ensuring he stayed weak by cutting his rations whenever he was displeased. It's gotten worse of late. He can't remember the last time he ate something.

He whistles a tune as he strides down the street, channeling his relief and satisfaction into it. It's more than the tune deserves—he despises the song's simple chords and monotonous melody, but it was easily learned and a favorite of tavern wench and noble alike, something anyone would know.

Attius wonders if anyone from the ship has pursued him. It could be hours before they notice his absence or discover the quartermaster's corpse. He doubts anyone will mourn the man. He demanded respect through harsh words, heavy hands, and cracking whips but only got grudging obedience and cringing servitude. Besides, no one on that ship has a lick of magic or common sense—all they care for is riches, whores, and wine.

The trickle of divine aura he felt in the harbor is a river now. He realizes he's been following it, wading upstream to find the source. The fingers of his right hand tingle painfully, a signal from his *pater* to pay attention. Here, tucked into a quiet alley, surrounded by small shops and food vendors, is a tavern.

Carved figures perch on the roof's corners—multi-tailed foxes and serpentine dragons. A painted sign glows with enchanted radiance in the fading daylight—a spring blossom glimmering in pink and white.

The flower's center blazes with yellow-white light. He knows this flower, those little elements of decoration, and for a moment, he misses his homeland.

Soutori in the spring. The words whisper through his head in a voice he does not recognize. It is feminine and inviting, almost motherly.

You wouldn't know, he tells himself. *You never had a mother.*

A different force tugs at him. Invariably, he is pulled forward, his hand reaching for the fine curtain in the doorway. Pushing through it, he walks through the threshold, squinting in the sudden radiance of the brightly lit room. Magic presses in all around him, almost suffocating in its intensity. It beckons him forward, his tired limbs operating of their own accord.

The scents of baking bread, spices, and roasting meat assault his senses. His shrunken stomach cramps painfully at the whiff of it. Attius stumbles into a high-backed booth, collapsing into the plush cushions. He trembles as his head droops and his eyes close. The tavern's interior is a warm, inviting heat that makes him want to do nothing more than lay his head on the table and finally rest, free of rough hands and sharp words.

"Finally, you have arrived, my child," a woman says in Soutorian.

The sound of his native language jolts him awake. He raises his head and tries to focus on the woman across from him. She is beautiful beyond words. Her sleek black hair is pinned with long bamboo sticks, and her brown eyes are impossibly radiant. She regards him with quiet amusement. She doesn't appear any older than he, but one glance sets off his senses so strongly that he nearly retches, realizing at once who she is.

The Queen of the Foxes. Oh gods, I'm going to die.

Her smile widens as if she can read his thoughts. "Do not fret. I will not harm you."

She will kill you. Run.

Attius' muscles betray him, refusing to respond to his mind's frantic urging. He trembles in the booth, his panicked breath rasping painfully in his throat. Animal fear courses through him, driving him to run and hide. His lips part in a grimace, teeth bared in a weak imitation of a feral snarl. The woman watches him patiently.

Run. Run. RUN!

Her aura is an overpowering mass of magic that clings to her like a mist. He digs his nails into his palms so hard they draw blood, trying to regain control over himself. He forces his throat to relax enough to speak.

"*O-sanribi*, please. Don't kill me. I will leave. I don't mean any harm. I swear it. I don't want to die. Please, don't kill me. *Please*." The words spill from him as tears flow over his cheeks. "I didn't want to kill him, any of them. I don't want to hurt anyone." *Lies. You loved your vengeance.*

The woman tilts her head. "Child," she gently chides. "I would have killed you the instant you arrived on my shore, should I want you dead. You surprise me. I thought you would have lost all will to live with what you have endured." She raises her left hand and snaps her fingers. "I am Ava. By the great moon that graces our sky and bathes us in her moonlight, I bid you welcome to my home. You will not come to harm here, I swear it."

The ceremonial invocation of hospitality ripples over his skin, the magic behind her words as thick as fog on a moonlit pond. Attius greedily mixes his magic with it, drinking in the soothing aura as if parched with thirst. He closes his eyes and takes a deep breath, holding it as he manually forces his body to relax. He lets it out and takes another deep breath, slowly counting to ten before he slumps forward, resting his head on his arms.

Ava watches him with cool patience. "Good. You have excellent control over your body. You are strong, child. I am pleased."

"I don't feel strong," he mumbles into his forearm.

"Ah, but you are. You have the strength to argue with *me*. You have made it far and arrived at last. Surely, you see it."

"I..." He wonders how much he should say. *Idiot, she's divine. She already knows everything about you.* "I don't want to get my hopes up."

Ava clucks at him in disapproval. "Now, now. Trust your instincts."

"My instincts told me to run as far away from you as possible."

"That is not instinct, that is fear. You would do well to continue to fight it. Not everyone bigger than you wants to hurt you. No, I speak of your intuition, child."

"Alright, *fine*." He sighs. "I'm at a crossroads. I don't know more than that. For all I can tell, one road could lead down to Ukton's realm."

"Ahh, perhaps you will dance through the heavens with Olomilo if you insist upon Gethki gods."

"Forgive me if I'm not particularly loyal to Soutorian ones."

"Loyalty is earned. My brethren have done nothing worthy of such. I wish to change that."

A shadow falls over the table. Attius cringes away from it as he looks up, wide-eyed, at a draconic form backlit by brilliant white light. Bright silver scales shimmer as clawed hands set a finely carved bamboo tray before him. The wyverni nods to Ava and walks away without a word. Attius stares at the tray, almost drooling. The smell of food is overwhelming.

"We must begin somewhere," Ava says. "Eat. Slowly now, it would not do to make yourself sick."

He weeps as his shaking hands pick up the chopsticks. The meal is meager—a cup of broth, a small plate of fermented cabbage, and a cup of pear juice. To him, it's a feast. He lets himself cry, his hands trembling as he savors the first hot meal in months. Ava's face blurs as the tears drip onto the table. He sips the juice, savoring the liquid that soothes his ragged throat.

"Thank you," he says after he finishes, wiping the tears from his cheeks. "I'm in your debt."

Ava scoffs. "You know your tales, child. 'Do not owe a fox a debt lest it takes your soul as payment.' Did you forget?"

"Of course not," he says. "However, if we listen to tales, I would be dead by your hand, *O-sanribi*. Not fed at your table."

"Is that so? Perhaps we are not thinking of the same tales. No matter. If I have allowed you to keep your life, why do you try to sell it back so cheaply?"

"It *was* good food. Divine, even."

"Charmer," she says, leaning toward him.

His eye is drawn to her outfit for the first time, the tops of her full breasts spilling out of her corset.

If only I could be so beautiful.

Ava clucks her tongue. "You can be whatever you wish."

The thought that she can read his mind unnerves but doesn't surprise him. He tries not to dwell on it. It's better than feeling the vile emotions of others. "Don't poke around in my brain too long, Ava," he says, trying to force humor into his tone. "It's not a happy place."

"You have the potential to be happy. You are meant for greater things than you think, child."

"Could have fooled me," he snaps, his resentment as sour as bad Gethki wine. "So far, all I've been is a vessel for disgusting men to empty their—"

"No," Ava's voice cracks like a whip. "*Stop.* I will not allow you to disparage yourself like this anymore."

She reaches across the table, laying her hand over his. It takes all his restraint not to yank it away. Her hand is warm and soft, and the emotions that brush against him are like a salve. When was the last time he'd felt anything like this? A year or more, surely.

Why am I so broken? Why am I so weak?

Ava sighs. "Listen to my words, child. Heed me and hold them close."

Her eyes flare, shifting from brown to brilliant violet. Her aura coalesces into a writhing mass of undulating shapes, twitching and flicking. More power than he has ever felt radiates from her, thickening the air so much that it hurts to breathe. Ethereal tails manifest behind her, around her, as his magic resonates with hers. It comes forth of its own accord, swirling around him in silvery tendrils threaded with soft pinks and reds. They embrace him like serpents, flowing around his body like a lover's caress.

What? What is this?

"You have climbed the mountain to touch the sky, dear one, but you are now weak. Your muscles tremble and threaten to collapse. The sky calls for you, and you do not have the strength to fly yet, but you will. Oh, you will."

Her hand grips his, and he gasps as power flows into him. The tendrils around him tighten their spin, dizzying shapes of blossoms and leaves appearing among them. They sprout up his arms and around his head and chest, soft and supple. A gentle breeze blows, cool and fragrant, rustling the flowers and brushing against his cheeks. Tears flow freely at the sight, the only thing he *ever* loved about his homeland. A young bard who had lost all hope until he saw the cherry trees bursting with color.

Soutori in the spring.

Ava's violet eyes hold him transfixed. "Lost soul of Soutori," she continues. "I see you behind your mask of flesh and pain. Your heart is steel, your soul like fire. Shapeshifter cursed and blessed by gods, I will now guide you. One moon, hence, your life will change. *You* are the wind, the promise of spring, and you will lift the greatest of this land."

She leans back. Her aura fades, and her violet eyes return to brown. He keeps watching her, unable to look away.

"Rest," she continues. "Regain your strength. I swear you will come to no harm while you reside under my roof. Your every want will be attended to, and your every need will be filled."

She rises, places a brass key on the table, and turns to leave.

"Ava," he manages to choke out.

She stops.

"What about after I leave?"

"Do not fret, my child," she says, tilting her head back. "When you leave my care, you will go with the strength of dragons."

Attius spins the key in his fingers, flipping it over his knuckles with practiced ease. Stopping before a door, he compares the handle's wrought brass and the key's base, both engraved with a stylized "5." Even he can figure this puzzle out.

He slips the key into the lock, and the door swings open, soundless on well-oiled hinges. Candles flare to life as he enters the cozy chamber, illuminating the room with cool white flame. He sinks to his knees, covering his mouth as the door swings shut behind him.

I don't deserve this. Any of this. I don't...

A flash of purple momentarily blinds him, and his thoughts stop. He reels from it, sitting back on his heels.

I decide if you deserve it, Ava says in his head. *Not you.*

The walls are painted with scenes from his favorite folktale, The Dance of the Suroribi, a story that resonates with him, fills him with hope and pain, and defines his existence.

The tale is old, returning to the murky days of early Soutorian folklore. While the tailed foxes are the core of his homeland's myths, the *suroribi* stands out—a shapeshifter whose presence signifies the world's end. According to the series of songs, she will be the beacon of light while everything turns to ash. Hope, beauty, love.

The five-tailed fox on the walls is almost alive as the scenes transition across the panels. Here, she plies a pair of travelers with song in return for fish stew. Orbs of silver foxfire surround her on this panel, the divine flame holding snarling demons at bay as she protects the two children cowering behind her. The last image is the most striking. The spirit dances, spinning elegant fans through the air, her body bowed as she weaves magic into her performance. All around her, the world burns, the dark red fire and destruction painted in garish, heavy detail.

I want to be her.

The thought comes clear and vibrant amid his muddy thoughts. Rising from the floor, he approaches the painting, his heart aching with a child's pain.

For the first time in three years, the shapeshifter allows themselves to transform into their true-born form, watching the skin on the back of their outstretched hand shift. Their fingers rest on the depiction of the spirit, their shade a near-perfect match to her painted fur. They are the flip side of the coin, the darkness to her light, the evil to her good. "The *suroribi* can't exist without the *sipu*." You can't have the good without the bad.

And they must be the bad—the *sipu*, the evil little shapeshifter who will scourge the earth of everything good and bright. Where the *suroribi* is harmony, they are discord. She is beautiful; they are shameful. Her arrival is anticipated, while the people of Soutori curse the *sipu's* existence. They are only here to mislead, confuse, and deceive like the cursed little creature they are.

All I can do is cause others pain.

Stop.

Their stomach roils, threatening to expel their first meal in ages. They force their stomach to relax and their throat to close on the bile, manually asserting control over their digestive system.

No. We are not doing that, they sternly tell their gut. *Don't be so ungrateful.*

They realize how skinny they are when they place their hands over their torso. The quartermaster's clothes shimmer into view as they release their illusion over them. The clothes hang as loose as empty sacks on their slight frame. They strip them off with contempt and throw them against the only unpainted wall in the room, next to a copper tub. Now naked, they look at themselves, trying to assess their body with clinical detachment.

I could use a mirror.

No sooner does the thought cross their mind than a full-length mirror nearly as tall as them appears. The frame is ornate, carved from thick, beautiful wood, and the metal's reflective surface is polished to a perfect sheen. They approach the mirror, frowning, forcing themselves to look at their reflection without letting the disgust overwhelm them.

Short and frail. Not strong at all. What good is being a shapeshifter if I can barely even lift-

They cut off their thoughts as the candles flare with violet light, casting wild shadows around the room.

Sorry, sorry. The candles flare white again. *No one's ever tried this hard for me before.*

Better get used to it, comes the wry reply. *I will not be the only one.*

What does that *mean?*

Ava doesn't answer. They scowl and let their gaze settle on the reflection of their torso. Their ribs show starkly under their thin skin. Their hip bones are equally prominent, sticking out sharply from their body. While usually slim, their stomach is concave now, their muscles wasted away to mere scraps. Bruises cover their thighs, abdomen, and arms, the angry ones from the quartermaster's earlier attentions blending into the ones from days past. Ragged wounds, old and new, wrap around from their back to their sides. Of course, they made it to their real form. Why would it be any other way? Like this, they resemble the depictions of the *sipu*—a shriveled thing. Disfigured. Ugly and disgusting.

They sigh. No use enduring the wounds any longer. They finally test their magic earnestly, plunging into its heart. It responds almost eagerly, rising to greet them like an old friend. Silvery-white sparkles surround them as they spin it into the air, mixing it with the residual magic of the place. It's like the first deep breath after emerging from underwater. The bruises fade as they blanket themselves in their healing magic. The newest wounds disappear, but the old ones leave ragged lines, marring their skin.

Never again, they promise their magic and themselves. *From now on, we fight.*

That sudden burst of hope makes them raise their head and look into the reflection of their face. Their eyes shimmer with radiance, ringed by thick, dark circles. Those eyes are the only thing they like about themselves, the only thing that, perhaps, the *suroribi* would possess. The rest of their features, however...

They scowl. The expression only highlights their sunken cheeks and gaunt face. They purse their cracked lips, pondering what they should do next.

Another candle flares to life, drawing their attention away from their reflection and to the tub. A bath. It's been months since they've had a real one, and cleaning spells only go so far. Their skin itches. They hurry to it, desperate to scrub away the filth coating their skin.

The metal thrums beneath their fingers as they grasp the curved lip. Despite the faint chill in the room, it's warm to the touch. The enchantment is easy to find, expertly threaded in loops of magic throughout the metal.

They climb in, stretch their emaciated body along the tub's length, and tap into the enchantment with a brush of magic. The water steams as it flows from the elegant spout, almost too hot for comfort. A few inches from the top, the water abruptly stops, triggered by yet another enchantment. There are four, a lot for such a mundane object. They only managed one with their prism.

While enchanting is not their favorite type of magic—learning it had been all but forced on them, after all—it is by far the most useful. Enchanting is stable, reliable, and, most importantly, doesn't require being born with magical ability. Like any scholarly pursuit, it takes time and dedication.

Too much dedication. They'd rather make music.

If enchanting is like knowledge, then natural magical ability—bloodline magic—is like music. One is from the mind, the other from the heart. They lift their hand above the surface and kindle a silver orb of flame, letting it whirl and spin in their palm like a tiny sun before extinguishing it.

There's a third kind of magic, too. Pacts with divine entities are rare and extremely varied. Some only require a few acts of service, like their pact with their *pater* Nylocke. Others are lifetime commitments in a temple. They've even heard of warriors serving under the imperial dragon of Geth.

They're the only one they know with access to all three. Their *pater* said it made them lucky. Trying their luck is all but required by the demigod as payment for their powers. They flip their hand over and stare at the back of it, where the demigod's sigil rests. The glyph, visible only to them, is a series of tiny concentric rings outlining the Soutorian character meaning 'Luck.'

Water swirls around their wrist and into their hand, whirling like a typhoon around their fingers. Absently, they form it into shapes—a bird, a branching tree, a fish. Nylocke hasn't demanded any payment lately. In fact, their *pater* has stayed suspiciously silent. Why did they end up on that ship if they were so lucky? Why didn't their *pater* do something? *Anything?*

They sigh and methodically clean themselves, scrubbing so hard they rub their skin raw. The water turns murky with months of grime before a pulse of magic sweeps it away. They wash until the water runs clear. If only they could wash away the years of shame and self-loathing so easily.

Fatigue presses in as the hot water pulls the tension from their limbs. It would be so easy to drift off, surrounded by enchanted water. They close their eyes and let their skeletal body float off the bottom. Magic soaks into their scarred skin. Time slows.

A flare of light blazes against their eyelids. Their eyes snap open, and instinctively, they cringe away from it, trying to make themselves as small as possible against the curve of the tub. Silver-white fire springs to life in their palm, sending a cloud of steam rolling over the tub's sides.

They'll fight, this time.

Two glowing eyes pierce the cloud before the steam dissipates, revealing the form of a purple fox sitting on the water's surface. They curse and douse the fire in the tub. The fox spirit—a familiar of Ava's —snorts and flicks its ears. In its mouth is a roll of fine linen—all that drama for a towel.

They take the towel and depart the tub. The water drains as they dry off. They pause and scratch the little spirit behind the ears, smiling for the first time in months.

The fox leaps to the floor, then turns and walks toward a small, single bed. The rich wooden posts hang with shimmering silver silk, accented with pink gems. The fox hops onto the mattress as they pull down the covers, caressing the soft fabric of the sheets.

The fox curls on the plush pillow. They groan with pleasure as they settle into the bed, pulling the covers to their ears. The soothing magic of the spirit surrounds their head, making their eyes close as soon as their face settles onto the pillow. The silence is heavy; no shouts of other men, no droning sailing song, no splash of oars, no roaring of waves.

Peace.

They're asleep before they finish the thought.

III

BRONZE

Dragon

Levnys watches the paladin settle into a bedroll. His large frame fills the space between the wall and the foot of the bed. He is not at all what she pictured a paladin would be like. He is a warrior of considerable stature and powerful build, blessed with a scarless face. His eyes are the most striking—irises of rich gold, backed by an internal light of flame. She has seen their likeness before, long ago, on a princess of his bloodline. His eyes seem to miss nothing, constantly monitoring his surroundings. Her mother had the same restless eyes.

Perhaps that is why she gave him a chance.

The hour is late, with the candles burning low on the table. Since arriving on this curious ship, she has spent most of her time sleeping. The paladin—Lucius—stayed out of the room for several hours, only returning after the din of the ship's crew died down.

Levnys bears her teeth. Things are not going as she expected. Stories of strange activity around her territory—the Sparkling Coast —drew her out on patrol for the first time in ten years. The other dragons kept order around their lairs, requiring very little direct interference on her part. It had gone so smoothly for one hundred years.

She agonized over the decision to investigate personally, but eventually, the stories became too much. Movement of sea serpents at the edges of her territory. Purple-finned razorbacks migrating early. Ships afraid to sail west due to macabre stories brought back by hollow-eyed witnesses. Evil spirits. A cloud of death that left no survivors. Corpses drained of their blood. Each tale is more extreme than the last.

Yet, as she reached the northern edge of her territory, she found no evidence for such tales. That's when the stories of a strange dragon creating trouble reached her ears. She assumed it was a routine territorial spat that the usual posturing and compromise could resolve. Young, ambitious dragons always moved into this area; this seemed no different. How wrong she had been.

Instead of an arrogant, barely grown youngster too confident for his scales, she met an enormous drake in his prime—a strange breed unknown to her. He lured her into a trap, and she had barely gotten away. She does not know how she managed to reach that island. Everything had been a blur until Lucius' magic brought her back from the brink.

She does remember the terror, the burn of that dragon's poison in her veins. A true warrior would not have been so afraid. Yet, instead of facing death with dignity, she ran. Perhaps she does not deserve the second chance placed on her back. No matter. Next time she will not be such a coward.

Lucius turns over, creaking the boards beneath him. Something about his presence energizes her, something she cannot put her claws into. She idly wonders if it is his magic. It radiates from him, warming the enchanted cabin. His paladin magic lingers in her blood, surprisingly soothing. It does not make sense that an enemy has such a comforting presence.

Unable to grasp it, she sets her mind to reviewing the information she has gleaned about *Raven's Flight* and her passengers. They head southwest to Caltava, her home, along the trade route that flows from Curia and winds along the populated islands within the shallow seas. Their next major port will be Dalos, only days off. She could part with them there, should her strength return in time, but she is determining if she should. The strange dragon could be searching for her, and hiding among paladins, ironically enough, could be the safest thing. She bares her teeth at the thought. A dragon such as her, forced to rely on humans for protection.

Their group is small, less than ten. They are all powerful individuals, stronger than most warriors, judging by the scraps of aura she can sense through her closed door. Aside from Lucius, the most curious among them is the half-dragon, a tall, stately young woman. Her lesser dragon heritage is not what caught Levnys' attention—her kind is not uncommon on the Coast. No, it is her magic. She seethes with angry electricity, primal and feral.

Lucius murmurs a spell to extinguish the candles, leaving them in darkness. The smell of the smoke intrudes her nose, driving away the lingering scent of Lucius' honey ginger soap and oiled hair. He cleaned up before returning—a bath, shave, and change of clothes transformed the rumpled warrior into an almost pretty man.

The weariness takes hold of her, and she sinks deeper under the soft blankets. She is nearly asleep when Lucius cries out.

"*No,*" he says, his voice muffled by the pillow. "*Please, no.*"

She turns her head, trying to catch a glimpse of him. All she can see is his legs thrashing under the blanket.

"*Blood,*" he murmurs. "*Don't make me….*"

Lucius jerks. Metal scrapes against wood, his retching deafening in the still night air. The smell hits her, sour and rank.

"Lucius?" she inquires. "Are you alright?"

"I...sorry. Be back."

He departs quickly through the door, hunched over, holding his stomach. The smell slowly dissipates as Levnys lies there, helpless to move.

Lucius returns after a time, holding the metal pot he was sick in. He sets it next to his bedroll before settling into the chair and burying his face in his hands. A long silence stretches before he speaks.

"Sorry, Levnys, I..." His deep voice is raspy, rough. "I hope I didn't wake you."

"You did not. What happened?"

"Dreams."

"Dreams? About what?"

"Things that...I can't talk about."

Lucius takes a long drink from a full skin. Levnys can smell the uncut wine, a rough vintage. In the near-blackness, she can see him trembling. He takes another pull of the wine, then coughs wetly.

Blood, he said. What had this man done, that it torments him in his sleep? Humans his age often serve in the empire's legions, but would a royal risk his life so?

She longs to know. He must have such unique stories. The curiosity wars with her wariness. "You have these dreams often," she says.

"Yes," he says in a pained voice.

"Why do you have them?"

"Drop it," he says roughly. After a few seconds, he adds, "Please."

A magpie chatters outside of the window. Lucius' head jerks up. He is half out of the chair before he pauses. The bird pecks at the window. Lucius sighs, leans over the bed, and opens the porthole. A rush of wings and cold air bursts through the room before Lucius quickly closes the window again.

"Your bird?" Levnys asks.

"Yeah." Lucius returns to the chair. The magpie lands on his knee. "I told him to stay outside so he wouldn't disturb you, but he doesn't listen." Levnys can hear the affection in his voice. "He, uh, when I dream he wants to...um, he stays near—"

Lucius gags, then starts coughing uncontrollably. Levnys stays silent through his struggle, unsure what she should do. "He may stay," she says, after Lucius' raspy breaths settle. "I do not mind."

"Thanks."

The silence stretches after that, punctuated only by rough coughs and the slosh of wine. Despite this show of vulnerability, Levnys cannot allow herself to forget the danger this paladin poses. She does not remember much of her struggle on that beach, or the subsequent healing, but she does recall the searing burn of flame, the stench of melting metal.

Never trust one who has once stood against you.

But how could her mother's words apply to this broken man?

Her eyes close against her will. His ragged breathing accompanies her uncontrolled descent into sleep.

When she wakes the following day, Lucius sits on the bed beside her, resting a hand on her arm. Warm magic flows into her like a swirling river. Part of her wants to reel away from his proximity, but her body does not move.

"Good morning," he says cheerily. "I brought you breakfast."

She yawns and opens her eyes. His face comes into focus, his golden eyes radiant, one almost hidden behind his hair. It spills over his forehead, raven-black and loosely curled, shiny in the morning light. He brushes it back and grins at her.

"Lucius," she says, her voice hoarse with sleep.

"That's me," he says.

A snort comes from behind him, dainty and delicate. The half-dragon sits in the chair. Her presence is a surprise—half-dragons generally avoid her kind, and for good reason. Some Greater Dragons are known to be intolerant of their presence.

"Ah, right. Levnys, this is Kisara, my sister."

Sister? How curious. "It is nice to meet you," Levnys says.

She means every word of it—Aea punish the dragons that are so narrow-minded to exclude their own offspring. Kisara turns her frilled head. Behind those eyes, Levnys sees it—the power she sensed. It cringes away from her, fleeing deep into the woman's body. Kisara drops her chin to stare at her clasped hands.

"It is nice to meet you, too, Levnys. I hope Lucius is treating you well."

"He is."

"Good."

Lucius grins. "Kisara would beat me up if I wasn't."

Kisara wrinkles her nose. "No, I'd tell Mother, and *she'd* beat you up."

"With her sandal," Lucius agrees. "No thanks."

"A warrior such as you is afraid of his mother?" Levnys inquires.

"Rightly so." Lucius stands and puts his hand over his chest. "A true warrior will admit that a battle is lost before it begins."

"I would love to see her chase you through the palace again," Kisara says.

Lucius wrinkles his nose and sticks out his tongue—a surprisingly juvenile expression. Levnys finds herself smiling. "I imagine that is a sight," she says. "You grew up in the palace, Kisara?"

The woman blanches at the question. "I did."

"You are a princess?"

"No."

Levnys waits for her to clarify, but the half-dragon stays silent—a sore point. The silence stretches for several awkward seconds before Lucius clears his throat.

"Can you sit up on your own, Levnys?" he asks.

"I will try."

She rises halfway before her body gives out. Lucius is there to help her within seconds, letting her grip his arms as he gently hauls her up.

"Guess not," he says, frowning.

Kisara watches them, her face a mask. The power inside her writhes again, flickering like a thunderhead. She swallows, then stands, turning to leave. "I'll see you later, Lucius," she says. She pauses by the door. "Hope you are better soon, Levnys."

"Thank you," Levnys responds, settling her back against the padded wall.

Lucius' frown deepens as he watches his sister depart. After a beat, he turns back to face Levnys. There is no trace of the cheerful smile—instead, he appears deflated, his eyes weary.

"Sorry, it's, um—"

Levnys holds up her hand. "No, it is my fault. I did not know it was a painful topic."

"Most things involving our mother are." He twists his face as if in pain. "For both of us."

Another moment of vulnerability. "Let us not speak more of it," she says.

Relief passes over Lucius' face. "Thanks." He pulls his arms back. "Um. You should eat."

"Yes, that would be wise."

He sets the tray over her lap, and she devours the bread and cheese she finds there. Lucius places his hand on her shoulder to send his magic into her. His eyes are unfocused by the time she finishes her meal.

"Lucius," she says.

He does not respond.

"Lucius," she repeats, nudging him with an elbow. "I am finished."

He twitches, one curling strand of hair falling over his forehead.

He brushes it away, puts a smile back onto his face, and retrieves the tray from her lap.

"Sorry. Won't happen again."

"Do not apologize." She watches him put the tray on the table. "Tell me, you have traveled much of this empire, correct?"

He settles back onto the bed and returns to healing her. "Only the mainland."

"Are you familiar with the Sparkling Coast?"

"No. I'm visiting lots of new places on this trip. It's beautiful so far."

"Indeed. Do you plan to stay long?"

He shakes his head. "No, passing through to Caltava, then west."

"What is the reason you are traveling like this?"

"Like what?" he asks, tilting his head.

"On a single trireme with no markings, not a royal procession of enormous warships," she clarifies. "I have seen them a few times in this sea. They are hard to miss."

"Ah, that. Well, I'm not on this mission as a prince."

"Mission?"

"You know we're paladins. This is an official Order mission. We're going to an island called Charris to the west."

"What is it that you are searching for?"

"Information. Strange things are happening on the Coast."

The same as her. Had news truly reached so far? "What things have you heard?"

"Ships disappearing, mainly. No letters from Charris in over a month." He tips his head. "What about you?"

"Why do you assume I have heard anything?"

Amusement touches Lucius' lips. "Once I mentioned it, your face changed. We're here to help figure it out. Anything you have is useful."

After a brief hesitation, she outlines her findings, leaving out the strange dragon and his attack. Lucius listens intently, his golden eyes turned up in thought.

"I see. Thank you, Levnys."

"Do not thank me, I am also trying to help." She studies his face. "Is information truly all you seek?"

"Well, I'm always searching for information on dragons."

A flutter of panic goes through her. *No, not again.* "Dragons. Like me?"

He raises an eyebrow. "No, not like you. You don't have feathers."

"Feathers. Are you always this cryptic?"

"Sorry. I'm used to people dismissing them as a myth. Yes, feathers. You know the Gethki sigil—the six-winged feathered dragon?"

"Yes. It is everywhere. I am well acquainted with the tale of your empire's founding."

"Ah, well, it's not a tale. The dragon is named Andereth, and she's real."

Levnys sighs. "Yes, I know that."

Lucius' eyebrows go up. "You do?"

"I am a dragon. We generally remember things humanity does not."

"Then you know she and her family disappeared."

"Yes."

She searches his expression as he stares at her. His magic surges within him, curling into the air like heat from cobblestones. Feathery wisps of yellow gold twist upward like half a hundred candles. It writhes behind his golden eyes, causing them to radiate with a pulsing energy.

There, the power she felt on the beach. "You are trying to find them," she says warily. "Why? What are your intentions?"

"I am sworn to protect them," he says. There is an edge to his voice that was not there before, a defensiveness.

"Protect?" She raises her chin. "They were gone long before you were born."

"I know that." He almost growls the words. More power surges from him as he clenches his eyes closed. "Trust me, I *know*."

"Why would you care so deeply about creatures you have never met?" she presses. "Do you truly wish to protect them?"

He abruptly stands and crosses the cabin in two strides. Outside, a bird's piercing whistle cuts the morning air. Lucius faces the wall, opening and closing his fingers, his shoulders heaving. The radiant heat of his magic becomes stifling.

Levnys braces herself. If his rage overflows and he attacks, she could transform. The ship would be destroyed, but even if she could not take to the air, she could overwhelm him, take him out before he could—

The paladin's head droops. The golden light pulses bright, but the heat recedes. He places one hand against the cabin's wall, bracing himself against it, taking long, measured breaths.

"That wasn't very polite," he says heavily.

Oh. Levnys' fingers curl as she digs her nails into the woolen blanket.

"I'm *sorry.* I didn't mean to burn you," he continues. "I didn't mean to hurt—" His teeth click together, audible even across the room. "You're right. I know it doesn't make sense. I'm aware that the dragons have been gone for a long time. But this oath is all I have left." Lucius turns to face her. Tears shimmer in the corners of his glowing eyes. "To me, it's everything—all that I am. My powers, my family line, my reason for fighting, it's all because of *them.*"

Levnys releases her grip on the blanket and slowly averts her eyes, staring at the empty wineskin on the table. Paladins are supposed to be vicious, uncompromising killers, drunk on their righteous rage. None of the paladins on the ship had displayed anything of the sort.

But if she gives him the few scraps of knowledge she knows about the Celestial dragons—her feather-winged cousins whom Lucius seeks —and it leads to their harm, she would not be able to forgive herself.

She wants to believe it is not a trick, that they are not here to repeat history. This small group could be scouts, a vanguard before death sweeps her Coast again. Her mother's tales were full of such deception. So is the history of this man's empire. She must remain vigilant.

That does not mean she should be rude. She does owe this man and his companions her life—a tangible reality against the shadows of suspicion and fear. She opens her mouth to apologize, but he turns away, toward the cabin door. It creaks open on salt-rusted hinges. He pauses at the threshold long enough to say, "Krakli is outside the window. Tell him if you need me."

The thud of the door cuts off any further comment. Levnys closes her eyes, her lips trembling. "I am sorry," she whispers, too late.

She lies helplessly as the morning sun warms the cabin, mixing with Lucius' lingering magic. They are similar, she muses—pleasant, uplifting, intensely hot. Perhaps there is a lesson in that. Levnys follows the thread of thought, letting herself ruminate. The same sun that sparkles off her sea's waters and coaxes plants to grow can also heat one's scales, burn sensitive skin. Too much sun and plants wither and dry out. She wants to believe she is wrong and the paladin— *Lucius, his name is Lucius, be polite*—will not turn out to be as destructive as she fears.

Eventually, she runs out of things to ponder and relaxes into the bed. There is not much else she can do—the scroll cases on the table are out of her reach, the muffled voices surrounding the ship too distorted to understand. Right now, all she can do is rest. Rest and recover, so she may face the dangers as she ought, teeth bared, claws extended. To do anything else would be unacceptable.

IV
GREEN

Pica

The first horn jolts Pica from his thoughts. He opens his eyes and stares at the red-striped canvas canopy above the bath, watching the steam curl against it. The enchanted tiles of the bath warm the water he lounges in. Although the construction seems simple—a knee-depth rectangular basin set into the stern of *Raven's Flight*—it teems with magic, with complex and layered runes too complicated for him to understand. Enchanting has always been like a foreign language to him. Seto, Kisara's lover and the group's wizard, tried to explain it to him once, to little success.

He can enjoy the luxury of it without knowing precisely how it works. He has too many other things to worry about, anyway. His dreams continue, along with an insidious restlessness. Often, he finds himself pacing the length of the ship or wandering the perimeter of the encampment, certain that danger lurks in the darkness.

So far, the most dangerous thing in the camp is him.

It's been several days since he saved the dragon currently sharing his cabin. Her suspicion of him hasn't abated, although they managed to settle into polite conversation after a few hours of agonizing silence. Once, after a little too much wine, he bluntly asked about why paladins were so reviled. He hadn't gotten much of an answer, to his exasperation.

He tries not to dwell on it. He'll continue to heal her until she regains her strength. What she does after that will be up to her. Part of him hopes she will stay around for a little while. She's a sharp and attentive conversation partner when she's not actively suspecting he will set her alight.

Another part of him resents that suspicion. He's sick of people assuming the worst based on things he has little control over.

Pica sighs and hauls himself from the bath, toweling off with fresh linen before gathering his clothes. Krakli completes his lap of the bath as Pica pulls his tunic over his chest. The magpie chirps at him.

"Yeah, fine," Pica says.

With a sharp whistle, Krakli flies to sit on Pica's head, working himself into his long hair. Pica's let it grow out over the last year in defiance of the short style forced upon him when he joined the legion. It was one of many things he and his uncle Monedula—the *proconsul* and commander of the northern regions—argued about.

He emerges from the tent into the cool air, watching the beach come alive around the ship. In the clear sky, seagulls scream and circle, building their courage to descend upon the morning meal. Every landing the ship makes brings out the human scavengers, too— beggars, thieves, and, worst of all, overpriced merchants selling shoddy trinkets and baubles. Ralex's officers generally run off the last two, but anyone searching for food finds their begging bowls filled with scraps of leftover bread or porridge.

Like all triremes, *Raven's Flight* must frequently be brought to shore to prevent the timbers from becoming waterlogged. Pica and his companions have settled into the ship's daily routine of hauling it onto the beach. Each island, each shore, each tiny town and settlement holds something unique, something to be cherished in these bustling waters.

A shout draws his attention. He goes to his Order's usual breakfast spot—a wooden table near the bonfires. Another special treatment Ralex insisted upon. It had taken Pica and Lucia three days to convince him to stop setting the table with a cloth every morning.

The scent of fresh-baked bread fills his nose. He procures a bowl of porridge and settles at the table with the gladiator twins. The 'twins' are not brothers, nor do they look anything alike. Petrus is a stocky man with long black hair, worn tied back, and a well-groomed beard.

His thick forearms are a forest crisscrossed with pale dueling scars. Sparax is his contrast, nearly as tall as Pica, with a lean build, a mop of curly red hair, and expressive blue eyes. A constellation of freckles scatters across his shoulders and arms and spans the bridge of his nose, darkened by the southern sun.

Both are his sworn shield brothers, members of the Order since the age of sixteen. Calvus took them in after they escaped a gladiator school, and the two proved to be fearsome and talented warriors. Most importantly to Pica, they accepted him as a friend without caring about his royal origins. In Sparax's case, it turned out to be more than friends. No more, though. Pica's actions saw to that. Since their reunion, Sparax has remained cordial but distant.

"Morning," Pica says, nodding at the two men. "Bread looks good today."

"They got flour without seeds this time," Petrus says, examining the dark brown chunk. "Not that I mind anyway—bread is bread."

"Did you forget about the sand in the garbage they fed us in gladiator training?" Sparax asks with a yawn.

"That's because there was sand in everything," Petrus retorts. "I bet there wasn't any sand in your fancy legionnaire bread, right Lucius?"

"You don't want to know the shit I ate," Pica says. "Mud comes to mind, not to mention actual shit."

"Disgusting. I bet you're happy to be free of that," Sparax says.

Pica smiles at him. "You have no idea how much."

Their eyes linger on each other's before Sparax averts his gaze. "How's the dragon, Lucius?"

"Better. She's walking around on her own now."

It had taken two more days of healing for Levnys to rise out of bed and another two for her not to cling to his arm while walking. He spots her standing on the beach, staring at the sky.

"You still sleeping on the floor?" Petrus asks.

"Yes."

Sparax opens his mouth to add something, but the second horn sounds—all hands cast off. The three of them finish their food without further conversation. A cook sweeps past, removing their bowls without pause as they rise from the table. It, too, is removed without ceremony. The three of them step out of the way. They quickly figured out that any help they would provide would disrupt the well-oiled routine of the ship's departure.

Fires are smothered, tents dismantled, supplies loaded. A splash as the bath is drained, the water returning to the sea from where it came. Rowers take position along the ship's flanks as Ralex bellows orders—first in Fresian, then Caltavian. Pica grins at the amount of good-natured profanity in his words.

Drums beat. The crew sings—a prayer of good fortune, beseeching the spirits of sky and sea to guide them safely to their next sandy shore. Ralex's voice joins, louder than a seasoned centurion and equally as vulgar.

The song reaches the chorus, and, as one, nearly 200 men lift the ship off the beach, shouldering its weight between them, and march in lockstep into the gently lapping surf. Row by row, they enter the water, submerging themselves to their chests before releasing their grip and climbing the heads of the retracted oars to the deck. The entire ritual takes only minutes. *Raven's Flight* rocks gently in the morning waves, at sea once more.

Pica and his companions head for the small rowboat beached for them nearby. Krakli rasps and fluffs himself out against the brisk morning breeze. Levnys' brow furrows, but she turns and approaches them, moving slowly over the beach. Pica helps her settle onto the bench before he and the others push the rowboat into the water and paddle to the waiting ship.

At odds with the beautiful morning, a foul unease coils in his gut. He frowns and scans the water and the sky. Nothing but wispy white clouds and sparkling turquoise water. Odd.

Levnys makes eye contact with him. Her face remains blank, but he can see the worry in her eyes.

Lucia's shield smacks Pica in the chest, and her feet sweep his legs from underneath him. Pica's shoulders hit the deck. The padding of his training armor softens the blow, but it still knocks the wind out of him with an explosion of breath. Lucia steps up beside him, levels her wooden sword at his throat, and calls, "Point!"

He lies there for a moment before pushing himself up, scowling. He can never beat her, no matter how hard he tries. He ignores her outstretched hand, and she glares at him.

"You're not improving," she says in a frosty tone. "You used to have such promise, Lucius."

Such a comment is unusual for her, and anger rises white-hot in Pica's core. How can he be expected to fight effectively when he can barely get half a night's sleep? He stomps away from the group of paladins.

Sparax's voice follows him. "Lucius? Where are you—?"

"Leave him," Lucia snaps. "Let him brood."

Pica closes his teeth before he can say something he'll regret. It's a near thing—the rage inside him continues to build like magma in a volcano. He reaches the rail, clenching the black wood.

Krakli perches nearby. Pica tries to ignore the magpie's concerned inquiry as he slams his fist down. Above, Levnys is in her dragon form for the first time since he rescued her, circling low over the water.

She turns her head and bellows. Something twinges at the sound, some instinct of danger, but he pushes it aside. He's too tired to care. Gods, he wishes the dreams would stop.

Krakli's shrill of alarm tears through the morning air, and the magpie takes wing. Levnys bellows again, flipping in the air. He follows the line of her vision, and his stomach churns. The anger inside him continues to rise, and the cause of it speeds toward them on dark wings.

"Dragon!" he calls out.

The dragon is green and shiny, its scales large and haphazardly covering its body, overlapping like feathers. A viscous fluid drips from its claws as they flex open and closed, falling into the water below. As more details become clear, Pica realizes it's not covered in scales; it's covered in *leaves*. Its tail is a thick bush with branches twisting together. More branches sprout from the back of its head, curling like horns to frame its narrow face.

To Pica's surprise, the dragon doesn't immediately attack. It turns and circles, flying around Levnys' flank. She mirrors it, snarling. Behind him, Ralex shouts orders. The drumbeat changes as the oars lift from the water in a synchronized motion. The other paladins join Pica at the rail as the giant green head turns to them.

"What's this?" the dragon muses in a deep male voice. "Are these humans bothering you?" He circles lower. "A deal, little *drakaina*," he says to Levnys. "I will help you kill them if you give me what I want."

Levnys growls low in her throat. "I will not."

"Shame," he says. He flaps his wings hard and turns sharply to shoot at Levnys like an arrow. She drops from his path, evading his talons by less than a foot.

Shit. She's too weak for this. "Hey!" Pica shouts. "Ugly!"

The dragon's head whips toward him. Beside Pica, Sparax sputters, "What are you doing?"

"She can't fight him!" Pica says, pushing along the rail to get closer to the hostile dragon.

"Neither can we!" Sparax's voice is almost shrill. "What are we going to do at this distance?"

What *is* he doing? His magic surges, insistent, building in his forearms and hands. Everything seems so sharp, so clear. Right there, someone trying to hurt another. He can do something about it. He can use his power to protect someone.

"I'll hit him," he says. "You support me."

The dragon pivots and slashes at Levnys again. A wicked gash opens across her flank as she screams in pain. The dragon's tail connects as he flips, sending Levnys careening into the water below. Pica's heart sinks—no, it can't be. Blood wells to the water's surface as the dragon turns to face the ship.

"Leave. My quarrel is not with you," the dragon says.

"She's our friend," Pica shouts. "We won't let you harm her."

The dragon comes a little closer and sneers. "*Friend*? Dragons don't make friends, human."

"You're wrong."

The other paladins come to the rail. Sparax's hand rests on Pica's back, between his shoulder blades, sending a blessing spell rippling through his limbs.

The dragon chuckles and tilts his head like a dog. "Oh. You're serious. Well, if you insist."

The dragon dives for the ship, pinning his wings back. Pica strikes, sending an orb of fire streaking from his outstretched hand. It explodes against the dragon's side, sending burning leaves spiraling away in the wind. He roars in surprise and reels to the side but continues his approach. The vegetation on his sides smokes, the rough wood pattern of his skin black and smoldering. The dragon sneers as Pica throws another orb at him. The explosion reels him again, but his tail sweeps across the deck as he passes low over the stern. Several deckhands, unable to dodge in time, collapse to the deck with dilated eyes, convulsing. Vicious thorns, six inches long, stick out from their exposed limbs, the skin around the wounds already red and inflamed.

Calvus and Lucia run to the stricken crewmen, struggling to move on the rocking ship. Pica jerks his attention back to the dragon flying over for another pass. Fire kindles in Pica's hand as he prepares another shot, but the dragon dodges away, flies low, and snatches Petrus straight off the deck. The ship rocks in his wake, sending Pica stumbling away from the rail.

Pica's heart surges. Part of him is screaming, begging the gods not to take another friend away from him. Another part calmly tracks the dragon's flight, waiting for a moment to strike. Sparax's fingers tighten on his tunic. "Petrus!" Sparax screams, his voice tinged with panic. "Lucius, do something! Please do something!"

New recruits always scream like that, in their first real battle. They learn eventually, like he had to. Sparax doesn't know. None of them do.

Oh gods, what is wrong with him? Sparax is his *friend*, not one of his soldiers.

Petrus' arm jerks, and the dragon's hand opens, sending the stout paladin flailing into the water. Blood sprays, along with a pale green fluid. As soon as he's clear, Pica strikes, driving the dragon away from Petrus' falling body.

"Pull oars!" Sparax shouts, then dives overboard. The oarsmen react with the speed of drilled routine, heaving the long oars into the ship. Not fast enough—Sparax's shoulder clips the edge of one, and he spins into the water with a splash. Pica grits his teeth and glares up at the circling dragon. He flies out of Pica's reach, studying him.

"What now, mage?" he taunts.

Ralex shouts another order and two officers dive into the churning water. The dragon makes another loop, casual in his patrol above them.

Shouts pull Pica's attention away for a breath. Sparax's soaked head surfaces. The dragon folds his wings and plunges during this momentary distraction, closing the distance too fast for Pica to attack. He dives to the deck as the dragon grabs for him and misses. The dragon chuckles as he turns back to face the ship.

Stalemate. He and the dragon stare at each other for a long second. Pica keeps his spell behind his teeth, waiting for him to make a move. The plant dragon isn't a fool. That much is clear. Inside Pica, his magic writhes and convulses, filling him with an anger that feels like a living thing.

Go away, he tells it. He tries to push the feeling down, but it only grows stronger.

He's so focused on it that he nearly misses the tiny black speck circling far above. Pica bears his teeth as Krakli dives. The magpie shrieks as he snatches a branch from the dragon's brow. The dragon jerks his head, snapping at the bird, but Krakli is well past, laughing in his *chak-chak-chak* call.

Pica unleashes fire from both hands, hitting the dragon squarely in the chest and neck. The fire doesn't catch, but a great swath of the dragon's leaves are scorched away, revealing a tangled network of thorns and branches and filling the air with acrid smoke. It fills him with a vicious sense of glee. *Protect*, his power seems to say.

Feet pound across the deck as Seto and Kisara join them. The wizard shouts and breaks a thin strip of bark between his hands. With a *pop*, energy spirals from the broken ends out toward the dragon's bark-covered head. It loops around his nose, snapping his jaws shut.

Levnys bursts from the water and slashes at him, her claws rippling with lightning. The plant dragon flaps his vast wings, sending a gust of wind across the deck and pushing *Raven's Flight* off her course. Levnys places herself between the ship and the dragon and roars defiantly, lightning sparking along her flanks and wings, her gashes leaking foaming blood. Pica lurches to his feet, preparing to strike. The dragon's eyes flick between Levnys and Pica, brilliant chartreuse, and fix on him. For a small moment, Pica sees a darkness in them, something haunted. He sees the same look in the mirror.

The roiling anger inside Pica fades. He slowly lowers his hands.

The dragon tips his head in concession and, heaving his great wings, flies away, his sides twitching in what can only be laughter.

* * *

Blood drips onto black wood as Pica's chest heaves with exertion. "Got him," he rasps as Petrus' body jerks. He slumps backward as the other paladins close in around the prone man, pressing their palms against his pallid skin. Petrus' eyes flutter under his lids as he jerks again. Pica watches his Order methodically assess his friend with half-closed eyes.

"Heartbeat confirmed," Calvus says. "Lucia, the poison?"

"Cleared," she replies.

"Sparax, is that gash closed?"

"Nearly, Grandmaster." Sparax appears half-dead himself, soaked and shivering, an enormous bruise forming on his bare shoulder. "Give me a minute."

Petrus thrashes again, his eyes flying open. A string of obscenities flows from his mouth as everyone on deck relaxes.

"...shit stain of a whore!" Petrus finishes. "Ow," he adds more quietly.

"No, don't move yet," Calvus says when Petrus tries to sit up. "Stay there."

Levnys' head appears over the railing as she watches the scene. Her eyes linger on Pica's bleeding fingers. He gives her a weak smile.

Not everyone was so lucky. Two of Ralex's stewards died before any of the paladins could help them. Their covered bodies lay near the bow, their shrouds hiding the destruction the poison wrought on their bodies.

They limp to the closest island and put to shore early afternoon. Levnys swims instead of flies, silent except for her heavy breaths. Thankfully, her wounds were shallow, and they were able to purge the poison quickly.

She drags herself ashore and flops onto the beach, sighing loudly. Pica climbs out of the rowboat and goes to her side, settling on the sand beside her head. Silence stretches between them like a vast chasm, perilous and dark. Questions press against Pica's lips. "We need to talk," he eventually says.

"Do we?" One turquoise eye watches him, half-lidded. "What is it that you wish to talk about?"

"What did that dragon want?"

The eyelid sinks lower. "My territory."

"And where is your territory?"

"The Sparkling Coast."

"*All* of it?" Pica asks in disbelief.

"Technically. Much of it is merely a formality. I do not rule over the other dragons here, but I am the one who inherited it; therefore, I am the one who protects the others."

"You protect them?"

"Most of the others would be killed in seconds if they faced a foe such as the dragon pursuing us. It is those dragons I defend." Her eyes close. "Or attempt to."

"If he kills you, does he get the territory?"

"No. Perhaps he assumes so."

"Can you defeat him?"

Levnys pulls her lips away from her teeth. "I do not know. I have failed twice now. The first time, he lured me into an ambush. This time, I am weakened. Yet even at my full strength, he is a dire threat, and I do not know if I will succeed."

"You will with our help."

Her head drags across the sand as she looks away from him. "I will not ask it of you. I *cannot*. A dragon of the Coast would never—" She cuts off. "I will not ask it of you," she repeats.

Pica purses his lips. He suspected this would be her reaction, but she's not the only one allowed to be stubborn. "You're not asking. We're doing it anyway."

A cloud of sand bursts into the air as she exhales heavily. "A true warrior does not need the assistance of others."

The laugh bursts from Pica's chest before he can stop it. Levnys lifts her head to look at him. Her indignant expression only makes him laugh harder.

"You think—you actually *believe*—" He leans forward, resting his palms on his knees, trying to contain it long enough to speak. Each time he tries, the more he can't contain it. He waves his hand in a feeble attempt at an apology.

Levnys snorts. Her breath blasts over him, smelling of ozone and salt, blowing his hair back. "That was not very polite," she says.

"Sorry. I don't mean to—" Another wave of laughter threatens to overcome him. "But you're wrong. Absolutely, completely wrong." He straightens, bringing his hand up to hide his smile, biting the knuckle of his forefinger. Levnys' eyes narrow, and her nostrils flare.

"Explain," she says flatly. The word rumbles like thunder in her chest.

Pica takes a deep breath and raises his chin until he stares straight into those huge turquoise eyes. "A true warrior knows the value of allies," he says solemnly. "A true warrior knows when to rely on the strength of others."

Levnys' expression changes, her eyes softening, her head tilting a bit. Pica holds the eye contact, stone-faced. He's heard not to lock eyes with a predator. Even though she could snap him up in two bites, he's not worried. In a way, she reminds him of a young patrician officer, head filled with stories of brave heroes and impossible odds. Eager to fight, but ultimately naive.

"A true warrior uses their strength to protect others," he continues. "They don't care about glory or power. Knowing they can stand up for what's right is more than enough."

Levnys turns her head away. "Are you a true warrior?" she asks after a long moment.

"No," Pica says emphatically. "Not after—"

His teeth close over the words. He doesn't try to speak them again. Instead, he follows Levnys' gaze out over the water, where *Raven's Flight* hunches dark against the bright winter sky.

They hold the funeral for the fallen crewmen that evening. The Caltavian rowers sing a haunting dirge as they carry the linen-wrapped bodies into the small graveyard. Pica and his companions observe in respectful silence, listening to the mournful words.

To the ground, return, free from pain and sorrow.

Pica's mouth goes dry.

"To the ground, return..."

Soldiers throw pale corpses, stripped bare, into a wooded ravine.

"...free..."

Blood pours from the mouth of a newly captured slave. He spits his severed tongue onto the sandal of his captor.

"...pain and sorrow."

A mother screams over the wrapped body of her son, clutching the amulet he wore.

He comes to at the edge of the water. Blood tinges the remnants of his afternoon meal. His stomach heaves again as water swirls around his wrists and knees. Acid bile burns him from stomach to throat, a fire he can't quench, can't control.

The sand behind him shifts. Kisara sits nearby, above the tide line. Pica coughs, spits bloody mucus into the retreating water, and settles beside her. She hands him a water skin. He drinks deeply, feeling bitterly nostalgic. Years ago, before he joined the Order, Pica and his sisters would be sent to the palace gardens whenever Pica's father paid their mother a visit. They'd sit in silence, hidden in a stand of manicured trees, listening to the sweet trilling of birds and the whispering wind. It became their refuge, their sanctuary from the reality of the royal harem. Pica leans against Kisara's slim shoulder as he did then.

"I miss Tiberia," Kisara says wistfully.

"Me too," Pica replies hoarsely.

They make their way to the camp when the smell of the evening meal wafts into the air. Pica sips broth in front of a small fire, pointedly ignoring the crewmen's murmurs and sidelong glances.

Levnys settles in human form on a blanket a few feet away from him. The firelight dances along the plaits of her metallic hair. Pica tries to hide his surprise, but the barest hint of a smile quirks the dragon's lips before she hides it behind her goblet of wine.

The next few days pass without incident. Neither branch nor leaf of the plant dragon shows itself. Pica often catches crewmen scanning the sky.

Levnys joins him at the fire each night. The conversation is tentative at first, but they soon find common ground on a topic dear to Pica's heart—history. Tales flow like water between them—anecdotes and myths mixed with tales from the past. Levnys seems to devour them all, listening more intently than anyone has in Pica's life. There's plenty to talk about, and the wine dries up before the conversation does.

He finds himself impatiently waiting for the evenings, spending the day thinking up new things to discuss. Levnys holds a unique perspective and nuanced opinions, neatly filling in the gaps in his knowledge, especially regarding her home of Caltava. When they're together, he's immersed in the moment, with the air cool on his skin and wine sweet on his tongue. For a few hours, he can forget about war, and put aside the fire and death. Still, distance remains between them, a chasm he can't bridge no matter how hard he tries.

She remains in their company, flying above *Raven's Flight* like an armored escort or standing at the bow in her human form, her face turned to the wind as if in prayer.

Pica finds Levnys standing at the ship's bow as *Raven's Flight* enters the crowded harbor of Dalos. The lamps of the early evening shine like fireflies against the dark shoulders of an ancient volcano. Pica steps up next to Levnys and follows her gaze to the low buildings surrounding the harbor. He finds the usual dock fare—shop fronts, inns, brothels, and market platforms nestle between each berth. It bustles with activity, the sound of half a hundred songs drifting over the water, accompanied by shouts from the deckhands and the bray of donkeys hauling cargo. The majority of the ships at the dock are trading vessels, wallowing tubs stuffed full with amphorae of wine and olive oil, sacks of grain, and fine fabrics. An unusual number of fishing boats rest here as well, toys compared to the larger ships, floating haphazardly in the open bay or tucked into whatever scrap of land or dock will fit them.

In the sky, nearly invisible in the growing darkness, a silhouette of a dragon circles above the quiet caldera. Levnys watches it with no visible concern.

"Good evening, Levnys," he greets her. "Are you well?"

"Yes. I am nearly whole. I am glad."

"Me too. You're strong—that helped a lot. Best patient I've ever had."

She snorts. "You attempt to flatter me by stating the obvious." She looks up at him, a smile on her lips. "It is like saying that the sun is hot or the ocean is deep. Can you not do better than that?"

He laughs. "You expect so much from me. I'm not a bard. How can I ever hope to describe the majesty that you are, Levnys? All I can do is try."

"Then you must try."

"Fine, fine." He spreads his arms wide and clears his throat. "A raging wildfire is but a dying candle to your flame-"

"I am a lightning dragon."

"Right. Olomilo's greatest tempest is but a tiny spark to your raging storm. You are lightning *incarnate*." He clenches his fist. "Blazing with blinding light, you strike awe into all that see you. Your visage is as grand as a thunderstorm." He glances down at her. "I'm running out of lightning examples. Is that good enough?" he asks, and winks.

She is laughing, her beautiful face radiant in the light of the docks. A thrill goes through him as he laughs, too.

"Lucius, I retract my question. Clearly, you cannot do better."

He puts his hand over his heart. "Ouch."

She winks back at him. He stares at her, speechless, as she turns back to face the harbor. "I have not been to Dalos in some time. I look forward to it. I have many people to speak to."

He looks at her in surprise. "You know this place well?"

"Yes, I spend much of my time on patrol here. There is a—." She stops. "You are going into town as well, is that correct?"

"Yeah, I won't return this evening."

"I have heard. Your friends are not discreet about their plans. You will drink too much wine and lay with courtesans. It sounds like a fine evening. You will tell me about it tomorrow."

That's not a question. Pica chokes at her bluntness. "Uh, yes, I'll do that if that's what you want."

"Yes. The best stories come from the best wine. I know of a place that has excellent *passum*. It is called the Gilded Amphora. You will find it most enjoyable."

A dragon giving him tavern suggestions. He never thought he'd see the day. "I'll make sure we go there. Thank you for the suggestion, Levnys."

"You do not need to thank me. I hope you enjoy your evening."

It's mid-morning by the time they make it out of the brothel. Pica's headache from the excellent wine last night has subsided, blessedly. The winter morning is cold but pleasant, and Pica is comfortable in a tunic and heavy cloak. In the south, the weather stays mild through the coldest months—so much better than the north at this time of year. The twins chatter next to him as the trio approaches the bathhouse. Pica only pays partial attention—they will rehash the entire evening, repeating stories and arguing about things they barely remember. Pica smiles wryly. Some things never change.

According to one of the courtesans, the bathhouse is the grandest on the Sparkling Coast. It looms in front of them, its entrance framed by grand white marble columns. The mosaic on the lintel is exquisite, depicting an ocean scene in patterned tile swirling with white, blue, and turquoise. A finely crafted fishing vessel faces an enormous sea serpent, coiling through the waves. Caltavian style, here? Interesting. It's an odd choice. The Fresian and Caltavian residents of the Coast are traditional enemies, or at least intense rivals. Perhaps 130 years of the Gethki rule over both have some benefits if only to keep a tentative peace.

They enter between the pillars into the bathhouse proper. Pica smiles at the attendant, a older man with wispy white hair and a stooped back. He doesn't worry too much about being recognized as royal off the ship—an enchanted tattoo holds an illusion over his upper chest, neck, and face, turning his draconic scales into an old burn scar and his golden eyes muddy brown. Another former soldier traveling the seas. Not a lie, but not the whole truth, either.

"Good morning, *secu*," he says, using the local honorific. The man looks at him in surprise. "The cost for three, please."

The man glances at the twins and back at Pica. "Do you require a private bath?"

"That won't be necessary. The public bath is fine."

"Four copper each."

Pica gives him five silver. "More than reasonable. Please keep the rest. This bathhouse is beautiful."

The man gives him a long look. "That it is. Are you some kind of noble?"

Pica laughs. "Just a retired soldier, *secu*," he lies. "Got lucky in a dice game last night and felt like passing it on."

The man shrugs and pockets the extra coin. "This way, please."

They follow him into an enormous, sunlit room. A huge pool rests in the middle, steam curling off the clear water's surface. Fruit trees surround the building—birds sing from somewhere in the branches, trilling a thousand different notes. Pica senses Krakli within them, nearby but out of sight. Pillars of marble ring the outer edges of the main chamber, holding up a vaulted dome ceiling. A scene from a myth wrought in a mosaic covers the entire concave construction. The craftsmanship is master class, nearly as intricate as the main mosaic in the Emperor's throne room. Olomilo, the god of sky and lightning, is depicted as a sinuous dragon, climbing his thunderclouds as lightning illuminates stormy skies. Flanking him are the gods of the sun and the moon—Solis, the golden ram, and Cetuna, the azure wolf. Pica studies it for a moment, perplexed—another odd choice. Olomilo is generally depicted with the sea goddess Naltia in such mosaics. The inclusion of Geth's silent gods is something Pica's never seen before.

Several people scrub in the main bath or soak in the hot water. In Geth, the baths are segregated between men and women, but here on the Coast, everyone bathes together without issue. Pica feels the gaze of a couple of them as he follows the attendant, who points out the towels and scrapers before leading them to an artificial waterfall. The clear water spills into a shallow pool before draining into a winding canal leading out of the building.

"Rinse off here before entering the main bath, if you please. There is a cooling pool in that alcove," he says. "If you need anything, *svetu*, please do not hesitate to ask." He bows and walks away.

Svetu. That's an even more formal honorific. *What a few extra coins buy you*, Pica thinks with bitterness.

He strips off his clothes, and the twins follow suit, placing their items in baskets. They all leave their amulets on, as they always do. The dented bronze medallions, inlaid with iron and brass, depict the six-winged Andereth, the symbol of the Gethki empire.

She is stylized as a gold and azure double-headed dragon with enormous feathered wings and winding roots for a tail. She emblazons the sides of the empire's ships, flaps on their flags, and accompanies his people wherever they go. The Celestial Shield does its best to uphold the original oath made with her by the first emperor, though the details have been lost. Too many years have passed, and, more importantly, the celestial dragons disappeared two centuries ago.

Lucia gave him the amulet on the day he was elevated to full paladin. It represents their oath, she said. It's to remind him what they fight for and, more practically, a focus for his paladin magic. Pica learned to be prepared for the worst at all times. A man could be caught naked or drunk without protection, but Pica will always have his paladin magic.

He steps under the waterfall to rinse in the tepid water. After a minute, he emerges, dripping wet, and heads toward the main bath, grabbing a towel as he passes. He foregoes the scraper—even magical cleaning wouldn't help one of those.

At the pool's edge, he sees the mosaic under the water for the first time. It is wrought in vibrant color, a more magnificent copy of the dragon on his amulet. Coiled around Andereth is a depiction of the sea goddess, wrapped around her as if in an embrace. He stands there, rendered speechless by its beauty.

"Move it, aurochs," Petrus says from behind him. He drops his voice. "People are staring."

Pica winces as the other patrons quickly avert their eyes. He submerges himself in the hot water, resting his head on the lip of the pool and closing his eyes. The twins join him, sliding into the water on either side. They talk over him as he relaxes, savoring the warmth soaking into his sore muscles.

"Hey, Lucius, look," Petrus says. Pica opens one eye, expecting mischief. Instead, Petrus points into the pool. "Doesn't it look like she only has one head?"

Pica squints at the distorted image, then takes a deep breath and sticks his head under the water. Petrus is right—the sigil only has one head instead of two. He notices that the tail is different, too. Instead of spreading out like a tree's roots, it spirals gracefully, intertwining with the sea serpent that embraces it.

Wait.

The serpent is not the sea goddess. Instead of turquoise scales, it is covered in auric plumage, the stones of the mosaic glinting like gold. Its wedge-shaped head is ringed with a crest of feathers sprouting from under an intricately carved stone crown. Four outstretched wings spread from its legless body, filling the background with gradients of red and orange. Fire surrounds the serpent in a blaze of light so realistic the floor appears to burn. Butterflies dance through the flames, their wings a complex pattern of orange and black.

Something inside Pica stirs at the sight. Magic roils in the depths of his body as if waking from a long slumber. The serpent's emerald eyes bore into his. He can't look away.

I'm...alive?

The voice is not his. Someone else is in his head—an unmistakable presence, like a dark corner of his mind had its curtain ripped away. The magic continues to writhe, building, heating his skin. The water around him churns, painfully hot. The serpent's pupils narrow.

Where am I?

Pica's stomach roils. His lungs protest. He needs air, but he's paralyzed, transfixed by those eyes. Darkness descends on him.

Heat presses in on their skin. Before them, a verdant jungle reclaims the slopes of a great stone pyramid. Blood—dried blood, fresh blood—cakes the stones and flows down its steps. A body is flung from the summit, tumbling down the sanguine stairs. The felina lands in a crumpled heap, her heart torn from her chest. The feathers of her golden headdress are dyed crimson, the polished bronze disc crumpled. The stench of blood lingers on their tongue. Her lifeless eyes stare blindly at the darkening sky.

The vision shifts—a flash of feathered starlight wings—a midnight-purple owl in a pool of vermilion, lifeless, her constellation plumage dimming. Her name bursts from their lips in an anguished scream.

Pain. A flash of white fangs in a crimson mouth. A deep, sinister laugh taunting them. Black eyes, triumphant as their strength fails. A great bat-like shape looms above them with outstretched wings, webbed and black as midnight. They thrash as a voice calls their name.

Name? What is my...?

Six wings of azure and gold, one hanging limply, resplendent feathers broken, bleeding from deep and wicked gashes. A clawed hand, reaching out.

Fingers entwine in Pica's hair and jerk his head out of the water. He gasps, filling his burning lungs with steam-filled air. Strong hands lock around his wrists, keeping him from flailing. Krakli shrieks from the trees before taking wing into the bathhouse, circling wildly below the mosaic.

"Lucius!" Sparax's voice cuts through his confusion. "What's wrong?"

Andereth! It was her! How? *Why?*

His chest heaves. The other bathers edge away from him, speaking in hushed voices.

"I-I-" His head falls back against Sparax's shoulder. How can he put into words what he witnessed? "It's...I saw...something."

"What did you see?"

He feels like a madman. "Can't. Later."

"Uh, sure," Sparax says. His hand lingers in Pica's hair, his fingers a familiar and comforting presence. "Lucius, are you alright?"

No, no, he's not alright. "I will be," he says, not sure if he's lying. "We need to leave."

The innkeeper squints up at Pica. "Are you sure, *secu*? That will be very expensive."

Pica sighs. "Yes, I'm sure. Do you have one or not?"

"I have one, but I can get three people in that room. You will pay for three people?"

"I already told you I would."

After several more minutes of dubious back-and-forth, Pica firmly presses the gold pieces into the innkeeper's hand and suffers through the man's insistence on proving their authenticity. Finally, with the man satisfied and the key relinquished, Pica climbs the narrow staircase to his room. The chamber is plain—the bedding rough but clean, the candles fresh, and the room itself free of the scent of mold or dampness.

Krakli settles onto a rafter, fluffing out his feathers. The bird is asleep within seconds. It's a relief—the poor familiar has been restless all day, echoing Pica's mental state. The memory of the bathhouse has Pica on edge, along with the unnerving sensation of another's presence. He attempted to explain the source of his anxiety to his familiar, but the truth is, he's not sure what happened himself.

Pica opens the window to let the breeze in, lights the candles, and settles onto the bed. As usual, it's too short for him, but he's able to angle himself so he lies diagonally, stretching his full length on a relatively soft mattress. Thus situated, he stares at the rough-hewn rafters. His gaze tracks the splinters and smoke stains.

What does it mean? He'd heard of jungles in stories, and nothing so vivid. He could smell the vegetation and the blood of that hapless felina, and felt the humidity press on his skin. Then, there was Andereth.

He doesn't know what to think. Deep down, part of him doubted that she and her kin were like the stories said. Seeing her alive, moving, with resplendent gold and azure feathers shifting in the sun, hearing her voice—she was so real, so vibrant, like he was there.

Because, maybe, in a way, part of him was.

He desperately wants to believe he imagined the voice inside his head. Was he hallucinating? Some soldiers did. Maybe the stress finally caught up to him. He didn't imagine the mosaic, though. Sparax and Petrus both confirmed the presence of the golden feathered serpent, with its emerald green eyes—

...you.

Oh, gods.

...protect...

Oh, *gods*. There can be no mistake. The voice is muffled, like someone shouting from a distance, but it's still *there*.

...wanted to...

Pica's eyes go unfocused. Something, some*one*, in his head. He wants to run, to drown the voice with wine, sleep until he's sure he'll wake up from the dream. It's pointless. He'd tire, sober up, wake up, and that voice would still be there. He *knows* it.

So, he steels himself, then tries to brush those hot coils of magic in his core. *Hello?* he asks. *Can you hear me?*

Vague confusion is the only response. It's not his emotion, but he feels tied to it, bound with strands like thread. He tries again, fortifying his greeting with paladin magic, weaving it into the words. More threads bridge the chasm. Relief, anguish, confusion all wash in.

I'm...live...

A horrid pain tears through Pica's body. Thousands of thick needles drive themselves into his flesh, everywhere, into his arms and legs and even his face. He grabs the pillow and bites down to muffle his scream. Chains burn into his skin, a vile, searing agony. His vision fills with pulsing crimson light.

Then, it's gone. The candles blaze orange against his eyelids. He lies there panting, whole, the only pain the familiar one in his gut. Shame worms into him along the threads wound around his chest.

...ry...

The entity's presence recedes into his core. He tries to draw it back out, picturing those emerald eyes, but it's beyond his reach.

Answer me. Gods curse you, answer me.

But nothing does.

He lies there, helpless, curled around the pillow. He doesn't want to be alone—not with his thoughts, or with the reality of his plight that drives nails into his skull. Krakli is there, up in the rafters, but it's not enough. All he wants is for someone to hold him, to feel another person's warmth, their breath, for someone to tell him it'll be alright.

It has to be alright. He has to get through this, for no other reason than to fulfill his oath. The vision of Andereth solidified his resolve to do whatever it takes to find her and her kin.

It doesn't matter if it doesn't make sense. This is the path *he* chose. Someone needs to help them, and it will be him, even if he does it alone.

Cool air fills his lungs. The pillow warms under the exhale. Repeat —in through his nose, out through his mouth. Again. *Figure it out. Put the pieces together.*

He pictures a large table, scratched and worn, stained with ink. On this mental surface, he carefully places each piece of information he's gathered since leaving the bathhouse.

A stone carved with a date: 4 ae, almost hidden by a thick bush.

The original owner of the bathhouse, noted only with the initials ADD.

Two artists who oversaw the mosaics—the very ones who crafted those in the emperor's throne room.

Why was a Gethki-style mosaic built *here*, on an island that wouldn't be part of the empire for another hundred years? Why include the sun and moon, and what was that serpent?

He wasn't able to find any additional information in Dalos' library beyond that. Tomorrow, he'll return to scour the old archives, searching for any information he can glean from the faded scrolls.

He lets his mental image fade, tucking each piece back into place. At least he can look forward to the library—something he dearly missed during his time in the legion. He can search for new information in earnest, now.

New clues regarding Andereth are exceedingly rare, and to have one so vague is a renewed torment. The entire situation frustrates him —finding information shouldn't be this difficult. His empire keeps meticulous records of everything *except* the celestial dragons. They are well documented for the first fifty years of the empire's history. After that, nothing—no trace, not a single document remains after that point. The records must have been purged somehow, but why? And by whom?

He has a theory, but even considering it makes his blood boil. If he's correct, the rulers of his empire, his birthright, are responsible for more than endless war. If true, he doesn't know if he can ever forgive them. But what does it matter? They're dead anyway, and he cannot confront them. All he can do is try to set things right. For the dragons, and all victims of his empire.

Old bitterness consumes him—he never wanted this. From his earliest days, he was groomed for the throne and despised every minute. He hates the senators, the politics, the posturing, and the constant passive-aggressive game that all royals must play. He also hates war, although he is exceedingly good at it. They gave him the highest accolades for the worst atrocities, and all he has to show for it is pain.

All he can do now is follow his oath. He will find those dragons. If they need freeing, he will release them, and if they need protection, he will protect them. He will fight for them, bleed for them, and suffer every miserable second of being emperor if it means he can see them fly free someday.

And if his empire truly is to blame, he is going to fix it. It's the least he can do.

V

AURORA

Shapeshifter

You must wake.

They don't want to. The bed feels too good. Every muscle is soaked in fatigue. Their heart labors, pounds in their head. It's so hot under the blankets, soggy with their sweat, but they can't move. It would be so wonderful to keep sleeping.

Their body shudders. Somehow, they know they're dying. Better it's here, in this soft bed, than on that ship. Ava will release their soul to dance among the spirits, and they will finally be free from their pain.

No. NO.

They don't want to die.

Sunlight presses against their eyelids. They bury their face in the pillow, trying to block the brightness. Darkness would be better.

A shadow falls across them. They try to protest when the blanket is peeled back, when strong hands turn them over. A wet cloth cools their burning skin, wiping the sweat from their face.

Someone lifts them into a sitting position. Metal presses against their lips—water. Their trembling hands rise to grip the cup, instinct taking over as they gulp the liquid. No, not water. Broth. The pain of their hunger is overwhelming. The cup is empty too soon—they want more. The cup is taken away. Whoever fed them returns them to bed, pulling the covers to their chin.

They sleep. Light fades, shifts to darkness. Each time they wake, someone is soon there with a cup of broth. They live for that cup, that thin liquid, that elixir of life.

Slowly, so slowly, their trembling ceases. Their fever cools. They can move their arms again, their legs, turn over in the bed. Finally, they open their eyes.

They're alive.

Sunlight bathes the room, dancing across the walls to highlight the forms of the *suroribi*. They stare at the spirit's depiction for a long time. It's an ancient art of painting that mixes magic into the pigment itself, giving the portraits a depth unachievable with mundane methods.

That's not all. The *suroribi* is different than her usual depiction. Her features are more fox-like, with a canine face, instead of a pretty human with tails and ears slapped on as an afterthought. It makes sense, considering the owner of this place.

It comforts them, in a way. Often, people forget the root of her story. She's meant to be a sign of hope when times get desperate, a spirit fighting for the lives of those around her. A protector of the weak, uplifter of the downtrodden. Her dark counterpart, the *sipu*, is her foil, trying to tear down all she holds dear.

Something about the mural catches their eye. They sit up to get a better view, squinting in the bright sunlight. In the candlelight, the *suroribi's* shadow wasn't visible. Now it's clear—a twisted shape, the form of the *sipu*, is present in each panel. Moreover, every shadow has a set of eyes, the sclera black as midnight, staring out across the room.

There is an even older tale.

Ava's voice is like a horn blast in their head. They cringe, instinctively putting their hands over their ears. *Good morning to you, too*, they reply, trying to compose themselves. *Well, what is it?*

Join me for breakfast, and I will tell you.

They scowl. It seems they won't get any reprieve for almost dying. Methodically, they put both feet on the floor. With an effort, they stand. The room spins a little, but only for a second. Step. Another step. Their legs don't collapse.

"Well. That's good," they say. They forgot what their real voice sounded like—a light tenor befitting their waifish form. It'll be good to use it again. It's been months since they sang anything. The men on the ship told them to stay silent after breaking the lute and throwing it overboard.

Miserable bunch of bastards. I hope they get plundered by pirates. Or sink in a storm. Or-

An oily sensation slides along their spine—dark, greasy, like something foul. Revenge would be a sweet wine they could savor. Their gaze falls on the *suroribi's* shadow. Their heart labors as they struggle to compose themselves.

Surely, they're going insane. It would make sense.

Their stomach growls. The longer they stand here, the longer before they can eat. They can't give in to the urge to stuff themselves, though, as much as they may want to. A lifetime ago, they studied healing under the stern tutelage of a Gethki cleric. It was while training with him that they encountered the first victims of a terrible famine: two hollow-eyed children, not much younger than them, all skin and bones and pleading cries for food. The cleric insisted on giving them tiny portions of bone broth and fermented vegetables when they would have fed them as much rice as possible. They hadn't understood why—until one day, some well-meaning person gave the little boy *dango*. They were forced to watch as his body deteriorated. It took two days for him to die, with seizures wracking his tiny frame. Through their recently awakened ability to read emotions, they felt his pain and confusion, watching helplessly as he faded. Not even the cleric could save him. "It happens when you give them too much too quickly," he said. "A starving body cannot handle such rich food right away."

They must be strong. No matter how hungry they are, they cannot give in to their body's demands. But some broth would be good.

There's another problem—they can't go downstairs naked. The thought of putting the quartermaster's clothes on makes their skin crawl. They could cast an illusion, but that prospect is equally unappealing. They're as unlikely to do that as they are to go out in their true form. They could become something with fur, but even felina wear clothes.

The quartermaster's uniform, then. It's intact, at least. They could craft a shape to fill it, but making their body bigger will only wear them out faster. It's better than nothing.

Resigned, they head toward the window, where they threw the uniform. It's gone. Instead, a drawstring pack of linen and leather rests on a small desk. A peek inside reveals a bundle of clothing. They carry it over to the bed, withdrawing each piece with reverence. A brown tunic, rough but well made—perfect for laborers or freedmen. A rich *exomis* dyed blue, with patterning along the hem. A red dress—a modified *stola* with a plunging neckline that makes their heart skip. There are accessories, too—Gethki-style sandals, a woven leather tunic belt, and a red shoulder drape with matching ribbon. The last thing from the bag is a pair of Soutorian *tabi* boots with a split toe, strung with golden laces.

They finish laying out the garments, too stunned to think. Ava reading thoughts is one thing, but this is something far deeper. These garments correspond to a theme they've crafted for their personas, aligning to the colors of a rainbow, a spectrum like the light their prism sheds on a wall. Now, they have a choice.

Their forms are another shield against the world, something to hide their true nature. Protection. They long for it to be more, to use their shapeshifting as an artistic expression, like their music. They long to be beautiful.

They run their fingers along the sloped collar of the *exomis*. Davros is their blue persona—a suave and charismatic duelist and performer. The form would be safer on a ship or in a crowded city. They wouldn't have to play the part in full—a little would do.

But their eye is drawn to the red *stola*. Aurora. They can be Aurora again—a confident woman ready to take on the world. Ava's promise of their safety lingers in their magic. They can be anyone they want. Here's the permission laid out on their sickbed. It's a chance to explore a side of themselves they rarely get.

Carefully, they fold the tunic and *exomis* and return it to the bag, along with the *tabi*. They face the mirror. Their skin shifts to pale smoothness as they fill out their form, transforming their starved male body into a curvaceous female one. The hair on Aurora's head lengthens to her waist and ripples to blonde, spilling around her heart-shaped face and over her shoulders. She studies her reflection in the mirror, frowning.

I wish I could feel as healthy as I look. Or as beautiful.

She puts on the *stola*, settling it over her body. The neckline plunges to her navel—an entertainer's dress. It fits perfectly, of course. She wouldn't expect anything less of Ava. She retrieves the matching wrap, draping it over her shoulders and chest.

Finally, she braids her hair and ties it with the ribbon. The weight of the braid settling between her shoulder blades makes her giddy. She loves how the dress looks—the curve of the fabric and the complex layers of the sleeves. The sandals are perfect, too. With her blonde hair and light brown eyes, she could be a Fresian entertainer. She adds that to Aurora's tale, weaving it together with her existing narrative like melodies in a ballad.

Her stomach growls. No use in keeping Ava waiting. Aurora pulls on her sandals, gives the mirror one last look, and heads through the door.

Aurora's legs shake with fatigue when she makes it down the stairs. She clings to the railing for a moment. How did she manage to make it off that ship? Whatever strength possessed her, it's gone now. After a few moments, she straightens and puts one foot in front of the other. Each step is a victory, and she will savor the reward.

A feast of smells washes over Aurora as she emerges into a small dining area. The scent of stewing vegetables is overwhelming. There's bread, too—a dangerous temptation.

Aurora finds Ava at a high table, perched like an elegant bird on a stool. She wears the same leather corset, showing flawless skin above the tightly laced garment. Aurora collapses on the stool across from her, bracing herself on the table.

"You are looking much better, my child," Ava croons. "I am pleased."

Aurora bites back a sarcastic response, choosing courtesy instead. Someone under Ava's employ nursed Aurora back to health. So, she tilts her head and says, "Thank you for caring for me. Your hospitality is second to none, and I wonder how this doesn't put me in your debt." *Or what I did to deserve it.*

"You may say the thoughts out loud, child." Ava studies Aurora's face. "A gift does not incur a debt, for we are not the fey. Perhaps the world owes *you* a debt. It has been most unkind to one of its most important saviors."

Aurora's stomach growls loudly. She places her hands on her belly, imagining her true form's emaciation. "No one owes me anything. I haven't saved anyone."

"Yet. Many will owe you their lives before long."

Aurora's stomach complains again. The smell of food is a torture she's struggling to ignore.

"Pardon me," Ava says. "You have been so patient, humoring me." She waves her hand, sending a spark of lavender foxfire from the small room. "We will make you whole, and you will fulfill your destiny."

"Great. The apocalypse," Aurora says. "Can't wait."

"*Sipu*," Ava says reproachfully.

Aurora cringes. The word hurts worse than the lash. Tears well as she stares at her hands, her strong fingers trained for the lute. Hands she's used to heal others since she was a child. She's tried so hard not to be that foul shadow, and the only thing her efforts have brought her is pain and abuse.

"Why do you call me that and allow me to live?" she demands. Her throat wants to close over the words, but she forces them out. "You saved me, fed me, and now you call me the worst thing possible." She raises her head and clenches her hands into fists. "*Why?*"

"To prove a point. Old tales are merely that—tales. Stories to teach, inform, thrill, and entertain. Reality is not an old tale; no one can be defined solely by words passed by ignorant lips." Ava's face is a statue, flawless and cold. "Time has twisted the story into falsehood. Long ago, the *sipu* and the *suroribi* were not mortal enemies, but inseparable. You cannot have one without the other."

Aurora stares at Ava. She swallows, trying to focus, but she's so hungry, so tired. Her head feels like someone packed wool between her ears. She has to eat *now*. The need overpowers every thought she has.

"I don't understand," she chokes.

"You will." Ava reaches across the table and grabs Aurora's chin, holding it fast. "You consider yourself unnatural, a creature apart from the cycle driving this world. Banish those thoughts. You are as natural as the moon in the sky and the sea which brought you here. You are flesh and blood, created from the union of male and female. A woman conceived you, grew you inside her, and delivered you with pain and blood. Your destiny is not to end this world, as you insist on believing. You are cursed only by your pain." Ava's eyes flare with violet foxfire. "I will not coddle you. You must face the truth and do it soon. Your future depends on it. Do not wallow in self-pity any longer."

She releases her grip. Aurora slumps over the table. "That doesn't explain anything," she manages.

"Impudent child," Ava says. Her words are softer now, with the slightest hint of affection. "Your fighting spirit is strong. Perhaps that is why your magic has grown."

"You're not going to explain, are you?"

Ava waves her hand in elegant dismissal. "I, like Nylocke, have decided to take a chance on you. You know I cannot tell you more."

"Of course, you know my *pater's* name. Why am I surprised?" Aurora manages to straighten. "Right, all this divine shit means I need to figure it out myself. How much time until my life 'changes,' anyway?"

"Three weeks."

Aurora shivers. She was out for a week. That long, and she feels like she still has one foot in the underworld. "Is there anything I can do around here?"

"Yes. When you return to your chambers, you will have what you need to assist me. Keep what you find. It is an investment." Ava stands as a hulking form fills the doorway. "We will continue to care for you, make you strong enough to fight. That is a promise. Join me for dinner."

She leaves before Aurora can reply, slipping past the new arrival. The felina is huge, with an enormous mane and piercing amber eyes. His tan tunic almost blends with his tawny fur, making the spotless white apron over it stand out like a beacon. He holds a tray that looks too small, stocked with covered bowls.

Aurora forces herself to remain still, resisting the urge to shrink away. He won't harm her — Ava wouldn't allow it. Besides, it's not his fault he was born big and terrifying. She shouldn't be rude.

"Uh, hi," she squeaks.

"Hello. This is for you," he says in a deep, accented voice, placing the tray in front of her. "It is good to see you moving around. I am pleased."

Someone cared for her while she was dying, someone who wasn't Ava. Perhaps it was him. "Thank you," she says.

"My brother has made a special meal for you."

Aurora smiles weakly as he pulls out the stool across from her and settles onto it. "You don't have to—"

Her stomach interrupts her, cramping so hard she doubles over. The felina's ears twitch as her face flushes scarlet. "Never mind."

"I will stay here. If you need more, I will bring it. Do not mind me."

Aurora tries to relax. She uncovers the bowls, revealing steamed leeks and a large bowl of broth. Setting in, the taste overwhelms her. The food is lightly spiced with subtle flavor, not bland at all. Warmth spreads through her body as she finishes the leeks and then the soup.

"It was delicious," she tells him.

Teeth flash in his scarred muzzle, causing her heart to jerk. She hides her reaction by grabbing the fruit juice and sipping it.

"I will tell my brother. His name is Gesur." He tilts his head. "I am Hayat. What is this form's name?"

That's right. If he cared for her, he would have seen her true form. The shame tries to sink its claws into her again. "Aurora. It's nice to meet you."

"Yes. Ava tells us that you have a good voice. Will you sing us a song at dinner?"

Aurora almost wants to cry. The thought of performing again makes her heart soar. "I'd love to."

"I look forward to it." He stands and moves to her side, holding out his hand. "Allow me to help you with the stairs."

After a few seconds of hesitation, Aurora places her hand in his. He leads her up the stairs, letting her lean on him as they reach the top. He remains until she recovers, then departs, letting her enter the room alone.

She stops inside the doorway when she sees Ava's gift. A lute rests on a small stand near the bed, the lacquered wood shining in the bright morning sun. It's plain but finely crafted, and its graceful lines bring fresh tears to Aurora's eyes. It thrums with power when she picks it up. Delicate enchantments permeate the instrument like the walls. Aurora tunes it, humming to herself, letting her fingers find the familiar patterns on the strings.

The tears flow freely now as music swells from the lute. She pours her soul into the music and fills the room with her light soprano, delighting in its return as if greeting an old friend.

Several days pass before Aurora can spend more than a few hours out of bed. She monitors her progress every morning, staring at her true form in the mirror. Consequently, she can look at it now without cringing, albeit barely. Sinking back into a healing role, if only for herself, has given her a new grasp on things and a sense of control amid so much uncertainty.

Ava and Gesur have her on broth and fermented vegetables, but she eats thrice daily and has far more energy than when she arrived. Then again, she almost died, so anything is an improvement over that.

Aurora finishes her letter and seals it with wax from one of the white-flamed candles. Later, she'll send it to Caltava. Hopefully, it's not too late.

Five months ago, a letter from her best friend Romero reached her in Geth. The wizard greeted her and wished her well in Gethki, updating her on his travels from Selucia across the continent to Carbay and tales of his new home. It stung to read his friendly words after almost a year.

Then, the letter switched to Soutorian—a language few in the Gethki empire could read. In it, he outlined a mission of utmost secrecy and unfathomable complexity. They could use a mage of her caliber, he said, if she could make it to Caltava and join the master wizard there. *It will change the world*, Romero finished. *Imagine traveling across the empire in an instant. Think of the possibilities!*

When she received the letter, she was one voice lost in the roaring din of Geth, barely managing to feed herself. Although she was suspicious, her trust in Romero won out. She left on the first ship she could find. Too bad it turned out to be a trap.

It doesn't matter now. She can move forward. Aurora longs for a reality where she can make a difference.

She stands, stretches, and reaches for the small bag containing her few things. Aurora plans to go out for the first time since arriving in

Notri, hoping to book passage on a ship. The thought of taking the risk terrifies her, but she can't live off Ava's hospitality forever. A quick change of clothes later, she faces the mirror wearing the brown tunic. Leaving the safety of Ava's tavern as Aurora is a step too far. So she shifts, adopting another of her favorite forms. Her body slims, changing from female to male, her hair shortening and her shoulders widening. Davros checks the mirror and sweeps his straight brown hair back from his face.

He picks up the letter and heads out into the terrifying world.

VI

LANDING

Pica

Pica shivers under his heavy cloak as the damp sand shifts beneath his weight. The first rays of light crest over the island's far side, lifting his spirits but not enough to drive away the deep despair in his bones.

A ship floats offshore—a trading vessel. Odd that it's not in the harbor. Perhaps they didn't want to pay the docking fee. Or they're smugglers. Either way, it's none of his business.

Last night, his dreams of blood and death haunted him more than usual. After three times trying to expel the contents of his stomach, he finds himself here on the beach, his feet moving with a purpose that surprises him.

They come!

It's that voice again. Anxiety starts to crest in his chest. *Who?* he asks it.

No response. He looks around the deserted beach, turning completely around. A figure follows him—a recognizable one, with that thin frame and billowing white cloak. Seto—Kisara's lover and their group's wizard—jogs up to him. The wizard's brown hair falls into his face as he leans to catch his breath, pale cheeks bright red with exertion.

"How'd I know I'd find you here, Draconius?" Seto says after a moment. He straightens and raises his chin. The wizard is a head shorter than him and considerably slimmer, but Pica knows better than to underestimate him. Seto's blue eyes squint in the morning light as he studies Pica's face. "You look rough."

"Good morning to you, too," Pica says wryly. He doesn't take his rudeness personally. Seto treats everyone like that—except Kisara. Pica always tries to be polite to him, if only to annoy the prickly wizard further. "I didn't sleep well. Something wrong?"

"The air is off," Seto says. He spins on a boot heel to stride along the beach. Pica marches in step with him as a matter of habit. The wizard stares straight ahead, keeping his back stiff. "The spirits are upset."

He would know. Seto is an expert in summoning magic, the art of calling divine or elemental entities to one's aid. His discomfort confirms what Pica can sense—something is wrong on a magical level. Explains Krakli's grumpiness this morning, too.

"What's that?" Seto asks, pointing ahead of them.

Further along the beach, half-submerged in the lapping surf, is a pale and twisted shape. Pica's stomach clenches as he realizes what it is.

A body.

He's running. Sand shifts beneath his heavy footfalls as Seto calls out in surprise. He braces himself for what awaits him. Drowned bodies have a certain appearance, a distinctive sight he can never scrub from his memories. Not after his cohort was forced to retreat across a flood-swollen river. He shoves the image away.

Upon approach, however, a different sight awaits him. The corpse isn't a drowning victim. Instead of a swollen and putrid mess, it's shriveled despite its watery tomb—desiccated, like the mummified kings of Tekan. Pica drops to his knees, steeling himself before inspecting it. Hundreds, no *thousands* of puncture wounds riddle every part of the hapless man's body. Just like...

Thousands of thick needles drive themselves into his flesh, everywhere, into his arms and legs and even his face.

The image from last night flashes through his head. He manages to push it back down, his jaw set. Seto crouches next to him, frowning. He holds out a hand, palm out. Pale blue magic swirls around his fingers. The wizard's frown deepens. "Draconius, what can you tell me?"

Pica grimaces and brushes the man's skin with the back of his fingers. He gags at what he finds. "His blood is gone," he says. His hand feels foul. He casts the cleaning spell, but the disgusting sensation lingers.

"There's a residue here. Divine origin but corrupted." Seto stands and steps away from the body. "We should get the town guard before they think we did this."

"Right." Pica stands, wiping his hand vigorously on his tunic.

They come! the voice inside him says, tinged with fear.

The ship groans as it hits something underwater. Pica turns and peers out at it. His blood burns with rage, primal and raw, from the deepest depths of him. Seto takes a step back, his mouth opening.

Krakli's panic washes over Pica, nearly bringing him to his knees. The familiar flees in silence as something sharp drives into Pica's forearm. A tiny bird sinks its beak to the hilt through his tunic sleeve. Crimson feathers flash in the weak sunlight as Pica's anger boils over. His magic reacts of its own accord, and the tiny bird bursts into flames, writhing before crumbling to ash. Pica looks around wildly, scanning the horizon.

"You should have let me look at that first," Seto complains. "That was a—"

Flame kindles to life in Pica's hands. He strides forward, unthinking, his magic burning fever-hot. It sweeps over him like a rushing river, pulling him under.

"—summon," the wizard finishes.

A smear of black, undulating unnaturally, rises from the stricken ship.

Burn them! The entity's voice is desperate, panicked.

Fire streaks from Pica's outstretched palms. The first shots sizzle in the water. He aims higher, strafing closer to the swarm. Another bird flashes past him, its wings humming. Maddening. These things must die. All of them must *die.*

"Draconius!" Seto calls out.

Pica pumps more fire into the approaching cloud, charring swaths of them to ash. One errant shot hits the sail of the stricken ship, igniting it.

Burn. Burn it. Kill them! The voice is pleading now.

Fire spreads rapidly along the sail. The birds circle into the air before heading straight for the beach—straight for him. Seto shouts. Streaks of lightning curve around Pica as the wizard summons his elemental spirits—miniature wyverns made of lightning which dart and weave through the swarm, turning them to charred ruins. The burning sail sags and lands on the deck of the hapless vessel, igniting it despite the dampness of the morning. The magical fire licks across the wood, consuming it. The mast lights. The figurehead follows shortly after. Pica watches numbly as Seto's summons turn the cloud to char. A pounding in his head. A pounding of fists against wood. Screams.

There are people alive on the ship.

Oh no. No no no no not again.

More birds pour out of the ship, heading for the shore. Thousands, tens of thousands. He glances at the desiccated body, riddled with puncture wounds, then his arm weeping blood. The horror creeps over him as realization dawns—if those birds get to the island and can spread through the population...

The ship burns. The birds approach. He looks between the two, the cold calculation already settling into place. He mutters a small apology to the souls he's about to condemn and turns his attention to the cloud.

"Seto!" he shouts, pointing. "Don't let it reach the island!"

More sparks, more wyverns, more flames. Pica grits his teeth as he burns through the cloud, relishing the roar as ash whirls like snow. They make quick work of the swarm with their elemental assault, the smell of smoke a choking send-off.

A bird flits in front of his face. Its black eyes, filled with malevolence, fix on his as it hovers, its tiny wings moving impossibly fast. Ruby feathers shimmer like gems at its throat below a long and wickedly sharp beak. The humming grows louder—deafening. Pica covers his ears as a snarling voice speaks in his mind, scraping across his brain like gravel. *So you return. So be it. You'll die just as well this time.*

Enemy, the voice inside him hisses. Hatred courses through him along those emotional threads, a cavernous sense of betrayal. Fire builds in him, begging to escape, to take revenge on the foul being behind the bird's eyes. Pica's skin burns hot, swirls up his arms to singe the sleeves of his tunic. The world narrows—all he can see is blurred wings and inky-black feathers.

A shout, and sparks surround the tiny creature. They swirl in a flashing orb before collapsing in a blaze of blue light, taking the bird with it. Seto holds a stone between two fingers, with a hastily scrawled rune painted in crimson on the smooth surface. Blood drips from his fingers onto the sand.

A crashing sound draws Pica's eyes back to the ship. The golden inferno chews through the wood to the waterline. The roar of the flames and the crash of burning timber can't drown out the screams. In his mind, he can see the twisted limbs, smell the stench of burning hair—the memory of villagers staggering forward, their skin splitting, before they collapse in a heap of black bones and charred meat.

Pica sinks to his knees, trying desperately to keep the memories at bay. People are dying—dying because of him. Again. So much blood. There's always so much blood. It runs in the cracks of a cobblestone street. It paints the sides of destroyed homes. It stains his hands, and it will remain no matter how much he scrubs. He is forever stained with the blood of innocents.

"Draconius! We have to go!"

Seto's voice sounds distant. The screams are louder. So loud. Water and bile hit the sand as he retches. Something inside him shatters like porcelain, and his stomach heaves again. The things he's tried to forget come flooding in—the stink of battle and the ruin he helped carve through a pristine land. His fingers scrape against wool as he tries to wipe the blood away.

Blood and shit pooled in spring furrows. A broken sandal. The endless rattle of steel armor and bronze chains, the cries of a hundred new slaves. A young man's eyes unfocused, unseeing, the pilum through his guts nailing him to a stone wall.

A jolt knocks every thought from Pica's head for a long and blessed second. Seto kneels in front of him, the two ends of broken bark in his hands smoldering, filling Pica's nose with an acrid scent. It's enough for him to realize Seto is speaking.

"—to get up!"

Seto shakes him. Pica grips his arm, centering himself. The visions fade as he locks them away. His throat burns with bile.

"We're out of time," Seto says, pulling fruitlessly on Pica's arm.

"Let's *go*."

"No. You go. I'll explain to the guards. We need to warn the island."

"Idiot. They'll arrest you."

"That's the *point*. They can't hold me. *Go*."

The guards arrest him, something Pica allows with exhausted apathy. When they try to put him in chains, though, he merely glares. One guard, a scrawny Fresian youth with the barest gasp of a mustache, wilts away from him. The other guard, an overweight Gethki man, stands well away, his sallow face florid ever since Pica's demonstration of his fire magic.

"D-don't run," the youth squeaks. "J-just come peacefully and—"

"Yes, yes, let's go," Pica grumbles and walks up the beach. When he reaches solid dirt, he waits for the struggling guards to catch up. They fall in step beside him, leading him through the narrow streets of Dalos' poor district. Their path is lined with frescoes defaced with graffiti and sagging awnings, long since faded to white. A few people watch them from dark windows and doorways. Pica raises his chin and endures their stares. There's no need for them to know how close they came to death.

They reach the modest guard station and escort him to a cell. The bars are made of wood, warped by dampness and age. He tries not to sigh as he settles onto the floor, disdaining the stained cot. The overweight guard slams the door with shaking hands, murmuring something about the guard captain and questions.

Pica closes his eyes and rests his head against the damp wall. The corpse of the ship burns against his eyelids, causing his empty stomach to churn. He swore he wouldn't take any more innocent lives with his fire. Yet, his power rose in him like a firestorm, and once again, people died at his hands. But this time, he can't blame it on duty.

His magic went out of control. The thing inside him took over, turned him into a weapon. It makes him sick to do so, but he clings desperately to the knowledge that his fire saved the island. It's the only solace he has. Not even his familiar is there to reassure him.

The fact that Krakli hasn't reappeared is worrying. The magpie is no stranger to violence or its aftermath. Krakli's reaction to those blood-drinking birds was extreme—Pica's never felt such fear from his familiar.

Warrior...

The sound is faint but unmistakable. Pica tries to establish a connection. It slips through his hands like a slimy eel. A slight brush of emotions—was that embarrassment?

Enemy...

Enemy. That's what the entity called that bird. Pica recalls the hate, the seething desire for revenge. Something is happening, something Pica doesn't have all the pieces to. What were those birds?

What *is* inside him?

His body relaxes against the wall as he slips into a light sleep. He only wakes when he hears commotion down the hall, a raspy voice overbearing the squeaking of the Fresian guard. Boots ring on stone and stop in front of his cell.

"What in Ulios' name are you doing here?" a familiar voice barks.

Pica opens his eyes. The guard captain is a stout man with broad shoulders and black hair shot with gray. His armor shines with oil, and his uniform cloak is without stain or wrinkle. Some legion habits never leave a man. "Axius," Pica says in a tired greeting, saluting with a fist to the chest. "Well met. Didn't know you were in the south."

"Hah! My wife and I decided Geth was too lively for our old bones. What are you doing here? Your uncle finally get sick of you?"

Pica's lips narrow at the understatement. Some of the arguments between Pica and his uncle had nearly come to blows. "Had to give me back to the Order."

The Fresian youth looks back and forth between them. "You know him, sir?"

"Know him! Hah! This big bastard was a whelp when he strode into my century's camp like he owned the place. Never did beat the pride out of him." Axius thumps the guard soundly on the back. "Cyamus, let him out. I trust you didn't give my men trouble, Regillus?" he asks Pica.

"Regillus? Did you say *Regillus*?" Cyamus' mouth gapes, opening and closing like a fish. The youth almost rips the door off the cell when he yanks it open.

"Congratulations. Not many can say they arrested the crown

prince," Axius says dryly. "Go get a basin ready so our 'captive' can freshen up. No offense, Regillus, but you look awful."

Cyamus bows so deeply that he almost tips over and disappears in a rush.

Pica hauls himself to his feet and exits the cell, clapping his hand on Axius' shoulder. "Thanks."

"Wine?" Axius asks. "You're going to need it, especially with all the questions I got for you."

Pica gives his old centurion a weary smile. "I certainly do."

Pica's muscles burn as he lifts the bag of sand and lowers it again. He repeats the gesture with the other arm: up, down, right hand, left hand, repeat. He throws his mind into the familiar task, sweating in the afternoon sun beaming on the open deck of *Raven's Flight*. Crewmen work around him, ignoring his presence. His daily workouts have become as routine to them as their tasks.

Some soldiers turn to drink to quiet the screams. Some gamble and whore until they're destitute. Others miss the thrill of battle so much they seek it at every opportunity, selling their swords to fill the holes in their hearts. Others quietly fade away. Some lucky bastards don't suffer—they return to their families whole and happy as if they were merely on a grand tour of whatever land they were stationed in.

Pica has always turned his inner turmoil into action. During active duty, it was so easy to push it to the next day and the one after that. Always something to do. Since leaving two months ago, the lack of activity has let the thoughts creep in.

Perhaps that's why his mind keeps returning to those birds. He turns the encounter over in his head, trying to view it from all angles, letting his brain pick apart the details. Where did the ship come from? What kind of bird was it?

Who spoke to him?

You'll die just as well this time.

There are surely pieces missing. He'd like to go to the library or ask around the docks for information, but Axius commanded him to stay around *Raven's Flight* in case they needed him for further questioning. He listened without argument—it seems other habits never leave a legionnaire.

Krakli was waiting for him when he returned to the ship. Pica found his familiar in his cabin, huddled behind his bag. No coaxing could draw him out, so Pica set out water and dried meat before leaving.

He finishes his routine and moves to lean against the mast. The enormous wooden pillar has been pulled and laid along the ship's length. Somewhere behind him, riggers repair the sails and replace worn ropes, chatting rapidly in a southern language he doesn't know.

The sweat on his face and upper body dries in the afternoon sun. He turns his face into it, savoring its warmth in the cool air of the day. The presence inside him stirs in the light, flushing his skin, almost as if it's enjoying the warmth, too.

A shadow falls over him. Pica opens his eyes and sees a tall figure, hair ablaze with red and gold. Pica's heart lifts a little.

"Heya, Lucius," Sparax says. "Copper for your thoughts?"

Pica snorts. "My thoughts are royal, therefore worth a gold." He pats the wood next to him. "Sit. You're in the way. My thoughts are powered by sunlight."

"Your thoughts are powered by muscle and audacity," Sparax retorts, settling beside Pica. "But seriously, are you alright? Seto told us what happened."

"I'm managing." Pica's gaze meets the blue eyes of the other paladin. "I thought you'd be drunk in the streets by now."

Sparax pauses before replying. "I wanted to talk to you alone. It's...been some time since I've gotten to."

The last time they had a conversation alone, it became an argument, and both said things that couldn't be retracted. That was six years ago—surely now, things will be better. Pica chooses to cling to that hope.

"Sure. What do you want to talk about?"

"Nothing specific. Just..." Sparax sighs. "I missed you, Lucius."

Pica winces. "Yeah. I know."

Sparax's face turns toward him. "That's it? An 'I know'?"

"I'm...sor—"

"I don't want an apology."

Stop being an idiot. "I...Sparax. I missed you, too."

Sparax pats him on the shoulder. "See? That wasn't so hard. Like taking meat from a hungry wolf." His smile falters. "Lucius, why did you change your mind?"

"Change my mind?"

"About being in the legion. About coming back to m—" He swallows. "Us."

"Oh." Pica stretches, knitting his fingers together and pushing them out before him. His knuckles crack loudly. "I didn't have a choice. My father commanded it, so my uncle had to let me leave. He wanted me to defy his orders, but I wanted out. It's the only good thing my father has done for me."

"I see. Is it...permanent?" Sparax's voice quavers a little.

Pica looks at him with a lump in his throat. "Yes, Sparax. I'm not going back to that."

Relief floods Sparax's face. "I'm...good. That's good. But why? You were so eager to leave when—" He closes his mouth, stifling the words.

"I didn't know—" The words falter. He tries again. "What I did was—"

"Lucius? I don't understand."

There, the tightening in his throat. He tries to figure out a way around it. Sparax deserves to know. "Did you—when you were a gladiator, did you ever have to—" He draws a thumb across his throat.

"Kill others?"

Pica nods.

"No, only animals." Sparax pauses. "I imagine you had to kill others, right? In a battle?"

Hundreds. Thousands. Pica tried to stick to his spear, but when his uncle ordered it, he had no choice but to use fire. He was nothing more than a weapon. A lot of them were helpless villagers. *Children.*

He should have said no. But he was young, eager to impress his uncle Monedula, driven to be a strong and powerful warrior—the opposite of his slovenly and lazy father. He'd been force-fed lies about the glory of his empire his entire life. Honorable battle between hardened warriors—that was a Gethki war, not wholesale slaughter and subjugation of an innocent population. By the time he realized it, it was too late. He was already a monster, stained by blood and ash.

That's when he started to defy Monedula—not openly, but in small ways. Evacuating a village before burning it. Ordering his cohort not to take slaves. It wasn't enough.

"Not just," he chokes out. "Lot more."

He blindly reaches out for Sparax's hand. They intertwine fingers like they used to, and he clings to the familiar warmth with all his might.

"How many more?" Sparax asks.

Pica jerks his thumb to the sky.

"Why didn't you tell me?"

The pain in Sparax's voice is like a dagger. "Can't," Pica says. He feels like screaming. How had it come to this?

"I would have been there for you," Sparax insists. "I would have *listened*."

"I can't," Pica says. "It won't—the words won't—" He draws a long breath and waits for a beat. "I wish I hadn't—"

"Hadn't left?"

Pica jerks his head in a nod.

"It's too late for that now."

The silence stretches for several minutes as Pica bows his head. Hundreds of hammers and thousands of shouts don't drown out his ragged breathing. This is it, then. Sparax surely can't forgive him after this.

It's inevitable. Everything is tainted now. He doesn't deserve Sparax's forgiveness. Beautiful Sparax, quick to laugh, who always had a smile for him. Sparax, who didn't care about social status or bloodlines. The chasm between the heir apparent and an escaped slave—it didn't matter when they were alone.

Now, that chasm is deeper than ever. Pica desperately wants to bridge it, to go back to the way things were before. But, as hard as he tries, the words won't come.

Eventually, Sparax sighs and pulls his hand away. He stands before turning to look at Pica, the sunlight dappling his face. "I'm sorry, Lucius. I thought I was ready for this, but I'm not. I need some time to think."

"Promise me something?" Pica manages.

"What's that?"

"Don't be a stranger."

Sparax sighs. "Despite my better judgment, you haven't gotten rid of me yet." He turns and heads toward the gangplank, then pauses. "You won't be a stranger either, right?"

Pica lays his head back on the mast. "Not anymore."

After two days of waiting, Axius arrives at dawn to dismiss his confinement to *Raven's Flight* with a somber summation of their investigation. No one was left alive. Most of the bodies were too burned to tell if they died from the fire or the birds.

"We tried to keep a lid on your identity, so the magistrate is calling for the punishment of such a 'reckless mage.' I'm holding him off as best I can, but Regillus." Axius' face falls. "I have to tell him soon."

Pica sighs. "Tiberia is going to *hate* this."

"Who?"

"My sister. Never mind. Thank you, Axius. We'll be off tomorrow. Tell them whatever you need."

The guard captain salutes him and is almost off the ship when Pica asks, "Where did the ship come from?"

"Charris," Axius says over his shoulder, then departs.

Pica's stomach drops. Charris. The disappearances, the rumors—those birds have to be the reason. It fits too well.

That ship he burned is only the beginning of their troubles. If it made it this far, swept east on the currents, there could be more scattered through the sea, pushed by wind and waves into the heart of Geth's trade network.

Pica sits hard on the mast, staring out over the water of Dalos' harbor. The implications of dozens of ships, each with their lethal cargo, landing amongst the people and dragons of the Coast—the destruction they'd cause is unfathomable.

Their Order had been sent on this mission to investigate the strange matters in the southern seas. Pica expected pirates, uprisings, or any other mundane reasons that waited across the turquoise water.

Now, perhaps all that waits for them is death.

It is midmorning when the first rumble of thunder echoes from the east. Pica sets down his weights and stares into the clear blue sky. He opens his senses and waits—the next flash, the next rumble, and the magic brushes past him. Another attack?

Krakli chirps and circles above his head—he feels it, too. Pica pulls on his tunic and slings his bag over his shoulder, digging through the side pocket. Sandals slap on wood as he hurries down the gangplank and out of the dry dock. People all around him stare at the sky as he pushes past them. After ducking into an alley and looking around, he withdraws an intricately carved horse statue from his bag, sets it on the ground, and whispers, "Eclipsis, heed."

The statue expands quickly to fill the narrow alley. The black warhorse tosses her head, her greeting an enthusiastic neigh. She's enormous, much taller than the biggest draft horse. Pica grabs her reins and strokes her nose.

"Hey, old friend," he says. "We're going for a ride."

A more enthusiastic squeal of excitement comes from the horse, echoed by Krakli's shrill whistle. The magpie flies in tight circles around them, calling out his raspy greeting. Pica basks in their reunion momentarily before pulling himself onto Eclipsis' riding pad using the thick leather straps, settling onto her back.

"Eclipsis, I need you to go east," he tells her.

She reaches around and nibbles his leg in response.

Pica sighs and pats her on the neck. "Treats later. It may be urgent."

Eclipsis tosses her head, snorts in derision, and canters over the cobblestones. Lightning flashes again, and she whinnies, pointing her nose at it.

"Yes, that's where you need to go. Very good."

She prances a few steps side to side at the praise. Emerging from the street onto a dirt road, she increases her speed. She gallops when they hit an open field, surging forward, her long legs covering the distance with deceptive ease. Pica watches the sky.

A bolt strikes the ground nearby. Eclipsis tosses her head but keeps running forward. A ripping sound immediately follows, a deafening peal of thunder like a solid object. Eclipsis vaults a bush, and another field comes into view. A bronze dragon crouches there, scales shimmering in the sunlight, neck arched in a graceful bow.

Levnys? It has to be.

A smaller dragon stands facing her, not a third of her size. It's silver-white and unlike any dragon Pica's ever seen. Ragged wings beat the air as it roars. A ball of lightning forms in its jaws, then screams into the sky, exploding with a blinding flash. Pica recognizes the magic at last.

Kisara!? How?

A crowd gathers at the edge of the field. A mix of awe and fear paints their faces as they point and shout. One man stands in the field with his back to Pica's approach, white cloak flapping in the wind. His brown hair stands straight on end as he stares forward, arms crossed.

Seto.

Lightning flickers and Kisara roars again, a feral bellow, before her head whips toward Seto. Her eyes blaze with uncontrolled rage before she leaps at the wizard, claws outstretched.

"Kisara!" Pica screams. He's too far away to stop her. Seto doesn't flinch as Levnys makes her move. Like a mother cat playing with her kitten, she pounces on Kisara, knocking her sideways and pinning the smaller dragon beneath her front legs. Lighting crackles in the air as Kisara struggles, snapping her jaws uselessly.

Eclipsis stops next to Seto, blowing hard and snorting. Pica slides off, running as soon as his sandals hit the ground.

"Wait!" Seto says. Pica halts abruptly, staring at the two dragons with apprehension twisting around his gut. Kisara stops struggling, bringing her head up to touch noses with Levnys. The bronze dragon nuzzles her and lets her up. "Good," she says. "You regained control faster, I am pleased." She crouches and adds, "Please do it again." Lightning swirls between Kisara's open jaws before flashing forward, bridging the gap between the two dragons. Levnys basks in it, running her claws through the elemental stream. "A good amount of power. The sky version, now, and do not lose control."

Kisara's voice fills the air with thrumming magic. Dark clouds form above her, then lightning arcs, tearing chunks from the ground as the thunder grows deafening. Pica tenses when his sister lunges forward, jaws wide, at Levnys' head. Then, she stumbles, cutting the attack short. Levnys' wings unfurl a little as she sweeps her front leg around Kisara and pulls her close, arching her neck around the shoulders of the smaller dragon. Kisara closes her eyes and leans into the embrace, visibly shaking.

Pica's shoulders relax. Relief drives away the apprehension, releasing the grip of adrenaline. Seto steps up next to him, never taking his eyes from Kisara.

"Well done," Levnys croons. "I am proud. Let us stop for now, so you may rest."

Kisara takes a step back as she shifts her form. She bows deeply to Levnys before turning to Pica and Seto with a broad smile, curly hair mussed and clothes rumpled, but eyes shining with child-like glee. Pica hugs her tightly, cherishing the rare happiness. How long had it been since he's seen her so happy? "Kisara, that was incredible." He pulls away and looks up at her. "Since when can you become a dragon?"

"Couple years ago. I couldn't control it, though. Not until Levnys helped me." She hugs him again. "I get to train like you do!"

"I'm delighted, Kisara, I mean it."

She turns from him and steps over to Seto. He looks at her with a wide smile. Pica smirks and steps away from the couple as Eclipsis snorts and stomps her foot. Turning, he sees Levnys approaching. He faces her as she stops before him and lowers her colossal head.

"Good morning, Lucius," she says.

"Good morning," he replies. "I see you're starting the day strong."

She snorts, causing the ground around his feet to puff in dust clouds crackling with static. Eclipsis lets out a startled whinny. "I am happy to see you. I am sorry for scaring your horse."

"She's fine. She's not truly a horse." He glances over his shoulder. "You can drop the act. No one cares."

The horse nickers and immediately calms, dropping her head to tear at the grass.

Levnys peers around him at his mount. "You have another familiar?"

"Yeah, she's like Krakli," he says. "Except Eclipsis decided to be an overly large horse for an overly large prince."

Levnys squints at him. "I have not heard this story yet."

"Well, no. I had no reason to mention it until now."

"I would like to hear it. You will go to town with me today and tell me. I will show you the best place to eat fresh fish."

"I don't get a choice in this, do I?" he asks.

Her huge eyes twinkle. "You always have a choice, Lucius. Perhaps you do not want to spend time with me?"

His heart lurches before he realizes the dragon is teasing him. "You know I do, Levnys, but what about Kisara?"

The dragon glances at the couple. Kisara has her arm around Seto's shoulders, talking breathlessly. "We will resume later. I do not wish to push her too hard." Levnys turns her gaze back to Pica expectantly.

He raises his hands. "You got me. I'll go with you to town, but I have places I want to go, too. You'll have to come along."

"Very well. Although..." She shifts her eyes to Eclipsis. "I have never ridden on a horse before."

Pica quirks his eyebrow. "You haven't? I find that hard to believe."

"Most horses do not tolerate a dragon's presence." She transforms, shrinking and twisting in a haze of magic. "We do eat them, after all."

"I see." Pica turns to Eclipsis. "Well, we have a bit of time for a ride before going to town, don't we, old friend?" Eclipsis' head jerks up. Her excitement washes back into Pica's senses, and he grins. "I knew you'd like that idea. Come, Levnys, stand next to me."

He picks her up, places her on Eclipsis' back, and gets on in front. Her hands grip his tunic as he turns the horse's head. Levnys nearly falls off when Eclipsis trots forward. Pica sighs and reaches to grab her, pulling her back up.

"You need to hold on to me. Lean against my back, and don't let go." Her arms wrap around his stomach, and something in him stirs. He does his best to ignore it as Eclipsis pulls at the bit. "Yeah, yeah, give us a minute. Be patient," he tells the horse.

"Is this better?" Levnys asks as she presses her face against his back.

"Better. Are you ready?"

"Yes. What am I ready fo-"

Pica lets slack into the reins. The horse surges forward, her legs churning as she races across the open field. Levnys' arms tighten around him. He lets Eclipsis run as fast as she likes, cherishing her joy as her long strides cover the ground between them and the city. It's been too long since he's ridden for any length—he's not made for so much ship travel.

Eclipsis slows to a trot as they approach the city. The horse pulls on the reins and tosses her head up and down.

"That did not last long," Levnys says. Her voice comes out a bit breathless. "Do we truly need to stop?"

Pica pats Eclipsis' neck. "Not at all. Eclipsis, go on."

The horse squeals, turns sharply, and races back across the field.

Two hours later, they return to the city via the main road. The sun peeks from behind white clouds, casting its light between the crowded buildings and onto smooth cobblestone streets. The air rests warm against Pica's face. Oxen rumble, and donkeys bray as they haul their overstuffed carts to the harbor. On the breeze is a myriad of smells, pleasant and not, mixing into the complex scent of a crowded city. Eclipsis strides with her head held high as the crowds part before her. Above them, Krakli floats on updrafts from the warming cobblestones and concrete.

Levnys leans against him as they ride, hugging his waist. Her heat is as soothing as the sun on his skin. He's missed it so much—the warmth of another's embrace, the quiet and unassuming comfort of an affectionate touch. Another thing the legions took from him. He wonders if he deserves it after all he's done.

Eclipsis brushes his thoughts with concern. It's enough to pull him back from the edge of his despair—for now. He needs to focus on something else. Anything else. "Thank you for training Kisara," he says to Levnys.

"Why do you thank me? It is not you that I am training," Levnys replies.

"Well, no, but it means a lot to her, I can tell. Did she ask you to?"

"No, it was my idea. I did not see Kisara train with the rest of you, and I wondered why. Her lightning will not harm me, so I thought it would help."

"You are helping, and you didn't have to."

"But I am happy to. She deserves it."

"She does. More than anyone."

He shifts his weight as Eclipsis neatly dodges a running child. Levnys' body moves in response, her lithe frame brushing pleasingly against his back. A wave of wicked amusement comes from the horse as she senses his response to the movement. When he realizes her next intentions, he taps her with his heel.

"Don't even think about it," he scolds. "I don't need your kind of help again."

"Help with what?" Levnys asks.

Shit. "Sorry. I was talking to my horse."

"What is it your horse wishes to help you with?"

Part of him wants to curl up and blow away in the wind. "Making friends," he says as casually as he can.

If the horse could snicker, he imagines she would.

"Friends," Levnys repeats slowly. "I see."

Pica's cheeks grow hot. She likely *does* see. There's no way a dragon nearly two centuries old doesn't pick up on these things. Not that she'd be interested anyway. The lingering distance between them rests heavily on his mind lately. Until he can get to the root of that expanse and bridge it, there's no reason to hope there can be more between them.

"Where are we going?" he asks, desperately trying to change the subject.

"You will need to go that way," Levnys says, pointing down a narrow lane between two buildings.

Before he can guide Eclipsis, the horse turns.

"What, you listen to her now?" he asks her.

Eclipsis snorts.

"She is wise," Levnys says. "I am the one who knows the way."

They arrive several minutes later at a small shop in a shaded side street. The awning is faded to near white, with patches of darker blue near the building. A lantern glows in each window as the smell of cooking fish wafts from the entrance. Pica's stomach growls as he dismounts and lifts Levnys from the horse. He sets her down gently and turns to face Eclipsis. The horse stares at him as he crosses his arms.

"What?" She tries to shove her nose against his bag. He blocks it with his left hand. "You don't trust me?"

Eclipsis stomps her foot. He stares her down for a minute, then reaches into his bag and pulls out a burlap sack. Her nostrils flare, and she shoves her nose forward again. He blocks it a second time, smiling.

"You're not fast enough anymore. Here." He pulls out the bunch of grapes and sets it on the ground. He turns to Levnys as Eclipsis happily munches her treat, pulling the grapes off individually. "She'll be fine out here. Shall we?"

VII
SWAN

Levnys

As often as she has visited this island, Levnys never entered the library. The building—a circular construction of marble and concrete on one corner of the city square—never drew more than a passing glance. Lucius fidgets upon their approach to the stately building, brimming with energy.

They hurry through the atrium and past a double row of concrete busts painted in bright colors, all with gold or azure eyes and black hair. Lucius glances at the last one with lips set in a line but does not stop to examine it. *Aquillus Pavo*, the description reads. The current emperor. Another plinth, empty, sits next to it.

Lucius does not stop moving until he reaches the oldest section. The scrolls are of thick leather or delicate papyrus, neatly filed into narrow niches. A librarian hovers nearby, but Lucius ignores him as he crouches and, after a minute of deliberation, gently pulls a few scrolls. Lucius carries the stack to a nearby table and settles in, ignoring Levnys completely.

Levnys should be upset at the sudden inattention, but she is more amused than offended. She waits for a few minutes more, but Lucius is well-engrossed in his scroll, digging through his bag while murmuring to himself, laying out a veritable arsenal of ink, writing implements, and rolls of parchment.

"I will look around the rest of the library," Levnys says.

She gets a quiet grunt of acknowledgment and leaves him to his work. Rows upon rows of shelves are stuffed with scrolls of every size, ranging from single letters to massive tomes. High above are enormous rolls of leather—half a dozen histories kept behind thick panels of tinted glass. Each one is the size of an oxcart. A lump forms in her throat—those tomes can only be made of one thing. Dragonhide.

The history of the dragons in this area is long, predating the humans by several thousand years. These scrolls are a relic of a time when war ravaged her Sparkling Coast—when dragons fought dragons for supremacy of the entire sea. Her mother was a general in that war. All Levnys knows is from her stories.

According to the tales, her mother led a brilliant campaign against the lesser dragons, thwarting every counter-attack they offered with brutal efficiency. In one story, she held off a trio of heavily armored ruby dragons, slaying two and grievously wounding the third without receiving a single burn.

Levnys, meanwhile, cannot defeat a single dragon with no elemental powers. Her mother would have turned the plant dragon into fertilizer for Caltava's vineyards. No matter how hard Levnys tries, she will never be a fearsome warrior or cunning strategist. She cannot protect her inheritance.

She sighs and pulls her attention away to wander further through quaint gardens and the quiet conversation of the library's patrons. Several statues are placed artfully, with short inscriptions. The largest —a depiction of Aquilus, the first Gethki emperor, stares pensively across the expanse of scrolls. He holds a shield in one hand, the other an olive branch. Not for the first time, she mulls over how she knows far more about the history of the humans here than her own.

Eventually, she amuses herself by approaching the librarians individually, asking for any stories they have to tell. She knows a few of them, whether from her infrequent visits to the island or their progenitors.

Two hours pass before she returns to Lucius' location. Krakli hops from shelf to shelf, chirping softly. Levnys settles into the chair across from Lucius. His eyes move over the writing as energetically as they did hours ago, devouring the text on the page, his precise handwriting filling a roll of papyrus in neat columns. Smears of black creep from his hairline, inky lines blending into his inky hair, refreshed as he pushes his curls from his forehead.

"Lucius," Levnys says, yawning.

The tip of the calamus returns to the ink pot and withdraws with fresh blackness. Lucius' eyes flick to her and back down. He writes several more words before belatedly saying, "One moment."

She waits several moments, studying him. His long fingers and broad palms dwarf the reed, but he holds it delicately between his calloused fingertips, wielding it as expertly as he wields the sword. Perhaps, she muses, more so.

The table is too small for him, as is the chair. He stretches out his legs, nudges her foot with his, and moves it away in a jerk, muttering an apology. The chair groans as he shifts, the table bending slightly under his elbow. He pays neither any mind.

He finishes his sentence and raises his head, eyes sunken and rimmed with red, yet bright with life against his dark skin. He tilts his head at her expression, the calamus hovering over the expanse past the dark marks on the papyrus.

"It has been two hours," she says. "Did you plan on being here much longer?"

"We could go if you want," he says, voice heavy with disappointment. "I thought you'd be right at home in a library with how much you love stories."

"I enjoy listening to them. Books cannot be emotional. They cannot change their vocal tone or show facial expressions. They are merely words on a page." She glances at the scroll. "I know you do not wish to leave. Tell me what it is that you are looking for."

He smiles as easily as he always does. The expression sets his face alight and lifts her spirits in a way that surprises her. She is no stranger to the feeling, but from a human that should be a foe—she is not ready to accept it. He touches the tip of the calamus with ink-blackened fingers. The stains disappear, as do the ones on his forehead.

"Sure, but you already know," he says, setting the reed down.

"The celestial dragons."

"Yes. They disappeared during the civil war between Anserus and Cygnus, so that's where I search."

"Have you found anything?"

His lips form a line. "Not yet. I've been searching for years."

Levnys glances at his thick roll of notes. "I see. Why do you keep searching if you have not found anything?"

"I will search *until* I find something," he says emphatically, following the line of her attention. "Until I find them, or I die."

The intensity of his conviction catches her off guard. She struggles to reply to such a passionate statement. "You say they disappeared during the war?" she asks instead. "Tell me about it."

"Didn't we already talk about it?"

"It was mentioned, but we did not go into depth. Tell me."

He leans back, causing the chair to protest loudly. "You know we use old Gethki to name princes and emperors, right?"

"Yes, after birds. You are the Magpie."

He grins. "That's me." He cracks his knuckles. "So. We have Anserus, the Gander, and Cygnus, the Swan, brothers. Anserus, being the elder, was chosen to be the heir. In year 52, he took the throne upon the death of Alauda, the Lark, after the poor bastard was stabbed in his bed. The prince was elevated the next day." Lucius raises his finger. "That's strange. There is a mourning period before the state funeral, and the ceremony to confirm the new emperor happens later."

Levnys leans forward, and he watches her, his excited smile growing wider as she does. He *knows* he has her attention and seems to revel in it.

"Anserus being in Geth when his father passed is not unusual," he continues, "but the speed with which he ascended is."

"As if he knew it would happen," Levnys says.

"Yes. Cygnus was on a long mission with the Celestial Shield at that time. He was rightfully suspicious when he returned to Geth to find his brother on the throne. Their father wasn't a controversial ruler and had obviously not died from natural means. Cygnus accused Anserus of kin slaying and regicide, and they began to amass their forces." He leans forward and rests his elbows on the table, laying one hand on the other. "Here is where I speculate."

Her lips spread into a smile despite her efforts to keep it from her face. He is so earnest in his enthusiasm for his findings that she cannot help but be charmed by it. Lucius' curls spill across his forehead, and he leans forward a little further, the brown of his disguised eyes like burnished copper.

"Right around this time, all seven celestial dragons disappear. The brothers were gathering their legions," he says, "and the bloodline was fighting internally for the first time. There wasn't a clear enemy, no outside force to contend with. So here's my theory. The dragons picked a side."

"How does that explain their disappearance?"

"Every scrap of information we have on the dragons tells us that they valued the health of the bloodline above all else. They would not abide a kin slayer, so I believe they sided with Cygnus. They are entities with fathomless powers, so whoever they sided with would likely win with little contest. The pragmatic solution would be to remove them from the fight before anyone could act." He turns his hands over and stares at his palms. "I believe Anserus did that and erased all evidence of it. The lack of any records in Geth is the most suspicious thing."

His hands twitch as if trying to catch something slipping through his fingers. Levnys reaches over and puts her hand on his arm. It is warm despite the cool air. Magic stirs at her touch, follows her fingertips along his soft skin, swirling like sparks around a cooking fire. She traces her eyes up his arm, along the muscles shadowed against his tunic sleeve, over the metallic scales on his neck, up to his disguised eyes. Surprise shines in them, but something else is beneath it—a longing, a hunger. She leans forward without thought, tracing the inner curve of his elbow, then back along the carved lines of his forearm. She likes the look in his eyes, the sharpness, the intensity.

But in an instant, it is gone. A quiet pain returns as his eyes grow distant. He looks down at his hands again, staring at his calloused fingers.

"Then," he says, and his voice catches. He trembles under her fingertips. "The brothers went to war. For six months, it was nothing but brutal fighting, Gethki against Gethki, thousands of deaths. No ground was gained. The war could have gone on for years, but one day, they found Cygnus in his tent, assassinated like his father. Not much to fight about after that."

"And the dragons were gone," Levnys says sadly.

"The dragons were gone, and no one knows the truth."

"I must ask—why do you search so hard when they are already gone?" Levnys asks. "Surely, there is more to it than your oath."

Lucius' lips twist into a half-smile. "If I were lost, I'd want someone to figure out what happened to me. I'd want someone to *care*." His eyes shift to her hand on his arm before he touches her fingers lightly. "For the celestial dragons, I want to be that someone." His brows furrow. He draws a quick breath. "There's something else to it, too. Something strange, and I'm not sure you're going to believe it."

"What is it?"

As Lucius relates the events of the bathhouse and his visions, Levnys' heart aches for him. This, in addition to his nightly dreams. No wonder he looks so weary.

"I'm going mad," he finishes. "If whatever this thing is inside me is the cause of my obsession, is it truly mine?"

"Your greatest philosophers could not answer that question properly," Levnys says. "Is this entity separate from you?"

"You believe me," he says, and the relief in his voice makes her heart ache more. "It could be part of me or not, but what matters is that it's *there* and influencing me. I hate it, Levnys."

Part of Levnys wants to remain suspicious of this man. She is less willing to listen to that caution with every passing day. The more she learns, the more she witnesses—it chips away pieces of her reservations. She should not judge him. Those paladins of her past, the purveyors of such suffering, should not influence her opinion so much. This man, in particular, saved her life with no hesitation. So far, Lucius met her suspicions with kindness and respect that she has not earned. He trusted her with the knowledge of the entity inside him. It is about time she attempts to trust him.

"I have met one of the celestial dragons which you seek," she says, and the words leaving her mouth lift a weight off her chest.

Lucius' head jerks toward her. He half rises out of his chair, placing his palms on the table. "What? When? *Where?*" The gold in his eyes threatens to leak through the illusion.

"I was very young," she explains, taken aback by the intensity of his magic. "Before your civil war." He slowly lowers himself back into the chair. "Chyriss was one of the youngest, almost a dragonette herself. She came to Caltava to meet my mother."

"What was she like?" Lucius presses. "Anything, no matter how small. I *need* to know."

"She had feathers instead of scales, and her wings were like a bird's. I remember finding her strange but so beautiful. Her plumage shimmered like golden coins, and she was nice to me. Warm. Being near her was like being in a courtyard at noon on Midsummer. She felt like the sun. I did not feel her likeness again until I met you."

"Makes sense. Her grandmother gave my bloodline its powers."

"You do not understand. I have met royals before. Some had golden eyes and scales and fire magic, like you. None of them gave me that same feeling. You are like the sun, too, *Utuka*." The old word comes unbidden from her lips, but when it does, she realizes how much it fits. At his puzzled expression, she explains, "It is an ancient draconic word for 'sunrise.' I find it fitting."

His expression softens, and he looks away. His blush deepens, visible in light filtering down from the slatted windows. "Thank you, Levnys."

"Do not thank me," she says. "I wish I knew more and that it could fill that void inside of you. I have seen your determination to find them. It consumes you and burns you like fire. Your aura blazes hot whenever you speak of them; whether it is you or the entity inside you, it does not matter." She takes his hand. "If anyone will find them, it will be you."

He turns back to look at her. Perhaps he is perceptive enough to know the weight of those words, perhaps not. Either way, he watches her with a tenderness she did not think possible for such a man. Warm magic presses against her fingers. She realizes she has been cherishing the feeling his magic gives her, ever since they drove off the plant dragon. The fire of his determination, the passionate look in his eyes—she has always found such things attractive.

Levnys wants to help him achieve his goal, to see the look in his eyes when he succeeds. "You are not finished with your book," she says. "I do not mind if you return to it."

"Are you sure? I don't want you to be bored."

She stands and heads to the shelf, poking through the scrolls until she finds one with a carved wooden swan on the binding cord. She withdraws it, carefully unrolls the delicate leather, and settles back into her chair.

"I thought you didn't like reading," Lucius says.

"Perhaps you should not question me," she replies, amused. "I do not mind helping you for a little while."

They settle to their respective scrolls. The one she chose is about Cygnus, an accounting of much of the information Lucius already mentioned. The words are faded, but legible Fresian, and she can read them with little difficulty.

"Anything yet?" Lucius asks after a while.

"It is a biography of Cygnus. He passed through here in year 53."

"He did?" Lucius leans over. "I didn't know that. Makes sense. Must have been before the civil war."

Levnys gives him an even look. "Naturally. He would not be alive afterward."

Lucius slaps his hand against his forehead. "Right. Sorry. Anything interesting?"

"You must let me read it," she says. "I promise I will tell you if I find something you have not mentioned."

Krakli continues his circuit of the bookshelves, peering into each niche. The bird is restless, fluttering his wings and rasping quietly to himself. Lucius glances at him every so often, watching his familiar with visible concern.

Levnys reaches the end of the document. There, scrawled in a different hand, is a message in Gethki.

"Lucius." When he looks up, she says, "This is strange. The last line of this scroll says, 'Beware the island of Charris.'

Krakli shrieks.

Lucius' head jerks toward his familiar as the bird takes to the air, flapping madly over the shelves. Lucius surges out of his chair, tipping it over with a crash. He tries in vain to catch the bird, but the magpie evades his outstretched hands. Levnys watches for a moment before standing and gently plucking the panicked Krakli out of the air. He struggles between her fingers, pecking and squirming, his distressed keening pulling at Levnys' heart like the calls of a crying hatchling.

Lucius' hands close over hers and he gently takes the trembling bird. He brings Krakli to face level and strokes his head. "It's alright," he murmurs soothingly. "Shh, shh, I'm right here." Slowly, Krakli gains control of himself.

"What happened?" Levnys asks after the magpie's vocalizations cease.

"He—I'll try to explain. He's not mortal like you or I. When their paladin dies, a bonded spirit can find another to aid if they choose to. Since they are reborn into a new form, what few memories they retain are hazy at best." Lucius gently sets Krakli on the table. "When you read those words, it triggered one of those memories."

Levnys stares at the bird. "Why?"

"Don't know yet." Lucius rights the chair and sits. Krakli shakes himself out, fluffing his feathers before raising his head and emitting a low rasp. "You're sure?" Lucius asks. After a few seconds, he adds, "Go on."

Krakli chirps and flies to a bookshelf sagging with scrolls, squeezing his pied body between the shelf and the plastered wall. When he emerges with a thin leather tube, Lucius emits a forceful breath. Krakli brings it to him, and he turns it over before holding it for Levnys to see. Stamped into the old scroll case is the Gethki crest, along with the letters REGILLVS CYGNVS. Lucius sets it on the table.

"Well. I suspected that Cygnus was one of the paladins Krakli served." He carefully unties the stiff leather cord. He frowns when pieces of it break off in his hands. "This may confirm that."

Lucius withdraws a single roll of parchment from the ancient leather. He unrolls it slowly, flattening it until a drawing comes clear: a bird in flight, wings sticking stiffly out from its body, with a long curved beak and flared tail.

His eyes widen, and he gags, pushing himself to his feet. His magic surges, as strong as Levnys has ever felt it, as he buries his face in his hands. Levnys stares at the drawing with her heart in her throat.

"Sorry," Lucius says. He settles back into his chair. "The entity it —it didn't like that at all." He rubs his eye with the heel of his hand. "It's the strongest I've felt its presence."

"Will you be alright?"

"Have to be." He reaches out and unrolls the parchment again. Both he and Levnys lean forward to read the neat letters inscribed there.

To my beloved friend, I hope you will find this in another life.

I leave this letter in desperation and shame, for I do not know if I can face my Order after all I've done.

We encountered a great evil on Charris—a swarm of horrid birds who drank the island's denizens dry. Not even the rats escaped. What's more, there was something else, a terrible creature from our worst nightmares—a vicious bat-like thing larger than any dragon.

It taunted us. It knew who we were. It knew Andereth. It said it was going to kill her and every living being in our lands.

We battled it and sealed it with old and dangerous magic. Only I survived. I'm too ashamed to write what unforgivable things I did, but the blood will forever stain my hands.

The seal can't hold forever. Someday, it will break, and that creature will be free to threaten us again. It must be stopped. The world may forget, but you must make it remember.

The scholars treated me like a madman. I don't know if my father will believe me. But on the few shreds of honor that remain to me, I swear it is all true.

I know what I must do. I must protect the dragons. I must protect Andereth. I will try to make them understand. I will scream it from the rooftops in Geth, but I fear it will not be enough.

My friend, please remember I will always love you, even after my bones are ash and my soul is with Ukton.

To the paladin who inherited him, I hope he is as dear to you as he is to me. Take care of him for me.

Cygnus

Krakli whistles, bowing his head over the letter. He underlines "beloved friend" with his beak and turns to Lucius. "Yeah," Lucius says. "I think it's for you, too."

Levnys' heart warms as she witnesses the tenderness on Lucius' face. Krakli settles next to the letter, setting his head on the ancient ink.

"Cygnus never returned to the Order. We never knew what happened," Lucius says. "The first words from him we've ever found and...and—" Lucius' voice catches. "Old magic. What old magic? He said the seal wouldn't hold. What if, what if—" Lucius stands and paces, wringing his hands into his hair. "I saw something bat-like in that vision. What if it's that thing the letter described?"

"Surely you do not plan to go to Charris," Levnys says.

"Do we have a choice? Defying a royal decree can mean execution."

"Even for you?"

Lucius stops pacing. He stares at the shelves for a long moment. "My father hates me. I imagine he'd light the pyre himself if he could." He drops his hands to his sides. "Besides. If some evil on Charris threatens our people, we must stop it."

Our people. Levnys does not miss the inclusion. "You plan to fight this evil?"

"Who in their right mind would stand by and *let* this happen?" He turns to face her. "The birds are already here. We need to get moving. I can send letters to the surrounding islands and the legions."

"I will put the word out to the other dragons." Levnys gently rolls the letter and slips it back into its case. Lucius takes it from her with trembling hands. "Do you plan on forcing Ralex to sail to every tiny island in this sea in search of these birds?"

Lucius shakes his head. "That's not practical. I'll tell Calvus and Lucia. Will you help me?"

"Yes, if you help me contact the dragons."

The words are out of her mouth before she realizes it. Lucius stares at her for a long moment. "It's a plan."

VIII

SEASON

Pica

After scouring the archives for further information without success, they leave the library to Pica's reluctance. Eclipsis takes them up the volcano's slopes to a town halfway up the side. "Wait here," Levnys says.

"Why?" Pica's eyes travel to the caldera looming above the city. Lights wink at the very top, visible despite the afternoon sun.

Levnys falters and turns away. "It is a dragon enclave—one of the last in our sea. I cannot take you there. Please try to understand."

Because he's a paladin. He hasn't figured out why their presence is such a sore point. The library hadn't been any help.

"I understand," he lies.

She melts into the crowd. He stares after her, then drops his eyes to Krakli, perched on Eclipsis' head. The magpie is fast asleep. Pica strokes the smooth feathers of his back and wings, relieved that his friend can rest.

His mind turns back to the letter. It's another piece of the puzzle, one he uses to distract himself from the reality of another residing in his head. It doesn't work. Eclipsis dances beneath him, sensing his anxiety. A long breath in through his nose, a longer breath out through his mouth. Another. Then another. The tightness in his throat increases.

What if it's not benevolent? If it has access to his magic, it could do untold damage before it—and he—are brought down. A healer turned foul could cause immense suffering. He's been trained to kill others. How much more blood would be on his hands?

It would finish destroying what little humanity he has left.

Pica clenches his teeth so hard they creak. Tears threaten to spill over his cheeks. People murmur as they pass. No wonder—he must be a sight, a big man crying on a bigger horse. Eclipsis' annoyance at the attention scrapes against him as she backs off the road, away from the crowd.

She takes them into the shade of a pear tree, behind a rough stucco wall only a few inches higher than Pica's head. Slowly, he gains control of himself, pushing the anxiety away while Eclipsis stands as a stalwart companion.

"Thank you," he says, patting her neck and raising his head. The pear tree is starting to bud. Above him, sparrows flit from branch to branch, singing their spring love songs. A dog barks somewhere behind him. The sound of children playing floats over the wall. Shouts from the road, the creak of carts, the snort of oxen and mules. The smell of baking bread. It would all cease to exist if those birds ever made it to the island. Anything in their path will be turned to desolation.

Cygnus' words stick in his head. *It knew Andereth. It said it was going to kill her.* Andereth. Pica's head spins. There's something he should be grasping, some truth hidden in the words. He's too tired. Night after night of violent dreams have dulled his senses, filed off the edge of his wit. One thing is clear, however. If whatever is behind those birds is a threat to Andereth, he is oath-sworn to do something about it.

Now, if only he knew where she was.

Pica sighs. For now, he can only protect what's in front of him. Once Levnys is back, they can update his group on their findings.

Eclipsis senses his urgency and emerges back into the open, making for the road. They don't have to wait long for Levnys to appear—in dragon form. He wonders if she will scoop them up, horse and all, but she lands in the space vacated for her and transforms.

"It is done," she says as he pulls her onto Eclipsis' back. "They will spread the word."

As she speaks, five dragons take to the air from the caldera, their metallic hides sparkling in the sun.

"Good," he says. "How will they relay information?"

"*Raven's Flight* is an unusual ship," she says. "It will find us."

Pica turns Eclipsis' head and lets the horse join the traffic back down the hill. The main city stretches below them. Pica shivers at the thought of all those people, turned to bloodless husks.

"I wish to eat before we meet your companions tonight," Levnys says. "I know a wonderful *thermopolium.*"

"Is that wise? We should get word to them as soon as possible."

"A few hours will not make the difference."

She leans against his back, wrapping her arms around his waist. The burst of affection surprises him. He's instantly aware of her heat, the strength in her arms. Part of him is distracted by how good it feels to be this close. When she brushes her hand across his chest, his magic roils, incongruous with the rest of his feelings. The image of them together, entangled in a candlelit room, flashes through his head.

Gods curse it, what is wrong with him? This isn't what he should be thinking about right now.

"Perhaps you're right," he says. "But we could talk to Ralex, at least. If we can leave earl—"

"You know as well as I do that his crew would not stand for it," Levnys interrupts. "This is not like you, Lucius. I have never seen you this stressed."

"I can't sit by," Pica says, clenching the reins. "The birds are—"

"Turned to ash by your magic. You have warned the magistrate. Ralex's crew is spreading the word in the harbor. There is nothing further we can do, Lucius."

Pica bows his head. "I'm missing something, Levnys. Something big."

"It will come to you. You are stubborn enough to wring milk from a bone should you be thirsty."

"Is that a compliment?" He sighs and leans back against her. Her entire body is pressed against him. He sinks into her comforting presence, letting her draconic aura mix with his own. "Fine. You're right. What do you suggest?"

"Some meat, then I will show you around the island."

"Alright. It's better than doing nothing."

He tries to relax, but his mind keeps wandering, mentally reviewing the preparations they'll need to make. One thing keeps dragging him back, his body insistent he pays attention—the dragon and her continued proximity to him. She always keeps in physical contact—arms around his waist, leaning against his side, hand on his back. She seems to know each time he drifts, bringing him back with a touch on his arm.

Thoughts of birds and long-dead princes slip into the background. All he can see is her—the curves he wants to follow with his hands, the shimmering hair he longs to entangle his fingers in.

His familiars, sensing the direction of his thoughts, gleefully conspire to push him and Levnys even closer, to Pica's exasperated amusement. Eclipsis stops short a few times too many, and Krakli seems convinced that trinkets will help his cause. Pica puts an end to that when the magpie brings him a smooth stone, carved and inset with metal—an ornate artificial eye.

"Go give that back this instant," Pica scolds as Levnys bursts into laughter. "What is wrong with you?"

It's an escape for all of them, Pica realizes, but he lets it draw him in. It's a taste of peace, a scrap of happiness for a few hours before reality must rush back in. If only it would never end.

Later, as the sun sets and the oil lamps bathe the streets with an auric glow, they stop in front of a richly decorated tavern. The smell of roasting meat draws Pica in immediately. He can't wait to have a drink and a filling meal. They dismount under an oil lamp, and, with a thump on her side, Pica sends Eclipsis to wander off—an activity the horse begs for each time he summons her.

Levnys watches her depart and turns to him. Pica's heart skips when she steps up and places her hand on his chest.

"I had a wonderful time today," she says.

He tries not to pay attention to how fast his heart beats or how beautiful she is in the lamplight. He places his hand over hers, stroking her fingers.

"The second half was fun," he replies. "Despite the circumstances."

She tilts her head, leaning forward. "I am glad I could make your day better."

He'd love to close the rest of the distance, to see what her lips taste like on his. Instead, he waits. There's so much unresolved, so much she hasn't told him. Should that stop him? Doesn't he have his secrets, too?

He runs two fingers over her cheek. She looks up at him but makes no further move.

What are you waiting for? he asks himself. He leans forward.

Someone clears their throat. Levnys lets out a small laugh and steps away. *Shit.* Lucia and Calvus stand behind them. His aunt crosses her arms and tries to look stern, but a smile twitches at the corners of her mouth. Calvus studies the tavern's sign with perfect disinterest.

"Ah, hello," Pica greets them. "You're early."

"We're last," Lucia says. She turns and heads for the tavern entrance. "Everyone else is already inside."

Pica curses and follows his aunt. Levnys laughs softly behind him.

The ship's languid routine returns after they depart Dalos, to Pica's annoyance. Of all his companions, only Seto seems to share his desire for urgency. Ralex, for his part, listens to their concerns but shakes his head at the request to move faster. "That'll wear out the crew," he says, crossing his arms. "They ain't gonna be no good to us then." He spits out the reed he was chewing. "I got my men going into each town to hear the news. You'll be the first to know if they find something."

With that paltry reassurance, Pica does what he can. Most islands don't have a library, so he is forced to wait, reviewing his notes and the copy he made of Cygnus' letter. Soon, he has them memorized.

...the blood will forever stain my hands.

I must protect the dragons.

Pica always admired Cygnus for standing up to his brother's tyranny. Now, he reflects bitterly, it seems he has more in common with his ancestor than he thought.

It said it was going to kill her.

The world may forget, but you must make it remember.

Pica touches his amulet, determined to do just that. But he can do little at the moment besides ruminate.

Today, the spring sun shines brightly over the glittering waves.

Two dragons circle above the ship, silhouettes against the brilliant sky. The larger of them dives, tucking her wings tight against her body. She streaks through the air toward the calm sea—a plummeting projectile of bronze and turquoise. Before impact, she unfurls her wings, arresting her momentum and setting down with a small splash.

Kisara tucks her wings as Levnys did, dramatically increasing her speed. Her wings open, but too late. Instead of landing gently, she impacts the water with an enormous splash. Levnys dives. A few seconds later, she surfaces with a shivering Kisara lying on her back.

Their training now includes flying lessons.

Pica reluctantly turns his attention back to his training. They started again within hours of *Raven's Flight* departing Dalos—no rest for the devoted, it seems. He works through his warm-up drills with his battered practice sword—thrust, parry, slash.

His mind wanders as his body goes through the motions he's performed daily for thirteen years. He's always found it a good way to think, to let his mind work on one problem or another. He turns the details of the last few days over in his mind, funneling his anxiety and stress into his limbs, trying to unpick the tangled web of details wrapped tightly around the obscured truth.

He glances again at the dragons. Kisara, recovered, takes to the air. Levnys watches momentarily, then dives. She breaches, propelled by her powerful tail. Her wings snap open, sending spray from the tips. The droplets catch the midday sun, casting dazzling rainbows in the air. He marvels every time he sees it. It's not like him to be so overwhelmed. He watches her flap hard to join Kisara in the sky.

The prince and the dragon. Sounds like a bard's tale.

Another sword taps against his—an invitation. Calvus steps across to mirror him, offering him a distraction he gratefully takes.

It's near dusk when the dragons land and join the ship already ashore for the evening. Levnys back-wings well away from the campfires, landing in the surf with a large splash. She walks regally up the beach and shakes herself off, sending water droplets into the air that refract the setting sun like molten gold.

Levnys detaches the leather straps and netting strung over her hindquarters, letting it and the struggling fish inside drop to the sand. She withdraws two and nods to one of the cooks waiting nearby. Pica takes the fish, and she transforms, settling in her human form next to him. Pica hands her one of his daggers, and she sets to cleaning her catch.

Pica cleans the other fish, tossing the guts aside for the ever-present gulls to fight over. The entrails attract different birds, too—crows and magpies descend from the trees, their feathers flashing in the setting sun. Krakli joins the feast, making fast friends and quick rivals, losing himself in the raucous crowd.

Both halves of his fish are soon roasting on an iron rack over the campfire. Kisara spreads out in her dragon form beside the ship, already asleep.

"She worked hard today," Pica says.

"She is doing well. I am pleased with her progress."

"Kisara's always been a quick learner, and you seem like a great teacher."

Levnys' fish joins his on the rack, outside the now-roaring campfire. Pica swallows when she joins him on the blanket. She's sitting a lot closer to him than usual. He's painfully aware of her—her heat, the fresh scent of her hair. The stench of burning flesh quickly replaces the latter, and Pica curses. He uses the poker to flip his fish—burned already.

"Kisara is like a hatchling learning how to fly," Levnys says, nobly ignoring his floundering attempts at cooking, "although they are smaller and do not hit the ground as hard. That is why we train over water."

Pica pulls his burned fish out of the fire and plops it onto his plate. Levnys' nose wrinkles at the charred meat, but she doesn't comment as he waves the smoke away.

"You've taught others to fly before?" he asks.

"Yes, I have raised two clutches."

"You have children?"

"Yes, but they can no longer be considered children—especially my sons. They are grown now, with territories."

Levnys flips the fish and sprinkles the perfectly browned scales with herbs from the clay pot near the fire. Pica stares at his fish. Should he tell her? The gnawing guilt that's followed him for years, the consequences of his choices, churns his gut as much as the stink of overcooked meat.

"I hope that it does not bother you," Levnys adds.

"No." He sets the plate on his knees. "It would make me a hypocrite if it did."

"You have a child."

"Yes," he admits. "It's not public knowledge. I'm telling you because I trust you. My son's name is Umile. I'm not involved in his life, but..." He pokes at the cooling fish on his plate. "I'd like to be someday. After this mission, with luck."

"Will you tell me the story?" Levnys asks, plucking her fish out of the fire with an iron poker. She puts it on a plate, removes the burned one from his lap, and replaces it with half of hers. Pica takes a grateful bite as Levnys tosses the blackened fish to the birds.

"I met his mother in a tavern south of Valri, where I was stationed. This was our first time away from the legion camp." He drinks a long pull of wine. "This is going to sound crass, but—I needed to release some, ah, tension. We'd been in the field too long, and I'm not one to lay with other soldiers." He blushes and looks away from her.

"Ah." Levnys says. "That is reasonable."

"When Elda walked into that tavern, noble and beautiful, I was smitten." Pica's blush deepens. "She was intelligent and had a wicked sense of humor. We snuck away from her entourage, and, well, let's say I didn't get a lot of sleep that week." He eats a bit more fish as Levnys snorts. "Of course, it couldn't last. She had to keep traveling, and I had to return to my legion. We'd taken precautions, so imagine my surprise when I got a letter saying she was pregnant, then another a few months later describing the appearance of the child. The bloodline traits manifested themselves strongly in him."

"The bloodline traits. The scales and the eyes."

"Yes, and in his case, feathers. Ah, and other things. He's unusual."

"Feathers. How is that possible? What else does he have?"

"Feathers, clawed feet, a tail. I assumed it happened sometimes. It's not in any records, but not every royal child is recorded."

"Those traits are like those of half-dragons, Lucius."

"I can see the similarities, but I'm a human. So is his mother. The bloodline is the only explanation." He sighs. "Umile is five now, and Elda married a nice man who is raising him like his own son. Elda writes me letters and keeps me informed, and I send them gifts—toys, trinkets, clothes, and things to help with his upbringing. I saw him before leaving on this mission. He's adorable—beautiful like his mother, talented in magic, already impressing his tutors." He pictures the boy's golden feathers contrasting his dark skin, his shy smile, and his eager explanation when Pica asked about his magic. "If I live through this mission, I will visit him more. I hope it's not too late to..." He trails off. Levnys leans against him now, giving him her silent support. "In any case, he's officially my heir, so he gets all the support from the crown that any royal child would. It means my father knows about him, but oh well. He hasn't decided to out him yet. He's waiting for the right moment, knowing him."

"Is that something you are concerned about?"

"Only if things get heated with him. More heated. We, uh, don't get along."

"That tale is known in the Coast," Levnys says. "I am honored you told me such a thing. It cannot be easy for you, choosing between this mission and seeing the child."

It *had* been easy, Pica notes, with more than a hint of remorse. Right now, Umile has a stable family—something he could never give him. He can't be a father for Umile, no matter how badly he wants to try. Something will always be broken inside him, shattered into thousands of pieces and scattered like a destroyed mosaic.

When Umile looked at him with those innocent golden eyes, Pica knew he had to keep him safe—safe from the vicious politics of the royal court, safe from the brutal reality of war. Pica wants to give him what he never had, even if that means protecting the boy from him and everything he represents. No child deserves a monster for a father.

Maybe someday, he can be that person. Right now, he can only swallow the guilt, nod, and eat the rest of the cooling fish.

Levnys stays close to Pica the rest of the evening, all but sitting on his lap at one point. The change in her demeanor is stark, and part of him wonders if there's something wrong.

Another part of him wants to kiss her right there without a care about who's watching. His magic writhes within him at her every touch, driving him to distraction. Finally, the evening winds down, and he excuses himself to his cabin. Despite the dragon's flirtatious demeanor, there are things he'd like to resolve before moving forward —regardless of his body's objections to the separation.

He is reading an old traveler's journal when his cabin door opens. He raises his head as Levnys walks in. Her bronze skin shimmers as she steps into the candlelight.

She is completely naked.

The dragon is devastatingly beautiful, moving with sensual grace. The sway of her hips is enough to drive him mad.

"Good evening," he says, trying to remain calm. "Nice outfit."

She doesn't respond. As she steps closer, he notices that her skin has tiny scales covering her shoulders, belly, and thighs. The firelight reaches her face. More scales ring her eyes, under her brows, and travel toward her ears. Her loose hair flows around her shoulders, framing her thin face. Her eyes lock onto his.

Oh, gods, her eyes.

They are draconic, her pupils slit and dilated. The turquoise iris obscures everything but the tiniest sliver of white. Heat rapidly rises in his belly as his magic stirs and growls in response to her approach —intense, hot, and feral. The burning warmth spreads through him, flushing his skin painfully hot. Sweat beads on his face and bare chest.

"Levnys?" he asks, his voice strained. "Are you alright?"

She remains silent when she climbs onto the bed. Pica puts the old journal on the table as she slides into his lap, straddling him. The heat inside him is white-hot as she places her hands on his shoulders, tracing her fingers along the lines of his muscles. His hands rise to caress her back, eagerly running over her naked skin.

He didn't ask his hands to do that. There's a disconnect between his mind and what his body is doing. That presence within him is overpowering, pressing against him with a force yet unseen.

"Levnys, what's going—"

She kisses him, cutting off his words. A howling wind of heat and lust roars within him, an overpowering tempest. He is immediately aroused at the heat of her, the weight of her pressed against him. She slides her fingers down his chest as his hands travel over her body. He can't *stop*. Something is wrong. He's losing control. This isn't how it should be happening.

She moves her hands down his stomach, fingers electric on his bare skin, and pulls at the laces of his breeches. His body twitches, his hips pushing greedily upwards. He summons the last scraps of his control and breaks off the kiss with a gasp.

"Levnys?" he manages. "This isn't like you—"

She thrusts her hand past his waistband and strokes him. The firestorm becomes incandescent. His mind goes white as he pulls her head to his, kissing her with urgent hunger.

Reason returns to him with a long moan as his body shudders in climax. The woman beneath him writhes and gasps, her breath hot on his neck and ear. She whispers his name as he registers his hand tangled in her hair and her legs clenched around his waist. His body shudders again as hers relaxes, her pleased sigh ruffling his hair.

What? How did I...?

He lays there for a minute, letting his skin cool before pushing himself up on an elbow. Levnys lies under him, their bodies entangled, her skin shining with sweat in the candlelight. The scales are gone now, replaced with flawless brown skin.

She touches his face. "That is not the expression I expected," she says, stroking his cheek. "Why do you look so confused?"

"I...um. What happened?"

She glances at their entwined bodies. "You have visited brothels. Surely, I do not need to explain."

He sighs. "No, not that." He detangles himself and sits up in the bed. "You came into my room already naked. You didn't say anything or respond to my questions. It's like you were in a trance. Your eyes were odd. Levnys, I blacked out. I don't remember anything after that."

"That is strange. I remember everything that happened."

"You do." He can't keep the anxiety out of his voice.

"You are upset. Why? Did you not want to lay with me?"

"It's not that...it's..."

"Is it better if I tell you it was wonderful?"

He stares at her, incredulous. "No. I mean, yes, a little, but....no." He finds his clothes crumpled against the wall and dresses. Levnys watches him with notable confusion. He pulls on his cloak over his unbelted tunic. "I'm...going to get some air. You're welcome to..." She's welcome to what? Stay? Go? What does he want her to do? "...do what you wish."

He leaves her there, naked in his bed, and wanders the length of the ship. What *had* happened? He can't deny that he would have welcomed this in another circumstance, but...why did he lose control? Was it his magic? Was it—

He stops walking. The thing in his head feels like it's standing next to him. Pica sits and rests his back against the rail, pulling his cloak around him and the hood over his head. Heat wells in him, endlessly moving, restless. He turns inward, trying to envision it and grasp that slippery presence. He cycles through things that have brought it forth before, to no avail. Finally, he pictures those emerald green eyes from the mosaic, and the entity's presence becomes sharper and more pronounced.

Why? he asks. It does not answer.

The minutes pass as he broods, trying to separate the myriad emotions that press on him from all sides. Levnys laughing, beautiful in the soft lamplight. Suspicion, wary looks. The sensation of her arms around his waist. The predatory look in her eyes as she entered his room. The heat of his release inside her, the warm breath, the soft sighs.

What is he supposed to do? Why doesn't he remember?

"Lucius?" Her soft voice cuts through his thoughts like a blade. She stands before him, her slim form lost in one of his tunics. "Would you like to speak about it?"

"I..." He sighs. "I don't know what to say."

She settles beside him and spreads a blanket over her bare knees and feet. She sits far enough away that no part of them touches, but he is hyper-aware of her. His magic stirs again, encouraging him to go to her, to—

Stop it.

He's never been so torn. What should have been a wonderful moment feels rotten, a blight, a creeping mold. The entity inside him senses his anger and cringes away like a disciplined animal, settling enough for him to think clearly.

"My magic has never gone wild before, not even as a child," he says softly. "It wasn't right."

Levnys stares hard at her knees. "There is a potential reason, but it may be strange to you."

"Tell me."

"It is dragon mating season."

"What could that possibly have to do with this?"

"This time affects us strongly. Lucius, I felt your draconic blood call to me, so I came to you." She sighs. "You are young, handsome, and strong—a powerful warrior. I have seen how well you move when you fight. I was already curious what laying with you would be like."

"I'm not a dragon," he says.

"Not in the strictest sense," she says. "However, compared to how a fire dragon feels, there is little difference." She looks away from him. "Young dragons who have never mated before often lose control of themselves."

Pica stares at his hands. What if they move on their own again? The thought of being so helpless—it almost breaks him. He's not a dragon—he's a human. Isn't he?

"How long until—?" he asks.

"Until?" Levnys prompts.

"Until this—" he waves his hand between them. "Until it's done."

"Ah. A few days, perhaps a week. I assume you do not want this to happen again?"

He has no idea what he wants. Everything is pressing at him from all sides. Does it even matter what he wants?

"No. I mean...I like you, but...this was..." Like his dreams, the words don't want to come out. He hauls himself to his feet. "Sorry, Levnys, I—I need to be alone."

The dreams jolt him out of fitful sleep. After he empties his stomach and drinks some water, he paces the tiny cabin—if one could call it pacing. Three short steps take him from chair to wall, three more back again. Back. Forth. At this rate, he's going to wear through the floorboards.

Anger, warm but not hot, simmers like a cauldron. He pokes at the entity with no success. Is it hiding from him? The concept is darkly funny—as though there would be an escape for either of them.

He returns to bed after nibbling a small piece of bread. Sour bile lingers despite the water and grain. His teeth hurt like someone ran a whetstone over them, his tongue fuzzy and vile.

He'll never get any rest. Everything he touches turns foul. He closes his eyes, but fire dances behind his eyelids, his nostrils recalling the stench of burning wood and roasted flesh. He caused such destruction. Why should he be happy when he's caused so much pain to others?

Tears course down his cheeks, flowing in a river he's helpless to stop. So much is out of his control. He longs for action, to meet those cursed birds again, to use his fire for something good. Something noble. The vicious urge to burn them all seethes like magma.

But it's not *his* anger—it belongs to the entity inside him. It's all so clear now. The same thing that forced him and Levnys together is the same thing that burns with hatred for the birds. It's the same drive he has for finding the dragons. None of it belongs to him.

Is there anything of him left?

Pica's stomach clenches, sending a knife of pain through his torso. He curls around it, gagging, barely keeping the bread and water down. He's lost weight despite his best efforts. His stomach has to be damaged by now. He could attempt to heal it. Yet, some part of him wants this, to experience pain and regret for what he did. Like Cygnus, blood stains his hands. This is the retribution he deserves.

A sob wracks his body, sending a fresh wave of pain through his guts. The pain is the only thing real. Even his oath, the rock he's clung to for half his life, crumbles beneath him. The dragons have been gone for almost two hundred years. His Order is reduced to mere errand boys for the crown, sent on missions that get them all killed. Who are they fooling, except for themselves? Who are they supporting but the very empire that has caused so much suffering, proclaiming themselves as shield to the sky, while all they are is another bloody limb of a corrupt system.

It would be better for everyone if he did die out here.

Then, Pica thinks, *I couldn't hurt anyone anymore.*

His sword is over there. He keeps it sharp.

The crack of impact on the shutters jolts Pica out of his reverie. Krakli slams his body against the wooden slats in blind anguish, throwing back his head and crowing in full voice. The magpie sticks his beak in through an opening, working open the latch from the outside. Pica watches him with fresh tears, unable to move, overwhelmed by the force of his familiar's emotions.

Krakli frees the latch and bursts in on a rush of wings and cold air, flying into Pica's face. The magpie pecks him hard enough to draw blood. Pica flinches, reaching to grab him. Krakli pecks him again and dances out of Pica's reach, scolding him in a loud *chak-chak* call.

"Stop," Pica says hoarsely. "You're going to wake everyone."

Krakli ceases, shifting to growling in a long, raspy note. Every feather on his pied body stands out, turning the bird into a ball of anger and grief. Pica reaches for him, but Krakli pecks his fingers. Though their bond doesn't express itself in words, the magpie's meaning is clear.

Take it back, he says. *I'm still here, idiot.*

Pica draws in a breath and holds it. He closes his eyes, focusing on his center, like his mother taught him—on his heart that thuds in his chest. Breathe out, breathe in. His limbs shake with fatigue and anxiety. Out. In.

Finally, Pica finds the strength to rise. He crosses his legs under him, resting his hands on his knees. Pain lingers like a blade in his guts, but the nausea fades enough for him to reach for the water skin.

He opens his eyes. Krakli watches him, mouth open—a silent witness. The bird is right. Krakli has been with him through everything, and the little familiar hasn't left him. Eclipsis, too, has remained. Spirits in service to Andereth herself haven't abandoned him. Who is he to give up so easily?

His sword will remain sheathed today.

He drains the rest of the water skin and stretches out as best he can on the too-short mattress. Krakli settles on the pillow next to his head, giving him one last peck before closing his eyes.

"Yeah. Love you too," Pica says.

It's a tiny spark of hope in the vast blackness surrounding him, but he clings to it. The specter of the blood-drinking birds looms large, like a thunderhead darkening the horizon. If, no, *when* the birds appear again, will they be as helpless to stop them as they would a summer tempest?

Despite the odds, he knows he will stand strong and fight to his last breath. Lucia will stand with him. The others, too, even Calvus. He doesn't have to do it alone. He has to cling to that hope—it's all that's left for him.

As for Levnys...

Pica sighs. A different pain arises when he thinks about what transpired a few hours ago. Another thing that's been tainted by forces beyond his control. Perhaps it's better this way—though they ended up as close as two beings could be, he feels the distance. He wouldn't be surprised if he finds her gone tomorrow, despite the lingering danger of the plant dragon.

He'd almost forgotten about the dragon since the birds appeared. Could the two be connected in some way? Stranger things have happened. There's so much uncertainty of late.

The fatigue eventually wins, and he slips into a fitful sleep, his mind free to torment him with violence once again.

IX

NIGHTSHADE

Levnys

Levnys barely speaks to Lucius for the next four days, striving to be where he is not. She does not want to risk hurting him again. His despair and confusion, the look he gave her when he regained his senses—she hopes she will never witness such a thing again.

The fire is not as bright in the evenings as when they share it. She misses his voice and how he smiles when speaking to her. She also, to her intense irritation, cannot get the intimate moment they shared out of her head. She catches herself approaching the ship, stumbling along the surf toward the warm aura calling to her. The buzzing desire and the memory of his soft skin are almost too much to bear. She sits on the cold sand, head bowed, watching the minuscule crabs emerge from the retreating tide. The water is calm, cold against her toes, a contrast to the tumult within her.

She only has to endure a few more days, but perhaps it is too late. The delicate connection may be damaged beyond repair. The thought of such a thing sits like a stone in her gut, a heavier burden than she would have thought possible. How has she come to care so deeply for this human?

A crab crawls onto her talon, and she lifts it to her nose, studying it as it waves its oversized claw in protest of her attention. She raises it into the air, its tiny form a shadow against the river of stars in the clear night sky. The moon's glow is silver on the low waves, rippling across the expanse of water in shimmering beauty. Levnys lowers the crab carefully back to the beach and stares at those stars. Somewhere under the same sky are her friends, the companions with whom she shares her territory, but also her newest enemy.

Levnys turns from the water and moves to the tree line to curl beneath the sheltering branches. Sleep inevitably takes her, the lullaby of the waves a salve to her troubled mind and aching heart.

When she wakes the following day, *Raven's Flight* is already in the water. She briefly considers letting it leave without her but finds herself rising, emerging onto the cold morning sand wet with dew. A crouch, a spring, and she is airborne, circling over the black ship as the drums beat time and oars flash like the fins of a great beast. Lucius turns his head to the sky and watches her for a long moment before something else grabs his attention—Calvus, his bald head shiny in the morning sun. Kisara joins her in the air not long after, and she throws herself wholeheartedly into the training, grateful for anything that could be considered a distraction. Thus, the following hours pass in a numbing routine.

Kisara flies low over *Raven's Flight* as Levnys flies high, brushing clouds. The waters below her are a fresco of greens and blues, the rocks rising from it blemishes on the smooth blend of the waves.

She feels the plant dragon's presence before she hears him. Levnys jukes to the side, folding in a wing and spiraling away as a dark green shape bursts from the clouds above, talons and thorns bristling. He misses her by inches. She dives. Her call of warning splits the air like a thunderclap. Below, figures scramble like ants over *Raven's Flight's* deck. The plant dragon flips in the air behind her. The thorns on his tail scrape her skin, opening stinging wounds on her side and tearing through the fabric of her netting. She evades his next strike by a scale's width. The poison makes her wounds burn in fiery agony.

Ralex screams orders over the wind, pushing his way to the bow as the drums pound. Kisara flies low over the ship, her wings pumping. Lucius sprints the length of the trireme before launching himself off the rail, out over the oars. Kisara snatches him out of the air before she labors into the sky with Lucius in her arms.

A roar wrenches Levnys' attention away. The plant dragon slashes her with claws this time, darting away as she turns to retaliate, his jaws cracked in a taunting grin. Kisara's voice cuts the air, and fire lights the sky, the explosion sending leaves scattering from the plant dragon's hide. A blaze of white scales and a sudden weight on her back, and Lucius is there, clinging to the leather around her body. His magic drives the heat of her wounds away. He screams her name.

"Lucius!" she cries out.

"Go!" is all she hears.

She flaps her wings hard as the plant dragon closes the distance, then folds them, diving and spiraling. She prays to Aea that Lucius has a good grip. Her foolish and brave paladin. Fire booms and lightning cracks, splitting the air with elemental fury.

"Ship!" Lucius screams, his voice nearly swallowed by the wind. She dives toward *Raven's Flight,* the enemy dragon behind her, and the reason for Lucius' direction is apparent. She hopes the plant dragon cannot react in time.

Black wood fills her vision. She banks hard. A ballista fires. The dragon's roar of surprise brings a savage glee to her chest. She circles low, flying around the ship. An enormous grappling hook—a harpax —is buried into the dragon's back, a steel rope spooling out from its metal-reinforced shaft. Another twang, another roar, another harpax. Lucius' flame explodes in front of the plant dragon's snout, reeling him backward, and a third finds purchase in his wooden skin.

"Now!" Ralex bellows, jumping away from the ballista and sprinting to the reinforced winch. Wooden gears scream in protest as he puts his weight into the lever, engaging the mechanism. Petrus and Sparax each run for another winch, and the ropes draw in. The dragon jerks as they strain against his weight.

And hold.

Levnys spares a glance over her shoulder at Lucius. He has worked his legs into the netting surrounding her, a rope tied around his waist and looped many times through the leather bands. He salutes her military style, fist to chest.

The winches drag the struggling dragon down. The drumbeat changes, and the rowers reverse their direction, bracing the ship against the weight of their catch. *Raven's Flight* bucks and rocks, sending unsecured crates sliding around the polished deck. The rocking lessens as the ropes tighten. Calvus and Lucia emerge from below with their steel swords drawn. They move forward with synchronized grace, their weapons glowing with magic, and sink them to the hilt in the dragon's leg. A white explosion sends splinters flying from the dragon. His scream of pain has a desperate, keening note. Lucius' magic falters.

Crackling lighting fills the air as Seto's wyverns dart around him in a sparking cloud. Kisara stoops in a dive, slashing at the captured dragon's flank and back. White light flashes again. The smell of spilled sap and freshly broken branches fills Levnys' nose. The dragon screams, trying to free himself. Levnys prepares to dive for his head to end his suffering and rid herself of her foe. Lucius' magic falters again.

The dragon flattens himself to the deck, folding his wings. Before the winches can take up the slack, he rips out first one hook, then another. Splintered green and brown wood juts from his back through foliage wet with his pale green blood. Lucia and Calvus close on him, but he spins, impacting them with his tail and sending them careening toward the rail. Sparax shouts and leaves his slackened winch, diving for the prone forms. The dragon rips out the last hook and lunges for the downed paladins. Lightning fills the air between the dragon and his quarry as Kisara and Seto cry out in unison, their combined magic a blinding wave of electricity. The dragon snarls, turns, and pushes off the ship with an enormous heave. Fury blazes bright in his eyes.

He peels his lips back from his jagged teeth. "You cheat," he says.

"I have friends," Levnys replies. "Come. Let us end this."

Lucius' magic shifts. A buzzing energy enters her body through his hand on her skin. It is as if someone bottled the rush of battle, the thrill of fighting. Her heart thumps hard in her chest, speeding to rabbit quickness, blood throbbing in her ears. Time slows as her foe closes the distance. She meets his rush with euphoric battle lust. Let him try to beat her now. She will turn him to kindling for Lucius' fire.

Red pulses at the edge of her vision. She has never felt so alive, so in tune with the elemental might a dragon can bring to bear. Lightning lives in her veins now, and it begs to escape. She opens her jaws and lets it spill forth at the oncoming dragon, filling the air with blinding light and an acrid stench. Her fingers flex with the need to dig her claws into flesh. Her foe emerges from the lightning with smoldering limbs, jaws spread wide. The next few seconds devolve into teeth and claws, snarling and bristling with the scent of blood in the air. *Her* blood—the plant dragon's claws dig into her shoulder, and she is caught. She whips her head around, but the enormous jaws close not on her, but Lucius.

No!

A man's scream. Blinding light. The dragon jerks his head back, his roar high and keening, distressed. His hold on her loosens. Lucius grips the leather with his left hand and a dagger with his right. He is drenched in sticky sap, his hair and clothes plastered to his skin, whole and alive.

"I thought you were a mage, not a paladin," the dragon says through his clenched teeth. He turns his head, revealing the ruin where his eye was, a trench of broken wood and gushing green blood.

"Guess what, ugly, I'm both." Lucius glares at the dragon through his limp hair. "Care to try again? You have another eye."

Levnys tears herself out of the plant dragon's grip and spins to face him. He is covered in burns, splintered wood, and drooping leaves. There is life in his remaining eye, clear and menacing. Lightning builds in her again. She arrows at him without thought, without consideration. She needs the kill, to make the lifeblood flow out between her teeth.

"Levnys!" Lucius screams.

They collide. Thousands of thorns dig into her skin. Lightning arcs between them as she drives him down to drown him in the very waters he seeks to steal.

Her entire body trembles. The dragon struggles, but she has him now, jaws tearing into his flesh, so much like wood. Blood gushes, numbing her tongue, but she does not care. Land fills her vision, drums pound behind her, her heart pounds in her ears. Lucius is screaming, too, his words lost to the howling wind. Impact, the sound of breaking bones and wood, a mighty splash. She drags the limp form onto the beach.

The blood lust leaves her. Her head hits the sand before she realizes she has collapsed. The poison is in her, everywhere. Her gums burn. Her muscles twitch. Somewhere distant, the sound of metal on leather and the weight on her back shifts.

Lucius' sandals hit the sand with a wet thump. He strides forward with a glowing dagger and seething flame. Levnys struggles to keep her eyes open. The plant dragon rises slowly to his feet, his sides heaving, opening his wings. His front leg hangs limp, and broken branches litter the ground around him. He takes a step back from Lucius. His hind leg collapses, eliciting a cry of pain. Lucius falters.

No. No, you must kill him.

The dagger dims, and the fire gutters out. Lucius lowers his arms. The dragon does not hesitate—he pushes into the air with a rush of wind and a storm of leaves.

Levnys is too weak to move. A deep cold settles into her. Her eyes close, and she cannot reopen them. Warm hands on her muzzle remind her she is in the realm of the living, not the frigid expanse of death.

"It's over, Levnys. It's alright," Lucius says. His hands are so gentle, his voice soothing. "I'm here."

Drums. Splashing. Shouting.

Cacophony.

Hands press against her skin. Levnys floats in the soothing waves of magic. Paladins—the enemy. No. *Friends.*

"...nightshade..." A raspy voice. The Grandmaster.

He sounds so distant.

"...your mouth. The poison..." Another voice. Lucius. Sweet, caring Lucius, who saved her life once, or is it twice, now?

He speaks more, but she cannot make out the words. The drums are too loud, so loud they could be a heartbeat. The taste of wood and pressure against her teeth sharpens the sounds around her. Her mouth. They want her to open her mouth—why? Yet, she does. Her tongue is swollen and useless like a fat slug in her mouth. A sharp pain in her gums causes her to groan, and the world inches further toward clarity.

"...bit him, yes."

"She must have ingested it. Everyone, hold her jaws."

"Understood."

Her mouth is wrenched open, her tongue pulled forward. An arm thrusts down her throat. She heaves her breakfast onto the sand. The sour stench makes her gag, and she brings the rest up on her own. Cool water, imbued with magic, bubbles against her tongue. Her throat works greedily, and soon, she drinks deep of it. A wet cloth wipes her cheeks around her mouth. Levnys opens an eye to focus on Lucia. The princess' sapphire eyes fix on her. A rare smile spreads across her face.

"She's awake," Lucia says.

Lucius is there within a second, nearly knocking his aunt over. He is shirtless, his remaining clothes and hair drenched. He closes his eyes briefly, exhales, and sits next to her head. His warm hand on her brow and tired smile are all she needs. Lucius is alright. She is alright.

"Hey," he says. "Can you talk?"

She tries, but her tongue does not move. She wobbles her head in the negative.

"Alright. We came down on an island too small for the ship. We'll heal you a bit more, but we need you to transform as soon as you can."

Levnys twitches her chin up and rests it back on the sand. Soon, five sets of warm hands press against her. The flood of magic lifts her and carries her along as if floating through a cloud. Lucius' eyes never leave hers. After several moments, her tongue feels less ungainly.

"Ready," she says thickly.

Lucius picks her up after she transforms, and she relaxes in his arms as they board the rowboat. She looks into eyes rimmed with dark circles, drooping with fatigue and worry, soft with relief. As the rest of the paladins man the oars, he presses his lips to the top of her head.

"Rest," he says against her hair.

When she next awakens, it is early evening. She is in a hammock strung between two enormous trees. The waning sunlight filters through the leaves, dappling the blanket under her chin. The activity around her slowly comes into focus. The smell of bread makes her stomach growl. She turns her head to regard the loaf on a small table beside her. Lucius reads one of his scrolls on a stump nearby. His rich blue tunic is unbelted, hanging loose around his waist. He raises his head as she reaches for the bread and gives her a weary smile.

Levnys mumbles a greeting around the bread in her mouth. By the time she finishes the loaf, she feels more like she is in the world of the living. The silence stretches between them. Questions press against her lips, but she does not know if she should ask them.

She does not have to. Lucius rolls the scroll and tucks it away into a leather case. "I imagine you're wondering why I didn't strike the dragon," he says.

Levnys frowns. "Correct."

"He wasn't a threat anymore." He taps his chest. "It's happened twice now—right before that dragon leaves, my anger evaporates."

"That does not mean you should have let him go."

"And what, killed him in cold blood? Why would I do that?"

"Why would you not do that? He has tried to kill me—us— multiple times."

"Once the intention to harm was gone, he was no longer an enemy. That's always how I've done things."

"So you will allow him to attack us? We will be at his mercy yet again."

"No. We know what he can do now. Next time, we'll be prepared."

"How are you sure it will be enough?"

"One can't be assured of victory but can always get as close as possible."

"You are gambling with lives," Levnys says flatly. "I did not think you would be so flippant about this."

"Everyone involved knows the stakes," Lucius snaps. His golden eyes flare bright. "No one else is holding a grudge about this, Levnys. Why do you?"

"Because it is *my* territory," Levnys snarls. "I do not tolerate challenges to it."

"Even when he wasn't fighting you anymore?"

"An enemy is always an enemy."

Lucius' face hardens further. "No. That view causes needless death."

"My mother did not think so."

"Then your mother was wrong."

"My mother was never wrong."

"Everyone is wrong sometimes," he counters. "You weren't the one who had the choice to kill him." Lucius flexes the fingers on his sword hand. "I made my decision. Agree or not, it was *mine*, and I would do it again."

She stares at him as the edge of her anger dulls. How can she deny it? It is not the choice she would have made, but he is right—it was not her decision.

"What was that spell you used on me?" she asks to change the subject. A wise dragon will step away when victory damages one more than defeat. She has already hurt him enough.

Lucius closes his eyes briefly. When he opens them again, the fierce glow has faded. "It's a vigor spell that sharpens abilities in combat. Standard paladin magic."

"Why did you choose to use it?"

"I wanted to show that dragon what teamwork can do. Although I got scolded for it."

"Lucia?"

"Kisara. She thought I was an idiot for making her grab me." He stands and stretches, causing his shoulders to pop. "I don't regret my choice there, either."

"Choice is important to you," Levnys says.

Lucius' jaw tightens. "It's the most important thing. A prince doesn't have much to start with, and lately, nothing is in my control."

"I am sorry for what happened, Lucius."

"I know," he says softly. "Doesn't mean I'm not upset about it." He turns his head to stare out over the camp. "I'm ready to talk about it, though, if you want."

"I am listening."

"You always do." He flexes the fingers on his right hand again—a motion he does to calm himself, Levnys realizes. "I know you didn't mean to...you had no idea I was..." He sighs. "Shit. It isn't your fault, but everyone must have a say in what happens. *Everyone.* I watched people around me get used and I couldn't stand it. I won't stand it. My father, that dragon—" Lucius' lip trembles. He bites it. "I refuse to be like them."

Levnys follows the line of his gaze at last. "Kisara," she whispers.

"Not only her." Lucius turns to face her. Pain contorts his face, twisting his handsome features into a grimace. "My mother was already married with two children when Toth, Kisara's father, did what he did. He wanted the child given to him and was willing to threaten Mother's family to ensure it. She was sent to the royal harem to 'protect' her and her 'honor.'" Lucius spits on the ground. "All they were protecting was their reputation. They didn't think the crown prince—my father—would want her. She's not his usual type. He prefers his women to be tiny and delicate, like a doll to play with. My mother is tall, proud, independent, and doesn't take grief from anyone. Perhaps he thought he could break her. After seven years and two children, he finally gave up. In the end, she's getting the last laugh— Tiberia and I despise our father's slimy guts. Mother taught us to respect everyone, no matter how low their station. She taught us to love and showed us how to be strong."

"She sounds like a wonderful woman."

Lucius' face softens. "No matter how dark things got, no matter how much my father abused her, she always had a smile for us. The least I can do is make her proud." He wipes his eyes with his tunic collar. "Though if she saw me dive off the ship's side, she'd use both sandals to beat sense into me."

"Hmm. Perhaps it is selfish, but I am glad you came to help me."

Lucius raises his head. His brown cheeks are dappled with red, his eyes swollen with tears. "I couldn't watch that dragon hurt you. Levnys, I—I can't forget it. I like you, but I wish it hadn't happened this way."

"I understand," Levnys says.

"When this 'mating season' thing ends, we should start over. A meal, some conversation, good wine. Is that something you'd like, too?"

"Yes, I would like that very much."

He stands, adjusting his tunic. "But I want answers. It doesn't have to be now, but if we're going to do this, I don't want the fact I'm a paladin to stand between us any longer. I deserve that much."

Levnys' gut clenches. "I understand."

He turns away. "I'll let you get your rest for now."

Through the efforts of the paladins, Levnys is airborne again within another day, training lightly with Kisara. The half-dragon's progress is remarkable, and Levnys' chest swells with pride for her stoic pupil.

One evening, she is greeted by one of Ralex's stewards as soon as she lands. "Regillus requests your presence on the stern," he says.

Levnys has to hide her smile after she shifts to her human form. "Tell him I will be there soon."

She approaches the stern of *Raven's Flight* with a small linen bag over one shoulder. Ralex's tent glows from within with soft yellow firelight. As she steps inside, Lucius smiles at her from the low table—crates covered with linen cloth—and raises a goblet.

The prince is in fine form, his raven hair oiled and curled, his azure tunic and golden eyes representing his royalty despite his casual dress. He is seated on a pillow, his legs curled under him.

"It's a bit more Soutorian than Gethki," he says as she settles across from him, "but I think I prefer this anyway. Are you comfortable?"

"Yes," she says with amusement. It does not surprise her that Lucius does not like the lounging couches of a high-class Gethki dining room. She picks up the goblet and savors the scent of the wine—*conditum,* she notes—sweetened with honey and dates and spiced with saffron. It is an excellent blend, she can already tell. The remainder of the table is set with simple but fine dishes—olive relish and goat cheese, bread, and roasted fish. She recalls the blackened fish from several days ago and asks coyly, "Did you prepare this meal yourself?"

Lucius laughs. "Of course not. I asked for assistance."

"Hmm. How did you manage to convince the cooks to do so? They are terribly busy."

"By taking over some of the burden," he replies. "I'm not good at cooking but can wield a knife. I helped carry that stone oven for them a few times, too."

He picks up a small bottle from the table and removes the cork. A briny fish smell wafts across Levnys' nose, and she wrinkles it. "Is that *garum*?"

"Of course," he says as he pours the fermented fish sauce over his meal—so much that the clear amber liquid pools on his plate. "Why wouldn't it be? Do you want some?"

"No," she says, waving her hand. "I do not like it."

He tilts his head. "You live in Geth and don't like *garum*? That's inconvenient."

"It is too salty by itself." She purses her lips. "I should not be surprised that the crown prince of Geth likes it. How typical of you."

He grins at her. "Guilty. Let's eat before the food gets cold, mm?"

They set to it. The fish is delightfully light and crispy, much to her taste. She catches Lucius watching her a few times. He smiles warmly as she meets his gaze.

"Why are we in Ralex's tent?" Levnys asks after finishing her food.

"An illusion of privacy," Lucius replies. "Easier for the crew to willfully ignore us. It isn't a secret, but sailors are like legionnaires in that way."

"I see. What is your companions' opinion on..." She gestures between them. "Do they know what transpired?"

Lucius' eyes drop to his goblet, and he swirls the liquid in it absently. "I talked to Kisara about it a few days ago. I told her everything."

"Everything?"

He blushes in the firelight. "I conveniently don't remember the parts I'd leave out, so, yes, everything." He sighs. "She helped me put a few things into perspective. She likes you a lot, you know."

"She has not expressed this to me," Levnys says.

"She won't, but I know her well enough." He smiles wistfully. "It's been good to spend time with her again."

"You are close."

He drinks. "We were, as children—it was me, her, and Tiberia." His face clouds. "Until I was twelve and joined the Order. The enclave was only a two-day ride from Geth, so I could visit, but it wasn't the same. Once I was out of the palace, I also realized how much I hated being there."

"It is fitting," Levnys agrees. "I could not imagine you lounging all day in the royal toga."

"You're right, but it's more than that. I've always despised my father, even as a child. When I got older and figured out what he did to those women forced to be in his harem, it became hatred. I couldn't hide it from him then and refuse to do so now. I wouldn't be surprised if he chooses my younger brother over me to succeed him. That little shit is cut from the same cloth as he is." Lucius looks like he wants to spit but drains his goblet instead.

"Would you object to that?" Levnys asks.

"It would be easier on me if I never ascended the throne, I admit. Regillus Noctua refused the throne for the sake of his books, and I'd love to do the same." Levnys smiles at the mention of that particular prince, one she met in Caltava so long ago. Lucius tips his head, acknowledging her recognition, and continues, "But I don't know if I'd be able to stomach standing aside as yet another selfish and cruel emperor took the throne." He coughs. "We're talking politics over a candlelit dinner. I'm sorry."

"No need to apologize, but perhaps we should not continue. I do not wish for you to reflect on negative things."

She reaches for the amphora of wine at the same time he does. Their fingers meet and linger before he pulls it from her grasp. He refills both of their goblets, emptying the vessel. Had they drank the whole thing?

"Should I call for dessert?" Lucius asks.

Levnys holds up the bag. "I had another thing in mind."

Lucius' eyes settle on it with bright interest. "Oh? What's that?"

"You will see."

She reaches for it, but Lucius places his hand over hers. "Would you like to continue in my cabin? It's getting late, and I'm sure Ralex wants his tent."

"Oh, that is a good idea."

He stands and holds out his hand to help her rise. They emerge into the night air together. Levnys stares at the stars momentarily while crewmen emerge from the darkness, entering Ralex's tent without a word. She looks at Lucius questioningly.

"They agreed to clean up tonight if I cut all the tubers tomorrow," he says with a shrug. "Shall we?"

They settle into the cabin, her in the chair, him cross-legged on the bed. She sets the bag on the table with a thunk.

"Close your eyes and hold out your hands," she says. She pulls out a blown glass bottle and places it in his outstretched palms. The small vessel appears tiny in his huge hands. "Open them now," she says.

His eyes widen. He turns the bottle over, studying it. The stylized stag, horns wicked and curving, catches the candlelight in gold metallic ink. Liquid swirls inside, its sparkle only hinted through the brown glass.

"How did you get Selucian ice mead?" he asks. "It's my favorite, and I—" He pauses. "I haven't had it for years."

"Dalos. Kisara helped me find it." She fishes into the bag, pulls out a small brass goblet, and hands it to him. Two feathered wings arc from the base and wrap around the sides of it. She retrieves its twin as his lips tremble.

"Why?" he asks so softly she can barely hear him.

"I wanted to thank you for saving my life."

He reaches out his hand. She puts hers into it, and he lifts it to his lips. Their warmth lingers on her skin. "I am happy I did, every day," he says. "Would you like to try it with me?"

"I would enjoy that."

He carves open the wax seal with his knife and removes the cork. Golden smoke wafts from the bottle, rich with a honey scent. He pours hers first, then his. The auric mist spills over the sides as the goblets' metal surface frosts over.

"It is enchanted."

"Yes." He holds up the goblet. "Care to give the dedication?"

"I will try." She holds up hers, mirroring him. "Here is to the time we have spent together. Here is to hearing every story in the world." She leans forward. "Here is to keeping to your path, even though it is difficult, and to oaths, duty, and those who must follow them."

"*Prosit*," he returns. They drink. The cold hits her tongue first, sharp and sudden as ice, then the strong honey and spice flavor. The tingling cold spreads to her nose and throat. Lucius sighs happily and rests his back against the wall.

She takes the bottle and pours them each another helping. Lucius sips it this time, his eyes closed, smiling. Levnys watches him for a moment. She does not want to break this precious mood but must do as he asked.

"Lucius, I must explain something to you."

"I'm listening." He heaves off the wall and sits on the bed's edge.

"First, I must tell you a secret that few humans know. South of Caltava, there is an island where young dragons go to live. It has been there for hundreds of years, since the Dragon War. One hundred fifty years ago, I was in the nest, living with my mother near Caltava. One day, we began to hear disturbing news from that island. Young dragons, barely older than I appeared near our cave with terrible injuries—skin burned off, limbs broken, covered with weapon wounds. Some of them died there in front of me." She bears her teeth at the old, old pain. "They spoke of human warriors clad in pure white, their shields adorned with a headless dragon."

Lucius' spine goes rigid. "Wait. That sounds familiar."

"Does the name Contradraco strike a chime?" Levnys asks.

"Yes, but..." His brow furrows. "It was something I read, a line in an old scroll somewhere. Please continue." He reaches out and lays his hand over hers.

"Those paladins did not care what the dragon's origin was—they killed every one they found. Individually, they could not hope to best a youngster, but there were a hundred of them. When they finished the island, they began to work their way north." The lump becomes an obstruction, causing her following words to come out strangled. "That was when my mother decided to confront them." Her fingers tighten in his. "She was the mightiest of dragons, an old warrior without peer. Yet they overcame her, chased her back to her lair. Her last words to my brother and I were to run and hide. I flew as far and fast as I could. I was so scared, and I knew I would never see my mother again. I lost my brother in the confusion. I do not know if he survived." She takes a drink, not from the goblet, but from the water skin on the table. "I returned to the lair to find my mother slain, pushed into the water. They took her head and left the rest to the fish. I sat in the destroyed lair for weeks until I got desperate enough to go to Caltava. The people there knew my mother well. They fed me and kept me safe until the paladins were gone. I never found out what happened to them."

"I remember now," Lucius says. "The Celestial Shield was sent after them, along with a legion. Emperor Passius ordered their arrest when they got to Gethki waters, but they resisted and were killed to the last."

"So your order saved us?"

Lucius sighs. "No, I can't give them credit. Most of the damage was done by the time we stepped in. No one recorded what happened on the Sparkling Coast. They were only acting in their best interest. Every organization does."

"Was saving me in your best interest?"

"That wasn't my intention, but it could be spun that way. We save the leader of the dragons on the Coast in an area distrustful of paladins, and after that, we're all friends. A true redemption story."

His bitterness lifts her spirits, assuaging the last of her fears. Of course, this man would disagree with the actions of those foul paladins. She is ashamed she had any doubts about it in the first place.

"I took over my mother's territory when I was old enough. I let the surviving dragons live in it, and we all benefit. The commune has young dragons again, including my daughters." Yet she is bitter all these years later. Will it ever indeed fade? "I took my mother's lair and made it my own. I will show it to you when we reach Caltava."

"I'd like that. Thank you for telling me this."

"You deserved to know, Lucius. I am sorry that I ever had doubts about you and your companions. None of you deserved to be treated with such suspicion."

"I can't blame you for that," he says. Sparkling golden liquid catches the firelight as he pours another serving of mead. "No hard feelings, truly."

"It is a relief to hear that." She sips the freezing alcohol. The burden on her shoulders has lifted, and the guilt assuaged as much as she could hope. She looks across at Lucius, at the slope of his relaxed shoulders and the lines that have mostly smoothed from his forehead. She finds him the most appealing when he is relaxed, and casual confidence permeates his body. She would like to lay with him again, to have his skin pressed against hers, her name on his breath. Yet, the bottle is not empty, and the mood is not right.

"It is your turn to tell me a story," she says instead. "Something from Gethki history?"

He sips his mead, inhaling the enchanted mist. "Sure, I have the perfect one."

X

MIGRATION

Pica

Two hours later, the bottle rests empty on the table. Levnys sits in Pica's lap, relating a tale from Caltava. The *praefectus urbi*, blind drunk, gave an impromptu speech in a brothel, accidentally replacing the word "propagate" with "fornicate," much to the amusement of the attendants. Pica laughs at her re-telling as golden mist spills from between her lips. She finishes her story and runs her fingers along his neck, causing him to shiver.

"This is nice," she says.

He lifts his hand to touch her cheek. "I agree."

"Would you like to lay with me?" she asks, a hopeful note in her voice.

He wonders if she knows how important that question is to him. Until now, he enjoyed her company with that remnant of doubt rankling him like an open sore. Now, at such a critical moment, she assuages his remaining fears with those simple words.

"I would," he says. "But there's something I need to ask first."

"What is it?"

"I know you didn't mind when I went to the brothel on Dalos, but now things are a bit, ah, further."

A sly smile quirks her lips. "You are asking if I mind you going to brothels? Only if you do not take me with you."

"Uh. Sure, that sounds fun. Beyond that, though."

"Ahh," Levnys says, and the smile broadens. "I did not think it needed to be stated. No, Lucius, I do not mind if you take other lovers. I would not wish to deprive another of your fine company." Her face softens. "You have a lot of love to give. I do not mind sharing it. But I am tired of delaying."

She shifts in his lap and kisses him eagerly. At his low chuckle and her returning inquisitive look, he says, "You *have* to know most women aren't so forward."

"There is no need to be shy about such things. Does it bother you?"

"Not at all." He moves his hands over her body, brushing his fingers along the tips of her breasts. "I like it a lot."

She puts her palms against his chest and pushes him backward. "Lay down," she whispers.

He spreads himself on the bed. She doesn't follow him. Instead, she strips her tunic and underclothes, leaving her lithe body covered with only flickering candlelight. Pica reaches to remove his clothes, but she shakes her head and pushes his hands away. Her fingers brush his skin as she undresses him—first his tunic, then his breeches, agonizingly slow. She removes his loincloth, leaving him naked. Her turquoise eyes travel over him, appraising him. He puts his arms behind his head, stretching himself out to enjoy the intensity of her attention.

"Like what you see?" he asks.

Her gaze lingers significantly. "Indeed I do. I must decide where I would like to start. Close your eyes. Do not move your hands."

A thrill of need courses through him, and he closes his eyes. The bed moves as her weight joins his. Cool fingers trace over his sternum and along his belly, stopping frustratingly short. He groans and arches his back. Her mouth replaces her hands, and she soon has him whimpering. Every move she makes is with purpose. He revels in the increasingly intense teasing, writhing under her attention. She keeps him guessing where her mouth will go next—lips against his ear, tongue on his nipples, breath on his thighs.

"Levnys," he gasps. "Gods, you're good at that."

"I have practice," she says wryly. "I must atone for you not remembering last time."

He feels a pang at the mention, but it is slight, a minor roughness, before her smooth fingers stroke him again.

"When do I get a turn?" he asks. "I'd love to know how you taste."

"Soon."

She takes her time, pleasuring him until he begs. His fingers tighten in his hair as he struggles to leave his hands where they are. He needs to touch her. The bed shifts again, and she's there, knees on either side of his head. Her heady scent fills his nose, and her heat warms his face. He turns his lips to her thigh and slowly kisses until he finds the sweet center of her, tasting her. She gasps, and her hips twitch.

"I need my hands," he says.

"Use them."

Pica grabs her hips and holds her still as he goes to work with tongue and lips. He loses himself in her softness, pleasuring her, driven on by her increasingly energetic cries. She shudders against his tongue, her hand tangled in his hair.

"Lucius," she gasps.

The way she says his name makes his heart soar. One more time, and she moves down his body. She's soon astride his hips, lowering herself onto him. A moan escapes him as she settles, him buried to the hilt in her, the quickness of her muscles edging him closer to release.

Gods, he wants nothing more than this. Finally, there's nothing left between them, no distance left to bridge. They move together with increasing rhythm, the graceful confidence in her lovemaking causing his body to arch beneath her. She's a vision of elegant beauty, her metallic skin shimmering in the faint candlelight. Pica channels magic into the flames, turning them gold. They send pulsing lights over the bed, dancing to their movements. She glances around, and a wondrous smile lights her face more brilliantly than any candlelight could. He can't get enough of her, the buzzing of her elemental intensity beneath his hands. She reaches release again, and he is lost, pulled along in her torrent. He climaxes hard into her heat, thrusting in as deep as he can, her name on his lips in desperate pleasure.

They coast down together. Levnys leans forward to rest her arms on his chest. Flecks of bronze in her irises catch the golden candlelight. He takes her face between his hands, drawing her down until their lips meet. They kiss until the candles burn low and the night's chill leaks through the cracked window. Levnys pulls away first. The smile she gives him sweeps away any lingering doubts.

"I'll remember it this time," he says.

"Is it worth remembering?"

He chuckles. "You know the answer, Lev."

"Lev." She traces his lips with a finger. "When a human shortens a name, it signifies affection."

"Sometimes not," Pica says, "but in this case..." He pulls her face down to kiss her gently. "Absolutely."

The giant blue and purple fish sails through the air toward Pica. He tries to catch it but misses. It flops on the deck, mouth gasping as a cook pulls it back from the railing. Pica watches him, noting with irritation that most men stand near him. No wonder. He hasn't caught a single one.

"What's wrong, Lucius? Your vision going bad?" Petrus teases him. The stocky man has caught every fish thrown his way, covering his arms with tiny cuts from the razor-sharp fins. He snatches another from the air and tosses it to the waiting crew.

Pica scowls at him. "I was trained to hit things."

A fish flies toward Sparax. The lanky man catches it effortlessly. He doesn't have a single cut on him. Water runs down his bare chest and arms, following the contours of his muscles. He notices Pica staring and quickly looks away.

Pica turns back to the water, squinting in the bright sunlight. The island of Notri rests on the horizon across a glittering blue expanse, churned choppy by thousands of enormous purple-finned fish. Boats scatter across the surface like toys, taking advantage of the bounty of life swimming below them.

A white streak comes from the sky, plunging into the thickest part of the school. Kisara surfaces, holding her wings straight as she struggles to bring the fish under control. Pica snickers. She looks like a seagull.

Kisara flaps mightily, emerging from the water with her prize. She wobbles as the fish flops violently in her claws.

"Hey! Aren't you supposed to kill it? Don't let go!" he shouts at her.

She tries to drop it on his head. He steps out of the way, letting it splat onto the deck. She waggles her wings at him and circles back out over the water.

Krakli swoops and dives, harassing the sea birds circling above the frenzy. Their protesting cries turn the skies into a cacophony, with Krakli's chattering laugh floating through it all.

A splash, and Levnys flips another one of the enormous fish straight at his face. He raises his arms to catch it but misses again. He ignores Petrus' jeering and watches the dragon. She moves gracefully among the swarming fish, the school arcing and swirling in its attempt to avoid her. She snaps out her neck and catches one, swallowing it whole, then darts again into the thick of it. She emerges with a struggling fish in each clawed forelimb and tosses them onto a nearby fishing boat as the occupants cheer her on. Pica watches her, transfixed. He hadn't imagined it like this when she mentioned the migration of purple-finned razorbacks.

It's been several days since they got together, and she's come to his cabin every night. He thinks of her soft voice in his ear and her soft skin on his as heat creeps up his cheeks.

Someone shouts his name. A fish smacks into his chest and knocks him backward onto the deck. Pain lances through his elbows as he lands with the fish flopping beside him.

Petrus' grinning face appears. "Struck by love, struck by fish. Classic."

"Shut up, Petrus." He pushes himself up, trying to head-butt the other man.

Petrus dances back with a hearty laugh. "Does this mean you're not joining us this evening since you belong to the dragon now?"

Pica stands and brushes off his tunic. Petrus doesn't have an ulterior motive for asking, but the look on Sparax's face—worried, anxious, but trying to hide it—catches Pica's attention.

"The opposite. She wants to come along," he says, trying to keep his face neutral. Pica wishes he could capture the twins' expressions in fresco. They both gape at him.

"Come along?" Sparax asks. "She knows what we *do*, right?"

"Of course. She demanded all the stories I could remember in detail." He grins as Sparax almost misses the next fish tossed at him.

Petrus recovers first. "She's welcome to, of course. I bet she knows some great places."

Pica takes the fish from Sparax's arms, gingerly avoiding the sharp fins. "She already has one in mind."

After the ship is hauled ashore, the four of them step off into the twilight air. The sea breeze is biting as they walk through the docks along the rich waterfront. The concrete and cobblestones are scrubbed clean of the dirt and debris of an active port. Bright frescoes turn the myriad buildings into a rainbow of color, surely refreshed more often than necessary—no graffiti, trash, or signs of the rowdy activities that generally define such a place. The cleanliness of the place unsettles Pica. The presence of the guard ships ringing this part of the harbor makes more sense. He frowns.

Pica catches a whiff of something fetid on a strong gust and glances down the docks. Guards stand vigil, facing the stretch of concrete toward a crowded set of ship berths and buildings. The guards turn away a stooped figure in a torn and filthy tunic, their feet wrapped with bloody bandages. Pica's spine stiffens as he watches the figure limp off. He almost intervenes but reluctantly turns away. He wouldn't get anywhere while in disguise, and his companions are moving on.

They walk along the main street for a while before turning. Levnys leads them through a twisting maze of side streets. The wind picks up, buffeting them and sending a ripple of goosebumps along Pica's bare arms. Levnys tosses her hair over her shoulders before pointing at a sign. "This is my favorite place to come in Notri. I stop here every migration."

The sign glows with enchanted light, a pink and white blossom with a bright yellow center. He'd seen a flower like that before. Was it his Grandmother's garden? Pica ponders it as Levnys holds open the curtain for them. They file through one by one, each carrying a razorback. The bright interior blazes with color: purple, blue, and pink orbs float through the air, sending their light scattering around the walls. A central ball of white light shines from the domed ceiling, illuminating the room with cool intensity. The lights are shaped like different types of fish. They chase each other around the ceiling, weaving in dizzying patterns. A rippling set of waves is painted on the dome's underside, pulsing in shades of blue and green as if lit by a sun.

The walls are bright white, and some panels are covered with traditional Soutorian murals painted in broad, elegant brush strokes.

"This way." Levnys steps out from around them and leads them through rows of tables. Pica can sense the attention of the few patrons on him. They pay his group momentary attention before returning to their own business. He likes this place already.

She takes them to a curtained-off area, firelight shining around the edges of the heavily embroidered fabric. "Please stay here," she says as she ducks through.

Music booms from a corner stage, a quintet of bards playing a driving tune. The heavy drums thump as several people dance to it wildly, arms in the air. Pica's gaze lingers on the pretty blonde woman singing at the front, her red *stola* swirling around her ankles as she dances. Her voice soars over the din of the crowd, as clear and pure as wind chimes. Pica's heart thuds along with the beat, quick, driving. For a moment, the music drives away the fatigue in his limbs, the pain in his gut. He forgets about the fish in his arms, the birds, everything but the voice.

Pica snaps back when Sparax nudges him with an elbow. Levnys emerges from behind the curtain, followed by a petite woman with black hair pulled into a tight bun. Her eyes are dark brown, accented by her elegant makeup. She wears an apron over a tightly-laced corset, and the skin above it is a smooth cream. Petrus swallows audibly.

"This is Ava, the owner of this tavern," Levnys says in introduction. "Ava, these are my friends Petrus, Sparax, and Corvus." She uses Pica's pseudonym without hesitation. "I am traveling with them. I wish to show them a good time."

The woman bows at the waist. "They are all so strong," she gushes in accented Gethki. "You found such beautiful men to carry your fish for you, Levnys."

"It is an added benefit," Levnys says. "They are your fish now."

"Yes, I always appreciate it when you bring me gifts. Please, come with me."

They follow her through the curtain. A huge brazier in the center of the room casts dancing firelight over the walls and ceiling. It is the only illumination, too intense to be natural fire—more magic. The entire place drips with it.

Leather couches surround polished wooden tables. One section is occupied—three figures sit in the furthest corner, talking in whispers. Two of them stand and approach—a pair of enormous felina with leonine manes. Ava directs them to take the fish. Pica watches them with interest as they depart—they could be from Tekan, that enormous continent far to the south. He has Tekani blood via his grandfather, though he knows little about that part of his family history. He dismisses his musings with his usual promise to research it more.

Ava chooses a couch and settles onto it. She perches on the edge, her back rigid in her corset. She gestures for the group to sit, then lifts her hand and snaps her fingers. The remaining figure stands and disappears through the curtain.

"Now, my lovelies, surely there is more to you than muscles," she purrs. "Otherwise, our Levnys would not bother with you." Her gaze lingers on Pica's disguised chest and neck. "You all buzz with magic, especially you, *notuda*."

Noble one, Pica mentally translates. He smiles at Ava.

"You understood the word, as I expected. You have Soutorian blood in your veins."

It's not the blood people usually care about. "Among other things, yes," he tells her. "Grandmother is from Soutori."

"Soutori is lovely in the spring. Have you ever been?"

"I wish. I've only heard stories."

"You should visit, *notuda*."

"I'll endeavor to try," Pica says.

"Do. You will have many reasons to go," Ava's eyes return to the twins. They fidget under her intense gaze. "You two. You are paladins, correct?"

Levnys chuckles. "Ava, you make them squirm in their seat. It is good to see these two sweat."

"Hey!" Petrus protests.

"I do not often get such visitors. And paladins! I thought I'd never see the day a dragon of the Coast would associate with such warriors." Ava leans forward, the firelight highlighting the curves of her breasts. "My lovelies, I request that you indulge me in some fun."

A shadow falls over their table. The wyverni's scales shine silver in the firelight, his draconic face peering over a large tray of drinks. He carefully sets a mug in front of each person. Frost forms on the hammered copper surface. He nods to Ava and retreats.

"Thank you, Zelkos. Please keep them coming." Ava takes the mug and raises it to her lips.

Pica picks up his mug, wincing at the shock of the cold surface. The others follow suit. Levnys inhales the mist that rises into her nose.

"To new friends and old," Ava says. "*Sita.*" She drinks deeply.

Pica follows her example, filling his mouth with the freezing liquid. Ice crystals form in his mouth, and the mint flavor makes his eyes water. He stares at his mug for a second, then drinks deeper.

"You like it?" Ava asks.

"It's delicious." The others express their agreement.

She claps her hands. "Excellent. It is my newest mixture. I am glad that the taste is pleasant. Now. I believe I was about to ask these two some questions."

Sparax is the one who swallows this time.

Zelkos brings another tray heaped with drinks and a bowl of bread. He leaves the whole tray.

Several hours later, the tavern fills with merry groups of attractive young patrons occupying most seats. Petrus and Sparax have someone under each arm, sharing drinks and more intimate things. A comely young man with black hair plays with Pica's tunic collar, his thin body pressed against his chest. He practically fell into his lap after Levnys caught him longingly staring at Pica.

The man, named Nerva, is from Geth—the merchant district. It doesn't surprise Pica that people from Geth don't recognize him. Levnys sits across their laps, intently listening to Nerva's drunken story. Pica's vision swims. It only took a few of the minty cocktails to intoxicate him.

A sound draws his attention, and he turns to look, trying to focus on Ava. She sits rigidly straight, sipping her misty mug. Magic radiates off her like waves of heat. Pica squints as her aura manifests.

The ethereal mist coalesces around her head into a canine shape with rounded ears and canted eyes. Several tail-like appendages appear behind her, their tips roundly tapered. They languidly lash, glowing with radiant lavender light. There's a sense of awe—not his—pressed against his consciousness.

Nine tails. His grandmother told him a story once. He struggles to remember what it was.

Ava's eyes lock onto him. All sensation disappears aside from her overpowering aura. His intoxication lifts, clearing the fog and stopping the room's spin.

Magpie, her voice says in his head.

She knows who he is.

Ava's aura pulses with a ghostly light. *Do not fear me,* notuda. *I am not an enemy. You must be made aware.* Her tails lash as her eyes glow with purple fire. *You will fight as people fall around you. One by one, they will die, but you must never stop fighting. You will fly high, Magpie, higher than you could ever imagine. Keep beating your wings. You must never stop. You cannot fail. The world is at stake.*

The room spins as Pica's vision blurs. His stomach churns at the sudden return of his intoxication. The warm bodies against him are impossibly heavy.

Levnys touches his cheek. "Lucius? Are you listening?"

"Um. What?"

Levnys snorts. "It is too early for you to sleep. Petrus and Sparax are going to a brothel. We should go with them. I want to bring Nerva with us." She leans over, kisses the Gethki man, and stands, swaying. She tries to bow to Ava but nearly topples over. "I thank you for the hospitality, my friend."

Ava stands and returns the bow. "My pleasure. Return here tomorrow. I have someone I'd like you to meet."

Levnys pulls at his hand, and he rises, unsteady. Nerva tucks himself under his arm, his hand drifting across Pica's back. Levnys leads them into the night, following the other paladins down the street.

The next afternoon, after some fruitless hours at the library, Pica and Levnys return to Ava's tavern. She greets them when the curtain settles, a drink in each hand. "Friends, you return. You are hungry. I have prepared a room for you, and food already awaits. You will find the accommodations most enjoyable."

The drink makes Pica's head fuzzy. It's rich and smoky, almost woody, and the flavor hides the bite of the alcohol. It warms him, making his fingers tingle. They finish their mugs by the time they climb the stairs.

Ava unlocks the door and hands him a key stamped with a blossom. "You may rest here until dinner." She bows and leaves.

They enter the room, and Pica stops to stare. Blue and gold silk hangs from the ceiling, interspersed with small golden lights. They float around of their own accord, weaving between the silk. A large blue rug covers a polished wooden floor. A bed with four posts sits at the center, expertly carved, the posts twisting into the branches of a flowering tree. Tiny motes of light glide along the raised edges, flickering over the polished surface. They fluctuate between brown, green, and pink as they move over the engraved leaves and flowers, distorted by the shimmering silk between the posts.

An enormous mural wraps around three walls, depicting a winding river in soft blues and greens. On the banks, pink-flowered trees explode with blooms, filling most of the painted surface. Heart-shaped petals blow through the treetops. Pink metal inlays frame each petal and tree, casting a rosy light into the room.

A reclining couch with enough space for two people rests under the open window. The table is made of sandstone rather than wood, carved in bas-relief with a woman's profile, flanked by pictorial glyphs. The last queen of the Negasi, Pica realizes. His grandfather has the same thing recreated on his villa's walls. To see it here—well, considering their host, he can't be surprised. Gethki, Negasi, and Soutorian mixed into something new. A message or a reminder. Who can say which?

Lights dance over a square ceramic plate, painted red and enameled to a shine. It is artfully arranged with roasted goat, steamed leeks, and, to Pica's delight, long-grained rice. An elegantly carved pair of chopsticks rests on a stand shaped like a delicate lotus flower. He and Levnys settle onto their sides to lounge, setting to their meal.

Rice. It's been so long since he's had it. The Soutorian import isn't rare, per se, but between the limited funds of the Order and the pragmatism of the legions, it's been out of his reach for longer than he'd like.

The meal is fantastic, as expected. Levnys chews thoughtfully, savoring each bite. Pica's eyes grow heavy. The glowing orbs pulse slightly, sending rippling light over the walls. It makes the trees appear like they are blowing in a gentle wind.

Soutori in the spring. Thanks, Ava.

Levnys pushes away her plate and stands. She tugs on his arm. "Come, Lucius, let us sleep for a bit."

"I'm fine, Levnys," he says, then yawns.

"Ava told you to rest. I will help you." She guides him to the bed and parts the curtains, settling onto it.

He stretches out next to her, then rolls on top of her, pushing her into the mattress. She lets out a pleased noise as her arms wrap around his shoulders.

The golden lights dance around them as they join together. After their lovemaking, Pica sleeps lightly. The alcohol warms his body to his toes.

Slowly, a world comes alive around him—that same enormous pyramid he saw in the bathhouse. The humidity presses on him, suffocating, the smell of vegetation an overpowering sensation. Stones crumble and fall with a crash that echoes through the jungle. Birds scream at the disturbance. One flies through his vision with brilliant green plumage and a bright red chest. Its tail feathers are twice as long as it, resplendent in their flashing color.

The golden orbs swarm like fireflies. He watches them as they coil around him. They coalesce into a long form—a serpent, its head rising to face him. Light radiates from the serpent in feathery wisps, floating around it like an ethereal flame. A forked tongue flicks with fiery orange as its emerald eyes raise to his.

The serpent is an exact copy of the bathhouse mosaic, minus the two sets of majestic wings. Pica's fingers open and close as he tries to contain the anxiety rising in him. Tension grips his shoulders, travels down his spine, curls in his gut. Here, in front of him, is the cause of his strife, the thing that insidiously wormed its way into his limbs, forced fire from his hands. Pica's throat closes on the questions pressing against his teeth. *Why?* he wants to demand. *What do you want from me?*

Those unblinking eyes study him for a long moment. The serpent's crest of red and orange feathers rises as their mouth opens wide—not in threat, but in an exuberant smile.

"We meet at last, warrior," the serpent says. Their voice is as warm as the heat radiating from their plumage, as relaxing as the summer sun. "I have been looking forward to it."

The serpent's joy catches Pica off guard. All of the questions he wanted to ask crumble away. "Uh, charmed," he replies instead. "What is your name?"

"That is a good question." The serpent turns their head away. "I do not remember."

A sense of despair rasps against Pica's senses. Like his familiars, he can feel this entity's emotions. Yet, it's different—while Krakli and Eclipsis can project how they feel, this serpent's emotions resonate in him, almost as strong as his own. It's as if the serpent is an extension of him. It supports a theory that Pica has been mulling over of late—although the serpent awoke recently, it seems they've always been there, slumbering.

"Ah. I'm, uh, sorry to hear that."

The serpent's glowing tongue slowly tastes the air. "Your condolences are appreciated, if not strictly necessary."

Pica swears he hears amusement in the entity's tone. "You can talk to me now," he states. "What changed?"

"Ah. It is the fox's doing. It was near impossible before."

Ava. Of course. "Why are you bothering to?"

The serpent jerks their head back. "You are surprised I wish to?"

"A little." Pica chews on the following words before spitting them out. "You took control of me. Why?"

"Oh. I do not know. It was not my intention to do so." The serpent bows their head. "I am deeply sorry for it."

They're not lying. A deep sense of shame claws at Pica's heart, mixed with desperate loneliness. What would he do, if he found himself trapped inside another's mind, unable to communicate, helpless to move? Pica sighs. It's impossible to stay mad at the entity. Like it or not, they're both stuck in the same bizarre situation. "Apology accepted. Please don't do it again."

The smile returns. Pica swears the serpent's feathers start glowing brighter. "I won't! I swear it!'

Once again, the serpent's voice rings with truth. All desire to cling to the grudge crumbles at the serpent's earnestness. Besides, it's for the best. Pica always believed that everyone deserves a chance. Better to make a friend than hold fast to a grudge. "So, you don't know who you are. Do you remember anything?"

"I have a few memories, but only scraps." The serpent indicates the scene around them. "Your land and its people are unfamiliar to me, except..." They raise their chin and regard Pica with a steady expression. "Your people worship Ah-Deh-Det. How is this possible?"

"Ah-Deh-Det?"

"The dragon with six wings. I have seen the depiction many times through your eyes. You, in particular, seem to be taken in."

Pica stares at the serpent in shock. "Do you mean *Andereth*?"

"Ah. Perhaps, yes."

"You...you know Andereth? *How*?"

"She is a...dear friend. I do not remember much besides that. How is it that she came to be here?"

"It was a long time ago," Pica says. "We've lost a lot of details, but I'll tell you what I know."

He tells the serpent the entire story, from her arrival in Geth and her pact with his ancestor to his suspicions about her and her family's disappearance. The serpent listens intently, never interrupting, tongue flicking in-out, in-out, each time leaving streaks of glowing orange light.

"So it is not worship, but reverence," the serpent says. "Especially in your case. Fascinating." Another flick. "She has grandchildren now. How wonderful. It pains me that they are missing."

"Promise me you'll let me know if you remember anything?"

"You have my word."

"Thank you." Something else occurs to him. "So, uh, how much can you see? Through my eyes, I mean."

"Everything, if I choose to perceive it."

"Oh. *Oh*. Shit." His face flushes hot. An audience, all the time. Gods curse it. The thought of it is mortifying.

"I have seen you do many things that young people enjoy. There is no shame in it." The serpent's mouth yawns as they twist their jaw back and forth. "I do not judge you for living."

"The fact that you can see what I do..." Pica swallows. "*That* feels wrong."

"There is little either of us can do about it," the serpent says. "I cannot read your mind nor see what makes you cry out in your sleep. Your thoughts are your own."

"I see. That's a small comfort, at least." Pica takes another long look at the pyramid. "So this is it? You say hi, then ride along and see the sights? Travel the empire in a prince's head?"

The serpent laughs. It is a deep laugh, warm and comforting. "Warrior, if only it could be so. We both know it is not that simple." The serpent's head tilts away. "I fear I have an enemy. Therefore, so do you."

"Who—" Pica's eyes widen. "The bat? The birds? The ones my ancestor spoke about? The ones that I—" His voice catches.

"Yes."

"When that voice said something about 'dying just as well this time,' it was *you* it was talking to."

"There can be no doubt."

"It's all connected. You, the birds, the bat, Andereth—all of it." Pica runs a hand back through his hair. "So what do we do?"

"We." The serpent repeats the word as if contemplating a puzzle. "We fight. The birds will come back. I am sure of it." The serpent shows their fangs. "I have a debt to repay to that foul bat."

"We're in agreement." Pica almost sticks out his hand for a handshake before he catches himself. "It's the best we can do, right?"

"Correct." The serpent's head jerks up. "Our time draws to an end, warrior."

Lights blaze around them. Golden butterflies manifest around the serpent. They weave in dizzying circles between him and the snake. They land on his head, arms, and chest, wreathing him in hundreds of fluttering scales of pure fire.

"Butterflies?"

"Are they not beautiful?" The fluttering wings gather around the serpent's head in an undulating crown. "I remember they are called 'Daughters of the Sun.'" Their emerald eyes glow bright. "We will speak again. Go and live."

The dream stutters. A soft touch sends a hot sensation through him, fingers following the lines of his chest and belly. His skin is soaked in sweat. Levnys is pressed against him. She runs her fingers down his spine as her mouth traces over the scales on his neck. He responds as he wakes, the heat and tension quickly building inside him. The dream fades into the back of his mind as he pulls her hips against his.

A knock comes at the door. "Go away," Pica says, his voice hoarse with sleep.

The knock comes again, louder and more insistent. Pica groans and rubs his eyes, then turns over and slides out of bed. Levnys rolls away from him, murmuring. "Who is it?" he asks through the door.

"The town guard. You are under arrest," a booming voice replies.

Pica hesitates for half a second, then rolls his eyes and opens the door. Petrus stands on the other side. His eyes flick quickly over Pica's nakedness as he smirks.

"Ah. I'm interrupting."

"Yes, you are. What do you want?"

Petrus pushes past him into the room. He looks around, whistling. "*That* is a beautifully crafted bed. Ava has great taste. Oh, my deepest apologies for the interruption, Levnys. I regret the need for it."

"You didn't apologize to *me*," Pica growls. He locates his clothes and moves toward them.

"It's a matter of respect. She can eat me, whereas you will only beat me up."

Levnys props herself on an elbow, watching the duo with a small smile. "I will not eat you, Petrus," she says. "You would not be tasty."

Petrus puts his hand on his chest. "I assure you that you'd find me most palatable."

Pica snorts. "No, really, what do you want?"

"It's almost dinner time. You don't want to besmirch your honor by being late, do you?"

"Where did you learn the word 'besmirch'?" Pica asks as he pulls on his clothes. "Did you accidentally pass out on a scroll?"

"Har har. Will you hurry? Everyone is already here." Petrus retrieves Levnys' clothes and tosses them toward the bed.

"Ahhh, I see. Why did they send *you* to get us?"

Petrus rolls his eyes. "No one would ever ask Kisara, Lucia, or Calvus to come to get you from a private room you're sharing with one of your lovers. Seto told us to leave you here. Sparax is more likely to join in than he is to retrieve you."

Then we would have been late for dinner. Pica hides his flushing face by pulling his tunic over his head.

"So it falls to me to drag your royal ass out of bed," Petrus continues. He crosses his arms and smiles. "And since I see one ass out of bed, I will call my duty complete. I'll let everyone know you're on your way."

Pica scowls good-naturedly at his friend. "You are thus released from your burdens. Get out of here."

Petrus laughs as he leaves, closing the door behind him.

Pica takes a long ride with Eclipsis after dinner, something he promised after much grief from the horse. Krakli sits on his shoulder rather than his head at Pica's insistence—he doesn't feel like detangling the results of his familiar's nesting. The setting sun turns the sky to fire as the wind blows cold off the harbor. Above him, the stars alight one by one. It's sweetly nostalgic, a reminder of when his dreams didn't haunt him and his world wasn't dangling over a precipice. He can almost return to that simpler time, save for one fundamental, irrefutable change.

What is that building? the serpent asks.

Another temple, Pica replies, peering at the mosaic above the entrance. *That one's for Ogtris, the goddess of music, art, and sex.*

She's a fox, the serpent notes. *Perhaps it is not a coincidence.*

It wouldn't surprise me in the slightest.

Eclipsis snorts, sensing his amusement. The serpent asked many such questions. Two hours of observations and inquiries have left Pica mentally worn out. The serpent's endless curiosity tests his abilities of explanation—the entity doesn't only want to know what and when but *why.* He answers the endless questions the best that he can.

Levnys believed him about the dream, thank the gods. Neither of them had an explanation for the strange things he saw, though Pica has some theories. Perhaps, were it earlier in the day, he would return to the library, although he doubts he'd find anything. The serpent made it clear they were not from anywhere near Geth.

Ava wasn't helpful when asked, which is a fact he should have expected. The divine fox—a *sanribi*, he remembered—gave him a vague but pleased reaction to his revelation about the serpent. She seemed more willing to answer the entity's questions he relayed but remained mum on what could have been the most helpful information. Alas, the nature of deities.

The anxiety surrounding the blood-drinking birds hasn't abated, either. Rumors are all they have. He's done his best to push it to the back of his mind, ready for action when it comes but not letting it foul his mood. It's for his sanity more than anything else—gods know there are plenty of other things he needs to worry about.

When the time comes, he will fight with all he has—yet another burden he's placed upon his shoulders like a yoke.

He scans their surroundings, more for the serpent than himself, and his mind wanders when there's a lull in the questions. Sparax has been at the front of it for most of the day, especially after Levnys decided to ask him many pointed questions about their prior relationship. He'd told her everything, of course.

They had gotten together at sixteen, at that tender age between boy and man, shortly after the twins joined the Order. Sparax was his first real relationship, something solid after the dalliances of a teenage prince. Except Pica left to join his uncle Monedula's army at nineteen, something Sparax begged him not to do. He did it anyway, and their relationship withered on the vine like unharvested grapes.

Pica vividly remembers the day his uncle convinced him to join. The elder prince—Lucia's twin, with salt-and-pepper hair and piercing brown eyes—sold him on the idea that he must learn to lead, and the best way was through military service. He was right on that point. But the rest...

The shame, heaped on the pile like discarded oil amphorae, only weighs on him further. *He* left Sparax. *He* chose something other than love and comfort in pursuit of duty. *He* broke his lover's heart.

He can't say he wouldn't do it again should they continue to Charris, leaving Levnys behind as he did Sparax. How can he face that when he's learned nothing from it?

Eclipsis, Krakli, and the serpent all brush against his consciousness with worried intrigue at his sudden anxiety. The attention is darkly funny to him. It's getting crowded in his head of late.

"I miss Sparax," he says. Admitting it out loud is refreshing, in a way. Eclipsis squeals and prances, almost knocking over a couple walking down the center of the street. Pica waves an apology as they gape at her. He pats her neck and mentally expresses his affection. The horse had always liked his former lover.

The serpent's reaction is simply curiosity. *The one with the hair like copper?* they ask.

Yes.

Tell me about him.

Pica is surprised by the request—it's the first time the entity has shown interest in someone other than him. So, as Eclipsis makes her way back to Ava's tavern, he does.

XI
DANCE

Aurora

Shadows stretch between the buildings when Aurora rises from the bath and dries herself with fresh linen. A breeze filters through the open window —warmer, with the promise of spring. Soon, the flowers will bloom, and the world will be released from winter's grip. She can't wait. She's constantly cold, no matter how much broth she drinks.

Since arriving, she's added more food to her diet—yesterday, Gesur served fresh fish, lightly seasoned and cooked Gethki-style. She had to stop herself from eating more than a small serving, it was so delicious. A week ago, she gave in to her cravings and ate a rye roll, and the experience made her sick for two days. It's made her more vigilant—she didn't survive the last year to die from eating bread.

Tomorrow, she leaves for Caltava. She sent several more letters, hoping it's not in vain. The anxiety gnaws at her—she'd be there already if not for that accursed ship.

She can't allow herself to wallow in maybes. Caltava is the best chance for her, a sizable city rich with trade and culture. In addition to Romero's job offer, one of the other musicians recommended several taverns where she could perform. It's enough to take a risk.

Aurora flinches when someone taps on the door. "There is messenger here for Davros," Gesur says. "From dock."

She notices the emphasis on her other form's name. After changing her throat, Aurora replies in Davros' voice, "I will be there in a moment, Gesur. Thank you."

She puts on the blue *exomis*. A quick shift later, Davros heads down the stairs with apprehension. He can't stop imagining the things that could be wrong. The prospect of leaving tomorrow already makes him nervous. An unexpected twist could crumble his tentative resolve like dried leaves.

Spirited conversation filters through the curtain to the public areas—a crowd partaking in Ava's hospitality. The messenger is one of the dock boys, no older than twelve or thirteen. He's out of place in his sweat-stained tunic. "Oh!" he says when he sees Davros. "*Dominus* says bring you to docks if you want to go to Caltava."

"What's this about?" Davros asks.

"Problem." The boy shifts from foot to foot. "*Dominus* said bring you."

Davros sighs. The boy wouldn't know anything. "Alright, let's go."

The boy sprints from Ava's tavern. Davros follows the best he can, but his body remains weaker than he'd like. By the time they reach the harbor, he's breathing hard, while the dock boy hardly looks tired.

When they turn toward the opulent section, Davros chokes. What is he doing? He doesn't belong here. His spine stiffens when he passes the guards. Surely, they can hear how hard his heart thuds, the ragged edge of his breaths. They'll stop him, turn him away.

Neither give him more than a cursory glance.

Davros keeps his attention forward, trying not to gawk at the colorful buildings. It's a different world on this side of the harbor. The setting sun glints off polished wood and bathes the cobblestones with warm light. Everything here is gilded.

The ship at the furthest edge of the harbor is a smear of ink on this golden tapestry. Her baleful red eye casts its gaze over the rest of the harbor like a waiting bird of prey. Even the sails are painted black. Compared to the bulky trade vessels, the ship is lithe—a predator, a shadow of the warships patrolling the water.

The dock boy leads him straight to it.

The dock master waits near the ram. Four guards in black leather armor stand watch. As Davros approaches, they eye him but remain stationary.

"Ah, you made it!" the dock master shouts.

Davros taps his fingers against his leg. Everything is fine. "Yes. What's going on?"

"Ah, well." The dock master holds up his hands. "The ship you paid for slipped out early. Captain heard some fool rumor and left. He was halfway out the harbor before I realized it."

Davros' heart sinks. "Oh," he manages.

"You're in luck! Got another ship going to Caltava. Could be over a week before we get another one."

"Uh, are you sure, um…"

The dock master turns as a rugged blonde man emerges from behind the ram with a wide swagger of authority. Davros raises his head in false confidence as the man crosses his arms. "This him?" the man asks. He steps forward at the dock master's nod, looking Davros up and down. "What're you good at, kid?"

"I'm a bard," Davros manages to say without squeaking. "I can clean things."

"Clean things and make pretty noises. Got anything else?"

The back of Davros' hand tingles. "I'm a mage, sir."

The captain's eyebrows raise. "Ah. What kind of magic you got, bard?"

"Um, fire and water. I can heal, too."

"Mmhmmm." The captain appraises him again. "That's good. We could use that. You strong?" After a beat, he adds, "At magic. You don't look like you can lift more than a twig."

"Strong enough," Davros admits. "I can hold my own."

"Right, right. We'll take you. Doubt you take up much space, anyhow. Or eat much."

Davros' head spins. He considers the ominous ship, the guards, the ballista on the rails. Every instinct screams danger, but what choice does he have? He doesn't want to wait. It's right in front of him. All he has to do is take it.

He won't survive if this ship proves the same as the last. His fingers pulse with magic. Nylocke. He wants to scream at his *pater*, to beg him why he pushes him like this. Will it be for the better?

There's only one way to find out. Davros pushes back his fear and tries to squash the anxiety begging him to run. "I'll do it."

The captain turns on a heel. "Welcome to *Raven's Flight*," he says over his shoulder. "We leave at dawn."

It's dark by the time Davros returns to the tavern. The moment he strips his *exomis*, Ava's voice chimes in his head, clear as a bell.

Join me in the dining area. Come as Aurora.

Davros sighs. No rest for the emaciated. He shifts and sets to preparing for the evening's performance—first, the *stola*. Aurora eyes the shoulder wrap but decides against it. She combs out her thick blonde hair, letting it flow over her shoulders like ocean waves. Lastly, she applies the makeup Ava gifted her, using bold tones to accent her eyes and lips.

She's almost convinced herself she's beautiful. Almost.

After heading downstairs, she scans the room for Ava. She spots her talking to a gorgeous woman. Ava turns to face her as she approaches, tilting her head.

"You needed me?" Aurora asks. She tries not to stare at the woman.

"Yes. This is my friend Levnys. I am hosting her and her companions. They will *all* comport themselves with honor in your presence. I swear it."

Magic thrums as she speaks the ritual. It's the first time since she arrived that Ava has done so. Aurora's spine stiffens.

"A pleasure to meet you," Aurora says, bowing at the waist.

The woman's bronze skin shimmers with metallic radiance. Levnys holds herself rigid, her shoulders and back confidently straight. Pouring from her is an aura unfamiliar to Aurora, something primal. She's not human, but Aurora can't determine more than that.

Ava steps forward and holds up her hand. Circling in her palm is a tiny ball of violet foxfire. It rises to orbit Aurora's head. "You need not perform tonight. Instead, I want you to keep Levnys and her companions company this evening."

Oh. Oh shit.

Ava's smile is vulpine. "She enjoys stories. Surely, you will provide excellently."

Levnys turns to Aurora. "I look forward to your tales. Will you have a drink with me?" Her voice is a musical alto that makes Aurora's skin tingle.

Confidence. Become the mask. "Absolutely," she says. "Follow me."

She directs the foxfire toward the bar where Gesur works before leading Levnys to a private booth. They settle onto the soft cushions.

"What is your name?" Levnys asks.

"Aurora."

"You work for Ava?"

"For now. Until my ship leaves."

"Using your magic, I presume."

"You can sense my magic?"

"Yes. Is that strange to you?"

"Yeah. Most people can't. You must be unusual to detect it so quickly."

"I am not unusual. There are many like me in these waters. *You* are unusual. Is it bloodline magic?"

"I assume so. I was born with it, but I never knew my parents."

"You are an orphan?"

"I don't know," Aurora says, trying to remain composed. "I was left in a tent. The leader of an acting troupe raised me."

She flinches in surprise as Gesur sets a mug of pear juice before her. She scowls at him. He twitches his whiskers in amusement and sets a bowl on the table. The foxfire circles over it, casting a dim purple light. Gesur places the second drink. Levnys watches them with a small smile, relaxing against the cushioned booth. Gesur motions toward Aurora.

"She will lie to you," he says. "She will say she is not good at things. It is not true."

Aurora chokes. "*Gesur!*"

Levnys nods solemnly. "I will keep that in mind."

Gesur flashes a toothy grin and leaves, his tail twitching with satisfaction. Aurora glares after him, then reluctantly turns toward Levnys. The woman sips her drink, her lips curled at the corners.

"Sorry, uh…"

Levnys holds up a hand. "Do not apologize. I can see he likes to embarrass you. He does it because he cares."

"Yes," Aurora says with a sigh. "Yes, he does."

"What is it he refers to?"

"My music. He likes it when I sing to him." Aurora leans her head back on the booth. "He's right. I'm good at it."

"You are a bard. Do you write songs?"

"I haven't for a long time."

"Why is that?"

Aurora watches the enchanted lights dart around the ceiling. "It's complicated."

"I do not mind a long explanation."

"It's not long." She sighs and raises her head. "My job is to entertain you. This story doesn't do that."

"That is for me to decide, is it not?"

Aurora resists the urge to shrink away at the firmness in her tone. Although Levnys is the portrait of casual grace, something lurks behind her calm facade—something dangerous. She swallows. "Well, if you put it that way..." She takes a bracing pull from her pear juice, emptying it. "I haven't had time since setting out on my own." She pauses, but Levnys remains silent. "I spent my time working, trying to make enough to survive. All anyone wanted to hear were the most popular songs. I stopped coming up with new ideas."

Levnys finishes her drink and sets the empty mug on the table. The foxfire shoots into the air toward the bar. She tracks it until it leaves her vision, and then her eyes settle on Aurora.

"Playing for Ava made me consider it again," Aurora continues.

"What is the first thing you will write a song about?" Levnys asks.

"I don't know," she admits. "No one wants to hear about the life of a starving bard when they're having fun."

"Starving. Is that true?" Levnys eyes the bread in front of them, then Aurora.

Aurora's stomach tries to climb into her mouth. "Uh, it's an expression," she lies.

Zelkos silently appears, sets two more drinks on the table, and departs without a word. Levnys' attention turns to the wyverni, and Aurora has time to breathe. *You're such an idiot,* she castigates herself. To Levnys, she says with the most level voice she can muster, "You're good at getting people to talk about themselves, Levnys. That's not very common."

Levnys' mouth splits into a smile. It lights her face, magnifying her beauty tenfold. Aurora can barely look at her. There's no way she deserves attention from a woman like this.

"I prefer to listen to those around me. It is the best way to learn about the world. Humans are interesting."

"I guess we are," Aurora says. She picks up the bowl of bread and holds it out to Levnys. "Sit back and relax. Allow this humble bard to entertain you."

"Do you want to dance?" Aurora asks an hour later. The words leave her mouth before she can stop them.

Levnys drains her drink. "I would like that."

They head for the dancing crowd. The musicians are excellent, as always. Part of her wishes she was on stage tonight, singing along with them.

Then again, she's wanted to dance since arriving at Ava's tavern. Tonight is the first time she's been brave enough to push her way into the press of bodies. The enchanted music resonates in her magic, a euphoric surge that paints a smile on her face. Levnys is as relaxed as she has been all evening, moving to the music with liquid grace. Although Ava mentioned others, no one else has joined them. Aurora wonders what companions a woman like Levnys travels with.

Power thrums through the crowd as a magical presence washes over Aurora's senses like an ocean swell. Her magic pulses in response to it, sending a wave of sensual pleasure coursing through her limbs. She bites back her exclamation. Levnys' face brightens and she turns to the source emerging from the crowd.

Oh.

The man towers over her, with broad shoulders and a confident stature. He is layered in thick muscle, especially over his chest and arms. His biceps are bigger than her thighs. Her magic surges at the sight of him, urging her to approach. She tells it to stop, but it refuses to do so.

Oh no.

She takes a step back as Levnys walks forward and kisses him, molding her body against his. The change in the woman is stark—

before, she was as relaxed as a lounging cat. Now, she's all sensual grace in the man's arms. Aurora takes another step back as Levnys turns to her.

"This is Lucius," Levnys says. "You will like him. He will dance with us."

"Charmed," Lucius says in a sonorous baritone. His voice is smooth like honeyed wine. "I'm not good at dancing, but I can try."

"Nonsense," Levnys replies. "You are good at lovemaking, so you must be good at dancing. Pretend we are in bed."

Aurora barely contains her reaction to *that*, managing to keep the flush from her face. Levnys is right—she does like him. She likes how his hair frames his face, the black waves of it spilling over his forehead. She likes how he holds himself and dominates the space around him, drawing long glances from the people dancing nearby. Aurora doesn't want to admit it but likes how her magic sings within her, calling out to him.

She's stuck in place, unsure what to do. She wants to flee to solitude so she can slow her pounding heart. She doesn't want to face the fact she craves the touch of another, a gentle hand that doesn't bruise or harm. She wants to trust, to be in another's arms without worrying that she will be used. The fear keeps paralyzing her—it kept her from dancing until tonight, and it keeps her rooted now.

Ava gave her an explicit order to stay with Levnys and her companions for the evening. Aurora wonders if this is precisely what she intended.

Levnys and Lucius watch her, their expressions growing concerned. It's wrong on their beautiful faces. They shouldn't bother with her. She's not worth it. She forces herself to think rationally. Ava was careful to include the woman's companions in her invocation. This isn't a trap. They're not going to hurt her.

If she wants to play the part of Aurora, she should be confident, even if it's fake. She takes a step toward them. Levnys moves forward to take her hand. She lets herself get pulled closer, close enough that their body heat warms her skin. No. His magic. The man seethes with it. His aura is like hers—bloodline magic and *strong*.

She chokes as Lucius puts an arm around her waist. He holds her lightly, barely touching her. A flicker of concern remains on Levnys' face, but as they dance, it fades. Aurora tentatively brushes the tendrils of the man's emotions. Lucius buzzes with happiness and a confidence so strong she's jealous. There's more beneath those surface emotions—a deep weariness that surprises her. She quickly withdraws her magic, embarrassed at her intrusion. Her magic protests. It wants more.

Lucius wasn't wrong—he's not good at dancing. Not that he's terrible, but it seems like he can't connect to the beat. He's not perfect, then. Aurora is relieved at the realization. It's like someone is playing a cruel joke on her, that this is an illusion, and reality will inevitably come crashing down.

She tries in vain not to focus on how close they are. Close enough to smell their sweat and the alcohol on Levnys' breath. Close enough to see the series of fine lines crisscrossing Lucius' left bicep—blade scars. A metal amulet is nestled into the black hair on his chest. She realizes what she's doing—cataloging minor details to calm her emotions. To keep from thinking too hard about how warm his body is or how the light plays off the muscles of his neck and chest. To keep from reaching up and-

"Hey, Lucius, looking good!"

She turns her head. A redhead as tall as Lucius stands there with a wide grin. He's also handsome, covered in lean muscle, his curly hair shining in the pulsing lights.

Two of them now, so much bigger than her. Big men like Lucius and this newcomer mean danger. Once, there was a man as big as them, a gladiator. He followed her into an alley and knocked her out, then dumped her into the river after he was finished. It was a miracle she woke up.

She shudders at the memory, trying to quell her sudden panic. She was so close. Doing so well. It couldn't last.

Ava. I can't do this, she thinks in desperation. *I'm too broken.*

You are not broken, the fox responds. *It's safe to enjoy yourself.*

Why are you doing this to me?

You must face your fear, child.

"Compliments of Ava," the redhead says as he holds a drink in each hand. "She says you are *much* too tense."

He hands a drink to Lucius. Aurora's eyes track over his face and neck as he rapidly drains it. The man gives Lucius the second drink.

Her mind reels. She has to go. She can't be here. She's about to move when Lucius looks down at her. His smile stops her dead in her tracks as he holds out the drink. She almost gives in, then shakes her head. He hands the drink to Levnys, who finishes it. A faint relief laps at the edge of her anxiety.

It's alright. They're not going to hurt me. I'm safe I'm-

The redhead presses himself against her back, running fingers across her waist before traveling along Lucius' forearm, pinning her between them. Her heart rate skyrockets as the two men share a significant look over her head. The complexity in their emotions is a dark melange—regret, bitterness, longing, affection. The air drips with the tension between them, the unspoken *need* in it. She can't keep the flush from spreading across her face this time. The bodies of the others press against her as they dance. It feels good—so, so good. It battles her panic enough that she can take several deep breaths.

Ava wouldn't be pushing her so hard without a reason. Aurora tentatively tests each of their auras, running her magic along the threads of their emotions like vibrating lute strings. Something is troubling them, some deep worry that winds through their surface emotions like ink drops in water. Her curiosity deepens. The nagging feeling she's had over the last month solidifies. Something is going on —something big. Something that has both Ava and Nylocke involved.

Part of her wants to defy them. What right do gods and spirits have to dictate what she does? The world can burn around her for all she cares.

Yet, isn't the world also moments like this? The music, the press of bodies around her, the swirl of joy and lust and love coursing through the room like a whirlpool—that's the kind of thing she cares about. Not Nylocke and his goals. Not Ava and her machinations. This.

She's returned to reality when the redhead cuts between Lucius and Levnys. "My turn, aurochs," he says. "You get her in the bedroom."

Lucius watches him lead Levnys away, then shrugs and turns to Aurora, giving her a smile that makes her knees weak. "He stole our dance partner. Mind being stuck with me?"

"N-no," she manages.

He puts his other arm around her waist. The weight of his full attention sends her magic surging again. This close, he's enormous.

Her head doesn't clear his collarbone. Should he mean her harm, none of her other forms would do any better against him. She swallows hard and watches him. Nothing predatory about his behavior. Not yet. She has to try. She *wants* to try.

She reaches out to the enchantment in the music and pulls it around them like a blanket, trying to find comfort and confidence in the beat. Something in Lucius responds, and his movements change. His body moves more naturally with the music, and he steps closer. Her body reacts to his touch with violent intensity. *Ata,* she curses in Soutorian. She wants his hands all over her. The thought almost makes her break into nervous laughter. How can she be having these thoughts after everything that's happened?

"Hey, I'm getting the hang of this." Lucius' smile is radiant and disarming. "You must be a good teacher."

"Or you're a quick learner," she says, trying to keep her voice even.

He laughs. "Charmer, I see." He winks, sending Aurora's heart into a fluttering stutter. "I'm enjoying your company. Keep dancing with me?"

"Alright," she says. She is surprised he asked at all. "I can stick around for a few."

"A few? We're going to be here all night. Have a drink with us."

"Fine, fine," She gives him a thin smile. "But only because you asked so nicely."

The music shifts as the beat becomes faster. She dances to it without a thought, letting it take control. Lucius puts his fingertips on her waist and leans back. Oh gods, she should have worn the wrap. He can see everything. His eyes travel over her body slowly, leaving a trail of heat in their wake.

Aurora braces herself for what comes next. His hands will roughly grab and grope as the press of bodies grows closer. He'll take what he wants, and she won't be able to stop him. She watches his face, wide-eyed and terrified, waiting for his next move.

He doesn't make one. He raises his eyes back to hers. "You know this song well," he states.

She swallows. "One of my favorites."

"I like it too," he says. "Though I'd rather watch you. You're much better at this than I am."

Aurora blushes at the compliment. "Who's the charmer, now?"

Lucius laughs. Slowly, so very slowly, she lets herself get lost in the music and enjoy this beautiful man's company.

I don't want it to end. Gods, please, this is all I want.

XII
PYRAMID

Pica

"My name is Aurora—since you finally asked," the blonde tells Pica.

The group sits together on one of the fire-lit couches. The thumping beat of the music punctuates their spirited conversation. Sparax sits beside him with Levnys on his lap. She plays with his hair as they whisper and giggle. Their presence is a pleasant weight on Pica's heightened senses. Their drinks are constantly refreshed, compliments of Ava's attendants.

Consequently, Pica is pleasantly inebriated, his head swimming with enchanted alcohol. Most of his attention is focused on the woman sitting beside him. Aurora is a contradiction, though he hasn't put together how. She has a nervous air of anxiety, alert to the slightest danger. He's seen it before, too many times.

On the other hand, she has a significant presence despite her small stature, a quality more fitting for a gladiator or politician. There's defiance in her, the air of a fighter. She's haunted by something, just like him. What is it she's battling?

"You are Lucius," Aurora continues. "Lucius, what?"

"Huh?"

"You're Gethki, so you have lots of names, right? What are the rest of them?"

"How do you know I'm Gethki?"

"Your name is *Lucius*. Everyone and the emperor's name is Lucius. Besides, your accent is so upper class it's wearing a toga."

Observant. "Pilius Corvus."

"You're lying," she says. She studies him with her honey-brown eyes. "You didn't say it naturally enough. What are you hiding?"

"If I'm trying to hide something, why would I tell you?" he asks, amused by her straightforwardness. "And you? You're not Gethki. You have an accent."

"I'm Fresian," she says.

"What district are you from?" he asks her in Fresian. He chuckles when she gives him a blank look and switches back to Gethki. "Didn't think so. You're lying, too. Is Aurora your real name?"

She grins at him, an expression that illuminates her face. "Shit, you got me. Smart, though; I like that. Tell me yours, and I'll tell you mine?"

"I won't tell you my secret so soon, Aurora." He raises his drink. "You need to get to know me better first."

Her grin falters. "You mean sex, don't you?"

"Mmm. Is that something you'd like?" He leans closer. She leans away. Interesting. Another mixed signal. She had given him plenty this evening. "Let me know if you would. I wouldn't mind."

Her eyes widen before she takes a drink. She recovers within seconds, her smile returning. It looks brittle.

Ah. So that's it. He glances away and leans back, giving her space. "But no, that's not what I meant," he continues. "I meant we should have a conversation and tell each other things about ourselves. I know —let's make it a game. You tell me something, then I'll take a turn. We need to guess if the other person is lying."

Aurora's smile turns genuine. The air around her stirs as she leans back toward him. "Let's make a wager. The first to guess correctly three times gets to hear the other's secret."

Zelkos puts more drinks on the table. The wyverni hands Aurora her drink, Pica notes. He catches the scent of something sweet. Levnys leans forward and grabs two full mugs, swaying as she does. Sparax laughs and pulls her back onto his lap.

Pica returns his attention to Aurora. "Fine, deal. I'll go first. I started training to fight when I was twelve."

"True. Twelve is a good age. Train the muscles as they develop."

"Correct."

Aurora takes a drink. "My turn. I was born in Sardiora."

"A lie."

"Why do you say that?"

"Sardiora is too far away. It takes a year to travel by ship. There's hardly any population movement, and the immigrants who do come here are wyverni."

Aurora gives him a puzzled look. "Good guess. Your turn."

"I am a mage of peerless power."

"A lie. I can sense strong magic in you, but peerless? An empty boast."

He shakes his head. "It's true—I'm the strongest in a family known for powerful mages."

"Prove it."

He wonders how he can do that without lighting the building on fire. He hesitates a second, thinking. A mental nudge and the serpent fills his senses with warmth.

I wish to help, they say.

Uh, sure. Just don't—

Heat radiates from him, leaking into the air surrounding the couch. Sweat springs forth on his bare arms. The enchanted brazier takes on golden-white flames, its auric glow turning Aurora's blonde hair to spun gold. The shimmering air envelops her. Their auras blend, hers mixing with his so intensely, so *exquisitely*. Her magic is so delicate, a cool breeze, a spring day to summer heat. Pica has never felt anything so extraordinary.

The breeze stills, and the air becomes stifling. Pica reels his magic back as Aurora stares at him with beads of sweat shimmering on her pale skin.

"Satisfied?" he asks.

Aurora swallows. "Uh. Wow. You're a lot stronger than me."

Pica doubts that's true. He merely brushed her magic with his, and it sent his senses reeling. He doesn't push, letting her recover from the demonstration. Aurora takes a long drink from her mug.

"My turn," she says. "I made a pact with an ancient entity,

gaining power from it."

"A lie. You use bloodline magic."

She waggles her finger. "Wrong. Yes, I use bloodline magic, but I *also* made a pact."

"Care to tell me more about it?"

Her eyes grow distant. "Not right now. Sorry."

"No problem, I get it." He moves closer to her and taps his mug against hers. "We've each earned a point. Shall we continue?"

"Oh yes." Her eyes glitter as she takes a drink.

Levnys rests her chin on Pica's shoulder. "Sparax wants to go with Petrus to a brothel, but I will stay here. What are you two talking about?"

"Getting to know each other," Pica says.

"Making a wager," Aurora says at the same time. Their eyes meet, and they laugh.

Levnys climbs onto Pica's lap and sits across them, putting her legs on Aurora's thighs. "I wish to listen. Do not mind me." She lays her head against Pica's chest.

Pica hooks his arm around Levnys' waist. "Where were we? Ah, right, my turn. I was born in Geth, but some of my ancestors are from Eugaria."

"True." She studies his face. "It's your eyes. Soutori, right? One of your grandparents. You can't be more than a quarter."

He tips his mug to her. "*Very* observant. I'm impressed."

"Noticing physical traits is essential to my abilities. Also, *I'm* from Soutori." She taps absentmindedly on Levnys' knee.

"You don't look Soutorian,"

"You're right, I don't. It's my turn." She lifts her hand, fingers closed. "I can take whatever form I wish, as long as it has two arms and two legs."

Her fingers open. A teardrop-shaped prism floats off her palm, scattering wild rainbows over her face. Her ears lengthen, arching back over her darkening hair. The red of her *stola* shifts to yellow. Her cream skin changes to gold, contrasting the green eyes that lift to meet his.

"A lie," he says. "I recognize the disguise spell."

In response, she takes his hand and guides it to her face. She presses it where her ears arch backward. Instead of passing through the illusion, as Pica expects, his fingers brush skin. She shivers when he runs them along the ear's tapered tip.

"You're a shapeshifter," Pica says, stunned. "You *changed* into an elf but also used the disguise spell. At the same time. That's—"

"Spooky?" she supplies. "Frightening?"

"*Amazing*. The timing was fantastic! Well done, you fooled me."

Her features shift back as she flushes pink. She holds his hand next to her head with clammy fingers. "Thank you. Most people think it's scary."

"If you are not doing anything to hurt them, what is the harm?" Levnys says. "It is not wrong to change your form."

"I don't find anything wrong with it," Aurora replies. "I refuse to hate myself for something I was born able to do."

He tells himself the same lie. "This wasn't your secret?"

"A little part of it. You don't know my real name or my real appearance."

"That matters more than the shapeshifting?" Pica asks.

"Yes. It's my most important secret, and I don't share it with anyone." She drops her hand from his. "It's your turn."

Pica is slow to remove his hand from her face. She stiffens. Her skin flushes beneath his hand. She's afraid of him. He leans back, withdrawing his hand.

"My turn," he agrees. "If you get this one, you win."

"Give me your best shot."

"Are you sure you want that?" he asks.

"Yes. This is a game. The goal is to win."

She trembles despite her bold words, so hard it shakes the couch. Her magic churns, writhing like eels around her slim form. Thin threads of distress and fear interweave with intense curiosity and thrum like plucked lyre strings. Her emotions. He can sense them, faint but distinct. The serpent takes notice, too, their interest joining his like they're both peering through the same window.

"Alright," he says, pulling her magic into him. He lets it linger there like a fine cloud. The fear drains from her expression as her curiosity grows. Good. "I'm also afraid, Aurora."

The confusion hits him first, then disbelief. "A lie," she says. "You *drip* with confidence. I bet you've never known fear in your life."

"I've been afraid plenty of times," he says. He calls to mind his first battle in the legion, the roaring chaos of the drums, the screams of horses and men, and the constant *thud-thud-thud* of his blood in his ears. At the time, he was sure it was the end of the world, but it was only a skirmish. He lets it color his words, pressing them against her magic. "Afraid for me, my family, my companions..." *For the dragons.*

Aurora's trembling ceases. She watches him with renewed interest, a stirring of concern, a pinch of empathy—as if seeing him for the first time. "What are you doing?" she whispers.

"You can sense my emotions," he states. "Through your magic."

"Y-yes. How do you know?"

"I can sense yours," he explains. "I tested it."

"Oh. Uh..." She glances at her right hand and laughs softly. "You're *way* more perceptive than you look. Yes, I can sense emotions. I've never had anyone say they can feel *mine,* though." A hint of pink colors her face. "So you can tell I'm terrified of you. That's embarrassing."

"We can stop if you want. You don't have to stay."

Aurora sighs. "No, I made the wager. I must continue. Besides, I'm enjoying this. You're fun to talk to. Interesting. Surprising." She ponders for a minute. "My best talent isn't magic. It's music."

"True," Pica says immediately.

"Yes, that was fast. How are you so sure?"

"I saw you on stage yesterday. Your music is incredible."

"It's true." Her smile returns to her pretty face. "Your turn."

Pica considers his next move. She'll win if she gets this, but why shouldn't she? Forcing her to reveal her deepest secret doesn't sit right with him.

"Alright," he says. "Magic is what defines me."

Her eyes trace a path over his shoulders and chest. The gaze is as analytical as a master painter judging a fresco, though something smolders in her eyes, something Pica likes immensely. "That's a lie. You look like you can throw boulders. It takes intense training to be that strong." She picks up his hand and traces the callouses on his fingers and palm. "These are sword callouses. My best friend is a wizard. His hands don't look like yours. His body doesn't look like yours." She reaches out to touch his arm. "Another thing. Your skin is pretty dark, so it's hard to see, but you have tan lines on your arms. You've spent a lot of time in the sun, in armor." She traces her fingers slowly across his bicep, sending pleasant sensations through his skin. "You say your magic is powerful, and I believe you, but you do not fight solely as a mage. And that's not what defines you." She looks up at him, her fingers lingering. "Do I win?"

"Yes, you win."

A magic ripple washes over Aurora's skin. She breathes a pleased sigh. "Thank you for your wager. What's your secret?"

"Not here. I can't show you in public."

Aurora leans back from him. "I knew it. You're trying to—"

Levnys leans forward. "No. Stop. That is not what he intends. He will show you his secret, as he promised, and after, you can go if you want. Ava has sworn your safety, has she not?"

"She did." She looks at Pica. "I'm sorry for making assumptions about you. I've learned to be cautious."

"Apology accepted, Aurora." He nudges Levnys. She swings her legs sideways and stands. Pica follows her. "How about this? Will you join us for one drink upstairs to continue our conversation? I swear that Levnys and I will comport ourselves with utmost grace and hospitality while you reside in our presence." He puts some magic into the words, fortifying their sincerity.

Aurora gapes at him. "Wow, that was a perfectly executed ritual oath. You continue to surprise me, Lucius." She stands, smoothing her *stola*. "I'd be happy to join you. As protocol demands, I'll bring the drinks."

Pica smiles as Aurora looks around the room before going to the mural and running her fingers over the metal inlays. "Ava," she breathes. "This is a masterpiece." She takes time to study it before settling onto the lounging couch, sitting with her back rigid. She sips her drink, staring at nothing. Levnys sits on the other end. Pica leans against the wall, far out of reach of the women, ensuring he's nowhere near the door. He hadn't missed Aurora's tension as she entered the room.

Eventually, Aurora raises her head. "Well?"

Pica sighs. "Give me your word that you won't tell anyone you saw me."

"I can be discreet."

"Your word, please."

"Fine, I give you my word. *Gods*, you make it sound like you're royalty or something."

"Precisely." He touches the tattoo on his chest to drop the illusion. He turns his eyes to meet Aurora's. "Do you know who I am?"

She almost drops her drink. "You're a Gethki prince. Wait, are you *that* prince? The next emperor? Oh, shit, I forgot what bird that is. *That's* embarrassing."

Pica chuckles. "Magpie. Don't worry about it." He twirls his hand in a flourish, bowing at the waist. "Lucius Draconius Regillus Pica, in the flesh. I'm the crown prince, firstborn son, next in line, and the next emperor, however you want to put it."

"You're telling the truth. You're a prince, and you're bothering with *me*? Why? No, wait, don't answer that." She shakes her head. "Alright, that's a huge secret. I see why you want to keep that hidden. I imagine people constantly want something from you."

"That and the assassination attempts."

"Ah. True." She drums her fingers on the mug. "How do you know I'm not here to kill you? This could be a clever ruse."

"Too complex. You're a shapeshifter. You could have pretended to be Ava, Levnys, or anyone else you've seen me with. In, stab, out, then blame whomever you want."

She watches him with one eyebrow raised. "Good point."

"In any case," he continues, "if you are here to kill me, don't try." He crosses his arms and tries to look stern. Levnys covers her mouth to hide her smile. "You won't succeed."

Aurora's eyes narrow. "Oh, you think you can get me before I get you?"

"Not me. But the dragon could."

He laughs as Aurora jerks her head toward Levnys. "*That's* what you are?" She looks between them. "A prince and a dragon. Gods, I'm way outside my social class." Her face turns thoughtful. "I should write a song about—"

Pica winces. "Please don't."

"I'm kidding. Thank you for trusting me. What can I call you?"

"Lucius is fine."

He takes a step toward her. She stiffens and goes pale, gripping the mug so hard her fingers creak. White shows in her widened eyes. It makes Pica's heart wrench. It's the look of animal fear, of someone waiting for a blow to fall—and resigned to it.

"You're a fascinating person, Aurora," he says gently. "I can see why Ava wanted us to meet."

"H-how do you know…"

"We both know it's something she'd do." He returns to his spot on the wall. "You've finished your drink. Would you like to stay for more?"

The silence stretches as Aurora stares at her hands. They tremble visibly—her breathing speeds, rasping and shallow. "I-I…" she stammers. "I-no. I…can't. I can't." She sets the mug on the table with a hollow thump, then stands, running to the door. She reaches it and pauses. "I…I enjoyed our game, Lucius. I'm sorry." The words come out in a rush, and she leaves, slamming the door behind her.

Pica's eyes drop. He stares at the floor, then his hands. It happened again. He tried to be so careful, and yet…

"Lucius," Levnys says softly. "Sit with me."

He settles onto the lounging couch. It's still warm. He leans his elbows on the table, staring at the carving of a long-dead queen.

"It is not your fault," Levnys says.

"It's always my fault." Pica's lips tremble. He thought it'd be different this time. "That was real terror in her eyes. What did I do wrong?" he whispers. "What did I say this time?"

"Nothing, Lucius. I spoke with her before you joined us. She has not had an easy life."

She rises and moves to stand next to him. He wraps his arms around her waist, resting his cheek against her stomach. "I could tell. I can't stand to see such a—" His voice trails off. How can he describe her? She made such an impression on him, like he was made of soft clay.

"Interesting person?" Levnys supplies.

"—interesting person be so afraid," he finishes. "Now she's gone. I can't explain myself. I can't…" He hugs her tighter. "Why this? What's Ava's goal?"

Levnys puts her fingers under his chin and turns his head to look up at her. The rosy reflection of the mural flickers across her skin. "Perhaps it is not for us to understand."

"What are we supposed to do now?"

"Rest. We must rise early." She brushes the tears from his cheek. "We must take each day as it comes. Perhaps, in time, we will know the answer."

The dreams that night are replaced with visions, scenes from a richly decorated temple. They stand at the apex, gazing out over a patchwork city. Patterned squares filled with buildings rise from the vast lake bed, sewn together with myriad canals. Like any city, it buzzes with activity — the populace crawls over the landscape like ants in their pole boats and palanquins. Felina work verdant fields dressed in vibrant hues over their spotted skins. Drums beat from behind them like the pulse of an enormous heart. Standing beside them is a serpentine creature, their upper body human-like, with sleek red scales banded with yellow and black. They crack their jaws in a smile, their green and gold feathered headdress flawless and brilliant.

Over it all, the sun bears down, glinting off the gilded stairs with a blinding golden light — warm, like a summer's day.

He and Levnys wake early, well before dawn, and set out after a light breakfast and some pointed yet vague words from Ava. Pica searches for Aurora before stopping himself. What would he say? The last thing he wants to do is make it worse.

The dawn air is crisp, the nascent spring sun doing little to drive away the chill. It's well into the morning before the ship pulls away from Notri and continues southwest.

No one on Notri could provide any new information about the blood-drinking birds. Rumors and exaggerated tales, but nothing concrete. Pica wrote letters until his hand cramped, but in the end, it did little to assuage his anxiety.

Three weeks to Caltava, barring further delays. After that, they'll decide whether or not to push on to Charris. Pica can't understand why it's even a choice. He can see the death looming on the horizon like a thunderhead. They have to fight it. What choice do they have?

If we do not go, these waters will become barren.

The serpent's words resonate with Pica's feelings on the matter. Perhaps it's the insidious helplessness. He wants to *do* something, anything. Yet Calvus remains cautious. Pica considers pulling rank and taking control of the mission and the ship but decides against it. It doesn't feel right. He'd rather set out on his own than wield his royalty like a blunt object. Lucia hasn't done so, despite her quiet agreement with Pica's worry. He'll follow her example—for now.

He sits alone in his cabin, Levnys already airborne and wasting little time training his sister. Krakli is fast asleep on his pillow, his damp feathers fluffed out. The magpie was in their cabin when they arrived, covered in something sticky and foul-smelling. Pica washed him in a bucket rather than using the cleaning spell, to the raucous protests of his familiar. Hopefully, he'll learn to stay away from the fish market this time. Pica doubts it. Whatever happened, it was likely Eclipsis' idea.

The rumble of distant thunder punctuates his thoughts. He nibbles on some dried meat while his calamus flows over a scroll. It's not his usual notes, but a drawing of that pyramid—a feeble attempt to document what he saw in the visions. A mental nudge, and a warm presence fills his senses.

A good likeness, the serpent says.

It's missing something, he replies. There's no way for him to capture the smell of the place, nor the oppressive humidity and the cacophony of birds. Chanting and singing also joined the vision last night—a strange language, the likes of which he'd never heard before. One thing that is clear is the ritual of it. Religion. Worship. Sacrifice. He shudders at the memory of the felina with no heart, thrown so callously from the heights.

He draws the figures from the vision, the feline, canine, and serpentine forms in their colorful garb and feathered headdresses. He doesn't waste time on artistry—his drawings will never grace the walls of a temple. He digs into his bag and pulls out the set of pigments and brushes he purchased yesterday. The feathers of one figure he fills in with yellow—it was more of a gold, in reality—the other with a blue that's not dark enough. It'll have to do for now.

Priests, the serpent says, cutting into his thoughts. *Sun and moon, I think.*

Pica makes note of it and moves on to the other figures. Green, the feathers of that resplendent bird. Black, like the rich soil he walked upon. Crimson, the color of—

His brush stutters across the page, smearing red.

—blood.

He sets it on the table and stares at the drawings. The concept of blood and religion is not foreign to Pica. Blood is featured in holy sacrifices, the grisly sport of gladiators, and the grim work of soldiers. Every spring, they hold festivals where the worshipers self-flagellate until they bleed. The goddess of war, Zalaris, is depicted as a crimson mare, drenched in the lifeblood of those she tramples beneath her hooves.

Ezhual, the serpent says, interrupting his thoughts again. At Pica's inquiry, the entity falters. *The word arose in my head*, they continue sheepishly. *I do not know more. Sorry.*

Pica writes the word on the parchment. He runs his finger carefully over the smeared red, leaving it clean in its wake. He holds up his hand and expects to see blood.

Don't be sorry, he says. *Do you remember anything else?*

Fragments, the serpent replies sheepishly. *Nothing useful.*

I would still like to know.

The serpent is silent for a long moment. Pica closes his eyes, tries to picture their golden plumage and emerald eyes. To his surprise, they appear, resplendent and shimmering, coiled around an ornate pillar. A narrow expanse of grass spreads before them, flanked by stone. Carved seats, like the amphitheater of Geth, attend the verdant strip. Pica settles onto one of those seats as the serpent cracks a smile.

The air is cool, the oppressive humidity of previous visions replaced by a brisk alpine wind. Two snow-topped peaks loom in the far distance, their sharp ridges outlined by the rising sun.

"This place is new," Pica states, unsure what else to say.

"Yes. Three places remain in my memories. Here, where the sun rises and paints the mountains gold." The serpent's feathered tail sweeps into Pica's vision, like an arm wiping a slate clean. The stone risers are replaced by a gilded pyramid rising above a vast city. Pica's skin heats in the blazing noonday sun. "This place, where the pyramid's radiance lights the path for the people below." Another sweep of the tail and that familiar humidity presses into Pica's lungs. "And here, where all crumbles to ruin under the baleful red sunset."

Pica recalls the pool of blood, the crumbling pyramid. "You died here."

"Yes." The serpent lashes their tail violently, returning them to the clear mountain air. "There was another. That owl we saw, but I do not remember who...."

Their voice falters. Their crest droops as they stare out over the empty risers. Pica reaches over without thought, lays his hand gently on their feathered back. "You'll remember," he says. "I'll be here for you when you do."

The serpent snorts. "You do not have much choice." Their fiery orange tongue tastes the sky. "But, thank you. You did not have to listen to me, especially after...what happened before."

"You're right. I didn't. But..." Pica leans back, watching the unfamiliar birds circling above them. "No one deserves to suffer alone, do they?"

"When you could not hear me, I did not know what to do," the serpent says softly. "I felt as if I was calling up from a vast chasm. Only when I burned the ship, and when Levnys and I..." Their coils tighten around the pillar. "It seemed like, every time I managed to break through, it hurt you. I thought you hated your magic. Hated *me*."

The nascent sun disappears behind a thick bank of clouds, casting a cold shadow over the abandoned risers. Bumps ripple along Pica's skin when the wind picks up, driving a chill into his bones.

"You had every right to hate me," they continue. "First, I tried to keep myself hidden but had nowhere to go. I desperately wished to explain it to you, to tell you I was sorry. I prayed to your unfamiliar gods, to anyone who would listen. Then, someone heard me."

"Ava."

The serpent nods. "Yes. She said she would help, for a price and a choice."

Pica sits up straighter, turning his eyes to the serpent. A cold mist blows over them.

"She said if I tore down the barrier between you and me, there would be no going back. Our fates would become intertwined, inseparable. She said more, but I did not understand what it meant."

Pica's fingers tighten around golden feathers. "That was the choice. What was the cost?"

"She...did not say." At Pica's dubious look, the serpent raises their tail like a shield. "Not in so many words! She told me the cost would be like dropping a few cacao seeds to the ground while the tree is ripe for picking."

"I don't know what 'cacao' is, but I understand." Pica pauses, pondering. "It also didn't answer your question, did it?" Pica stands, suddenly restless. The memory of Ava's glowing eyes lingers, as do her words.

You will fight as people fall around you.

You must never stop.

"Gods," he says. "What a pain."

"Quite."

Pica paces a few steps down the stone riser and looks up into the clearing sky. Distantly, a magpie whistles a greeting. "I should get back, uh, out," Pica says. He looks back over his shoulder to see the serpent watching him. "It was good to talk to you, uh—what should I call you? Is serpent fine?"

"Whatever you like. It will be moot when I remember my name."

Pica puts his fist over his chest in salute. The serpent mirrors it with their tail. "To our—"

The cool alpine air shifts to a salt-filled breeze, threaded with the scent of burning candles.

"—fate," he murmurs into his forearm.

Sunlight presses on his eyelids. Sensation floods in, making his sleep-fogged mind reel. Pain in his gut. Krakli's insistent chatter. The ship's drumbeat heart. Drool pooled under his cheek. A warm, heavy hand on his shoulder. Familiar.

Strong fingers glide over sweat-slicked skin, electric, to tangle in his hair. Soft lips brush his ear, a sigh of pleasure, whispering—

"Lucius?"

Pica murmurs a greeting and lifts his head. "'Raxie," he says groggily.

Sparax's fingers twitch. "It's been a long time since you called me that," he says. "Is everything all right? What's all this?"

"All what—oh." Pica stares down at his notes still spread out on the table. "Long story."

Sparax leans over and runs his fingers over a drawing of the serpent. "This is the one from the bathhouse, right?"

"Sort of. It's the one in my…." Pica swallows. "I'm not sure you're going to believe me."

Sparax sits down on the bed. "I'm listening."

He always does. Pica relates what he's seen to the other man—everything. His voice falters a few times, but the serpent supports him, their presence a soothing bulwark.

"Huh," Sparax says at the end of his story. "You don't do anything by halves, do you, Lucius?"

Pica sputters for a second, then laughs ruefully. "I know it sounds insane," he says. "I would hardly believe it myself, except the serpent hasn't shut up since Ava's place."

That is not true, the serpent says, with enough indignation that Pica has to hide his smile.

"But you're still…you, right?"

The pain in Sparax's voice makes Pica want to cross the distance to the bed. Instead, he busies himself by tidying his notes and stowing them neatly in a scroll case. "As far as I can tell," Pica says truthfully. "But who am I now, truly?"

Sparax watches for a few seconds before rising to his feet, joining Pica at the table to clean the brushes and pigments. They both stare at the neat pile in a cavernous silence. A thousand tiny things battle in Pica's head, everything he wants to say to Sparax but can't.

I never wanted this.

Please forgive me.

"Do you remember the first time I joined you in the library?" Sparax asks.

How could he ever forget? Sparax had spent hours with him, looking through old scrolls, marveling at the intricate diagrams and drawings made by the Order's scholars, immersed despite his inability to read. "Of course."

"After you left, I kept going back. I practiced my letters like you taught me." His voice grows thick. "Being there reminded me of you. I wanted—I thought if I could be good at it, you'd—" The thickness becomes a quaver. Pica looks up to see tears gathering in bloodshot blue eyes. "I was an idiot. Why would you return just because I could write a few words? You had important things to do. Once I realized that, I wanted to give up, but Calvus wouldn't let me."

"Sparax, I—"

"Don't." Sparax turns to face him. "I'm not saying all this to make you feel guilty, Lucius. You're doing that to yourself." He raises his chin as the first tear flows down his cheek. "I was able to read some of your notes before you woke up. You're throwing yourself into this new mystery with everything you are. You're still doing all these important things. That's how I know you're still the same Lucius."

Sparax's face blurs. Pica's fingers curl inward. He longs to reach out to his former lover, to bury his face in soft curls. He can't move. "I —I—alright," is the only thing he manages.

A warm hand falls on his shoulder again, a brief squeeze. Sparax leaves his vision, his fingers leave Pica's shoulder. There's a squeal of rusted hinges, a wash of cool air.

"Come to the deck when you're ready," Sparax adds softly. "And wear your boots. It's going to rain."

The light sprinkles of rain when Pica first emerges into the late morning air turn into heavy drops by the time he faces Lucia. His aunt wins, as always, but Pica manages to keep his feet. They hold their practice shields over their heads as Pica scans the small crowd of people watching—the non-rowing crew observes their sparring, as usual. One is unfamiliar to him. Pica's gaze lingers on a handsome face with a day's worth of stubble, brown hair, and slightly tapered ears. The newcomer's eyes meet his for the briefest of moments before quickly glancing away.

The other paladins stand under Ralex's tent. Calvus leans on his cane, scowling, his arthritis surely bothering him in this rain. Sparax's hair is plastered to his head, his padded armor soaked. Petrus is the only one dry.

Lucia notices. "Petrus!" she shouts. "Time to be miserable like the rest of us. Choose who you want to fight."

The stout man scowls but heads into the rain. "Oh, good. Choices. I can be picked up and thrown across the deck or be hit so many times I lose count. One big bruise or lots of tiny ones. How fortunate for me." His boots splash on the deck as he glares at Pica. "Why don't you ever throw Lucia, you ox?"

"She's too fast to grab." Pica steps forward and addresses Calvus. "I have an idea, Grandmaster, but it's dangerous."

Calvus motions for him to continue. "Let's hear it."

"We train our physical fighting, but I believe it's insufficient. We're going about it in the wrong way."

Lucia's head jerks up. "What do you mean?"

"We're not going to fight other warriors," Pica explains. "We are likelier to face a magical foe. We all have magic—we should be practicing *that*."

"Didn't we decide that it was too dangerous?" Petrus asks him. "We could hurt each other."

"Yes. It's dangerous, but your foe tries to kill or maim you in a real fight. We need to train with that fact in mind." He steps toward the tent and raises his chin. "We are all healers. The best way to train magic is to use it, and the best way to use healing magic is to have something to heal. So here is my proposal. We fight each other, as usual, but this time, we use magic. Whoever is not sparring heals the ones fighting. Knock over two soldiers with one strike."

"Does this mean you'll light us on fire, Lucius?" Sparax shouts from under the tent.

Pica grins at him. "Paladin magic only. Lucia and I can train the rest on our own. That way, we're all on even footing. Sound good?"

All eyes turn to Calvus. "You have a dangerous idea, Pica. One strike can be devastating should we make a mistake." He taps his cane on the wood. "You have it correct, though. We must continue to grow. The fight with the dragon proved we are not prepared enough." Calvus studies Pica's face. "You and Petrus will go first. Lucia, Sparax, and I will heal you. Is that acceptable?" Both men nod in acknowledgment.

They face each other as the rain pours around them. "Are you ready, shield brother?" Pica asks.

Petrus' face hardens. "Yes. Let's go."

Seconds pass as they circle each other. Petrus rushes first, his wooden sword blazing with white light. Pica makes a nominal effort to block. It's been years since he's faced Petrus with magic, and he is curious about what he can do.

Smoke fills his nostrils as the brilliant sword slams into his shield. White-hot pain flares from deep inside his arm, causing his forearm to shatter. He drops to his knee as his arm flops to his side. He nearly brings up his breakfast—an excellent strike.

Petrus falters when he sees Pica's arm drop. He opens his mouth to speak.

"No," Pica growls through the pain. "Don't. Stop."

Petrus advances. Healing magic descends on them. The bones in Pica's arm snap together, and he turns the strike. The magical discharge tears a furrow into the black wood. The gash spits and steams in the rain before filling with water.

Pica retaliates. He winces at the sound of bones breaking under his strike. Petrus gasps as he is healed, hesitating a second before lunging back toward Pica.

Swords shine. Bones break. Magic sweeps over them each time, mending them seconds after each agony. Pica's world narrows to burning light and searing pain. He picks out each person's magic. A prickling sensation, like the start of frostbitten fingers. *Lucia.* A rippling wave of tiny pulses, almost electrical. *Sparax.* A whirlwind of hot magic, tightly leashed. *Calvus.* An airy swarm of thousands of tiny motes.

That aura. Was that—?

Petrus is relentless. They continue their battle, taking turns driving each other across the narrow deck. A sharp rap of a cane on wood ends the bout. "Match!" Calvus calls. Pica drops to a knee. Murmurs roll through the watching crowd. Pica looks at Petrus through his rain-soaked hair before rising. Petrus claps him solidly on the back.

"You didn't throw me," Petrus says. "Good fight."

"I *couldn't* throw you. You fight a lot differently with your magic, Petrus."

"Yeah, I've always been better with it." He squints up at Pica. "You didn't hold back, did you?"

"Only the first hit."

They turn and stumble toward the tent. Calvus watches them approach, his expression full of pride and something darker. "Good job, both of you. Are you ready for your turn at healing?"

Pica rolls his shoulder, wincing as it clicks. His arms ache mightily. "Yes, Grandmaster."

"Good. Sparax and Lucia next."

The rain relents as Lucia and Sparax face each other. Where Petrus and Pica fought with slow and heavy strikes, the pair fighting now move so quickly that Pica can barely track them. He channels his magic into the air, blanketing the area in a cloud of warm mist.

Lucia doesn't hold back, finding increasingly creative ways to knock Sparax to the deck. Each time, he springs back up, sword glowing. Pica puts his affection into his magic as he heals each new bruise.

The match ends when Sparax hits the deck again. This time, he lies there, blinking rapidly. "Alright, I'm done getting my ass kicked now." When Lucia kneels next to him and places her hand on his forehead, he tries to push it away. "No pity from you, madam."

"Shut up, Sparax, you fought fine." Her hand blazes with light. "The way you weave your magic into your movements is excellent. I'm proud of you."

Sparax grins at her. "Alright, mother—OW!" He jumps as Lucia kicks him in the shin. "Sorry! Please don't hurt me."

Pica stands and scans the crowd. The newcomer is gone. Pica leaves the matter be—it's not like anyone can leave a moving ship. He'll have plenty of chances to confirm what he hopes is true.

You felt that too, right? he asks the serpent. *That aura?*

I felt many things. That fight was exhilarating! The entity's enthusiasm catches him off guard.

Oh, uh, I'm glad you enjoyed it.

I am sad it is over, the serpent says wistfully. *But you asked about an aura? Perhaps one or two were familiar, but I do not know now. I'm sorry.*

Don't worry about it, Pica says.

They spar for the rest of the afternoon. By the time the ship is put to shore, Pica's limbs hurt so badly he can barely walk. They eat heartily that night, the cooks having found a dozen chickens for sale in the island's town.

He settles onto a blanket with Levnys as the sun sinks below the horizon. Ralex and two of his officers drag an empty crate over by the main bonfire. The captain beckons a fourth person standing outside of the fire's light. Ralex thumps the slight figure on the back, sending them stumbling forward as the captain's uproarious laughter carries across the sand. The figure hops onto the crate. It's the same person Pica spotted earlier. Their blue *exomis* is belted at the waist with braided leather. The bard steps forward, placing one foot on the crate's edge. Their boots are odd, split in half at the toes and tied with golden laces. Music swells from their lute, clear and vibrant.

The conversation around the smaller campfires subsides as heads turn to face the new sound. Krakli, picking at the remnants of their meal, raises his head and chirps inquiringly. Pica stares. He can't help it. He opens his senses and the aura washes across him, light, airy, familiar now. Levnys' hand settles on his.

The bard is excellent, their voice a lilting tenor amplified by their magic. The complex tapestry of the chords and spells weaved together takes Pica's breath away. He's transfixed, staring at the slender musician with rapturous interest. Music fills him, permeates through his muscles and skin, making him as light as air. The smell of the campfire and the warmth of Levnys' body at his side come into keen focus, almost overwhelming. Did the bread always smell that good? He washes the lump in his throat down with a swallow of spiced wine and shivers as it passes over his tongue, each flavor lingering before the next sip.

Is this what he's been missing?

His muscles unwind, the tension swept away by the river of music. The fog in his brain lifts as the notes swell to the song's climax. The lapping waves are the bard's accompaniment, the moon their pale spotlight. A white mist spreads like an incoming tide, swirling around campfires and crewmen like currents. It laps at his feet, surrounds his legs, rolls up his arms and folds around his chest in an embrace. He pulls the magic into him, down into his core, drinking deeply of its cool essence. The serpent's tired contentment rises, mixes their heat with the mist in a pleasing melange. The bard's head falls back as they finish the song, their eyes slipping closed on the final chord. Starlight shines on their oiled hair, firelight caresses their pale skin. A faint smile touches their lips, their satisfaction echoed in the magic permeating Pica's body.

They open their eyes and shift their weight. Time starts up again with a complex chord. The next song is one Pica is familiar with—a Negasi ballad his grandfather taught him. The bard's eyes drift over to him, holding eye contact for a few seconds. Their aura tugs at him, urging him to get closer. He stays in his place by the fire, but a few rowers move toward the music, settling onto the sand. Calvus sings along in a steady voice, enriching the difficult notes of the tune. The bard tips their head ever so slightly and looks away again.

"You are pleased," Levnys states, intertwining her fingers with his.

"Relieved."

They settle into contented observation. A steward named Sethre passes around wooden goblets of wine and things to eat while the bard moves from song to song—a Gethki tavern tune here, a Caltavian drinking verse there. The latter draws in most rowers, and their voices join in, blending into a chorus that fills the sky with its own magic.

Pica and Levnys watch until the last rowers are in their tents, until the fire burns low and the cooks retire. At last, the bard's voice leaves the singing to the seagulls and the lapping of the waves. Pica hopes they will approach, but the bard disappears into the darkness, slipping into the encroaching shadows.

"I believe it is time to retire, Lucius," Levnys says, squeezing Pica's hand.

The departure of the bard's magic leaves a longing within Pica's gut. "That's an excellent idea," he says wistfully. "Let's go."

XIII
THORNS

Levnys

The next day, they barely settle on the beach when Levnys feels the plant dragon's presence. She rises to her feet and roars a challenge. The humans around her recoil from her sudden anger.

Lucius is on his feet in seconds, following her line of sight. "Levnys, wait."

In the back of her mind, she hears him, but her blood is up. There, approaching them, her enemy. The plant dragon dips and weaves, flying so low his tail drags through the spray. His wings barely flap.

"Levnys!" Lucius shouts, thumping her on the side. "Look how he's flying!"

The plant dragon's head droops as he drops from the sky. He lands with a crash onto the sandy beach, the dry sound of snapping wood and breaking branches like thunder in the cool evening air. His sides heave with creaking breath, a dry rattle that causes dying leaves to flutter on his sides. His remaining eye focuses on Levnys with a narrowing pupil. "Peace, *drakaina*, or make it quick," he rasps.

Levnys steps forward, jaws cracking open. Lucius reaches the dragon first, placing one hand on his wooden snout. He turns his face to her with defiance in his eyes.

"What are you doing?" Levnys demands.

"He called for peace," Lucius replies.

"You believe him?"

He sets his feet. "I believe that he's lying helpless on our beach and is about to die." A pale yellow glow surrounds his fingers.

"What if he attacks again?"

"Then we will fight him again." He presents his back to her. "I can't stop you if you're going to kill him, but I will do what is right."

A tendril of doubt worms through Levnys' anger. Letting him leave is one thing, but now Lucius is healing the enemy. He nearly lost his companions to this creature, yet he did not hesitate. Levnys' rump hits the sand as the raw edge of her anger dulls.

Lucius' words burn in her head. *Your mother was wrong.*

Sparax passes her, then Petrus. Both lay their hands on the dragon's head. Neither look at her.

"His heart is laboring," Lucius says. "The blood, ah sap, is almost gone."

"Rear leg shattered," Petrus adds in a level tone. "Lots of healed fractures."

"Thousands of holes." Sparax slips his hands under the drooping foliage. "Lucius, he needs water."

"Good thinking. Lucia!" Lucius calls. "We need you!"

Lucia wavers, clenching her jaw. "You're sure."

Lucius raises his chin. "Yes."

Lucia joins them at the dragon's side. Levnys takes a step back. Even Lucia barely hesitated to help the dragon. They will save him just as Lucius saved her. She bares her teeth in distress, torn between the need to protect her territory and the guilt of slaying a helpless foe.

One who offered peace.

Lucia's hands are lost in a deep blue mist. The dragon's skin cracks and groans as water soaks back into it—drooping leaves uncurl and turn their faces to the waning sun. Levnys catches a yellow leaf skittering across the sand and studies it. Strange, but a dragon—one of Aea's children. Like her, and she wanted to kill him in cold blood. Why? Because it would have been convenient? She wanted Lucius to kill him on her behalf. What is wrong with her? Has she truly become this bloodthirsty?

She retreats from the working paladins, dropping to lie some distance away. The dragon's ruined eye is visible from this angle. The skull around the wound is green with new growth, sleek and shiny, contrasting his wooden skin. In the socket is a bud nearly the size of his good eye.

Levnys scans the rest of the campsite, watching the crew. Calvus remains back, observing but not interfering. Ralex stands nearby with arms crossed, frowning. His officers are at ease, some sitting, some lounging, watching the scene with marginal attention. The crew are mixed in their reactions—there is more than one empty campfire nearby.

She almost does not spot the shapeshifter in the tree nearest the dragon. Their eyes are not on Lucius, as Levnys would expect, but on Lucia. Water surrounds Lucia's hands, dripping onto the sand with a soft *plop*.

It takes nearly an hour, but eventually, the paladins step back from the dragon. His good eye opens slightly, focusing on Lucius' face.

"So," the dragon says. "I am to live, then." His voice has lost its rattling quality.

"This time," Lucius says. "What is your name?"

"I am Sehuti."

"Sehuti," Lucius repeats. "Rest now. I'll have some questions for you later."

Sehuti's rumbling chuckle vibrates the sand around him as his eye closes again. "I'm sure you will."

"I cannot believe you saved him," Levnys says as Lucius plops on the sand beside her. There is no heat in it—her anger has faded, replaced by sickening shame.

"I can," he says and bites into his bread.

Levnys noses at him. He pats her snout. His eyes remain on Sehuti, curled like a cat in sleep, his branched head tucked under a wing. From here, he could be a huge stand of bushes, incongruous on the sandy beach. Near him, the shapeshifter is almost invisible behind the vegetation, sitting cross-legged and staring hard at the enormous dragon. A fine mist clings to them as Sehuti's chest heaves, sending his leaves fluttering with every breath.

Lucius looks up at her. "Would grafting bronze onto your skin heal you?"

She huffs at the unexpected question. "Yes, any metal, if done properly. It was how they did it during the Dragon War. Why do you ask?"

"Lucia's water helped Sehuti more than the rest of our magic. I wondered if it had to do with what dragons are made of." He nods at the slight figure. "Someone else realized it, too."

"That mist is healing magic?"

"I can't be sure unless I check. I'm afraid they'll sense my magic and bolt."

"Ah. That means they have not approached you." She assumed as much.

Lucius' eyes drop. "No. I catch them looking at me sometimes. Watching like I'm a predator."

She nudges him. "Would you like my opinion?"

He sighs. "Yeah."

"The fear is not personal. They will overcome it, and you will get to speak to them again."

"I hope so."

The silence stretches between them after that. Levnys does not mind. Eventually, Kisara and Seto join them at the fire, then the other paladins, and polite conversation occupies the next two hours. Music threads through the evening air not long after the bard leaves their sight.

The conversation pauses when Sehuti stirs, raising his head to scan his surroundings before his gaze settles on their group. He hauls to his feet, shaking himself, causing the birds perched on his branches to take wing with noisy protest. Levnys braces herself as Sehuti approaches them directly, but the dragon merely settles on his haunches and lowers his head, peering first at her, then Lucius.

"You have questions," Sehuti says, digging idly into the sand. "Ask."

"I see you're getting right to the point," Lucius says wryly.

Sehuti sneers at him, but there is no malice in it. "I will participate in pleasantries if you insist."

"No need." Lucius looks around the fire, but none of his companions seem inclined to speak. "What almost killed you?" he asks.

Sehuti's lips twitch back from his teeth. "A foul cloud of tiny birds. Red and black. They surrounded me before I knew their intentions."

As they suspected. The irony of a shared enemy is not lost on Levnys. "You were lucky to escape them," she says.

Sehuti gives her a feral smile. "It was not luck, *drakaina*."

"Why would they go after you?" Lucius asks. At Sehuti's confused expression, he clarifies, "We've come across these birds, too. They drink blood."

"Ah, yes, something I lack. Yet they drank from me with no issue."

Seto sits up straight. "Not blood, but life force." All heads, draconic and human, turn to face the wizard.

"How do you know?" Lucius asks.

Seto blanches, then crosses his arms and scowls. "I captured one of the birds on that beach and had an opportunity to study it."

"And you didn't mention it until now?"

The wizard's back straightens. "I wanted to be sure of my findings first."

"It would have been nice to hear about it earlier." Lucius sighs. "Fine. What do you have?"

Sehuti stretches out on the sand, outside the group but close enough to listen. Seto produces a roll of parchment and hands it to Lucius.

"Here are my findings. The constructs are a celestial link, strong nodes with a straight source path and no agency." Seto scowls again as the faces around him settle into various expressions of confusion. Except for Lucius, who nods along, his finger tracing the parchment.

"Care to dumb that down a little, *ocelle*?" Kisara asks, quirking her lips.

"They're divine summons," Lucius says, glancing at the other paladins. "Like our familiars but, ah, spread thinner." He shrugs as all the eyes turn to him. "I don't understand the rest."

Seto sighs. "Close enough, I guess. There's one big difference, however." He leans over and points at something on the parchment. "Your familiars are weakly tied to the divine power of Andereth, pretty much their independent entities."

"Especially Lucius' familiars," Sparax mutters. Lucia silences him with a glare. Krakli squawks indignantly from a nearby tree.

"These birds are tied much more strongly to their source. So much that they're almost complete conduits. Anything these birds consume goes directly back to whatever controls them."

"What is controlling them?" Petrus asks.

"I'm not sure, something strong," Seto admits. "I also don't know how they replicate. Yet."

"Can you get more answers from that bird you captured?" Lucia asks.

Seto shakes his head. "I destroyed it. The conduit goes both ways —I didn't want to risk being observed."

"Smart," Sehuti rumbles.

Lucius rolls the parchment and hands it back to the wizard. "Thank you, Seto."

Seto takes it and tucks it back into his bag. He mutters a few words in polite response before he and Kisara depart the circle of firelight. The other paladins drift away, too, to drink or to sleep, leaving Levnys and Lucius alone with Sehuti. The dragon does not make any move to leave.

"What will you do now?" Lucius asks him.

Sehuti's eye squints as he smiles. "It seems smart to travel along with you." Levnys' throat rumbles in protest. Sehuti's eye turns to her, watching. Calculating.

"I thought dragons don't make friends," Lucius says.

"Traveling together does not mean friendship. I'm no fool. I have no defense against those birds. You, however, do." He tilts his head at Levnys. "Think of it as a transaction if it soothes you. I will help where I can, and you will turn those birds to ash." He scratches the ground again. "Which you are inclined to do anyway, so your burden is not increased."

"You're right. How do we know you won't turn on us?"

"You don't." Leaves rustle as he stretches, cracking open his great jaws in a yawn. "And I don't know if you'll turn on me. We'll help each other until it's no longer an advantage. Simple that way, don't you think?"

"Pragmatic. Fine." Lucius flicks his hand as if brushing away crumbs. "What do you have to offer?"

"Minor things, I admit," Sehuti says. "Scouting, when my strength has returned. Foraging, if such a thing is required."

"Scouting? What if the birds find you?" Levnys asks.

Sehuti's claws flex into the sand. "They will not catch me again."

Lucius leans forward. "Do you have a human form? How will we feed you?"

"Do not worry about providing sustenance for me. As for your first question, hmm." He tilts his head. "Human is not an accurate description, but I have such a form. The goddess has blessed all her children with them, after all." He gives Levnys a pointed look at that comment as if challenging her to remark upon it.

Lucius does instead. "The goddess?"

"Indeed." Sehuti's lip twitches. "All dragons are children of the land mother. Where I am from, she is Ulene of the great lifetree. Here, she is Aea of the rocky earth. What her children call her does not matter. She is one and the same."

"According to legend," Levnys adds, "Aea gave us our other forms when humans began to spread. She changes each to match those around us so we may mingle with them."

"Mingle," Sehuti snorts. "In my land, it is simply to survive."

"Why did you come to us knowing we would possibly kill you?" Levnys asks, forcing herself to examine Sehuti's ruined face. There is something deeper behind his calm facade—a fathomless darkness.

"Surely you've seen how plants wither in a drought, *drakaina*? It's not a pleasant way to die. I knew if I came here, you'd save me or kill me, and either would be better than that torturous end."

"How can you be so casual about death?" she demands.

"Death is cheap in Tekan."

Lucius' head snaps up. "You're from Tekan?"

Sehuti's lips twitch. "Indeed. The Agymah region." His gaze lingers on Lucius with lazy interest. "Is that going to be a problem, mage?"

There, again. A prod. Sehuti is testing his boundaries and trying to find a sore spot. Lucius grins at him. "Of course not. My grandfather is Negasi."

The branches over Sehuti's brow twitch. "Is that so." He makes a show of inspecting Lucius, turning his head this way and that, before nodding assent. "I suppose that is possible—I heard the Negasi fled to this land. Do you wish to tell me more about it? Relate to me in some way?"

I would like to hear it. The possibility of collecting another precious story from Lucius excites her. Sehuti notices her interest and sneers ever so slightly.

"You're going to travel with us, so I may as well." Lucius yawns loudly. "But I won't force you to listen to my family history." He slowly stands. "They could use my help taking down the galley, anyway."

He turns and takes two steps before Sehuti says, "Wait."

Lucius pauses.

Branches droop as Sehuti sighs and looks out over the water. "It's been too long since I've heard a story about Tekan."

"In that case, would you like some wine?"

By the end of the evening, Levnys is convinced Lucius could talk anyone into peace. The nightshade dragon—Sehuti confirmed the Grandmaster's theory—soon regales them with tales from his homeland and exile from it. The dragon is old, much older than she, well into his fourth century of life. And what a life it has been, if half of the stories he tells are true. While she cannot say she has forgiven Sehuti for his actions, she can say she understands him a bit more.

His pride is as prickly as the thorns nestled under his leaves, that much is clear. Upon her first tentative offers of sanctuary within her territory, he bristles and snaps before settling into quiet disbelief. It is not outright rejection, but it is also not acceptance. She will need to keep an eye on him.

The crew of *Raven's Flight* eye the dragon less suspiciously over the course of the evening, perhaps taking solace from the prince's relaxation around him. Their captain is also nonchalant, and it does not take long for the usual routine to settle in. The music winds down and stops as the fires burn lower.

Finally, Sehuti wanders into the tree line to sleep. Lucius yawns and sags against Levnys' chest. She wraps her foreleg around him and lowers her head to the sand. It would be so easy to fall asleep like this, under the stars, with the sea breeze cool on her skin. She drifts before Lucius' voice cuts through her drowsing.

"We're going to see those birds again soon." He absently drums his fingers on her foreleg. "Both of us think so."

"Both?"

"Oh, uh, me and the serpent." He averts his eyes, as he always does when speaking about the strange entity. "Sehuti's appearance makes that clear."

She moves her head closer to him, wrapping herself around him. Hearing the anxiety in his voice is a vivid pain, a sharp wound.

He slumps against her foreleg. "I'm so tired, Lev. What I wouldn't give for one good night's sleep without expelling my guts." His nails scrape across her scales as his fingers curl into a fist. "Am I going mad? I *sound* like I'm going mad. Who else babbles about amnesiac fire serpents in their head beside someone a few bones short of a Tali game?"

"You are not going mad," Levnys assures him. "Ava confirmed it."

Lucius laughs, a bitter chuckle that makes his shoulders shake. "Another thing that sounds insane. 'No, I'm not crazy; a divine fox told me I'm perfectly fine.'"

"Have your companions questioned it?"

"I haven't told them. Only you and Sparax."

"I see. Did he believe you?"

Lucius sighs. "Perhaps he was humoring me."

A soft noise comes from nearby—a stone shifting across the sand. Levnys spots the slim form crouching outside the light of the fire. Their eyes widen and they shrink back at her attention. She deliberately turns her gaze away.

"Perhaps you should trust Sparax to be honest with you," Levnys says. "It helps that you are not prone to fits of madness."

"You seem so sure about that," Lucius replies. "That's reassuring. I'm going to the cabin, care to join me?"

"I would enjoy that," Levnys says.

He stands and heads toward the ship and his—*their*—warm bed. She rises to follow, turning away from everything—the treacherous dragon who may turn on them at any moment, the nervous form hiding in the shadows, and the softly lapping seas of her precious home.

PART TWO

BLOOD

XIV

BUTTERFLIES

Pica

Pica's femur shatters under Sparax's precise blow. Pain lances through his limbs and along his spine. He puts his weight back on his unbroken leg, waiting. The agony of it has gotten routine, much like the healing wave that will snap his bones together.

Sparax circles him with his face drawn. His friend broke his legs three times this match, along with an arm, a kneecap, and left wrist. Pica inflicted similar injuries upon his former lover, each time regretting the grim routine he inflicted on them with his hare-brained idea.

They all benefit from the unusual training, especially Petrus and Sparax. Sparax proved himself an expert in timing his most powerful strikes from impossible angles, weaving magic and melee together into poetic agony. One such blow shattered Pica's collarbone on the second day, knocking him unconscious, after which he emptied his stomach of a regretfully delicious breakfast. Pica proved to himself how dangerous this endeavor was after nearly shattering Sparax's skull. No amount of healing would have brought him back from that, a fact that Pica tries not to dwell on as the magic around him takes effect.

The paladins' auras intermingle with his, each of his companions choosing different parts to heal. Threaded through it all is the shapeshifter's airy presence, stitching together the disparate pieces to create something greater than the sum of its parts.

The shapeshifter heals him every time he fights. That quiet presence is comforting and frustrating in equal measure—the shy bard keeps observing him from a distance, never approaching. The terror he sensed in Ava's tavern lingers in their magic, but there's something else there, too—curiosity.

A silver cloud of mist curls around his newly mended femur. It lingers, leaving Pica with a distinct impression of a warning.

Be ready.

Pica keeps himself from looking around, focusing on his opponent. Sparax rushes him again, sensing when he is healed. Pica is grimly amused at the lack of pragmatism. Were Sparax truly his foe, he would have pushed his advantage while his opponent was incapacitated, seeking to kill or cripple his enemy.

Krakli's shriek pierces the air. The familiar's panic is like a dagger to Pica's temple.

Warrior! The serpent's voice calls. *Ware! He is here!*

A flit of red flashes across Pica's vision. His head whips around to focus on it, his opponent forgotten. Fire rises in him. Lucia beats him to it. Crackling ice freezes the tiny bird solid, its feathers flashing blood-red before it *thunks* to the deck. Time takes a collective breath as everyone turns toward the sound. Pica frantically searches for what he hopes is not there.

His heart leaps into his throat when he sees the black cloud undulating unnaturally off the bow. He turns and, fueled by years of training and hard-won experience, barks orders in a loud, precise voice.

"Crew members, retreat now! Block the gaps with whatever you can find. Pitch, cloth, anything. Move!" He turns and unleashes a streak of fire that explodes inside the approaching swarm. "Burn, squash, trap them. Go!"

He grabs anyone standing still and shoves them toward the stern, punctuating his words with blasts of fire. Ralex takes up Pica's call, shouting orders at the people streaming inside. A quick brush of magic pulls his attention. The shapeshifter catches his gaze across the deck, their expression set like steel.

"Protect the rowers!" Pica shouts. Magic flares to life as the paladins activate battle spells. They surge through his aching limbs, invigorating him. He's going to pay for this later. No matter. If he doesn't fight now, there won't *be* a later.

Krakli's panic tears at the edges of his sanity. At Pica's urging, the magpie takes wing and flies high above the cloud of death hanging before them.

Levnys' bellow splits the air, a defiant voice answered by Kisara's higher tone. Lightning flashes from both, tearing through a chunk of the swarming mass.

There's a groan of wood, and the timbers shudder beneath Pica's feet. *Raven's Flight's* forward movement slows. Sehuti is at the stern, holding the curl of it between his claws, huge wings outstretched. Sehuti flaps hard, and the ship slows further. Ralex bellows out another order. An officer takes up his call, and the drum shifts. Oars dip back into the water but push instead of pull. The slender oars groan at the strain. Several snap, sending splinters spinning through the air.

Pica turns back to the swarm. He drops his practice shield and holds up his hands, palms out. *Serpent, are you ready?* he asks.

Yes.

The magic rises in him like a living thing, coiling through his limbs. A flaming wall appears between the bow and the swarm, hovering in the sky. Birds in their thousands impact it, burning to crumbling ash. Each impact fuels the vicious hate inside him. An enormous stream of lightning tears through the cloud as Levnys flies by, carving a swath through the swarm that quickly fills behind her pass. A cloud of birds breaks away and surrounds her as she swings upward, nearly obscuring her. She cries out in pain, a long, shrill sound that tears Pica's heart from his chest. He watches helplessly as she spirals and dives, trying to shake off the tiny creatures. Kisara calls out. Lightning surrounds Levnys in a cloud of sparks.

He can't afford to watch. All he can do is hope. His attention returns to his wall of flame, sizzling under the constant barrage of birds hitting it. They move mindlessly, ever forward, spilling around the outer edges of his barrier.

A trapdoor slams. The drums beat. *Raven's Flight* comes to a shuddering stop. Five paladins stand against the swarm that now obscures the curl of the bow. Pica sends as much fire as he can at it, but his best efforts don't make a dent.

The swarm descends upon them. Pica swats at them desperately, trying to keep them from landing on him. Some sink home as he cannot knock them away fast enough.

I'm going to die.

"Paladins!" Lucia's clarion call cuts through his panic. "On me!"

He reacts out of instinct, diving toward his aunt's voice. All five paladins cluster in the middle of the deck as a howling wind rises, countless chunks of ice swirling madly within it. The crystals tear into the birds, driving the swarm back. Pica blindly launches fire out of their icy shield, snarling as his magic burns more birds to ash. Thunder booms as lightning rains all around them.

Below, the screaming starts. He closes his mind to it, sectioning it off into that place reserved for these situations.

Warrior, hold up your hand.

The idea appears in his head, as sharp and clear as a sunbeam. He nudges Lucia and holds out his hand, palm up. A white-hot ball of flame appears above his palm. He winces as his skin blisters. Lucia's hand supports his, an icy mist forming under the sphere. Three more hands join hers, glowing with pale yellow light, their magic spiraling around the orb like foam circling a whirlpool. Pica channels all his rage and pain into that ball, his frustrations, anger, and hate. The orb burns blue-white and grows as Lucia's mist keeps his skin from melting. It swells to twice the size of his head before he raises it to the sky, over Lucia's ice barrier that cuts into his skin, and launches it into the swarm's heart with a snarled curse.

He huddles under the swirling ice as a shock wave pulses through him. The boards beneath him creak as the group stumbles, barely keeping their feet. The world goes white as the orb explodes with a massive roar of flame. The firestorm expands rapidly, consuming thousands of tiny birds in one enormous blast. Streaks of light spiral from it, fluttering and weaving as they home in on the birds, delicate wings blazing as they turn them to ash. *Butterflies,* Pica realizes as he slumps against Sparax.

A slap rattles his teeth. He tries to focus on everything at once. Energy courses through his body, sending his heart rate surging.

"Sorry," Sparax says grimly. "It was the only thing I could do."

Pica grips his forearm, then turns and launches waves of fire from both hands into the remaining swarm. He is relentless, pouring everything he has into his flames. The swarm dwindles rapidly under the magical onslaught.

The battle turns in an instant. The birds swirl upwards and streak off toward the west. Levnys and Kisara give chase, harrying them with bursts of lightning. The butterflies follow.

Screams echo from below. Pica spins on his heel. As he turns, a cloud of birds rises from behind the forward sail. They swirl around a center point, then merge into one enormous shape. Crimson eyes fix on him and an eagle—on black wings wider than Pica is tall—dives at him with talons spread.

You have not won, vessel, it says in his head.

The voice scrapes against him like a rasp deep in his bones. Pica manages to get his left arm up. Its talons sink into the meat of his forearm. Its beak plunges toward his eye. He jerks his head away in time, gouging his forehead. Hot blood sheets down his face.

Enemy, the serpent hisses. *What do you want?*

Fire rises within Pica's core. The eagle's talons tear at his arm as something foul flows into him, something heavy and cold like steel.

Weakling, the eagle says. *You should have stayed dead.*

Pica's heart pounds like he sprinted up a hill. The slithering sensation wraps itself around his heart, coiling through his guts. The fire in him abruptly dies. The serpent cries out. Pica's legs buckle, and the eagle drives him to the ground.

Heed, vessel. This is how your parasite died.

Talons tighten. His bones snap like twigs. He screams as his vision goes crimson.

A grand pyramid, its steps reaching high into the sky, looms above them. Humid air presses down, heavy with the stench of blood. They try to move their body, the long coils of it scraping across rough basalt. Their wings are broken. Their skin burns under their feathers—thousands of shiny black chains hold them fast.

Before their nose stretches a great courtyard, its dark gray stone marred by a lake of blood. In the center of that lake, an enormous crimson bat, dripping and visceral, pins an owl made of starlight beneath his wicked claws. The bat peels back his teeth to reveal fangs as sharp as obsidian. Wings webbed with craggy black skin spread wide. Birds—those accursed servants of blood—pour forth and surround the owl. She screams in pain. The sound wrenches at their heart—they're helpless to save her. Ah-Uaya-Nih, their sister, their opposite, the moon to their sun, tries to defend herself. White moths, glowing with silver light, rise in a shimmering cloud, but it is too late. The birds descend, turning her starry feathers into a foul black smear.

The moment she perishes, the sky itself shudders, joining in their anguished wail. They call her name and curse the bat with every bit of strength that remains to them.

"Thus the moon wanes," the bat crows. "Now the sun will set."

The cloud of birds surrounds them. They're too weak for fire, too weak to call their daughters with their wings of flame. The bat's wings spread. Foul talons sink into their flesh as thousands of beaks—tens of thousands, hundreds of thousands—drive into their body like needles.

Movement at the edge of their vision. Ah-Deh-Det reaches out to them. Something gold shimmers in her hand, pulsing and writhing, and the fire within them dies. "I'll see you again soon, my friend," she says.

The bat's fangs descend, and they know no more.

The eagle screeches, dragging Pica from the vision. Lucia yanks her dagger out of its back and plunges it in again. Again. Her face twists in rage, tears streaming down her soot-stained cheeks. The eagle is wrenched from him, followed by bones snapping.

Pica turns his head to look at the eagle limp under Lucia's feet. He focuses on it, willing the conjured flesh to catch flame. Nothing happens. He tries again. Again. No fire comes forth.

Serpent? he inquires. They don't answer. *Serpent, are you there?* Still no answer.

Blood flows into his left eye from his torn skin. The cuts on his arms throb. He feels like something is broken in him, shattered like pottery. When did it become so cold? His skin burns with the pain of a thousand needles.

Lucia kicks the eagle's body across the deck. Her bare arms are red with frostbite; her eyes are rimmed with dark circles like bruises. She looks at him with undisguised anguish.

"Lucia," he rasps. His heart pounds too hard in his chest—something in his blood tears at him. Bruises spread across his arm like an incoming tide.

Her dagger clatters to the deck. She drops to her knees. "Lucius, thank the gods." Magic flares in her hand—weakly. "When I saw the eagle go for your face, I thought—" She makes a choking sound. "Oh, gods. What's happening?"

Footsteps pound on the deck. "Lucia!" Sparax calls. "Are yo—"

He stops. Pica's vision goes white as his bones creak and snap like twigs. The sticky wetness of blood courses from his nose and his ears. Cold. Why is he so cold? Why does no fire come to him? Black and white feathers flash in front of his eyes. Krakli's panicked cries are loud—so loud. Pain screams through every muscle, every bone.

Serpent? Talk to me!

There is no answer. Both the serpent—and his magic—are gone.

XV

DARKNESS

Davros

Birds stream through an open oar hole. They descend upon the closest rowers and surround them. Davros gags as beaks sink to their hilt in the exposed flesh of the rowers. Men scream in agony and fall, painted black by the swarm.

Oh gods, oh gods, oh gods.

He wants to run. He could get to the back, into a cabin. Seal the window. Ignore the screams. He could get away, get away, GET AWA—

No. He *can't.*

Silver fire flares in his hand. He aims it at the swarm, turning the foul creatures into ash. They keep coming. Shouts from above harden his resolve. Oh gods, the paladins.

"You!" he barks at the nearest oarsman. "Plug the holes. I'll protect you."

The man scrambles at his order. Davros sends flame ahead of him with both hands, driving the birds back as the oarsman reaches the opening. The man shoves linen into the gap. Birds dive for him, but Davros burns them off and sends a cloud of his healing magic after, closing the wounds. The oarsman gapes at him.

"MOVE!" he shouts. He pushes forward, driving the birds against the bulkhead. They struggle, darting manically, trying to find openings in his waves of fire.

Some men at his feet moan. Some are dead silent.

An oar catches fire. He grits his teeth—nothing for it. His body shakes under the strain of the magic, but he can't stop now. People are depending on him.

"Bard!" a voice cuts the air. Ralex. "Push 'em back. I'll get the leak."

Davros strides forward with Ralex at his heels. A group of birds breaks past his fire and surrounds a groaning rower. He burns them off a second too late—the man goes silent. Ralex curses in a strangled voice.

"On my signal," Davros says. White mist rises around them, flickering with silver sparks. He gathers it, lets it swirl around him in a whirlwind, and sends it forward. "Now!" he shouts.

Ralex surges ahead, leaping through the oars and benches. He lunges for the hole as the birds circle and dive at him. Davros meets them with fire. Ralex reels back from the plugged hole with several birds buried in his arm. He yanks one and crushes it. The hair on the back of Davros' neck rises as something dark and twisted coalesces before him, turning the white mist crimson.

You cannot stop me forever, herald.

Davros trembles at the voice. Herald? Herald of what?

An enormous explosion rocks the ship, sending him careening against the wall. *Raven's Flight* trembles, her timbers creaking as the remaining birds crumble. Dragons roar, paladins shout, and the foul presence vanishes. He leans against the wall for a long moment, stunned, as people push past him.

"Where's the bard?" Calvus' shout rings into the rower's compartment.

"Here!" Ralex calls.

"We need him. It's bad."

Ralex grabs Davros' collar and shoves him toward the exit. "Go."

Davros numbly scales the ladder. Seto emerges from the other end of the ship, his white cloak stained with blood.

"Here!" Calvus is next to him, yanking on his arm. "Hurry!"

Lucius lies on his side, staring at nothing. Blood streams from his nose and mouth. Petrus and Sparax crouch next to him, their hands glowing with magic. Lucia has her hands pressed against his chest. Her sandals are smeared with crimson blood.

Bruises mar Lucius' skin, growing as Davros watches. The bones of Lucius' left forearm jut out of a vicious gash. Sparax cradles the limb between his hands. The bones glow with an eerie blue light. Sparax's hands jerk, and the arm snaps straight. The ragged ends of the bones disappear back into rapidly healing flesh. Lucius barely reacts, letting out a small grunt of pain.

The prince's magpie tugs at Lucius' clothes, his hair, crowing and squawking, pacing around in small circles, his anguished calls tearing through the air.

Davros hesitates. Four people crowd around Lucius, all seasoned warriors. Getting too close could allow any of them to turn on him, to overwhelm him despite their injuries. It's the last ship all over again.

"Bard!" Calvus' voice is like a whip crack. "Help him. Please!"

Davros clenches his teeth and pushes into the group, wedging between Sparax and Lucia. They make way for him as he presses both hands to Lucius' side, sending his magic pouring in.

He gasps. There's a great void in Lucius, a cavernous chill where there was once warmth. Where is Lucius' magic? Where is his fire?

Lucius' pain is an inferno threatening to consume him. Davros can't do this. He's too weak. Lucius' body shudders beneath his palms. Davros curls forward as the anguish of four people tears at the edges of his sanity.

Lucia's hand settles on Davros' shoulder. He desperately grasps at the determination within her emotions. She hasn't given up—neither should he. Davros gathers the four rivers of paladin magic and weaves them like cloth through Lucius' body. Something in the prince's blood resists the wave of healing. A cruel affliction courses through Lucius' veins, tearing through him like twisted brambles. Davros goes after it.

No. You can't have him.

Davros' magic responds with its own will as righteous rage burns from his core. The affliction lashes back like a cornered animal. Davros' body shakes under the strain. Sweat beads on his arms and forehead. The pounding of his heart is all he hears.

"Keep going!" Calvus shouts from somewhere far away. "We almost have him!"

Please don't go, Davros pleads silently. *I promise I won't run anymore.*

He's sobbing now, his entire body aflame. Lucius groans as the affliction relents, and their combined magic sweeps the dregs of it from his body. Blood vessels mend, bones snap together, and Lucius' body stops trembling. Davros slumps over Lucius' prone form, his chest heaving.

They did it.

Paladins shout to each other. The affliction is gone, but Lucius isn't out of danger yet. Fever. Swelling. Blood loss.

But alive.

After a long moment, Calvus rises to his feet, leaning heavily on his cane. "Come," he says, tapping Lucia on the shoulder. "He's stable. Let's see to the crew."

Lucia's brow furrows, but she rises and follows Calvus out of Davros' vision. Petrus and Sparax remain. Davros' mist clings to their hair and clothes. Both men look worse for wear, with their own sets of puncture wounds and bruises. Sparax raises his head, his blue eyes tinged red, skin flushed. Their eyes meet for a long breath, Davros' worry and relief mirrored in Sparax's pained expression. His gaze shifts. Davros flinches when a rough hand lands on his shoulder. Ralex.

"How is he?" the captain asks. His voice remains steady, but his grief is a fresh wave of agony against Davros' senses.

"Not well," Petrus says. "Through the worst of it."

"Good," Ralex says. After a pause, he adds, "Petrus, Sparax—I need your help when you can. Heavy lifting."

"We'll be there soon," Sparax says.

"I—uh. I got him if you need to go," Davros says. He regrets the words as soon as they leave his mouth. What is he thinking, saying stuff like that? If anything, he should be the one to go. Sparax's eyes settle on him, and he shrinks back. "I—I—um. Never mind."

"You promise you'll take care of him?" Sparax asks softly.

"I promise."

Petrus and Sparax share a look and rise. "We'll be back as soon as possible," Sparax says.

Davros tries to center his thoughts, gathering the mist back around him. It's so thick that it muffles the background noise, even the raspy keening of Lucius' familiar.

His heart slows as he focuses on his breathing. In. Out. This is something he must face—he can't run anymore.

In. Out.

Gods spit on his fear. Right now, it's getting in the way.

In. Out.

He takes Lucius' hand, distancing himself from his anxiety. He turns the hand over, examining it. It's covered in blisters, burns, and bruises. Not dire. Davros delves deeper into Lucius' broken body.

He once healed a boy who missed his tightrope jump and fell to the ground in a crumpled heap. Lucius' body feels like that shattered boy's—as if every wound he'd received in the last several days returned at once.

It'll take hours to mend his bones so they won't simply break again. Davros is reaching the limits of his magic—he will need the paladins' help before they try to move him. Not to mention the toll extended healing takes on the patient's body. Already, Lucius' fever is starting to rise. Davros doesn't know if Lucius will wake again.

A man like him doesn't deserve to die like this. Lucius is never quarrelsome, never raises his hand against another, and always treats everyone around him with the same amount of respect regardless of their social standing. There are other things—the way he fights, the way his muscles ripple when he works out shirtless on a sunny morning, his easy laugh and beautiful smile. How could Davros do anything *but* fall for him?

Shit.

Regret threatens to break his concentration. Davros should have approached him sooner. He shouldn't have denied his feelings. Gods curse him; now, he may never get to talk to him again.

A great shadow falls over the ship. Sehuti circles above until Ralex acknowledges him near the stern. His voice rumbles, but he's too far away to make out the words. The enormous dragon flies off again.

Where are Kisara and Levnys? Davros prays they're alright. If anything happened to them, Lucius would surely be distraught. The shock may well finish what the affliction failed to accomplish.

Krakli's chirp and a scrape of boots alert him to another's presence. Sparax enters the mist and kneels across Lucius' body from him, picking up Lucius' hand. Davros feels Sparax's magic join his—tingling energy, like Levnys' lightning.

"How is he?" Sparax asks. "Can I help?"

"Still bad," Davros replies. "Can you heal his bones? I'll try to lower his fever."

"Got it."

Both of them settle into it. Davros watches Sparax warily for several long minutes, his fear setting him on edge. The paladin barely pays attention to him, keeping his eyes on Lucius' face. Through the magic, Sparax's anxiety is keen, as is a deep worry. Davros tries to ignore the other emotion he finds there—a quiet affection as solid as a city wall. It's like he's peeping through a window and witnessing something private.

Eventually, his wariness relents, and he relaxes. Sparax's magic is strong, and together, they make progress.

"So, who are you?" Sparax asks after a while, breaking the silence.

Davros started to drift. He jolts and looks up to see Sparax studying him.

"Um, a bard," Davros manages.

"Yes, but that's not all there is to you, right?"

A lump obstructs Davros' throat. He wants to run. He always wants to run. "No."

"So tell me."

"Why?"

"Because I want to know." Sparax shifts his weight, settling into a different position. "You care about Lucius somehow, but you've been noticeably avoiding him. Can't figure out why."

"Ah. Uh. Well." Davros rubs the back of his neck. "I met him in Ava's tavern the night before *Raven's Flight* left Notri."

Sparax's brow furrows. "I don't remember you."

Davros' stomach tries to do a flip. "I was the blonde girl."

"The one we danced with? How?"

"It's—" The flush creeps along his neck. "I can change what I look like."

"Is it magic?"

"No. Physical."

Sparax is silent for a long moment, studying Davros' face with tired eyes. "Huh," he finally says, his gaze dropping back to Lucius' face. "That's not the strangest thing I've heard this week. Well, if dragons can do it, why not you?"

Davros was expecting disbelief, fear, or any number of other extreme reactions, but Sparax had accepted it without a second thought.

Lucius groans loudly and stirs. Davros and Sparax lean forward, conversation forgotten.

"*Shit*," Lucius says weakly. He tries to raise his head. "'Raxie?"

"I'm here," Sparax replies. Davros registers the relief and tenderness in his emotions.

"Kisara? Levnys?"

Sparax swallows. "Took off after the remaining birds. Sehuti went to search for them."

"Oh." He turns it into an exhalation, and his worry is a knife against Davros' magic. "Shit."

"I'm sure they're alright, Lucius," Sparax says.

Lucius groans again, and a fresh wave of pain hits Davros's senses. He reacts with a flood of magic, trying to mitigate it. He can't stand it. Without a word, he and Sparax roll Lucius onto his back. Golden eyes, barely open, slowly track until they land on Davros. His lips curl into a small smile. "Hello," he says. "'Bout time."

"Sorry." Davros finds himself smiling back. "Call me Davros."

"Charmed." Lucius' voice comes out slurred. "How'm I doing?"

"Not well," Davros admits. "Something got into your blood, almost killed you."

"It was that eagle," Sparax says. At Davros' inquiring look, he adds, "The blood birds changed form and attacked him. He collapsed after that."

"Mhm." Lucius' fingers twitch. His eyes grow distant. "No fire..." he mumbles. "Gone..." Lucius closes his eyes. He exhales and relaxes into unconsciousness.

"What happened to his magic?" Davros asks Sparax.

"I don't know," the paladin says. "It disappeared when he collapsed."

"Oh." Davros ponders that. How was it even possible? Was it that affliction? If so, why hadn't his magic come back?

Silence settles between them. *Raven's Flight* floats serenely in the water. Ralex's usual bellow is subdued in the late morning air. Clouds gather on the horizon, weaving together before slowly rolling over the sea. A light rain falls as the sky turns somber. Davros keeps up his magic through it all, wishing he had more to give.

Calvus returns, limping heavily along the deck. In a low voice, he relays news from the other end of the ship. They lost around forty crewmen—two cooks and one of Ralex's officers. The rest were rowers. Sehuti found a nearby island with a harbor. The old paladin waves off Sparax's inquiries about his health before slowly returning to the stern.

Forty people. Can they make it to shore with those losses? Davros' question is soon answered when the remaining rowers take staggered positions along the ship's length, spreading themselves out to balance the labor. Like a wounded beast, *Raven's Flight* limps for refuge.

Davros shivers in the cold wind, trying to ignore his numb fingers. The hours pass in a haze as he blocks everything but Lucius' hand between his palms and Sparax's steadfast magic. Slowly, Lucius' body stabilizes. His breathing steadies and his heart doesn't labor as hard. Finally, shouts float over the thud of the drums—land.

The island has a small port, with ship berths and hands to help. *Raven's Flight* is hauled ashore into an isolated slip at the harbor's edge, separated from the docks by a rough sand beach. Davros cranes his neck to watch the activity as the rowers carry their fallen kin to the sand.

"You can go look," Sparax says. "I'll stay here."

"But—"

"Listen—Davros, was it? You're worried about him. I am, too. But you need a break."

"I'm fine," he lies.

"You're not," Sparax says. The redhead smiles at him. "Lucius has never been able to fool me, and neither can you."

Davros falters. Sparax is handsome, too, tall and lean, and the charm in his smile is disarming. No wonder Lucius likes him. Davros sighs and rises to his feet on unsteady legs. Sparax is correct— between the battle and healing Lucius, he's burned through his shallow energy reserves. The words of his teacher echo in his head. *To care for others properly, a healer must first attend to themselves.*

Davros takes one last look at Lucius' sleeping face and heads down the gangplank. The activity on deck has lessened—most people now mill around the wooden berth or coarse sandy beach. Long lumps, lined up like cordwood under a tattered black sail, lie in silent witness to their living companions. Davros' throat tightens. This morning, the men under that funerary shroud ate their porridge and bread, not knowing it would be their last meal. They sang their cheerful sailing song to their gods, and their gods did not protect them.

He hesitates when he sees the galley surrounded by rowers. The lead drummer—a wide-set man with dark skin, tightly-curled black hair, and more scars than Davros can count—spots him. Davros balks as the man's arm settles around his shoulders but lets himself get led through the crowd.

He receives his usual meal of sun-dried olives and vegetable broth. When he asks for a loaf of bread and water, the cook gives him a sideways look and hands him two loaves, a bulging water skin, and a covered clay bowl. The smell of roasted meat makes his stomach protest. He stumbles away, arms laden and face burning hot. The rowers let him pass unencumbered aside for the feast that he cannot eat.

Sparax's head droops when he returns to the deck. Petrus has joined him in healing Lucius. Davros sets down the meat, bread, and water for them and settles against a railing post to eat his tiny portion.

"Should we wake him?" Petrus asks Sparax. "He should eat this meat."

"Yes, let's do it," Sparax responds.

Both paladins look like they need a good meal themselves. Davros watches them go to work with eyes swollen from stress and fatigue, ruminating.

What is he doing, anyway? Lucius has so many people who love him already—he doesn't need a broken little bard with no social standing. The man is heir to the entire might of the Gethki for Ogtris' sake. Power, influence, and nobility—all things Davros will never possess. All he has is his voice; bards like him are as common as house sparrows.

Lucius stirs and opens his eyes. "Smells good," he says. His voice is much clearer. Petrus and Sparax lift him into a sitting position before carefully feeding him the meat one piece at a time. Lucius tries to take the skewer, but his friends don't let him.

"Davros," Sparax says, cutting into his thoughts. "Any ideas where we should put him?"

They're asking *him*? Why? They're healers, too—they don't need his opinion. Still, he scans his surroundings, pondering. Lucius will want to be present for the dragons' return, so his cabin is out. Ralex's tent is another option, but the grieving captain will need a refuge. His gaze travels to the tree line, which overlooks the beach—shaded and out of the way but with a view of the activity. "Up there," he says, pointing. "If we can get a canopy and a lounging chair, we can take turns monitoring him."

"Does the patient get a say?" Lucius murmurs.

Davros flushes and starts to respond, but Petrus answers first. "No," he says. "The patient needs to eat his meat and rest."

Lucius tries to take the skewer again. This time, they let him. It falls into his lap. "Fine," he sighs.

Ralex sets two of his surviving officers on the task, and soon, they have Lucius settled. So the afternoon passes—Lucius sleeps, then wakes, then sleeps again. Davros stays by his side, healing him the entire time.

Others come to check on them: Lucia, her fierce sapphire eyes clouded with worry; Calvus, a bastion of quiet authority and grandfatherly concern; Ralex, his eyes eternally wet with tears but bellowing voice as loud as ever; Seto, who lingers nearby with eyes on the sea.

Davros dozes off at some point. Someone covers him with a blanket. He only wakes when shouting heralds the return of the dragons. Levnys and Sehuti land near the silent bodies under their black shroud. Kisara rests in human form in Levnys' upturned hand. Seto runs to her as she carefully sets down the sleeping half-dragon.

Levnys comes directly to their tent and sticks her head into it. Her head droops with fatigue. Puncture wounds riddle the skin between her scales. Lucius raises his hand weakly to her, and the smile he gives her causes Davros to melt. Lucius has her—why would he need anyone else?

"Do you need healing?" Davros asks her.

"No, I am doing well enough. I will ask the paladins later. Please keep healing Lucius." She settles to lie next to the pavilion. "Tell me what transpired."

Lucius drifts off again as Davros relays the events in a monotone voice. "He should be moved to his cabin soon," he finishes. "He's stable enough for the night."

Levnys puts her nose an inch from Lucius' side. "Thank you for all you have done. Perhaps it is also time for you to rest."

Davros wants to argue, but she's right. He's been working on dregs for hours now. "I should at least play for the crew." At Levnys' pointed look, he hurriedly adds, "I won't use my magic."

"If you insist. You and Lucius have that in common, it seems."

"Have what in common?"

Her lips curl in a terrifying draconic smile. "The inability to rest."

They take Lucius to his cabin not long after Davros leaves the tent. The solemn vigil for the fallen continues, but one by one, the remaining crew of *Raven's Flight* drifts away, either into the town or their tents. Davros matches the mood with a somber tone.

He's set himself to overlook the bodies. The night is a cold one, the better to keep them from festering. Several bodies swell already, contrasting their desiccated companions. Davros wonders how long they'll stay out there, lonely on the sand with only the crabs for company. Rot will set in sooner rather than later, with disease quickly following through the fetid stench. He'd rather burn them and be done with it, as the Gethki would. The music master at Ava's tavern gave him an overview of Caltavian funerary customs. Caltavians—of which the crew is mainly comprised—do not burn their dead, preferring to inter them in carved stone tombs. Davros grimaces. He doesn't hold much faith in such rituals.

The moon rises over the quiet sea before he finishes. He stares at her silver beauty. In Geth, the moon is a wolf, fierce and snarling. In Soutori, she's a fox, pale and lovely. Sometimes, she paints her face black, sometimes white. Davros finds all aspects of the moon equally appealing—ever-shifting, ever-changing, ever-beautiful.

If only he could apply that same acceptance to himself.

Davros steps from the rock and moves silently over the beach. He's gotten good at being quiet over the years. It's how he learned the secrets he would hoard like a little gray squirrel. It's how he avoided violence against him. Davros found it best if others forgot he existed. The performing troupe tolerated him only because the man who raised him also ensured they were fed. Once that man died, stabbed in a tavern brawl, Davros was nearly stoned to death. It was only with the intervention of two foreign wizards he survived. He left Soutori for good after that.

The cleric who taught him healing, the bard who taught him music, the wizards who saved his life—none of them were Soutorian. They had seen past the superstition of his existence, and to them, he is grateful. Gods spit on the rest.

Davros chews his lip and pushes the thoughts away. The tent they set up for Lucius is deserted, as he hoped. He stashed a tattered bedroll and blanket nearby. He spreads them out next to the lounging chair. Added to the shelter of the tent and the blanket someone gave him before, it's almost cozy. He crawls under the covers and nibbles on a piece of dried fish.

He finds the half-eaten piece the next morning. A vast wall of leaves greets him as he slowly opens his eyes. Belatedly, he feels Sehuti's presence. The enormous dragon sleeps beside his shelter, curled around several young trees. Davros jolts out of his makeshift bed before catching himself. If Sehuti meant him harm, he would be dead already.

The dragon murmurs in his sleep in a strange language. His body shudders, causing the tent to tremble. Davros freezes. The dragon shakes harder. "*Sila. Sila!*" He repeats the word with anguish.

"Sehuti?" Davros inquires. "Sehuti!" he repeats. "Wake up!"

The dragon's sides heave. Sehuti raises his head and looks around wildly, his eye tinged with green and crimson. "*Medis!*" He spots Davros and goes still. "Bard? What is happening?"

"You, um, you were talking in your sleep," Davros says timidly. "Are you alright?"

"I—yes. I am fine." Sehuti looks away.

He's lying. Davros decides not to pry. "Er, good," he manages, then withdraws deeper into the tent.

Sehuti leaves without another word. The paladins bring Lucius not long after. The prince brightens when he sees him, and Davros flushes anew. He sets to healing the injured man, pouring everything he can into his magic. It seems Lucius' body benefited greatly from sleep. Lucius is more alert, and he's able to speak in complete sentences. They talk quietly, slipping into polite conversation. Davros' fear lingers like a stain, but he's more relaxed in Lucius' presence than he thought possible.

Lucius falls asleep after his midday meal. Davros lingers, reluctant to leave. He should walk around and stretch his weary legs, but what if Lucius needs him? His body remains so broken.

The decision is made for him when Calvus enters the tent. The Grandmaster gives Davros an appraising look and says, "You need a break."

"I'm f—"

With a sigh, Calvus settles onto a stool. "I wish to evaluate him without distraction," he says. "You may return later." After a pause, he adds, "Shoo. Let an old man work."

Davros chews his lip, rises to his feet, and exits the tent. His knees protest as he tries to work out the stiffness in his legs. His stomach growls—which is nothing new—but with a desperation that highlights his fatigue. He's pushed himself hard, but for Lucius, it's worth it. He glances at the galley, but rowers surround it. Davros sighs. Gods know he can wait.

Further along the tree line is a small shelter, much like the one Lucius occupies. Davros pauses when he sees Kisara resting on a blanket. He balks when she turns her head. "Hi," she says. "Care to join me?" She indicates the spot next to her. "Sit. I don't bite."

After a breath of hesitation, Davros ducks into the tent and settles cross-legged on the blanket. Kisara folds her hands over her knees. The half-dragon has a good foot and a half on him. Her splayed feet with their wicked claws dwarf his head, and surely her tail would do some damage.

"Fruit?" she asks, indicating a bowl.

Davros' stomach flips. He takes a fig and nibbles on it, savoring the sweetness. One won't hurt, surely.

"Thank you for saving my brother's life," she says. Davros jerks his head to find her smiling at him. She and Lucius have the same smile and crinkling of their eyes. "He means the world to me."

Davros' lip trembles. What is he supposed to say to that? He cycles through several responses before he says, "I'm glad I could."

"Seto told me you helped save the rowers, too," she continues. "He won't admit it, but he's curious about you. As am I."

"I'm just a bard," Davros says.

"Mmhmmm," Kisara says. "And I'm just a half-dragon."

Davros smiles despite himself. "You got me there."

The afternoon passes quickly as they settle into polite conversation. Davros finds himself relaxing in her presence as they observe the activity on the beach. It seems she's as softhearted as her brother.

"I should check on Lucius," he eventually says. Though he enjoys Kisara's company, he's anxious to return to the prince's side.

"I'll walk with you," Kisara says.

Lucius is awake when they return to his tent. "I was wondering where you went," he says, glancing between Davros and Kisara. "Everything alright?"

"Wanted to request a song," Kisara says dryly. "How're you doing?"

"Never better," Lucius says. "According to Calvus, only half of my bones are broken."

Kisara blanches. "Gods, Lucius."

"It's alright. Davros has been taking great care of me."

Davros blushes and settles on the cushion next to Lucius' chair. "I'm doing my best."

By late afternoon, he and the other paladins have Lucius standing, supported on either side by Sparax and Kisara. Another hour, and he's taking tentative steps, his legs trembling violently. Lucius' jaw is set in determination, and he insists on trying again and again.

The sun brushes the horizon when Seto approaches, his lips set in a grim line. The wizard's face is ashen gray. "Draconius," he says. "There's something you need to see."

XVI
FUNERAL

Pica

Pica manages two steps on his own before he has to be carried to the beach. He tries to shove the insidious helplessness to the back of his mind, but it's impossible. Davros lingers nearby with his lute hanging from his shoulder, his eyes darting around like a watchful deer.

Seto leads them to the bodies lying under the sail. Sparax and Petrus pull it back, revealing the results of yesterday's violence. Most of the bodies are desiccated husks. Several of them are far different— swollen to near-bursting. The woolen tunics have split at the seams, exposing the distended flesh beneath. Under the skin, dark shapes move like slugs through garden dirt. Seto kneels and holds out his hand. The shapes push toward him, congregating as if drawn to his warmth. Sharp points push at the skin like needles under cloth. Pica tries to distance himself from his emotions. He almost can't do it. Between the pain and the loss of his magic, he's walking the edge of a precipice, ready to plunge at any moment.

"Is this what I think it is?" he asks.

"Likely." Seto moves his hand over the body. The slug-like shapes follow. "Now we know, though." Seto looks at Pica. "We have to burn them."

Ralex, standing behind him, strides forward. "No," he says.

"It wasn't a suggestion," Seto says, facing the captain.

"I said no." Ralex's fingers flex. "Not these men. They're not Gethki. We bury them."

Seto's spine stiffens. He gives Pica a long look and steps forward. "Captain Ralex. Don't misunderstand. This has nothing to do with death rites." He points at the swollen body. "More birds like the ones who attacked us are forming. If we wait any longer, they will finish their development, then—" Seto spreads his fingers like a blooming flower. "We have to destroy the physical construct. Burying them will do nothing but ensure they spread."

Ralex's stern expression falters. He looks at the body of the oarsman. "How long?"

"No more than a day."

The captain curses in Caltavian. Ralex stares for a long moment at the swollen bodies, then at his remaining crew. Through clenched teeth, he says, "Do it."

Seto moves to walk forward, but Pica holds up a hand. "No. Let me do it."

Petrus hands him a torch. Pica leans on Sparax heavily as they walk forward. As they approach the first of the bodies, regret claws at his gut. He barely knows the words of the Caltavian rites, but it's wrong to say nothing. So he murmurs the prayer to Ukton, modifying it.

Farewell, beloved souls of Caltava, of Fresa, of the Sparkling Coast,
you will remain in our memories throughout this life.
Honored Ukton, though they do not know you,
guide these hallowed souls to their rest,
and soar with them forevermore.

He lights the first body. It takes a second to catch. He directs his magic to the blaze to spread it. Nothing happens. He tries again. Nothing. It's truly gone. He wants to scream. What good is he without his fire? It was his identity, his pride, his shame.

The fire blazes hotter as airy magic winds around him. He glances at Davros, and the bard gives him a slight nod. The flames take on a silver tint, casting dazzling light along the beach.

Beloved souls, may your memory be everlasting.

Shouting rises behind him. Crewmen rush forward. Lucia and Petrus put themselves between him and the oncoming crowd.

"Hold!" Ralex bellows.

At the sound of their captain's voice, they stop their advance. "Why do you do this?" one man shouts.

"Stop!" calls another.

"Gethki bastard!"

"Ralex, why?"

Pica and Sparax continue their grisly work. The next body is one swarming with those slug-like shapes. Pica gags but holds the torch until what was once a man ignites.

Beloved souls, may your memory be everlasting.

He hadn't bothered to learn everyone's name. He knew some of them—those who had spoken to him—but he hadn't sought them out. The number of crewmen wasn't an excuse. He'd taken time to learn the names of each man who served under him in the legion. What makes this any different?

One by one, the bodies burn. Ralex bellows for order, but the crowd becomes unruly. Calvus joins the other paladins. Seto's face goes white, but he also holds fast, standing at Ralex's elbow.

A drum booms slow and steady, like a heartbeat. The lute joins it several beats later, then Davros' voice swells in guttural Caltavian—a funeral dirge. At the sound of his voice, the crew falls silent.

Pica sets the last body alight.

Beloved souls, may your memory be everlasting.

He drops his torch onto the sand.

Pica scans the crowd. Behind him, their fallen burn, filling the air with acrid smoke. He must look like a monster to them—a Gethki backlit by the burning bodies of a subject population. He's been here before.

Ralex moves next to him. The captain grips Pica's shoulder, digging his fingers painfully into his skin. "Speak to them, Regillus," he says.

Sparax's magic flows into him—the vigor spell. His legs stop shaking long enough to take a step forward. He'll suffer for it later, he has no doubt. His muscles scream in agony, but he bites back the pain and straightens. The nearest crew members are a few feet away, close enough to overwhelm him, should they choose to. But they are not his enemy, and he is not theirs.

"Crew of *Raven's Flight*," he says, using his centurion's voice to carry over the crowd. "It is my deepest regret to have sent these souls to the gods in the manner of my people and not yours. It is not to defile your fallen, nor is it to disrespect them. It is for our continued survival and to save the Coast."

Shouts swallow his following words as the last rowers join their brethren. One tries to lunge for him but is dragged back. A scuffle breaks out somewhere near the back of the crowd. There's an unmistakable sound of impact. Pica's gut churns.

He's tired of being a monster.

"We burned them to prevent those vile birds from spreading," he shouts. The din lowers to a roar. "Had we waited, they would have used your fallen against you! They would have consumed us all. They would have spread across this island, then the next, then the next. Our Coast will perish if we do not *burn them all!*"

There's more venom in his voice than he intended. A man bursts from the crowd with tears streaming down his cheeks. Pica reacts without thinking, bringing up his left arm to block the blow. The impact of the club shatters his forearm. Pain roars through Pica's body, narrowing his vision until magic snaps his bones back into place. His stomach heaves. Petrus grabs the assailant's tunic and takes him to the sand. The rower looks at Pica in terror.

"HOLD!" Ralex screams. Desperation tinges his voice. The crowd takes a collective breath. "Please, Regillus, have mercy," he says hoarsely.

Mercy? It takes Pica a second to realize what Ralex fears. Violence against a royal is an executable offense. His father would do it with no hesitation. So would his uncle.

He will *never* be like them.

"Petrus. Let him go," he says.

Petrus releases the rower. The assailant is pulled to his feet and swallowed by the crowd. Pica's pain is a living thing now, gnawing at his limbs and chewing through his strength. Sparax ducks under his arm, supporting him. The vigor spell will wear off soon. Pica needs to get through to them somehow. How can he show them he's not their enemy?

"No words from me will be enough," he shouts. "I want to hear *your* stories. Tell me everything about their lives, their loves, their dreams. Tell me, and I'll remember. As long as it takes, I will pour your drink and listen. That's a *promise*."

Murmurs now. Ralex steps next to Pica and shouts, "The Regillus has taken the yoke of responsibility. Do not forget that this man saved our lives with his heresy. Forgive him, or don't. Either way, we must rest. Dismissed!" The captain strides off in the direction of the galley. Two of his officers move around the edge of the crowd, urging them away from Pica and the bodies behind him.

Gods, what a nightmare.

Pica's legs turn to liquid. When he opens his mouth to scream, Sparax shoves something between his teeth. He bites hard into the roll of linen as they lower him to the ground.

He withdraws as hands press against him. Paladin magic floods in. It is the only thing that keeps him sane. His stomach heaves, but there's nothing to expel. Voices surround him—shouts, sobs, murmurs. It all blends into a buzzing noise.

Everything is so cold. Pica misses the warmth of his magic. He misses the serpent. He'd gotten used to their presence, the quiet weight of their joy under the noon sun. Where had they gone? Did they die again before ever learning their name? Pica clings to life, broken, lost. If their fates are entwined, as Ava said, what will happen to him?

Finally, the pain relents. He lies on the sand as his breathing slows. Soft music swirls around him. When he opens his eyes, Davros sits cross-legged, plucking his lute.

Davros looks exhausted himself, with eyes rimmed red from fatigue and smoke. Mist curls around them as he plays, filled with the bard's airy magic. It soothes Pica's pain further—enough that he tries to push himself up.

"Oops, no, you don't," Sparax says from beside him. "Petrus, bring that crate."

They prop him against the wood. Pica's throat burns—he could use some water. When he expresses his need, Petrus adds, "Let's get you something to eat, too."

Sparax looks toward the galley. "Should we leave him unguarded, though?"

"If anyone tries anything, I'll burn them," Davros says flatly, his expression dark with anger. Pica is surprised by the venom in his tone. "No one will touch him."

"I believe him," Petrus says. "Come on, Sparax."

Sparax hesitates, then follows Petrus into the crowd. Pica turns his attention back to Davros. "Burn them? After what happened?"

Davros' jaw works. "I don't care. You saved them twice, and that's how they thank you? One of them broke your arm!"

"I broke their funeral rites."

"If those birds emerged, there'd be no one to bury them. Spit on their funeral rites."

"You say that, but you know their funeral dirge."

"Yes, and what about it? Doesn't mean I believe in it." Davros glances at the crowd. "The music master at Ava's tavern taught it to me. He said I'd need it. I didn't think it'd be this soon."

"Things would have been even worse without it. Thank you. I'm glad you're on our ship."

"I almost didn't get on it."

"Why not?"

"A warship painted black, even the sails. Armed guards. A captain who asked how strong my magic was." His lips quirk. "Imagine my surprise the next morning when you rode that huge horse straight up the gangplank. Part of me wanted to run when I saw you, but..." He sighs. "I didn't."

"What made you decide to stay?"

He shrugs, "I figured a captain would hold his crew to higher standards if royalty were on board. I was right."

"That's pragmatic of you," Pica says.

"Thanks." They're both silent for a moment. Davros' eyes drop away.

Pica sighs and says, "I hope they're back soon. I have a lot of stories to listen to and—"

"No," Davros interrupts. His head snaps up. "You need to rest."

"I'm fine," Pica lies.

"You are *not* fine. We've been healing you non-stop for a day and a half, and you can barely stand. You should be unconscious, but your pain tolerance is as insane as the rest of you. That doesn't mean you should push yourself harder."

"I made a promise," Pica counters. "I can't tell them I'm going to listen and hide in my cabin."

"If you insist on this, fine, but you can't do it here."

"Where else would I go? That tent you have me in isn't big enough."

"Leave that to me," Davros says. "There's Levnys. She can eat anyone who tries to hurt you." He stands without skipping a note. "Go to the bow once you've eaten."

He walks away before Pica can respond.

Levnys' head descends into his vision. "Hey, Lev," Pica says.

She gently prods him with her nose. He winces, and she draws her head back. "Sorry. What has happened? The bodies have been burned. There is tension in the crowd. Ralex does not look happy." Pica tells her, and she bears her teeth. "It is good I was not here."

Both she and Davros want to protect him, enough that they're willing to resort to violence. A dark corner of him wonders why he's worth it. Sparax, too—what is it they see in him?

Levnys' head swings to observe the galley. "Sparax and Petrus come. There is someone with them."

Sparax and Petrus enter his view carrying a spread of food, using a practice shield as a makeshift tray. Accompanying them is the lead cook, a tall and rangy Caltavian man with short blonde hair and an aquiline nose. Laxu, Pica remembers.

"You're lucky you're getting food at all, *Regillus*." Laxu turns the princely honorific into a curse. "Giving pretty little speeches while you defile my brother's body."

"I'm sorry for your loss," Pica says. "I wish I had another choice."

"Sorry. You're *sorry*? Save it, Gethki bastard. You don't care about us. You used this opportunity to—"

One of Ralex's officers—Itavus—grabs Laxu's arm. "Hey, stop it. You think he summoned those awful things? I saw him fight before we went below. Look at him. Look at his *hands*, Laxu."

Pica resists the urge to hold them up. His brown skin is an angry mass of purple and crimson. He can't imagine his face looks much better.

"Those hands burned my brother. Now, we can't bury him properly." Laxu jabs his finger at Pica. "He took that away from his family. Away from me."

He takes a threatening step forward. Levnys lowers her head.

Laxu balls his fists but stops.

"I saw them bodies," Itavus says. "I heard what that wizard said. We had to burn them, or more of them birds would come out."

"Horse shit," Laxu says, but looks unsure.

"Ralex gave them the go-ahead." Itavus puts his hand on Laxu's shoulder. "I'm sorry. I know you loved him, but don't take it out on the guy who saved our lives."

Laxu's face falls. "I don't care how good your reasons are, Regillus. My brother was all I had. All that's left is my pride. Don't take that away, too."

He allows Itavus to lead him away, back through the crowd. Sparax moves to put the food down, but Pica holds up a hand.

"Wait. Take me to the bow. I can eat it there."

"What's on the bow?"

"A place to keep my promise."

Levnys carries him in an upturned palm over to *Raven's Flight*. Sparax and Petrus lift and carry him up the gangplank and down the long ship. Levnys follows in her human form. Nestled into the curved V of the bow are several large cushions—bedrolls covered by linen sheets—surrounding an oil lamp on a small table. Three more oil lamps are placed around, sending flickering orange light dancing off the curves of several amphorae of wine.

"Wow," Sparax says.

They put Pica on the largest cushion, and he relaxes against the pillows propped on the wooden wall. Petrus leaves, but Sparax stays, settling outside of the firelight. Levnys sits next to Pica, glancing around, before turning her eyes to the carved curl of wood above them.

"Is this your doing?" she asks the darkness.

"Yeah," Davros' voice floats down. He's barely visible, perched cross-legged on the sleek timbers. "Will it work? Are you comfortable, Lucius?"

"Quite."

Levnys hands him his plate as Davros hums—a soft, sweet sound. The bard's magic surrounds them. Between Davros, Sparax, and Levnys, he's as secure as ever. He sighs. Why did it come to this?

They eat silently. Pica struggles to hold the bread with his blistered hands. Levnys finishes before him and disappears back down the gangplank. Several moments later, she returns with a steaming plate of roasted chicken and several goblets. She puts one goblet next to Pica, one next to her, and the last in front of the empty cushion.

Pica watches her with faint amusement. "We look like we are about to conduct an interview," he tells her.

She points at the food. "Eat. You need it."

He does, savoring the flavorful meat. He quickly finishes the second plate. Pica feels like he could curl up and sleep where he sits.

The first man emerges into the firelight after Pica finishes his first goblet of wine. He looks at the newcomer—an oarsman whose name Pica does not know. He settles onto the cushion. The man's left arm is a mess of tiny puncture wounds, his light skin turning into a giant purple bruise. He shakes, his face ashen.

"Wine?" Pica asks.

The rower drinks from the goblet. It takes nearly a full minute for the man to gather his nerves. "Hello, Regillus. My name is Nerie. You said we can tell you about those who died?"

"Please."

"I sit five rows back, I'm a *zygius*. Er, that's second level." He drinks with a shaking hand. "Been rowing for twenty years. Been on *Raven's Flight* for ten of them years. Tarxi sat above me, six of them. I know him real well. Knew him." His eyes mist over as he stares at the goblet clenched between his bruised fingers. "We heard the shouting about plugging them gaps. We was fast enough, them in front of us weren't. Those things burst in like nothing I seen before. They got Tarxi. I had my head down, so I don't see what happened, 'cept someone started shouting, making fire appear out of nowhere. I got the birds burned off me but in front of us...." He downs the entire contents of his goblet in one gulp. Levnys pours him another serving.

"Tarxi had no family," Nerie continues. "He was a slave before, like most of us. He was taken as a boy from somewhere north. Whole family was killed. Ralex bought him, freed him, gave him a job."

North. Fetocia. Pica wonders if it was his legion that took him. Likely. He tries to keep the sorrow from his face.

Nerie looks up from his goblet. His blue irises stand out sharply from the red of his sclera. Their pain is fathomless, and the terror is as sharp as a dagger.

"You said you're going to remember everyone. I want to believe you. I know people are real mad at you. We don't like seeing bodies burn on the Coast. But you did what you had to, so no more of them birds would come out. So I'm going to trust you. Remember Tarxi. He wanted to go to Isca and see that famous lighthouse. Go there and see it for him."

Pica drinks some of his wine. "I will do that as soon as possible, I promise."

"Thank you." Nerie drinks the rest of his goblet and departs.

Pica finishes his wine. Sparax comes over to refresh it. Pica cherishes the blessed numbness spreading through his limbs. He wipes his eyes with his wrists, trying to avoid the blisters on his palms. It doesn't take long for another crew member to approach them, then another. Pica converses with each one, committing each name and story to memory. Sparax and Levnys occasionally fetch more wine as the night stretches on.

Shouts come from the rower's camp, followed by the sounds of a scuffle. Ralex's voice carries through the cold night air, the words unintelligible. Pica longs to check, but he's helpless to move. What would he do? His presence would only make it worse. He drinks a long pull from his wine. This is his fault. Even without his magic, his fire causes pain. Perhaps he's better off without it, after all.

But if that's true, why does he feel useless?

Footsteps ring on wood. Sparax rises to block Laxu as the Caltavian steps into the firelight.

"Peace, Regillus," Laxu says. "I came to talk."

"Have a seat," Pica says.

Sparax gives the cook a long look before settling back down. Laxu sits across from Pica. His eyes remain angry, and the dark circles around them make them appear sunken. "Some of the crew tried to turn on Ralex."

Pica clenches his teeth. "Did anyone—"

"Yes, three. Itavus and Venel had no choice."

"I'm sorry it came to this."

"There's that word again. Sorry." Laxu sighs. "I don't like you," he says. "But you're good to your word. You didn't have to do this for us.

You could have retired to your cabin, but here you are." He takes a drink. "My brother's name was Cai. He wanted to go to sea ever since he was a boy. I wanted to follow him wherever he went. He was six years older than me and my role model." Laxu's eyes finally soften. "We are from a patrician family in Caltava, senate-class. Our father was upset when we left, but we promised to return as better men. We would get to see the world. We've done that, that's for sure. Ralex taught Cai to row, but I couldn't. Bad back. Cai was in the front when those things came through."

Pica tries not to wince. The man hadn't stood a chance.

"I heard he was drained instantly. An entire life like his is gone, and now I must pick up the pieces. I followed my brother around my whole life. I don't know where to go. How will I tell our family I couldn't bury him? They don't get to see his face as he goes underground." He clenches his fist on the table. "I want to be furious with you for burning those bodies. I want to tell myself it's some twisted sense of Gethki superiority, turning our tragedy into a chance to give a rousing speech. I can't, though. The more I think about it, the more I realize you're just a man, nothing more. You're doing what you think best. I can't hate you for that." He drains his wine, then reaches out his hand.

Pica takes it. Though the other man squeezes lightly, it sends agony rippling down his arm.

"I don't want any words of comfort," Laxu continues. "I don't want pity or reassurance. Remember my brother's name, and visit his grave in Caltava when we make one."

"I can do that," Pica tells him.

"Thank you." He rises and strides back down the ship without a second glance.

XVII
SCHOOL

Levnys

They do not fly out to hunt the next day. There is no need—thousands of fish gather offshore as an undulating mass under the spring waves. The razorback migration heads north to the Bay of Curia, where they will breed in the deep waters off the Gethki mainland. Fishing boats cast their nets into the bounty of life, hoping to harvest enough to feed their families for another year.

When the wind shifts, the scent of garum factories sometimes blows in from the island's north side, far away from the tiny town at its southern tip. Before they depart, she will brave the stench and inquire about purchasing more briny fish sauce for Lucius. Perhaps it will lift his spirits some after the loss of his magic. Seeing him in such a dejected state tears at Levnys' heart, and she finds herself lost about reassuring him.

The sound of claws on sand makes her turn her head. Kisara walks up to her, staring out over the sea. "Are we training today?" she asks.

"No," Levnys replies. "We should stay on the island."

"Are you sure? I'm feeling better."

"I am sure. It is important to get your rest." Levnys places a hand on her pupil's arm. "Spend the day with Seto."

Kisara glances over her shoulder. The wizard is hunched over a scroll, scowling, scribbling furiously with one hand while holding a hunk of bread with the other. "He's obsessed with figuring out the nature of those birds," Kisara says. "I'm not sure I could pull him away if I tried."

"Perhaps I can help you convince him."

A few minutes later, Kisara and Seto walk together hand-in-hand up the beach. Levnys smiles as she watches them. She has come to care deeply for Kisara, and it lifts her spirits to see her so happy, especially after learning what she went through.

It took Levnys many days to coax the story out of the pair. Even then, she only got the barest details. Seto was called to the royal harem to seal a rogue storm spirit some fool let loose, meeting Kisara in the process. The ritual of capturing it went awry, and instead of sealing it safely in the vessel Seto intended for it, the spirit's essence was fused into Kisara. The strange draconic form Kisara assumes is like lightning made flesh, a primal storm spirit which writhes and struggles on a psychic leash. Kisara locked it away, only letting it out when she was solitary or desperate.

That is until Levnys tore the thing out of its cage and cowed it, demonstrating her dominance and forcing it to listen. Kisara has taken over that dominance, and the two work together for now.

Levnys reaches the tent to find Davros at Lucius' side. The smell of steeping green tea fills the little pavilion. Magic hangs like a fog bank, tingling in Levnys' lungs. The bard is slumped against the side of the lounging chair, his eyes half closed, with his hand on Lucius' arm. Lucius' skin is clearer today, with less bruising. When he turns his head, his eyes are bright like polished coins. Levnys glances down at Davros, then back up. Lucius gives her a slight nod.

"Davros," she says, kneeling in front of him.

He twitches. A small smile plays on his lips. "Hi Levnys. Tea?"

"Yes, I will get it. You do not look well."

"'M alright." He yawns. "Waking up."

"Are you sure you are not using your magic too much?" Levnys presses. "You should not push yourself this hard."

"It's worth it." Davros sits a little straighter.

Lucius shrugs. "I tried to convince him. He's being stubborn."

"Ah. So you two are similar," Levnys says dryly.

Davros flushes. "This is important."

"She means it as a compliment," Lucius says. Davros turns his head to him. "She's right. You've been spending a lot of energy on me."

"I will go into the town today," Levnys says. "Would you like to accompany me?"

Davros blanches. He looks between her and Lucius, biting his lip.

"You should go," Lucius says. "I'll be alright for a few hours."

"Are you sure? I can get Sparax."

"He's busy. I'm doing better." Lucius puts his hand over his heart. "Promise. You know I can't lie to you with your magic inside me."

"Alright." Davros stares at Lucius for another long beat. "I'll go with you, Levnys. Can we have some tea first?"

Levnys carries Davros on her back along the wide cobblestone street. She expected him to balk at the suggestion, but he merely smiled and said, "That's a good idea."

Townsfolk call her name as she strides into the square. Children swarm around her while their parents call half-hearted warnings to be careful underfoot. Levnys crouches, lowering her head to let tiny hands pat her nose.

Davros plucks a few notes on his lute from her back, drawing more onlookers forward. "Would you like to hear a story?" he projects over the cheerful din. He does not raise his voice; instead, he uses magic to amplify it, letting it echo off the concrete buildings and thread through the morning air.

Stories. Of course. The bard must be full of tales from his homeland. The idea of hearing every single one thrills Levnys, and if he pairs it with a tune, that would be so much better.

"Gather around and listen to a tale of three little foxes." Davros' voice sails over the crowd, expertly weaving words and magic together. She gently noses aside the children and lifts her head to observe, unable to keep the smile from her face.

He is vibrant and flush with energy, as he is every time he performs. The lute is alive in his hands. The crowd reacts to every revelation, every twist and tangle, gasping when the little fox kits are in danger and cheering when they triumph.

When he finishes the story and plucks the last flourish, the crowd demands another. Then another. Davros plays for an hour before he begs off, bowing deeply from the elevated stage of her back.

"That was wonderful," Levnys says, putting her nose close to him.

Davros grins. "Thanks. It's always nice to have a new audience. Hold this, please."

He loops his lute strap over one of her horns. The magic of the enchanted instrument hums against her neck, intense and ethereal. Ava's magic. Davros slides down her leg and picks up the coins scattered on the cobblestones. She lowers her head, and he gently retrieves the instrument, inspecting it before slinging it onto his shoulder.

"Want to go to some shops?" he asks. "I have a bit more coin than expected."

"Very well." Levnys transforms, shrinking to her human form. They make their way to the plaza's edge, weaving through the loose groups of townsfolk. "What is it you want to purchase?"

"Clothes, mainly," he says wistfully. "What about you?"

"I was hoping to get something for Umile," she says, testing a theory.

"Oh. That's a good idea," Davros says, standing on his toes to look at the painted signs above the shops.

"You know who that is?"

Davros glances at her. "Lucius told me yesterday."

"How did you react?"

They reach the nearest shop. Davros peers in through the curtain and continues on. "I told him he's revealed two secrets now, without any in return." His mouth curls into a wry smile. "Other than that, it's good for a prince to already have an heir, right?"

"So it does not bother you?"

"Nah. Kids are alright." He ducks his head into another shop. "Bah, everything is too dull. I need bright colors."

She can hardly believe this relaxed person is the same nervous wreck they met a week ago. Davros slid so neatly into their lives. She can well understand Lucius' attraction to the enigmatic bard.

Davros hums as they move along the storefronts. They work their way through the town, visiting some and passing others. Davros purchases an orange *stola* and a set of bronze hairpins. Levnys finds a gift for Umile—a finely carved horse figure painted black. Davros snorts when he sees it.

"Perfect," he says.

They go north, walking along the cliffs overlooking the sea. When they are not far from the camp, Davros stops and looks over the water, chewing his lip.

"What is it?" Levnys asks.

"I'm sorry for running away," he says.

It takes Levnys a breath to realize what he speaks of. "At Ava's tavern." When he nods, she asks, "You reacted out of fear, did you not?"

"Yeah, but I was wrong. It wasn't fair."

"May I be straightforward?"

Davros chuckles and turns to face her. "Sure, why not?"

"You are correct. It was not fair. But you did not know us. Now, you do, and you have not fled again."

"But I'm still scared." He sighs. "I don't want to be afraid anymore, Levnys. How can I stop?"

Levnys holds out her hand. After a beat, he takes it, giving her an inquisitive look. "Come with me," she says.

She leads him down the beach to a rock jutting out into the water, where the surf swirls in eddies and whirlpools. Seafoam clings to its edges, reaching in tendrils like grasping fingers. The table of the stone is dry and flat and easily large enough for both of them. Davros falters for a breath, but he climbs onto the rock after her.

They settle so they look out over the water. The cliff's shadow falls over them, casting a cool shade and cutting the heat of the afternoon sun. They sit silently for a long moment, letting the sea sing her song— the rush of the waves, the crack of the surf. Seagulls add their voices, along with the splashing of migrating razorbacks, breaching to escape whatever is hunting them.

"What do you see?" she asks Davros.

"Beauty. Life," he says wistfully. "Death, for those fish."

"Could you empty the sea with a bucket?"

He gives her a sideways look. "Is this a trick question?"

"It is not."

"If you had a big enough bucket, I suppose." He taps his fingers on the rock in a quick rhythm. "It'd take a long time."

"Time," she muses, "answers your question."

"What question—oh." He stops tapping. "Shit."

"Also, like those razorbacks, you must do everything possible to survive. Fear is not a curse. It has kept you alive until now. I did not blame you for your fear that night, and I do not do so now."

Davros drops his eyes. "Ava told me not everyone bigger than me means me harm. She was right—again." His fingers scrape across the stone. "Why do this for me?"

"Are you not worth it?"

"No," he says emphatically.

"Why do you think so?"

"I—" He bites his lip. "I'm cursed. I don't deserve it."

"Hmmm." Levnys suspected as much. "There are many who disagree with you."

"Do you?"

She reaches out and puts her hand over his. He flinches but does not pull away. "Yes," she answers. She, too, has grown fond of him—perhaps with Lucius' influence, perhaps not—and wishes he would see that.

"Why?" he asks again, so softly she almost cannot hear him. "You and Lucius both. I haven't done anything special."

"You do not need to do anything to be loved, Davros," Levnys says. "You must merely be yourself."

"Yeah. I can't believe that anyone would like *me* the way I am." He stares out over the water. "No one wanted anything to do with me in Soutori. In Geth, everyone wanted to use me. It's a new feeling, being wanted with no bad intentions. This is my reality now, and I—" Davros voice catches. "It's taking a while to sink in."

"Time." Levnys watches the fish offshore swirl in an intricate dance. "It will get better, Davros. Trust me."

"I hope you're right."

They fall into a comfortable silence, letting the sound of the surf speak for a while. The splashing increases. All the razorbacks breach now. Some of them beach themselves as a silver shape catches Levnys' eye. Levnys cannot keep the smile from her face. "Do not be afraid,

Davros. She is a friend." She stands, her heart singing in her chest. How long has it been? "I will return shortly."

She dives off of the rock into the surf. Razorbacks crowd around her until she transforms, then dart away in alarm. She bellows her greeting with a full voice.

The return greeting is higher and joyful, and an old friend emerges from the school in a cloud of iridescent bubbles. The silver dragon is slender, long, and sinuous like a sea serpent, with short webbed limbs and elegant fins. They entwine together in an embrace, rising to the surface in their greeting dance.

"Levnys," she says. Her voice is as sweet and musical as Levnys remembers. "It is so good to see you."

"Zaitun," Levnys says, nuzzling her friend's cheek. "I was hoping to find you." She looks over at Davros. The bard watches them with widened eyes. "Come, join me at our camp. There are those I would like you to meet."

Davros bows deeply to Zaitun when introduced, Soutorian style. If the bard is afraid, he hides it, giving the silver dragon a polite smile. He seems to relax after she assumes her human form. Zaitun stands almost a head shorter than Levnys, as slender and delicate now as she is as a dragon. Her long silver hair falls nearly to her ankles in a shimmering braid. Midnight blue eyes, as deep as the sea, shine in the afternoon light. They make their way along the beach toward the ship's camp.

"Can we check on Lucius first?" Davros asks. Anxiety creeps into his voice. "I want to make sure he's alright."

"Of course," Levnys says. "I would also like to check on him."

"Who is this Lucius?" Zaitun asks.

"Levnys' lover and my—" Davros bites his lip and glances away. "Um, friend."

"Hmm. I see." Zaitun studies Davros for a few breaths. The bard's face flushes. As they crest the little hill and Lucius comes into view, Zaitun stops to stare. "Is that him, Levnys? What is he doing?"

Levnys peers into the tent. Lucius is leaning forward in his lounging chair, pondering a *lantriculi* board. Krakli stands over his pieces before picking up one of the flat wooden disks. He hops across the board and sets it carefully in a square.

Lucius squints. "Bastard," he says, a smile twitching at his lips.

The bird cackles at him.

"That's him," Davros says. "Looks like he found something to pass the time."

At the sound of his voice, Lucius raises his head. The smile he gives them makes Levnys' heart sing. "Hey, you're back. How was the walk?" He tips his head to Zaitun in greeting.

"Lucius, this is Zaitun, an old friend. Zaitun, this is Lucius, my lover."

"And prince," Zaitun says dryly. "You did not mention you are bedding a prince."

"It slipped my mind."

Davros hurries to Lucius' side, crouching beside his chair to place a hand on his arm. When they give each other a small smile, Levnys' heart soars.

"Tea?" Lucius waves his hand at the teapot, then stares at it for a breath. "Er, you'll have to heat it. Sorry. I'm unable to at the moment."

There is a catch in his voice. Davros' fingers tighten on Lucius' forearm. Krakli chirps and flies to his head, sending the painted *lantriculi* pieces scattering off the small table. Lucius drops his eyes to the ground.

"We will get you fresh tea," Levnys says gently.

"Alright," Lucius says, though it looks like he wishes to argue. He settles back onto the lounging couch with a groan. Davros' magic fills the small tent.

"Come, Zaitun," Levnys says.

They walk halfway to the galley before Zaitun says, "That man is in pain."

"Yes." Levnys glances back up the hill. "I am worried for him."

"The currents are not right," the water dragon continues. "I have heard rumors but nothing complete. Do you know what is happening?"

"Some." Levnys glances at the pavilion again. "I will tell you all I know."

Levnys joins Zaitun in her hunt that afternoon. They take turns driving the school into a tight ball and snatching fish that stray too close to their jaws. Her muscles burn with the exertion, but the thrill of the chase always energizes her, and doing this dance with Zaitun again means more than she can express.

Not long after her mother died, Levnys met the silver dragon in a hunt much like this one. Water dragons such as Zaitun fared the best against the paladin's scourge. Many of the eldest fled these waters when humans began traveling the seas, but the younger ones stayed behind. Zaitun was her first dragon friend, showing her many secrets of the Coast that Levnys' mother did not have a chance to.

Juvenile sea serpents join them, a rare sight so close to human habitation. Their presence concerns Levnys. While not as intelligent as dragons, her aquatic cousins—children of the sea goddess—are clever, resourceful, and opportunistic, to the bane of many a hapless ship. Their presence is a shift in the balance, a change in the delicate system of life in these seas. Such things do not happen without a reason. It is another sign that something dark transpires in those vast waters to the west, where the serpents call home.

The sinuous purple and black serpents grow bolder as the hunt continues. More than once, Levnys snaps at them when they try to take a bite out of her instead. One—the largest, nearly full-grown and covered in scars—throws its weight around, snarling at its comrades, and the others settle into an uneasy truce.

Their gills vibrate with low thrums in quick bursts and long tones. Only when Zaitun responds with the same strange noises does Levnys realize they are speaking. Her silver form is blinding against their dark hides, shimmering in the sunlight streaming through the water. Though they are much bigger than her, they seem to defer to her.

The serpents slip away after eating their fill. Levnys and Zaitun return to shore, hauling themselves onto the beach. They settle onto the sand close to the central fire. Zaitun nestles herself into the crook of Levnys' body, and Levnys covers her with a wing, cherishing the other dragon's sleek metal scales on hers.

"There is something I must ask, Levnys," Zaitun says after they are settled. "How is it you travel with paladins? Surely, their presence disturbs you."

"At first," Levnys admits. She relays the events of the last several weeks to her friend. "I have come to trust them with my life," she finishes.

Zaitun turns her head to regard the pavilion where Lucius rests. "I see. I will trust your judgment, Levnys, but perhaps the others will not be so understanding." Zaitun lifts her head to touch noses with Levnys—a comforting gesture. "I saw Okalth not a fortnight ago."

Levnys' heart sinks. While she would love to see Okalth again, she hopes they will not encounter him. This fragile thing she created, this peace with the paladins, may not survive the fire of Okalth's anger.

"We will swim that sea if we must, Zaitun," she says.

A *woosh* of air makes her raise her head. Sehuti backwings and lands on the beach, fanning his wings wide. Zaitun makes a low noise deep in her throat, a small growl of distress. "Levnys, what is that?"

"Sehuti is a plant dragon," Levnys says. "From Tekan."

"Is he a friend?"

"No," she replies, though she cannot call him an enemy now. "He tried to kill me three times. I do not recommend biting him."

Zaitun's lips peel back, revealing her curving, needle-like teeth. "Why is he here?"

Levnys nuzzles Zaitun's cheek. "It is complex. Do not be so alarmed." Levnys watches the nightshade dragon shake himself and fold his wings. "The paladins saved his life after that swarm of birds attacked him. He has not tried to kill me since."

Zaitun growls again. "I would not trust him."

"I do not."

"Yet you tolerate his presence."

"Yes. I believe that he will not act while the birds are a threat. He cannot fight them. I can."

Sehuti approaches them but settles on his haunches at a respectable distance. He bows his head. "A new face. Care to introduce me to your...friend, *drakaina*?"

"I am Zaitun," the silver dragon says. Zaitun trembles beneath her wing and no wonder. Sehuti is easily twice her size. Yet, she holds her head high, daring the nightshade dragon to try something.

"I am Sehuti." He grins fiercely at her. "It is good to see a water dragon. Perhaps I will need a drink later. There is so much poison water around."

Zaitun raises her chin. "You will find plenty of fresh water elsewhere. You must be a fool to fly where you cannot drink freely."

"Peace, Zaitun," Levnys says. She rests her head on top of her friend's muzzle. "He is trying to provoke you. Do not give him the pleasure."

"A little fun, *drakaina*, that is all." Sehuti dips his head again. "How is your recovery? Those birds did not treat you well."

"Kisara saved me in time. Some meat, some rest, and I will be whole soon," Levnys says, wondering if it is a genuine inquiry.

"Ah. I see." Sehuti shifts from foot to foot. He glances away, watching the camp activity. After a long silence, he sighs, turns, and walks away. What are his intentions? Although Sehuti has been nothing but polite, something remains off. Perhaps it is how he calls out in his sleep or the look in his eye when he stays at the group's perimeter. But Lucius also calls out, and Levnys has not been as welcoming to the old dragon as she could be.

Zaitun breaks into her thoughts with a nudge. "Did you not hear me?"

Levnys' skin twitches. "Sorry."

"I asked, where will you go from here?"

"Caltava, Aea willing. And you?"

"I was following the migration, but…" Zaitun turns her head to observe Sehuti, now wandering along the beach. "If those birds are as dangerous as you say, perhaps Sehuti is right. I want to travel with you if that is not too much of a burden."

Levnys' heart soars. "Of course, you may travel with us. I will be glad for every second of your company."

XVIII
LULLABY

Davros

Night creeps in as Davros plays from the rail of *Raven's Flight*. There's a chill in the air, sending rowers into their tents early. Davros listens intently to the stories of the crew as Lucius meets with each person in turn. Levnys sits at their makeshift table, sipping from a wooden goblet. The dragon appears relaxed but watches the scene with an intensity incongruous with her casual posture. Further down the deck, Sparax and Petrus play dice, placed squarely between the gangplank and the bow.

Lucius' outward ease in the face of lingering hostility baffles Davros. No matter how vicious the words against him get, no matter how many glares he receives, Lucius maintains his polite facade. And it is a facade. Davros can sense the weariness and quiet frustration that permeates Lucius' emotions.

Over the last day, several more of *Raven's Flight's* crew slipped away, bringing the ship's losses to over fifty. Ralex's only response was, "They are free men and may do as they wish."

Lucius isn't the only one presenting a facade. At least there's been no more violence, but only time will tell if that holds.

The last crewman departs. Lucius slumps on his cushion, leaning against the wooden bow wall. He has to be weary.

"Is it time to retire?" Levnys asks.

"Not yet," Lucius replies. "Let's sit a bit longer. Davros, would you like to join us?"

Yes. Yes, he would. Davros wavers. Levnys' eyes settle on him, softening. A war rages in his heart—there's danger in getting too close. Yet, Lucius' breath labors. Surely, he's in pain.

Concern wins out. He sets the lute on the deck and heads into the firelight. There's a space next to Lucius on the big cushion. Davros settles and tentatively places his fingers on Lucius' arm. His skin is warm to the touch. Inviting.

"Wine?" Lucius asks.

"No, thank you," Davros replies.

Lucius hands him a water skin. Davros drinks deep of the cool water—magically imbued. Lucia's doing, no doubt. Krakli lands on the table and shoves his head into a linen drawstring bag. The bird draws out an acorn and slams it onto the table several times before pecking it apart.

Davros raises his eyes to see Lucius watching him. "I wanted to thank you for everything you've done," he says.

"It's nothing," Davros says. A blush creeps along his cheeks as the intimacy of the situation sinks in. He's not sitting next to a sickbed, administering treatment. No, he and Lucius sit on the same cushion, sharing a drink, as the firelight dances around them. "I didn't do anything special," he adds, trying to deflect.

"Horse shit," Lucius says emphatically. Davros flinches. "You've been vital, and don't let yourself believe otherwise."

Davros takes a big swallow of water with shaking hands. No, it's not true. He lifts his head, drawn in by Lucius' earnest expression. Gods, he's so beautiful, so kind, so caring. Lucius lays his hand over Davros' fingers. *Ata*, the emotions within him make Davros lightheaded.

"Do you need to hear me say it?"

"Please," Davros says.

"Petrus told me how you saved my life. You have a special gift for healing. I've never seen anything like it."

Davros bites his lip. He can't stop looking into Lucius' eyes.

"*Raven's Flight's* crew is indebted to you. Surely, you've heard the picture they paint of you protecting them with silver fire and white mist. You're like a character in a folktale. Listen to me, Davros. You are a *hero*."

The conviction in Lucius' tone gathers tears in Davros' eyes. He wants to protest, opening his mouth to deny it all. He can't be a hero. Not him.

But Lucius believes it wholeheartedly.

"You're so hard on yourself," Lucius continues. "I want to get through to you. I want you to see what I do—someone beautiful, talented, and goodhearted. Gods, Davros, you overwhelm me. I find you endlessly fascinating and will never hide that from you. *Ever.*"

Davros lifts Lucius' hand to his lips. "I don't know what to do with a prince's affection, Lucius. Especially not one like you. I'm overwhelmed, too." He gives Lucius a trembling smile. "I'm getting better. Keep being you."

"I'm not the one who needs to hear that, Dav."

Dav. The nickname makes Davros' heart skip again. He glances over at Levnys. The dragon smiles at him. "I guess you're right. Both of you have been so good to me. I'm having trouble believing it."

"I'll tell you as often as I need to, darling bard," Lucius says. "I have no shortage of words for you."

Davros rests his forehead on Lucius' fingers. His face burns hot enough to make his cheeks hurt. "You're such a sweet talker."

Krakli chirps and looks up from his acorn. "*Sweet,*" he says.

Surprise threads through Lucius' emotions. He turns to stare at the bird. Krakli hops to the edge of the table to peer at their conjoined hands, then up at Lucius, who chuckles and rubs his familiar's head.

"What is it?" Davros asks.

"*Sweet. Bard,*" Krakli repeats.

"You have no idea how rare it is for him to say actual words."

"Oh. What does it mean?"

"Believe it or not, Krakli has a rather high opinion of you, being that you saved my life. Also, he likes your music. He knows my feelings for you and wants to ensure you get the point."

"That I'm, uh, sweet?"

"Well, you are."

Levnys moves to sit next to them. Their proximity would normally make him panic, but tonight is different. The last thing he wants to do is break this spell. How can both of them care so much about him? "I'm glad—" Davros stares at Lucius' fingers resting on his. "I'm glad you think I'm sweet. Can you—is it possible that you could say it sometimes?"

"I'd love to."

A loud *tink* causes them to look at Krakli. The magpie stands on Levnys' goblet, drinking the last dregs of wine. Davros finds himself smiling. "Thank you, too. Both of you. For understanding."

Levnys places her palm over Lucius' fingers, forming a stack of their hands. "I have said it before. It will take time for you to heal," she says. "Remember, you do not have to do it alone."

Davros' throat tightens. Tears form and fall unbidden, splashing on their conjoined hands. "I'll remember."

Ralex's hammer strikes with a clang on the bronze chain strung between the slave's wrists, ringing across the beach. The young man —a slender youth with matted brown curls and olive skin—stares at the captain with shock and anticipation. The cuffs drop to the sand as Ralex unlatches one, then the other. The youth lifts his head with trembling lips. Ralex thumps him on the shoulder.

"Why?" the youth asks. "You paid for me."

"Ain't no one a slave on my ship. You're a rower now. What's your name, kid?"

"Kafele, *dominus*."

"I ain't your *dominus*. Call me Captain. Kafele, you're gonna work hard, but we'll feed you, pay you. Hope you don't mind dragons." One of Ralex's officers steps forward, and Ralex addresses him. "Get him cleaned up, get a meal in him. Have one of them paladins check his health." Ralex nods to Kafele as Kisara lands nearby with another youth. This one's face is ashen white. "Next!"

Davros watches the proceedings with interest. Yesterday, Ralex started his search for new rowers. A motley mix of local boys, former slaves, and adventure seekers now mill about on shore, each with a new woolen tunic. Should the arrival be a slave, Ralex makes a show of striking their chains. In Geth, a freed slave would wear a special cap showing their status, but here, they blend in with the rest, free and equal.

Rowing practice begins the next day. At first, the rowers sit on shore, familiarizing themselves with the different commands and drumbeats. Each new rower is paired with a veteran. Most of the recruits are asleep before dark.

Davros is awake before dawn, gathering the dirty linens. Anxiety drove him out of bed early, so he makes the best of his time by cleaning—something he promised Ralex he'd do anyway.

Even with his magic, it's hard work. He has no strength, so carrying more than a few is impossible. Scrubbing each piece in a tub leaves his hands raw. Halfway through, he looks wistfully at the remaining pile—there's no way he can finish it by sunrise.

"Good morning."

He twitches. Kisara yawns and stretches as she walks down the gangplank. "You're up early," he says, trying to recover.

"So are you." She eyes his soaked clothes, then the pile. "Want some help?"

Davros almost declines, but the twinge in his shoulders makes him say, "Yes, please."

With Kisara's help, they finish as the sun lifts off the horizon. "Same time tomorrow?" she asks.

He grins at her. The work had gone a lot smoother with her help. "Sounds good."

When he reaches Lucius' tent, the prince greets him with a set of polished knuckle bones. "Ever played Tali?" he asks.

Davros nods. During his time in Geth, he trawled through the gambling dens and back-alley betting pools to scrape together enough coin to survive. He always had a knack for it, an extra sense for how the game would proceed. He picks up one of the bones, spinning it over his fingers. Real bone, not weighted—made for play, not for desperation. He flicks the knucklebone into the wooden bowl. Four carved dots stare at the sky. The clatter of bone on wood sounds as good as music. The fingers of his right hand tingle.

What do you want now? he asks his *pater*. Nylocke doesn't answer.

"Four right away, that's fortunate," Lucius says. He plucks the bone out of the bowl and joins it with three more in his hand.

"Want to wager?" Davros asks. The glyph on his hand pulses painfully. It wants him to take a risk. Of course, what is considered a risk in the demigod's eyes has always been a mystery.

Lucius laughs. "Sure, but I'm out of secrets."

They settle on coin—tiny copper pieces stamped with the profile of a dead emperor. Lucius' grandfather, Davros realizes. Will Lucius' face be the one on these coins someday? It's strange that the man sitting across the makeshift table is destined for the dragon throne. The most princely thing about him are those golden eyes that are always full of affection.

Davros wins every round. His little pile of copper coins grows into a heap. Krakli, observing from a nearby branch, chatters.

"Hush, you," Lucius says, waving his fingers dismissively. "One more?" he asks.

"All or nothing," Davros says.

Lucius puts a single gold coin on the table. Davros stares at it. He could buy food for a month with the coppers and that gold coin. If he saved them, he could afford the cheapest room in an *insula*. As sharply as a slap to the face, he realizes he no longer needs that. The circumstances changed so fast that his mind hadn't kept up. Even if the growing tension between him and the prince never blossoms, Lucius won't let him slip through the cracks.

He rolls and, for the first time, doesn't care if he wins. 4,2,1,1. Not bad. Lucius picks up the bones and rolls. 4,3,2,1. The best score. Davros lost. He *lost*.

Lucius looks up with a broad smile. Davros grins back as his glyph burns hot against his skin. Shivering pleasure courses through his magic. Payment made.

He doesn't care when Krakli shrills and flies to the table, stacking the copper coins one by one. Instead, he kneels next to Lucius' chair. The prince stretches out with a grunt of pain, folding his hands over his chest.

"That was fun," Lucius says. "You pick the next one."

Davros leans against the wood of the lounging chair. "Alright."

Another evening passes with music and Lucius' nightly conversations with the crew. In the morning, *Raven's Flight* wallows in the bay as the drums echo across the water. Davros can hear Ralex's bellowing from the beach. By sundown, the ship glides across the water with few hiccups. Some new rowers don't even reach their tents, slumping into sleep around a campfire.

It's late when Ralex comes to speak to Lucius at the bow. "There have been more casualties from those birds," he says. "Trading vessel was found adrift. No one survived."

Lucius' lips set in a line. "Did anyone burn the bodies?"

Ralex grits his teeth. "Yes."

Davros has trouble sleeping that night. Every time he closes his eyes, he sees the birds surrounding the rowers, the screams.

Seto joins him and Kisara the following day. The wizard doesn't help clean—instead, he sorts through the crate of scrolls delivered to their ship—missives and mail. Most of them are for Lucius, but one—a rich parchment letter sealed with wax—is for Davros. A quick inspection reveals the seal is enchanted with a simple yet elegant loop. Davros severs it with a tiny flick of magic, and the letter springs open.

Davros bites his lip as he reads the letter and rolls it up. Relief releases some of the tension in his shoulders—he still has a job waiting in Caltava. Another tiny burst of magic repairs the seal—Seto's eyebrow quirks at that.

"That's a master wizard's seal," he says. "How do you know how to use it?"

"My mentor is a wizard," Davros says. "I'm not, though," he adds hurriedly.

"Mm. But you know how to enchant." Seto turns on a heel, carrying the crate of letters. "Looks like you're useful after all."

Davros glances at Kisara. "Uh? Is he alright?"

"That's the happiest I've seen him in days."

After the midday meal, Lucius walks under his own power along a cobblestone street. Davros keeps his hand on his back, monitoring him. He can't help but notice how Lucius' muscles move under his hand. He keeps pondering it, stuck in his head like a catchy tune. His fingers trace Lucius' spine. Would he like it if Davros did this in the throes of lovemaking? The thought sends a pulse of need through him, quick as lightning and soft as a sigh.

Lucius' steps falter. He looks back over his shoulder in surprise, and Davros blanches. The magical connection is open. Lucius felt that, no doubt. Davros bites his lip and braces himself for the return of emotions. Will he push now that he's felt it? Davros can't stop him. All he could do is run away.

A thin hope plays along the threads of Lucius' emotions like a softly plucked note. He turns, lifting his hand slowly. Davros' heart speeds and the panic spreads through his chest like a creeping mold. Lucius' hand stops an inch from his cheek. His lips form a line when he sees Davros' expression. He withdraws his fingers. Lucius' concern, pain, and sympathy grow more acute as Davros struggles to control his breathing. Lucius' head drops. He turns away and takes another step forward, his eyes downcast.

Lucius avoids Davros' eyes on the way back to the pavilion. When he settles onto the lounging chair, he curls in on himself, putting his body as far away from Davros as the narrow space allows. Davros settles on the stool, tapping his fingers against his leg.

"You don't have to stay," Lucius says after a long pause. "I'll be alright."

He's lying. Davros doesn't need his magic to know that. But Lucius is giving him a way out. It'd be easier to leave. Levnys will be by soon. Surely, she'll lift Lucius' spirits. Davros sighs. No, this won't do at all. He rises from the stool, leans over, and tugs on Lucius' arm. "Come on. You need to lie flat. How are you going to walk tomorrow if you get a cramp?"

Surprise floods into Davros through their skin contact. "You're sure?" Lucius asks.

"No," Davros says truthfully. "But I promised not to run anymore."

Lucius slowly re-adjusts his position, settling onto his back with a groan. Dark circles emphasize the puzzled look in his eyes. "When did you promise that?"

Davros picks up the stool and moves it closer to the bed. His heart quickens as he sets it down at Lucius' side, close enough to touch his arm without leaning over. It's not the first time he's been this close to him. Why does he want to run?

Because now Lucius knows about the depth of his feelings, the breadth of his longing. His fingers tremble when he places them on Lucius' hand. "When we almost lost you," he says quietly.

"I see." Lucius' face softens. "I'm glad you stayed," he murmurs.

He closes his eyes and soon slips into sleep. Davros sets to healing him, mulling over the interaction. He wishes his fear wouldn't linger like a festering wound. The guilt every time he cringes from a sudden movement, when a raised voice sends him into panic—it only deepens the pain. Lucius' affection is as terrifying as it is thrilling. Lucius keeps his desire locked beneath the surface, never letting it rise above a low simmer. The reality that Lucius wants *him* sinks in the more time they spend together. It's there to read, as bright as the full moon.

What if, one day, he gets tired of waiting? What if it's all a lie, a ploy to make Davros vulnerable? No matter what he does, Davros can't shake that insidious paranoia.

The feeling lingers through the afternoon and gnaws at his sanity during his evening performance. After Lucius returns to his cabin, he sleeps on the lounging couch, curling around the pillow. It smells of honey and ginger—like Lucius after his bath.

You can't trust him. He'll hurt you eventually.

Even fitful sleep can't drive the feeling away. The pale dawn paints the eastern horizon with pastel softness. Davros bites his lip and scrubs the deck harder. The color bleeds from his knuckles as he grips the brush. If only he could wash away his doubts as easily as he does the daily dirt from *Raven's Flight's* deck.

He sends a wave of water across the wood with force, washing the grime over a pair of white draconic feet.

"Shit," he says. "Sorry, Kisara."

The half-dragon steps from the puddle and crouches next to him. "Need a break?" she asks.

Davros leans back on his heels. His back and arms ache from the exertion. It's bittersweet, a reminder that he's getting stronger.

"Yeah," Davros says.

They walk the narrow length of the trireme. The cooks move about, baking bread before the rowers awaken, filling the air with hearty aroma. Davros can't wait until he can eat it. Soon.

Kisara leans against the curved wall of the bow. Davros tries to relax, but anxiety gnaws at the edges of his sanity. He shifts from foot to foot, tapping his fingers together in a rapid series of mimed notes.

"Is everything alright?" Kisara asks after a long silence. "You seem on edge."

Davros' lip trembles. Lying at this point would be obvious. He feels fit to burst, of late. "No," he says. He puts his back on the wooden wall and slides down, bringing his knees to his chest. "I don't know what to do."

Kisara sits next to him, folding her legs under her and wrapping her tail around her knees. "It's about my brother, isn't it?"

Davros flinches. "How did you know?"

"Come now," she says. "I've seen the way you look at him."

"I'm afraid of him, Kisara," Davros admits.

"I know. I wanted you to say it."

Davros sighs. "Gods, I can't hide anything, can I?"

"Growing up in a palace means you learn to read people," Kisara says wistfully. "Why are you afraid?"

Shame clenches around Davros' heart like a fist. "He's big and strong. A lot of big and strong people have hurt me."

Kisara is quiet for a long moment. "Yesterday, Lucius said to me, 'I'm tired of looking like I'll hurt someone.'" Her lips form a line. "I understand how he feels."

Davros buries his face in his knees. "Shit. I didn't mean—"

"I know," Kisara says. "It's just—I hate it when people misunderstand him. I want to shake them and shout that he's not like that. He's been forced to fight, but the Lucius I know only wants to love. We grew up watching that rotten emperor abuse our mother. I'm only alive because some dragon wanted something that wasn't his. We were raised in a *harem*, Davros. Every day was a new horror." Davros raises his head. Kisara has hers bowed, staring at her clenched fists. "I tell you this so you can understand that Lucius will *never* hurt you. He'll never force you to do anything you don't want to because he'd rather die than cause that kind of suffering." She pauses. "Sorry. I want him to be happy. Levnys makes him happy. *You* make him happy."

"I want that, too," Davros says softly.

"Then let him in. Give him a chance to prove he's different."

Levnys often visits the pavilion. Sometimes, she curls as a dragon next to the tent, and sometimes, she sits with them in her human form. At first, Davros tried to slip away, but both objected. Davros' heart always warms when he sees how they interact and how comfortable they are together. As usual, Levnys manages to extract new stories from them. Davros had no idea how much knowledge Lucius had about the history of his empire, and sometimes he can't keep up with the complexity of their conversations. Still, he lingers, enjoying the company, never bored. Sometimes, they ask his opinion—something he feels thoroughly unqualified to give—but they always treat his words respectfully. The three of them settle into a comfortable companionship, and Davros' reality shifts once again.

News about the birds trickles in through trade ships and the occasional Gethki navy patrol. The letters increase, and Lucius spends most of his time reading. Ralex brings a mage to the tent, a woman in her late thirties with black hair braided and pinned, light brown skin, and a fresh set of puncture wounds. She wears a sky-blue cloak over a set of bronze ring mail, both stained with blood. When she sees Lucius, she drops to one knee in a crouching bow, right fist over her chest, in a military salute.

"Honored Regillus," she says. "I am Desmis, *Fulmina* of III Caltavia Auxilia."

Lucius returns the salute from his reclining couch. "Report, *Fulmina*."

"My unit was dispatched on a distress signal. We've encountered three swarms of hostile birds in the last two weeks," she says.

"How many war mages were deployed?" Lucius asks.

"Twenty, Regillus."

"How many in your unit are fit to fight?"

Desmis clenches her jaw. "Five, Regillus."

Lucius keeps his face stony, but Davros feels a surge of anguish through his hand on his arm. "Can you determine any pattern to their movements?" Lucius asks.

"We can't be sure, but all signs say they're moving toward Caltava."

Lucius does react now, sucking air through his teeth. "Shit," he says.

The war mage twitches. "Orders, Regillus?"

Lucius issues commands, and Davros' attention drifts. He doesn't want to imagine what those birds would do to the city. The very thought makes his blood cold. Surely, they can't let this happen.

After the mage departs, Ralex approaches. "We're leaving

tomorrow," he says.

Lucius leans back into the chair. "Good."

The next day, Davros tucks himself at the bow, out of the spray and wind. The air is crisp after the false promise of spring. Above, dragons circle—bronze, white, green. Zaitun paces the ship alongside a pod of dolphins, breaching every so often, the sun glinting off her silver scales.

Davros wonders where he will sleep that evening. Lucius walks under his own power now, albeit with a limp, so the pavilion will not be needed. There are little spaces on *Raven's Flight* into which he could tuck himself, but half the time, he's too anxious to be stuck in a place with no escape.

There's one option he's considered, but the mere thought of it causes his heart to clench. Lucius and Levnys would undoubtedly welcome him into their cabin. He could sleep on the floor, warm and cozy. Doing so would put himself at their mercy, but...haven't they shown him they mean no harm?

He hugs his lute closer to his chest, watching the paladins mill about on deck. Upon his insistence, Lucius remains in his cabin. The cold will do his body no favors. The prince relented, but sent Krakli with him, just in case.

Krakli chatters from nearby, as if sensing Davros' thoughts. The magpie ruffles his feathers and hops toward him, cocking his head.

"Hi," Davros says.

He taps his shoulder. Krakli settles onto it, fluffing himself out. Davros taps his fingers to the beat of the drums and hums softly, composing the first scraps of a tune. There's an idea forming, tiny and nebulous, and he pokes it around in his brain. It could work. Krakli whistles along, the magpie's quiet joy radiating through Davros' shoulder.

"Hey, that's pretty good," Davros says. "You like to sing, too?" At the *chirrup* of confirmation, Davros smiles. "You want to help me write a song?"

They spend the next two hours trading hums and whistles, and the idea coalesces. For the first time in months, Davros feels the special kind of contentment he gets from writing music. It's terrifying and breathtaking. He's going to play it for an audience one day. It's a goal he can cling to.

He dozes, waking when the ship leaves the water. *Raven's Flight* comes to rest on a tiny island with a narrow beach. Crewmen buzz with activity like industrious bees. There's more shouting than usual —the new members of Ralex's crew need to be shoved and moved about, and the preparations for the evening take twice as long. Davros spots Lucius moving slowly toward them.

"Don't tell him about the song," he whispers to Krakli. "It's a surprise."

Krakli chatters softly with an accompanying wave of amusement.

"He didn't give you too much trouble, I hope," Lucius says.

"Are you talking to me or the bird?" Davros asks.

Lucius laughs. "Good question."

The evening passes calmly once everyone is settled. There's no town on the island, only a few houses, and dinner that night is dried fish and lentils around small fires. A fight breaks out among the new recruits when one tries to steal from another. It's quickly suppressed with loud demands and even louder scolding. No whips, Davros notes with relief. Still, it makes the anxiety rise within him like a swelling sore.

"Good discipline," Lucius says softly. Levnys makes a small noise of agreement.

Davros plays his set. Fires smolder, and conversations fade. Davros tries to settle for the night in the crook of the bow. The shouting put him on edge, preventing him from entering a confined space. He hunkers into the thin bedroll and tries to sleep.

He dozes for a while, but every sound jerks him awake. He listens each time with his heart in his mouth, waiting. Nothing happens. He needs distance. He needs to get away.

A small chirp makes his heart wrench. He freezes. Heavy steps, uneven footfalls. He sneaks a peek above the edge of his bedroll. Tall, broad shoulders, long curly hair backlit by the wan light of the moon.

"Lucius?" he inquires.

The footsteps stop. "Davros? Why are you out here?"

Davros slowly sits up. "I could ask you the same thing."

"Couldn't sleep. You?"

"Couldn't sleep."

Lucius shifts his cloak and sits next to him, leaning against the wooden wall. "You first."

"Why me?"

"Princely privilege."

Davros sighs. "You have a lot of nerve. Fine. Most of the time, I can't sleep unless I'm hidden. I'm safe if people don't know I'm there. Sometimes I sleep there." He points at the storage hatch. "I couldn't tonight."

"Why not?"

"Don't feel safe. The arguing and shouting put me on edge."

"I see." Lucius pauses. "That's not all there is to it, is there?"

"No. People used me. Everywhere I went, someone hurt me."

"Is that why you're afraid of me?"

The sadness in his voice sends a lance through Davros' chest. "Yeah."

"What can I do?"

Davros shivers as the wind shifts, buffeting them with a cold blast. Lucius' heat radiates across the short distance between them. He wants to share that heat. Kisara's words whisper back at him: *Let him in. Give him a chance.*

He scoots over and leans against Lucius' arm. Surely, this is fine, right? His heart flutters, but this time, it's not fear. "Nothing," he says. "It's me. I'm trying, Lucius, I promise."

"I know."

"What about you?"

"Dreams," Lucius says. "Bad ones."

"What kind of dreams."

"I—" Lucius makes a frustrated noise in his throat. "I can't describe them. When I try, the words don't come out."

"So that means...."

"I can't talk about them. Not to Levnys, or Sparax, or my family — no one. Words fail me every time."

"There's nothing I can do to help?"

"I don't know."

Davros can sense the pain pouring off of him. Lucius is hurting, too. Wait. There *is* something. He pushes away the panic. He's realized that he will do anything if it helps this man. "Lucius," he says. "Can I...can I give you a hug?"

"Yeah. I'd like that a lot."

Davros rises to his knees and wraps his arms around the prince's shoulders. Lucius' arm comes up slowly, carefully. His hand rests light on Davros' back, so lightly it could be a feather.

"Is this alright?" Lucius asks. "Not too much?"

"A little more would be…would be alright."

The hand moves, and Lucius' arm wraps all the way around him. Lucius rests his forehead against Davros' shoulder, trembling. Davros' magic stirs at the touch, ready and waiting. He tries to ignore how good Lucius' arm around him feels.

"If you can't say the words, can I do it for you?"

"How?"

"I can read your emotions. I could express them for you."

"Will that work?"

"It could," Davros says. "Even if you can't say it, someone else feeling them will help."

Lucius is silent for a long moment. "Please."

Davros lets his magic flow in, steeling himself against the tide. He turns his senses to his magic, letting the world fade into a hazy blur.

"What is it you dream about?" he asks.

Lucius' breath catches—a stab of anguish. Regret. Remorse.

"Death," Lucius says through clenched teeth. "Blood."

Davros understands. "You've killed people."

Lucius sobs and nods against his shoulder. "Legion," he chokes out.

He finds his fingers in Lucius' hair. "You didn't want to fight."

Another nod, another sob. Davros' shoulder grows wet with the prince's tears. More emotion rises like a spring flood.

"Guilt," he says gently, and tears spill down his cheeks. "Gods, you're carrying so much of it."

"Blood," Lucius says again. "My…hands. My…fault."

"It's *not* your fault."

At those words, the dam breaks. Emotion as deep as the sea washes over him as Lucius breaks into ragged sobs. Davros is engulfed in it, drifting along, letting the tides of this man's despair spin him around. He distantly senses Lucius' other arm wrap around him and feels himself moving. He waits for panic to set in but feels nothing but Lucius' pain.

He runs his fingers through the prince's hair, whispering to him gently in Soutorian, letting the words flow from him. He recalls the words of an old lullaby, lilting, comforting, turning the speech into a quiet song, weaving his magic into it. Silver mist rises, shot through with pink, swirling in clouds around them.

Slowly, the tempest fades. Lucius' sobs lessen, slowing to deep and steady breaths. The tide of emotion ebbs, leaving Davros numb at the lack of it.

Davros becomes aware that he is sitting in Lucius' lap, leaning against his chest. His face heats as more intimate feelings brush against his senses. He fights the urge to shy away.

"Thank you," Lucius says softly.

He turns his head. The expression in Lucius' eyes is so soft, so tender. Davros can't look away. How long has he been craving something like this? To be cared for, needed, desired. He could have it. All it would take is for him to lean forward.

He can't. It's right there, and he can't. The pain rises in him again, the frustration at his inability to do *anything*.

The moment passes. Lucius releases him and turns his head away. Davros misses his arms already, a realization that makes him flush harder. He's glad for the darkness. He stands, lifting himself reluctantly out of Lucius' lap.

"Anytime."

"It's getting cold," Lucius says. "You shouldn't stay out here."

He's right, of course, but if anyone knows where he is, they could trap him. He'd have to fight.

"The best place would be in my cabin where it's warm, but..." Lucius stands slowly. "I understand that's too much."

"Y-yes," Davros says. "Sorry, I—" He bites off his apology. "I'll go into the ship, but what if someone tries to..."

Krakli whistles from the railing. Lucius holds up his hand, and the magpie flies to perch on his fingers.

"You're sure?" Lucius asks the bird. Krakli chatters. "Krakli will take watch and sound the alarm if something happens. His whistle can wake an entire cohort. Trust me."

Davros can't believe it. Even the bird wants to help him. He fights back the tears and nods. Lucius opens the storage hatch. Davros lights the candle perched on the ledge below. Yellow light flickers over the bags of flour and amphorae. Davros carries his belongings down and spreads out his bedroll. Lucius watches him from the top of the ladder.

"You can come down," he says.

Lucius does, stooping in the cramped space. "Smart. This is a good place to hide for someone your size."

"I'm not sure whether to be offended by that."

Lucius kneels and puts a hand on Davros' shoulder. Davros expects to find mirth in Lucius' eyes, but his face is stone-serious.

"I don't mean it like that. I like you the way you are and whatever form you choose to take."

"Even if I'm small?"

"What's wrong with that? You're closer to average than I am."

"I like you the way you are, too," Davros says. The words leave his mouth before he can stop them. His face grows hot.

Lucius smiles, and Davros smiles back. When did things shift? Here he is, inside this tiny space, with the man who scared him witless, and he's not panicking.

"We should both try to sleep," Lucius says.

"Yeah." Davros crawls into the bedroll, laying his head on the lumpy pillow.

Lucius watches him before he unclasps his cloak. He covers Davros with it, carefully stretching it out over his body. It's a rich man's cloak, thick and heavy, lined with fleece. Davros finds the subtle enchantment in it—a simple loop of magic meant to shed water. Lucius tucks the cloak under his chin. His fingers brush Davros' face and linger there.

"Sorry," he says.

Davros leans his cheek into them. "No, it's alright."

This close, he can't help but notice the curve of Lucius' cheek in the candlelight and golden eyes behind elegant lashes. Lucius leans forward. Davros can't look away. His lips get closer. Loose black curls shine in the flickering light as they fall to frame Lucius' face. Davros wants to entwine his fingers in them.

He can't move.

Closer. Lucius' jaw is dark with stubble. What would it be like, brushing against the skin of Davros' neck? He wants to see desire in Lucius' face, to read it in his magic.

He can't breathe.

Lucius' lips press gently against his brow. The kiss lingers before he pulls away. He strokes Davros' cheek, brushes his jaw, touches his lips. Davros feels it deep inside him, the fragile seed of something that wishes to grow —if only he would let it.

"Sleep well, sweet bard. See you tomorrow."

Davros watches him leave with his heart in his throat and turmoil in his chest.

XIX

CASUALTIES

Pica

Pica finishes belting his tunic as someone knocks on his door. "Come in," he says.

It opens slowly. Davros slips in and pushes it closed behind him. Krakli flies from his shoulder to the ledge of the window. The bird is asleep within seconds.

"I wanted to bring your cloak back," Davros says, holding it out.

Pica gently takes it, running his fingers over the soft fabric. "Your magic is in it," he says.

Davros' face flushes pink. "Um, I added another enchantment."

Pica looks at him in surprise. "You know how to enchant things?"

Davros grows redder. "Yeah, uh, kind of. I'm not very good at it, but I know the basics and..." He swallows. "I can do a few things."

"Well, don't keep me in suspense. Tell me."

"Oh, uh, you can't look?"

"Mm, no," Pica says. "I don't know anything about enchanting."

"Truly?" Davros raises his head. "Nothing at all?"

"Nothing at all."

"Oh, it's easy," Davros says and steps forward. "Lay your hand flat on the fabric, palm down."

Pica does as he says, spreading his fingers out over the wool.

Davros slides his fingertips along the back of Pica's hand before intertwining their fingers. The soft touch of his skin sends a thrill through Pica's chest.

"Put little magic into the fabric," Davros says.

"I don't have any right now, remember?" Pica reminds him.

"You do. Your paladin powers work. You're used to having so much that you can't sense what's left, huh?"

Pica smiles at Davros' earnest expression. "Let me try."

He focuses on his amulet. After a few seconds, the magic trickles from his fingers.

"Oh! There it is," Davros says.

A river of warmth sweeps his magic along with it. Davros steps closer and tucks himself next to Pica's side, pressing his body against his flank and hip. Pica realizes Davros doesn't notice what he's done. He tries to focus on what Davros is saying, pushing aside the glee at his proximity.

"...and then you find the core of the enchantment. They always have a base. Here it is, got it?" When Pica nods, Davros grins. "And from here, the enchanter pulls 'loops' and threads the magic through the object. The more starting points, the more complex the enchantment. This one's a single-loop."

Pica's magic brushes the delicate threads. They hum against his weakened powers, faint but detectable. Davros' fingers tighten on his, and he feels a stronger enchantment, a braided rope instead of a single strand. It buzzes against his senses, vibrating like a plucked lute string.

"Here's what I did," Davros says. "I made it easy to find when your magic returns to full strength. The other stuff may be too subtle for you. Ah, no offense."

"None taken. If it comes back to full strength."

"It will," Davros says, waving his hand. "Alright, here's the access point. Touch the thread with your magic and concentrate on the word 'lullaby.'"

Pica does as he is told. The song Davros sang to him last night plays in his mind. The voice is similar but higher and more delicate. Something in Pica stirs at the sound, a sensation of longing and deep comfort. His heart soars at the gentle Soutorian words, lilting and modulating. Perfect.

"I hear it," he says softly. "It's beautiful."

"I thought it would help," Davros says. "Whenever you're hurting and can't express the words, you can listen to the lullaby."

"You did all this for me?"

Davros swallows and lowers his eyes. "It's the least I can do for someone like you."

"Davros, listen to me," Pica says, leaning forward. "I'm just a man. My birth doesn't make me special."

"No. It doesn't." The corner of Davros' mouth curls into a smile. "It's everything else about you that does."

Pica pulls his hand away, sets the cloak on the bed, and then turns to face Davros. Pica gently hooks a finger under his chin as Davros tilts his face up.

"Thank you," Pica says. "It means way more than I can express."

Davros leans closer, sliding soft fingers along his cheek. "Try?"

The tiny quirk of his lips captures Pica's attention, holding it fast. He wants to trace their curves, feel his breath, taste the longing in his magic. He bends forward slowly enough for Davros to pull away. He doesn't. Their lips meet—soft, tentative, trembling. Pica can sense his fear, the simmering anxiety. He'll run. Pica is sure of it. He immerses himself in the moment, cherishing every second he can before the inevitable parting. The coarse brush of stubble against his chin. A quickening heart pulsing against his fingers. The surge of anxiety, of excitement, of a growing need mirrored between them.

Davros' fingers travel along Pica's cheek to tangle in his hair. Lips part, eagerness surges, sweet like honey. Davros presses close, standing on his toes to kiss Pica harder. The moment stretches, expands, and Pica is consumed by it, forgetting everything but their lips and tongues exploring each other for the first time. Tension builds like a drawn bowstring, taut and quivering. Electric pleasure chases Davros' fingers as they travel over Pica's chest, down his stomach. The whispering hunger in Davros' aura grows until it engulfs them both.

Pica's body responds with force—he wants to spread Davros' lithe body beneath him on the bed, to kiss and touch him until he begs for release. Davros' whimper of need nearly makes the urge a reality.

He holds it back. Beneath the growing desire in Davros' aura, beneath the delicious electricity and tantalizing pulse of his magic, the fear and anxiety lurk like a hungry creature in the fathomless depths of the ocean, ready to rise and consume the traumatized soul in his arms. Pica pulls away slowly, letting Davros catch his breath.

"Lucius," he whispers. "Gods, Lucius...you..." He mutters a few words in Soutorian.

"Hmm?" Pica inquires. "What was that?"

"Brain scrambled. Give me a minute." He leans his forehead against Pica's chest.

"That good, huh?"

Davros laughs softly. "You're such a bastard sometimes—you know that, right?"

"I know my father, unfortunately." He brushes his lips against Davros' hair. "I understand if you don't want me yet."

"I—" He looks up and sets his jaw. "I do want you. I want every part of you. You're charming and goodhearted and so beautiful you almost blind me. But...but I'm not *ready*." His fingers tighten on Pica's tunic. "I know you won't hurt me, but part of me won't listen. I know how much you want me. I want it to, but...I can't. I'm sorry. Gods, I wish I weren't so weak."

"Hey, don't talk like that," Pica says. "If all you ever want from me is a hug, I'll be happy."

"I want a lot more than that, Lucius," he says. "The way you kissed me, I...I want to know what else those lips can do."

Gods. When he talks like that, it drives Pica mad. He pulls Davros' magic into him, letting him experience the pang of need those words elicited. "Don't tempt me, sweet bard."

Davros inhales sharply and bites his lip. "Mm. Uh. I asked for that."

Pica chuckles. "Yes." He cups Davros' chin. "Even if you told me I could have you right now, no holding back..." He leans forward and kisses him again slowly, sensually. Davros melts, leaning into Pica with half-closed eyes. "...we don't have time."

Davros swallows. "We don't?"

"We're expected out there." He tilts his head in the direction of the door. "If you think I'm going to rush through the first time making love to you, you are sorely mistaken."

Davros flushes scarlet. "Oh."

"But that's for later. If you decide to be with me, tell me exactly what you want to do. Then, and *only* then, will I act on it. Clear?"

Davros seems a little taken aback. "I-yes. Of course, very clear." He gives Pica a small smile. "Sorry, uh, I'm not used to the lack of pressure."

"Get used to it from me," Pica says. "This is the way I am. *Gods*, Davros, you're right. I want you so badly it's painful, but that doesn't mean I get to have you. That fact should *not* be unusual."

Davros straightens and raises his chin. "No. But it is, and so are you."

Pica shivers as he sits beside Levnys on the beach, pulling his cloak around him. She's in her dragon form, eating a sea creature. He positions himself so her body blocks the biting north wind.

"You are cold," she observes.

"You're not?"

"It is not pleasant, but I am fine."

"How? Aren't you cold-blooded?"

"No."

"Oh." He waits for her to explain, but she takes another bite of her...whatever it is. He changes the subject. "I got a kiss today."

"Sparax?" she asks absently.

"Davros."

She pauses mid-bite, her bloody teeth gleaming, then turns her head. "Truly?"

"Yeah. He also enchanted my cloak with the song he sang last night." Pica touches his cloak with reverence. The effort must have taken Davros hours.

"I am pleased," she says, showing him a terrifying smile.

"I'm going to believe you."

"I hope that you get more from him."

"Me too."

She's about to reply when her eyes grow wide. She jerks her head to stare at the sky. Pica squints but sees nothing.

"Levnys?" he inquires, nudging her.

"Okalth," she says with apprehension. "He is here."

"Who is Okalth?"

"A survivor of the paladins' purge," she says. "He will not be happy you are here."

"What makes him any different than you?"

"You will see," she says. After a beat, she adds, "He is also the father of three of my children."

"Oh. So I'll like him." When Levnys looks at him sideways, he shrugs. "What, you have good taste."

"This is not a joking matter, Lucius," she says. "He does not like paladins."

"Not much I can do about it. I could hide, but that only delays the inevitable."

The silhouette of a dragon is visible. Levnys rises to a sitting position and bellows a greeting. Okalth responds with a resounding roar. His scales are pinkish-orange, gem-like, fading to red at the tip of his tail and clawed feet. The webbing of his wings sparkles with gold, back-lit by the sun. His horns are dull black and wickedly curved, matching the spurs on his wing joints. A "lesser dragon," as Levnys would call them, but there's nothing lesser about this one. Marring his skin are ragged scars along his flank and legs, along with swaths of scar tissue—burns, on a fire dragon.

Pica feels naked without his senses. Now would be a wonderful time to know if the big dragon means him harm. He stands, settling his cloak around his shoulders, and raises his chin.

"Orange?" he asks Levnys. "That's an unusual color for a dragon."

"Okalth is an unusual dragon." She glances at him. "Lucius, do not antagonize him. Leave if things get heated."

"Um, I didn't plan on starting a fight."

"It is not you I am worried about."

Okalth's wings send the dead leaves into a gale. They curl and blacken as he lands. Fire ripples over his body with flickering flames of red and orange.

Zaitun beaches herself, dripping water onto the cold sand. "I found him while hunting. I have told him about the birds."

"Okalth," Levnys says. She steps forward. "You came."

"Levnys, it is good to see you." Okalth's voice is a deep bass that rumbles the ground. "Thirty years, is it? How do our daughters fare?"

"They are well in the commune. Have you been lately?"

"I do not want to scare the young ones. I know what I am."

Okalth's yellow eyes turn to Pica. Flame curls from his nose and mouth as he peels his lips back from his jagged black teeth. Pica doesn't look away, doesn't *move*. Some of those teeth are bigger than his hand.

"Explain, Levnys, why you are standing five feet from a paladin?" he growls. "Several paladins," he adds.

Petrus and Sparax step up behind Pica. Sparax puts a hand on Pica's shoulder. Okalth's lips peel back a little more. He regards Pica's scales, then he lowers his head. Sparax's fingers tighten.

"A prince. How quaint. I don't sense your fire, Regillus. Are you one of the weak ones?"

Pica suppresses his irritation. "It's temporarily unavailable," he says. *I hope.*

Okalth snorts. Fire licks the air inches from Pica's face. "I see. Tell me, have you ever killed a dragon?"

Levnys takes a step forward. "Okalth, this is not the time for —"

"Yes," Pica says.

A low growl trembles the ground. "You are bold to admit this, knowing what waters you sail."

"No need to lie. You didn't ask what the dragon did to deserve it," Pica says, raising his chin.

"By all means, defend your deed. If you can."

Pica ticks off numbers on his fingers. "One, he took young humans from the local villages and used them as servants. He either forgot they needed to be fed or didn't care." Okalth's eye twitches. "Two, he increased his hoard by taxing the local populace. Those who didn't pay got eaten. Three." Pica's voice catches. "Three. He wouldn't stop when my legion confronted him. We tried everything. Each time we offered, he would destroy another village. After the third attempt, I led the team that killed him. I begged him to see reason, that he could live in peace if he stopped doing cruel things. He refused."

Okalth's lips descend. "Tell me his name."

"Mozzia," Pica says. "Mercury dragon of the Shumoth bloodline, in the north. His mother cursed me for killing him and thanked me for returning his bones to their family's lake."

"How noble. What do you think about Contradraco and their... mission?" He spits the last word.

Pica sneers. "I'm happy *my* Order got to kill every last one of those murdering bastards."

Okalth pulls his head back. He studies Pica for a moment longer. "Very well. I was curious why Zaitun and Levnys would willingly travel with a group of paladins. I do not understand, but no matter." He flexes a clawed hand. "Know this. I will tolerate your presence. I will work with you to rid my Coast of those foul birds." Flame kindles to life in his palm. "But if I decide you are a harm to my friends, I will burn you to black bones. Is that clear?"

Pica tilts his head in acknowledgment. "Perfectly."

Only after the dragon departs does Pica let himself relax. Sparax and Petrus both slump. Levnys' rump hits the sand.

"*Shit*," Sparax says. "Let's stay on his good side, or at least his not-bad side."

Pica's attention is on Levnys. Her head droops, watching Okalth go.

"Hey," he says. She glances at him. "It's alright. No one got burned."

"I did not want to choose between you," she says softly. "I am glad that I did not have to."

Petrus and Sparax each pat him on the shoulder and slip away. Pica walks toward her and lays a hand on her foreleg. "You care about him."

"He is dear to me. It pains me he is so angry, especially when it is directed at you."

Pica sighs. "I'm not particularly happy about it either."

"You are not upset?"

"I'm annoyed I'm being judged based on the actions of some bastards who died 150 years ago." He leans against her. "I'll work with him. He wants to protect his home. That's all I need."

Late that evening, Pica is about to extinguish the candles when Levnys gasps. "Lucius," she whispers. "Davros is outside our door."

Pica rises out of bed. "You have good ears," he whispers back.

"I did not hear him. It is his magic."

Pica cracks the door. The cold air outside of the enchanted cabin instantly chills his bare skin.

"C-cold," Davros stutters. "Help."

Pica pulls the door open. Davros stumbles in, and Pica quickly closes it again. Davros stands there, shivering uncontrollably, clutching a bedroll and a thin blanket. Pica gingerly takes it from him, setting it aside. Davros' face has turned gray, and his pupils are dilated. Pica recognizes the signs at once.

"We need to get you warm," Pica says in a gentle but affirmative tone. "We'll take off everything but your loincloth. No, don't try, let me."

Davros doesn't protest; instead, he nods. Pica leads him to the bed and guides him to sit. The complex laces of his split-toed boots give Pica trouble, but he manages to get them off, then the other clothes. Davros' chest is pale and drawn, with gray veins standing out sharply from his skin.

"L-Lu—"

"Don't try to talk yet," Pica says. "Lay down."

Davros does as he is told. Pica stretches out next to him, pulling him close to his body. Davros buries his face against Pica's chest.

"Levnys, the blankets. Everything you can cover us with."

She piles Davros' blanket and bedroll on top of the covers. Time passes with agonizing sluggishness as Davros' violent shudders turn into shivers, then slow.

"Davros," Pica says. "Try talking now."

"H-hi," he says, his voice muffled. "'M alright."

"Can I check?"

"Mhm."

Pica conjures what magic he can. "You were good to come in when you did," he says. "Your body temperature is low but not deadly."

He frowns. Although today was unusually cold, Davros' temperature is *too* low. His body shows many signs of extreme stress —a laboring heart and weakened muscles, tiny signs forming a big picture. Pica doesn't pry. Instead, he goes through a familiar routine, checking Davros' extremities for frostbite. Finding none, he withdraws his magic.

"You're going to be alright," he says. "You get to keep your fingers."

"That's good," Davros says. "I need my fingers."

Levnys makes noise for the first time since Davros arrived, chuckling softly.

"Sorry to intrude, Levnys," Davros says to her.

"You should have come here sooner," she replies. "Had I heard of your situation, you would not have slept another second in the cold." Pica shrinks from her pointed look. "You will *not* be doing so again."

Davros makes a choking noise. "*Zata*, Levnys."

At Levnys' inquiring look, Pica clarifies, "That's an affirmative."

"Um. I'll sleep on the floor, though," Davros says in a small voice. "Once I'm warm."

"Let me know when you're ready," Pica says.

"Not yet." He snuggles deeper against Pica's body. "This is very nice."

His cheek against his chest, the weight and presence of his magic— nice doesn't come close to how good Davros feels in his arms. "It is," Pica agrees.

Within a minute, Davros' breathing deepens. Pica looks up to see Levnys watching him. Her smile grows. He doesn't want to move a single muscle lest he shatter this moment. Levnys—beautiful, wise Levnys—gets it. She kisses him on the temple before she rises from the bed and sets to spreading bedrolls out on the floor. Pica rests his lips against Davros' hair.

He drifts. Levnys leaves the room and returns with more blankets, and Pica knows he must soon let go, if only for the night.

He stumbles through fire and death, scenes of carnage wrought by his hand. Everywhere he turns, there's more. His hands, burning. His hair, soaked. His heart, heavy. He pushes on, trying to run from the piles of bodies stacked like wood along a dirt lane. Away from the clouds of crows that call out in the charred air. Away. He can't get away.

"Bathe in moonlight, blessed suroribi.*"*

Music. A voice like delicate porcelain, singing the Soutorian lullaby. It fills his senses like an airy cloud, shimmering, sparkling. Cherry blossoms surround him as branches sprout to shield his view of the bloodshed.

"Sing, sweet suroribi. *Dance, sweet* suroribi.*"*

The fires fade. His whole body tingles. The panic subsides. Through the blooms, a snow-white fox spirit in a pink kimono dances with a pair of finely wrought fans. Five tapered tails move like water behind her, restless. Long hair floats like spider silk, shimmering white in the swirling winds. She looks at him with silver eyes and smiles.

"Bathe in moonlight, blessed suroribi."

Pica feels the dream slide away. Instead of his stomach clenching, the nausea fades. Davros lays across his chest, singing softly, as Levnys' cool hand moves hair out of his face.

"Sing, sweet *suroribi*. Dance, sweet *suroribi*." Davros' voice trembles as Pica's arms tighten around him. "I have you, Lucius. It's going to be alright."

Time passes quickly as *Raven's Flight* moves from island to island. They travel further southwest each day, chasing the birds along the rich trade network, ever closer to Caltava. Every morning, Levnys and Pica have breakfast together, eating fresh-baked bread and stew — fish one day, vegetable the next. Davros always makes himself scarce at these times, finding one excuse or another to disappear. Pica resists the urge to pry, but is saved from the necessity by Laxu. The Caltavian, who has remained icily cordial to Pica, mentions offhand one day that Davros only takes tiny portions, requesting dried meats and fermented vegetables.

Each afternoon, they land and scour the island for supplies to feed their crew and prepare for further encounters with the blood-drinking birds. Often, Pica is brought along to a wizard tower here, a mage's shop there, as Seto, Davros, and Kisara purchase raw materials for enchanting. Most of it is carried on *his* back, which Pica accepts with amusement. At least he's useful for something.

After the music is done and the fires smolder to embers at the end of each evening, Pica reads his new books by candlelight. Levnys joins him occasionally, but equally often, she lingers with her friends until deep into the night, appearing in their bed long after the candles are extinguished. Davros sits with him every time, reading along or asking for translations. The bard's confidence grows with each passing day and, with it, the tension between them. Pica lets Davros make each move, and what starts with tentative kisses soon turns into wandering hands and eager lips.

Pica's dreams continue. Davros joins them in bed, pulling Pica from the dreams without waking. Pica's stomach is grateful for the break. It's the first time he's gotten a whole night's rest in months.

When Pica's not sparring with his Order, he keeps Seto and Davros company as they enchant, stacking strips of bark in a neat and ever-growing pile. After the third day, Kisara joins him with two sets of bone needles and several rolls of leather. They cleaned out most of the tanneries they encountered, and now they set to work. Pica cuts the leather to shape while Kisara stitches the pieces together. Crewmen openly stare when he takes a needle and sets to helping Kisara with the tedious task.

One day, a commotion draws Pica's attention. Okalth and Sehuti face off down the beach—the fire dragon's nostrils streaming flame, the plant dragon cringing away from him, thorns bristling. Both have their teeth bared. Pica approaches, unsure what he plans to do. It's not like he could stop them.

"—surrounded by enemies!" Okalth snarls. His black teeth are backlit by roiling flame. "I should roast you where you stand, you overgrown weed."

Sehuti's tail lashes, dragging lines through the sand. "You don't understand!" he growls back. "None of you understand."

"Then enlighten me. Quickly."

"You would not listen to me." Sehuti's wings spread threateningly, his thorns bristling, tail lashing. Crimson rings the dragon's chartreuse iris, pulsing like a heartbeat. His legs tense, quiver like he plans to lunge at Okalth. Sehuti clenches his eye shut for a long breath. When he opens it again, the crimson is gone, and he rocks back, defensive again.

What was that? Now is hardly the time to ask. Pica stands well away from the quarreling dragons, pondering the situation. On one hand, Okalth has the right to be angry, given what Sehuti did. Conversely, the nightshade dragon has been civil, albeit a touch standoffish. At what point do a dragon's—or human's—past deeds stop reflecting on their current selves?

A stream of water shoots from the sea. Both dragons recoil away from it. Zaitun storms up the beach, dripping. "Are you two hatchlings? Stop this at once." She interposes herself between the two much larger dragons. Sehuti ceases immediately, his thorns disappearing beneath his foliage.

Okalth continues to snarl. "What is the meaning of this, Zaitun?"

Levnys appears next to her. "I did not tell you what happened so you could fight like animals, Okalth," she says, blocking Okalth's path. "Come, do not do such ugly things."

Sehuti eyes the rest of the dragons for a long moment, slowly backing away. He keeps his head high as he turns his back, then strides down the beach to lie in the thick vegetation.

Pica follows him. The nightshade dragon turns his head away. "Do not bother with empty words, mage," he says. "They are your friends. I am not."

"Okalth isn't exactly a friend," Pica says. "What happened?"

"He threatened me. That is all." Sehuti curls tighter on himself. "I am fine. You do not have to comfort me like I am a brooding sproutling."

Pica recalls the crimson in the dragon's eye. "You sure there's not something bothering you?"

"Leave me be, mage."

Pica sighs. "Alright. If you want to talk, you know where to find me."

Sehuti gives no reply, shoving his head beneath his wing.

No further incidents occur. The paladins and Sehuti stay well away from Okalth and him from them. The orange dragon proves helpful to their efforts, especially when Seto convinces him to contribute his magic to their enchanting efforts—it turns out the fire dragon is also a fire mage. Pica is doubly glad things didn't escalate. He often catches Okalth watching him, tracking his every move.

Several days into their travel, a booming roar makes Pica look up from his scroll. An enormous dragon, black as jet, approaches their beach. Sunlight shines off a hide made of jagged rock—a mineral dragon, obsidian, no doubt. The dragon back wings, sending sand and debris careening over the beach. Eyes the color of flint shot through with orange track the movement of the camp. The dragon dips her head as Pica introduces himself.

"Greetings, Regillus," she says in an enormous, feminine voice. "I am Gythu." Her rock-encrusted head sweeps side-to-side, observing the activity on the beach. Most of the crew stare open-mouthed at the dragon. Nose to tip of tail, she is almost as long as *Raven's Flight*. Sehuti watches the new arrival with one widened eye.

"I'd offer you wine," Pica says, "but I'm afraid I don't have a goblet your size."

Gythu snorts. "You have a sense of humor, Regillus. Perhaps we will get along."

Pica laughs. "I don't want to see what happens if we don't."

"Worry not. You will find me agreeable." She dips her head. "I must greet Levnys. We will speak later, Regillus."

"Call me Pica."

"Very well. Excuse me."

Gythu appears at their fire that evening. Pica almost misses the diminutive human form in the darkness. Her ink-black skin shimmers in the firelight. Instead of hair, jagged slivers of black glass sprout from her head in rough spikes. Pica hands her a goblet of wine.

Soon, the colossal dragon is a regular at their nightly gatherings. She takes to Calvus especially, quietly discussing the finer points of religion and culture. Pica has never seen the Grandmaster so cheerful.

Levnys and Davros grow closer, too. They spend much of their time in the cabin listening to one story or another. Davros always has a new folktale, poem, or anecdote. One morning, Pica returns from his bath to find Levnys seated at Davros' feet, the latter braiding the former's shimmering hair. Pica's never heard Levnys giggle like that before. Sometimes, the two of them whisper as they snuggle along Pica's body, one on either side. He doesn't mention it, but he finds the most peace in those moments.

After a week, they encounter the first casualty of the birds. The dragons circle above, ready for danger, but the battered trading ship is silent. As they pull next to it, Davros gasps.

"Oh. Oh gods," he whispers. His fingers tighten on the rail. "I know that ship."

Pica puts a hand on his shoulder, expecting to find sorrow in his emotions. Instead, he finds vicious glee. "Davros?" he inquires. "Are you—?"

Davros hops on the rail, then leaps the distance between the two ships. Pica curses. Ralex shouts orders as draconic shadows fall over the doomed ship like funerary shrouds.

Pica is about to follow Davros when a hand lands on his shoulder. "Wait," Lucia says firmly. "Don't be rash. They're bringing the gangplank."

"But—"

"You'll be the first across." Her voice softens. "He'll be fine, Lucius."

An eternity later, the crew finally has the gangplank balanced over the railings of both ships. Pica crosses as soon as it settles. Bodies litter the deck, drained dry.

He finds Davros at the stern, standing over a slumped figure garbed in finery soaked with blood. Pica puts his arms around his shoulders. Behind them, voices float somberly in the still air.

"He asked me to drink wine with him," Davros says. "It was drugged. When I woke up, I was locked in a cabin. He gave me to the quartermaster the next day." Black anger rises in his emotions. "I hope he suffered," he hisses. "I hope they all suffered for what they did to me." He kicks the desiccated body. "Now I get to have the last laugh. Good riddance." Pica bends forward, pressing his face into Davros' hair. "I don't care if it makes me evil. They deserved it."

"I believe you," Pica whispers.

At those words, Davros slumps. The anger drains from him. Davros turns around and buries his face into Pica's tunic. "Gods curse it," he says. "They did so many bad things. Why does it hurt?"

"Because you're not evil, Dav," Pica says. He strokes Davros' cheek. "They hurt you, but they were also human. It could have been you. You lived because you got away. You can't feel guilty about that."

Davros' fingers tighten on Pica's tunic. "How did you know?"

"I've...been there, too." The words come out easier than Pica expected. "If you want to talk about it, I'm here."

"Not yet," Davros says. He raises his head. "Can we go? I...don't want to be here anymore."

"Do you want to watch it burn?" Pica asks softly.

Davros shakes his head. "No."

They return to their cabin. Davros curls in Pica's lap as the roar of the burning ship fills the afternoon air. Drums pound as *Raven's Flight* moves forward, and Davros slips into fitful sleep. Pica holds him until they put ashore.

Not long after, Levnys enters the cabin and settles beside them on the bed. "We gathered supplies from the ship," she says. "It is good you did not witness what was below decks." She gingerly touches Davros' cheek. "How is he doing?"

"Coping," Pica says. "It's done, then?"

"It is done. Okalth and Gythu left nothing but ash."

"Good."

They find more stricken vessels the next day. Each time, the ships burn, and each time, Davros' funeral dirge casts its somber tone. Pica stands by him with smoke-swollen eyes. That night, the dirge joins his dreams.

One night, Pica and Davros begin their evening with their usual reading session, but this time, something shifts. The scroll they were reading lies forgotten as they stretch out together. Davros' head tilts back, and Pica's mouth explores the lines of his neck and shoulders, running fingers along the smooth skin of his upper chest. Davros' fingers entwine into his hair, his breathy gasps and alluring aura driving pleasure straight to Pica's groin. He wants more, so much more. Pica's fingers trace down Davros' slim stomach, over a hipbone, along the hem of his *exomis*. A gasp turns into a soft moan. The intensity of his magic turns Pica's vision white. The hand in his hair tightens. His fingers slide along Davros' thigh.

"Lucius," Davros whispers. "Do you want me?"

Pica presses his hips against his lithe body. The desire is a living thing now, pulsing red behind his eyelids. He brushes his lips along Davros' ear and whispers, "Does that answer your question?"

Davros' fingers tighten on Pica's forearm. "*Oh*. Lucius...." Davros turns his name into an exhalation. "What do you want to do...with me?" The question is tentative, halting, but with an eagerness to it.

The way Davros moves, how his magic engulfs Pica's body—he's so exquisite, so alluring. "I want to pleasure you," Pica whispers. "I want to know what your body does when we make love."

Davros moans again, the sound as sweet as his music. He tugs on Pica's hair, meeting his lips with an eager mouth, kissing him with an edge of desperation. Nails dig into his forearm, followed by a rush of magic so strong Pica's body shudders. It floods into every muscle and bone as Pica draws it deep into his hollow core. Davros pulls some of it back, mixing, churning their auras into a melange. "*Suya*," Davros pleads, tugging on Pica's breeches, maneuvering his body so their hips are pressed together. Layers of clothes remain between their bodies, but they may as well be bathed in only moonlight. Davros' need is the only thing Pica can feel, that intoxicating brightness.

Gods. If it's already this intense, what will it be like when they push it further? Pica's fingers tighten on the soft skin of Davros' thigh, savoring the bard's hungry lips, the hard press of his erection against Pica's hip.

Davros shifts, pulling, tugging, and Pica's body follows without consideration, landing half on top of his slim form. He groans and puts some of his weight down, pushing him into the mattress. A stab of fear cuts through the lust. Davros' breath hitches. Pica freezes. The fear becomes panic as Davros' breathing grows ragged.

Pica rolls back, pulling his arms away. "Sorry," he says. "I'm so sorry."

"N-no," Davros stammers. His voice trembles, and the fear morphs into frustration. "Gods *curse* it!"

"It's not your fault, Davros." Pica wants to reach out to him but refrains, giving him space. "I should have known not to—"

"No!" Davros interrupts emphatically. "*I* ruined it. It was so good, and I *ruined* it." Davros' face twists. He clenches his eyes closed, sending the welling tears down his cheeks. "I hate it, Lucius. I hate it so much. I want you so badly. I don't want to be broken."

"You're not broken," Pica says. "Thrown around by the tumult of life perhaps, but never broken."

"Tumult of life. Such fancy words," Davros says with a sigh. "You're not mad at me?"

Pica brushes away a line of his tears with his thumb. "Of course not."

Davros runs his fingers over Pica's lips. "Do we have to stop?" he asks. "You're so gentle. I'm, uh…I'm not used to that."

When he asks like that, when his expression is so earnest, Pica can't resist. "No," he says. "What if I lie on my back? Would that be better?"

"Maybe." Davros rises and kisses Pica, putting his hand on his chest and pushing, following Pica as he rolls over.

The raw lust is replaced by something more tender as Davros kneels over him, touching, kissing, exploring, letting his hands wander. He lingers on Pica's chest and belly, tracing lines and curves of muscle and skin. The quiet intimacy of it is simple and sweet—Pica could spend hours with him like this.

"You're not like those statues of great warriors," Davros says quietly, running fingertips down Pica's stomach. "You could scrub clothes on their bodies, but you're different. Softer."

"That's because I like eating," Pica says, smiling.

"I don't mean it as a bad thing!" Davros adds hurriedly. "I like it."

"I'm not offended. I know what it takes to look like that." He strokes Davros' cheek. "We had men come into the legion who took great pride in their physique. They would refuse bread and wine and insist on meat. At first."

"At first?"

"A few days of hard march in full gear changed their tune. That bread looked much more appealing after that."

"I can imagine."

Davros' fingers trace under Pica's cinched waistband, lingering on the cusp. Pica groans, resisting the urge to grab his hand and move it lower. He tries to suppress the need, but there's no way to hide it, not when Davros' magic permeates every muscle. Threaded through it is fearful anticipation, longing, nervous hesitation. Pica lifts his eyes to Davros' face, meeting widened pupils and white-rimmed irises. "Hey," he says softly. He reaches down and grasps Davros' fingers. The color drains from the bard's face. Pica tugs, guiding the trembling hand up to his lips. "Don't do it if you're not ready."

"But I—you've been so patient and—"

"Shh, it's alright. Come here." Pica takes him into his arms, letting him settle along his body—his usual spot. "You don't owe me anything, my sweet."

Davros buries his face in Pica's chest. "I'm sorry." The words are muffled, his breath warm on bare skin.

Pica threads fingers gently into his hair in lieu of a reply. Davros' fingers curl inwards as his body shudders with suppressed sobs. *It's alright.* He wants to repeat those words over and over until it *is* alright, until the darkness which haunts them both lifts away. *You're safe.*

You don't have to fight this alone.

But words can be twisted, falsified, empty. So Pica stays silent, letting Davros read his intentions and feelings with his magic instead. They lie together in that silence for a long time as Davros' tension releases and his anxiety fades. It's replaced by a quiet pain, a sense of longing, and eventually, Davros says, "I wish I was as strong as you."

Pica doesn't need to ask why. Instead, he replies, "I wish I could sing like you."

"You can't sing?"

"Not at all."

"But your speaking voice is so beautiful." Davros runs his fingers through the hair on Pica's chest. "I could teach you. Anyone can learn to sing a little, even if it's not the best—oh." He sits up and peers at Pica's face, squinting. "I know what you're doing, you sly bastard."

Pica grins at him. "Join us for sparring sometime. I promise Lucia won't go easy on you."

"Oh. I'll think about it. Promise." He lowers himself back down, and Pica's arms go around him tighter.

The candles burn low when Levnys slips through the door, letting it settle gently behind her. Pica gives her a drowsy smile. Davros sleeps against his chest, curled under Pica's arm. Levnys extinguishes the candles and joins them in the bed. Davros murmurs and shifts but doesn't wake.

Levnys kisses him, then also settles against his body. He runs his fingers along her braided hair as her breath warms his skin. Outside, the sea sings its soft lullaby, lulling him to sleep as much as the two bodies pressed against him. Something in his heart settles, and he realizes how much he craved this. He could have it. Although he's never been to Caltava, the thought of staying in the southern city, finally resting, and being able to spend his days with those he holds dear tempts him. In another life, he'd be a scholar like his mother and eldest sister, researching and learning about Geth. About Tekan and Soutori. About the tribes in the north and the nomads to the east. He'd visit those places, speak with those living there, and see the world outside the empire.

That's not his reality. Being Emperor is his path. He feels the pull of his oath, and he knows he will never break it. Not for gold, nor power, nor love. He won't rest until the dragons are free, but after—

perhaps he can live the life he wants. He clings to the sliver of hope like a shipwrecked man to driftwood.

XX

SKEWER

Levnys

Levnys finds herself alone for the first time in days, sitting on the beach watching the sun drop toward the horizon. There always seems to be someone around, whether it is Zaitun with her calming presence, Okalth's grumpy stoicism, or Lucius' warmth. Everyone has some task to occupy them, except for her. Even Sehuti goes out scouting, serving as a warning eye against the birds. The reports pour in now—dozens of ships found with their crews drained. Okalth and Gythu salvage what they can before sending the charred husks to the sea's depths.

According to the reports, the birds get ever closer to Caltava. Levnys awakens each morning with a sense of dread—will today be the day she receives word of her home's destruction? Part of her wants to forge ahead, to witness the city's wellbeing with her own eyes. It would not be wise, for what would she do if she encountered the birds? Surely, they would overwhelm her. It is safer to stay together.

White mist billows around her feet, curling around her toes and caressing her scales. She settles to lie on the sand, lowering her head as Davros approaches, munching on skewered carrots and leeks. The scent of pepper and honey fills her nose as he plops onto the ground to sit cross-legged in the shadow of her body. She curls around him, wrapping her tail around her front legs and laying her head beside his knee.

"Hi," he says, putting a hand on her nose.

"Hello, Dav," she replies. "I expected you would be with Lucius."

Davros sighs. "A few of those mages from the legion showed up, so he's in leader mode. I felt useless. I wanted to see what you were doing."

"Also feeling useless," Levnys admits.

"Want to talk about it?"

"I do not wish to burden you."

Davros runs his fingers along her nose, a soft touch that sends shivers over her skin. "Someone else's burden would be a good change," he says wryly. "You've done so much to help me, Lev. I want to return the favor."

"Alright." She glances down the beach at the green form curled on the sand. "It is about Sehuti."

"You don't trust him."

"I—do not know. He has behaved perfectly since—" She curls her lips. "Since Lucius saved his life."

"Ah. I understand."

"You do?"

"You wanted to subdue him yourself. Then, this handsome, powerful, wonderful human does it without a sweat. Er, do dragons sweat?"

Levnys tilts her head to bring Davros' face into focus. A smile threatens her lips. "Perhaps you are right." She ponders it for a moment. "I could not best Sehuti. I am not strong enough to defend my home."

"What would he have done if he killed you?"

"Before he asked for peace, I was convinced he would challenge all the dragons he found." Her eye tracks to the nightshade dragon. "Now, I am not so sure. That is not the point. The point is I was not strong enough. I do not deserve to inherit my mother's territory if I cannot protect what she fought for. She was a leader. I am not."

"What made her a leader?"

"According to the tales, she was a natural. Hundreds of dragons would follow her to the underworld should she ask it. She was a warrior without peer. The lesser dragons trembled when they heard her name. Every battle she fought was a victory. I will never achieve such heights. I will never inspire that type of loyalty."

"Hmm." Davros' fingers trace the scales between her brows. "Do you want that kind of loyalty?"

"Why would I not?"

"I don't know. I would prefer friends to subordinates." He taps a rhythm absentmindedly on her skull. She noses his knee, nearly knocking him over. "Sorry. Thinking. Trying to figure out how to phrase this."

"Perhaps you should simply say it," she says. "You will not upset me."

Davros swallows. "Fine. Your mother didn't sound like a nice, er, dragon. 'Trembled when they heard her name?' Does that give you warm feelings?" His fingers trace her forehead to the base of her horn. "If you were that scary, I wouldn't want anything to do with you." His fingers stop. "Er. No offense."

She drops her gaze. Had her mother been warm? She tended to her children and made sure they were fed. No danger came their way until the paladins arrived.

Mama, tell me a story!

You are too big for stories. Should you not practice your flying?

Her mother's words, locked behind time, come back now.

You will never be a warrior if you do not practice.

Not now. Go play with your brother.

If you cannot keep up, I will not take you to Caltava.

The skewer falls to the sand. "Levnys!" Davros puts his arms around her horns. "Oh. Oh gods, I'm sorry, I didn't mean to—"

"No," she says. "No, please do not apologize."

He tugs at her head, pulling it into his lap. It is almost comical—her head is larger than him—but she appreciates the sentiment.

"You don't have to be a mighty warrior or anything. I'm glad you're the type of dragon who would rather share a drink and a fire than a battlefield."

She leans her forehead against his slim body as much as she dares, lips trembling. Perhaps, if dragons could cry, she would be shedding tears.

"I am afraid I will not be able to protect you," she admits.

"Everyone protects everyone, right? We're all fighting those stupid birds." He folds his arms and leans on her head. "What was it you said to me? 'You do not need to do anything to be loved?' Well, same to you."

"You turn my words back at me," she says wryly. "I am proud of you."

Davros is quiet for a long breath. "Thanks," he says. He picks the fallen skewer up and brushes away the sand clinging to the vegetables, inspecting it from all angles before lifting it to his mouth.

"Surely you do not intend to eat that," Levnys says.

"A little sand never hurt anyone," Davros replies. "It's still good."

"We can easily get you more. The cooks—"

"No," Davros snaps. "I don't waste food."

She raises her head from his lap and turns her eyes on him. He grips the skewer so hard his knuckles creak. White shows around his blue irises—defensive, almost feral. He stares up at her for a long breath before he turns his head away and takes a bite.

The urge to pry almost overtakes her, but she refrains and lowers her head back to the sand. "I suppose I, too, use the beach as a plate," she says feebly.

Davros' laugh is barely audible, but its presence soothes Levnys' anxiety. His hand returns to her nose, with fingers resting lightly on the ridge of her snout. Silence stretches. Levnys basks in his quiet comfort as he finishes his meal. She recalls when he was a cowering figure watching from the shadows—how far he has come in only a few weeks.

A dark shadow and a rush of wings heralds a dragon's return. Gythu lands on the narrow strip of sand further down the beach, nearly too large for the space. The obsidian dragon is the eldest she has ever met, after her mother.

Gythu arrived in Levnys' territory one hundred years ago, well after the paladins' scourge. Levnys, barely an adult, feared for her life, but Gythu asked for refuge. In the years since, the dragon deferred to her, to Levnys' continuing confusion. In her mother's tales, a dragon only submitted to those stronger than it. Gythu could rule the entire coast if she wished.

Your mother was wrong.

Levnys had not considered it a possibility until Lucius spoke those words. The more she witnesses, the more she is inclined to believe him.

"She *is* pretty scary," Davros whispers. Levnys holds back her snort.

"Levnys," Gythu says, dipping her head in greeting. "Davros. It is a fine evening."

Her voice has an undertone of weariness, and no wonder. She has been airborne for most of the day. "Hello, Gythu. Would you like to join us?"

"Perhaps later. I must speak to Pica. We found more ships." Gythu transforms, shifting her bulk into her diminutive human form, to better move through the maze of tents and campfires spread along the beach. "Until then."

Levnys watches her go. Gythu is reporting to Lucius, not her. She pushes back her sudden pang of jealousy with a vengeance. This is not like her. Lucius is an experienced leader, used to the type of coordination demanded of such a role. It is better that he lead.

"Hey," Davros says. "Did you hear me?"

"No, I am sorry," she says.

"I said we should go see what Lucius is doing. I don't want to leave him alone for too long."

Davros is right. The loss of his magic continues to weigh heavily on Lucius. She cannot blame him for it—what would she do if, one day, she could no longer harness lightning? What would she do if her wings no longer lifted her into the clouds?

What if she lost the way to protect the ones she loves?

Levnys rises to her feet, then transforms. Davros threads his fingers with hers. They follow Gythu through the camp hand-in-hand.

XXI
MARKET

Pica

Two days later, they encounter the first stricken island. No birdsong greets them as they beach the ship, no stray dogs begging for scraps, no islanders plying their wares. A quick scout by the dragons confirms the fate of the quaint town. Kisara lands and empties her stomach into the surf.

Pica follows a stream tinged red with blood through a pear orchard along a groomed cobblestone path. The first body he finds was a man in his prime, tanned and dressed in a rough spun tunic. Whatever its original hue, the garment is now crimson. His rictus scream distorts what may have been a handsome face.

Pica moves on, each step weighing a thousand pounds, as his feet carry him past more lost souls. A young girl, no more than twelve. An elderly man, his attempts to shield the mass of fur beneath him ultimately futile. A cat, Pica realizes numbly. Birds litter the ground beneath the leafless trees. Krakli, perched on Pica's head, emits a thin whistle of dismay.

His resolve breaks when he makes it to the square. It was market day. The thick smell of clotting blood drives into his nose. He slumps to sit on a rock placed artfully on the side of the path, staring at the sky, the trees—*anything* but the pale forms strewn like discarded toys.

The trees rattle like bones in the western wind. Shutters bang against stone buildings, and tents try to shake themselves free of their poles. A turnip rests in a small pool of water, the source, a wooden cart overturned when its oxen attempted to flee. One remains in the harness, sagging like an empty wineskin. The other broke free, making it as far as the other side of the square.

He misses the crows. Even they are silent.

A hand settles on his shoulder, and he flinches. It's Lucia. "Are you alright?" she asks.

"We need to burn them. Burn the town," he says, staring at his hands. "Keep them from spreading. I can't, Lucia. I can't make fire. What good am I if I can't make fire?"

Lucia's lips form a line. She tugs at his arm. "Come. Walk with me."

He stands automatically at the authority in her tone, matching her strides with routine cadence. They skirt the edge of the square and travel down a shaded street. Pica clenches his jaw and stares forward, avoiding the darkened doorways and the smell of food mixed with the ever-present blood. They emerge into a second square—the temple district. Surely, no gods cast their gaze on this accursed place. Pica is hardly religious, only doing the bare minimum of sacrifice and service to Geth's myriad gods, but he wonders how they could let such things happen. Even Ukton's messengers—a majestic breed of raven with white-tipped wings—lie dead outside their black-bricked temple.

They enter the temple of Solis. The gilded marble floor is defiled by crimson, thick blood staining the grout black. The priests are strewn around the opulent temple to their silent god. The old routine settles in, that grim stoicism that carried him through six years of bloody conquest.

Lucia's fingers drum on the hilt of her sword. Her *steel* sword. He can't remember when his aunt went out armed with more than a dagger. The usual tan of her face is pale, drawn.

Something on the walls catches Pica's attention. He stares at the bloody glyphs that mar the frescoes with dawning horror. He's seen them before, in his visions of that lost place. Every depiction of the Sun God is defiled in the same way. He wishes the serpent could see them. They would know what it means.

"Shieldmaiden Draconia," a voice greets them. "Draconius."

Seto emerges from behind a pillar. His white cloak is immaculate, but his boots are shiny with fresh blood. The dark circles around his eyes look like bruises.

Pica nods at him. "Seto."

The wizard squares his shoulders. "I thought you'd want to see this. Mind the mess." He pauses, then adds in a hollow voice. "Sorry in advance."

He leads Pica around the pillar. Pica's stomach churns hard at the sight, and he clenches his eyes shut. Lucia gags.

It's exactly as they feared. The swollen bodies acted as incubators for the birds, and now the aftermath of their emergence is strewn across the fine marble floor. He barely manages to keep his lunch down.

"Cetuna's temple is similarly defiled," Seto says. "None of the others are. We haven't found any birds yet. We think they've continued southwest."

Something about Seto's words sticks in his head. The sun and moon temples were singled out. Why? He can't think. The smell of blood and viscera is too much. He needs air. He turns and walks out of the temple into the weak spring sun. Footsteps sound behind him, and Lucia's arm goes around his shoulders in a half-hug.

"We need to make sure the town is safe for the crew," Lucia says after a long silence.

"Right." Requisition of supplies from those who no longer need them. It makes sense. He pulls several thick strips of bark from his pocket and stares at them. Davros slipped them to him this morning. "I'll take east if you take west."

Lucia glances at the bark. "Will that be enough?"

"It has to be."

"Don't do anything stupid, Lucius. Be safe."

Pica kicks the door to the house off its brass hinges. Stress gnaws at him, creeping up his spine and into his shoulders. Each house, shop, bakery, and merchant has been the same. Bodies drained dry or burst open, and no birds in sight. The silence gets to him as much as the slippery blood beneath his sandals.

This is the last house on this side of the island. The sun disappears behind the buildings, blazing orange. A huge silhouette passes overhead, casting him in shadow briefly—one of the dragons, flying patrol. He ducks inside and squints in the waning light before going deeper into the house. Bodies, as before, are crumpled in the corner. One was an incubator. Pica doesn't have it in him to gag anymore. He turns to leave, desperate to return to camp and speak with his companions, to hear a friendly voice and fill the heavy silence.

A noise—a hum of wings. He spins on his heel and backs away from the sound, raising his hands to conjure fire.

Nothing comes.

He tries again, desperately searching for the familiar heat. Nothing. He fumbles into his bag, grasping a thin piece of bark in his fingers. 'Just break it' is the only instruction he received. He should have practiced, at least tried it out, gods curse him. The cloud of birds swirls out of an overturned amphora. They were waiting for him, he realizes—an ambush.

"Krakli, go!" he shouts. The magpie shrills and darts for the window, disappearing in a rush of wings.

He snaps the first strip of bark. Flame leaps from it, flashing forward from his fingers and licking at the swarm. Several tiny forms crumble to ash, along with a good portion of a wooden chair. Flame catches in the dry leaves that scatter over the floor. The cloud reels back, then reforms and comes for him.

They're almost upon him when he snaps his second strip. He tries to form it, to send it into the heart of the cloud. The flame catches on the straw-stuffed mattress of a child's bed. Smoke rapidly fills the room and obscures his vision, stinging his eyes and filling them with tears.

No fire. He has no fire. He's going to die. *Where is his fire?*

Beaks sink into his skin. He stumbles toward where he thinks the exit is, slapping away the birds. He breaks the last strip in desperation. It misses the birds completely.

Darkness intrudes his vision as he falls to his knees and gasps the cool air by the floor. He crawls slowly, too slowly, the strength draining from him. More beaks like daggers drive home. Blood—*his* blood—darkens the dirt floor.

Vessel, a horrid voice rasps. *You cannot stop me.*

"You haven't won," Pica wheezes.

The end is inevitable. I will consume you all.

"I'm not—dead yet." The world blurs. Despite his defiance, Pica knows the end is coming.

If only he had fire.

Andereth, I'm sorry. I was too weak.

The house trembles. A scream of tortured wood and shattering clay rips through the air. The waning sun is as bright as noon as it streams through the torn-off roof. Claws close around him, and he is airborne with the *woosh* of giant wings. The destroyed house shrinks below him as the wind whistles through thousands of leaves. Birds pour out after them—hundreds. *Thousands.* All hidden in an innocuous little house.

"Heal yourself, mage," Sehuti says. Roots twine around him, knocking away birds and engulfing him in pulsing wooden armor.

Pica taps into his magic, but he's so weak. Only the barest trickle greets him, enough to keep his laboring heart beating. The cloud rises after them.

Sehuti spreads his wings wide, then closes them. He jukes and dodges as the birds catch up, weaving through the undulating cloud with blazing speed. Pica's stomach heaves at the drop. He nearly blacks out, managing barely to hang on. None of the birds find purchase in Sehuti's skin. He hadn't flown like that during their battles.

Three dragons rise in the distance. Sehuti comes out of his descent and calls to them before he rises sharply, drawing the cloud thin behind him. Flame and lightning fill the air as Gythu, Okalth, and Levnys close in. Pica's vision pulses red. The dragons flash by as he slumps in Sehuti's claws. Sehuti enters another dive, then speeds for camp, leaving the battle in their wake.

They touch down, blowing tents over and scattering coals to the crew's shouts of alarm. The roots unwind, and Pica tumbles onto the sand. Silver flame blazes from above him. Sehuti takes several long steps back. Pica struggles to focus, finding his swollen eyes increasingly hard to keep open. Davros plants his feet and stands defiantly between him and Sehuti.

"I won't let you hurt him," he says, silver fire swirling around his outstretched hand. Davros is panting, visibly trembling, but he stares at the enormous dragon without backing down.

"Davros," Pica wheezes. "Stop. He saved me."

The flame goes out. Davros spins on his heel and throws himself on Pica's chest. White mist as thick as a cloud surrounds them as Davros shakes with shuddering sobs. The emotions pushing against Pica are painful—raw anguish and fathomless worry fill his veins as strongly as the magic that flows into him.

Pica closes his eyes. The sand shifts. A scaled nose brushes against his arm—Levnys' voice above him, worried. A deeper voice answers her. Krakli squawks.

He drifts for a long time, floating in that flood of magic. The torrent gradually slows, settling into a stream, then a trickle. He opens his eyes to see Davros crouched beside him, his hands glowing with ethereal silver light. The bonfire reflects blindingly off the wall of bronze scales surrounding him. He begins to sit up.

"No! Stay *down*, you stubborn mule," Davros says, pushing on his chest. "I swear to all of your stupid gods if you think you're walking around—"

"Alright, alright," Pica says as he obliges him. "I'll behave."

"*Good.* Please don't make me worry like that again."

Pica takes his hand. "I'll try, promise. Can you find Sehuti for me?"

"I am here," the nightshade dragon says from nearby. His head appears above them, peering into the protective circle of Levnys' body. Levnys' lips peel back at his proximity, but she makes no move to stop him.

"Thank you," Pica says, weakly saluting the dragon. "I would have died if you hadn't grabbed me."

"Likely."

"Why did you do it?"

Sehuti half-sneers, half-grins at him, showing his terrifying teeth. "I owed you my life. Now we are even."

Roaring flames lick the sky as the town burns, an enormous funerary pyre for its population. They found no survivors. Five hundred helpless people, all told—a small number in the grand scheme of things, perhaps, but Pica feels sorrow for each lost soul.

They found another nest of birds hiding on the opposite side of the island. Unfortunately for that swarm, Okalth was nearby and made quick work of it. Good riddance.

It should have been that easy for him. It would have been if he had his fire.

Pica lies propped on cushions with his back resting against Levnys' chest. Davros plays his songs from her back instead of his usual makeshift stage, refusing to let Pica out of his sight. Between the two of them, Pica doubts a fly could get close to him, let alone a cloud of birds. Krakli perches on his head, grumpy and exhausted. The magpie scolded him fiercely, chattering so fast that Pica was surprised the bird had any voice left.

Lucia hadn't scolded him, only hugged him, which was worse. She hadn't called him an idiot or a child or even chided him for his recklessness. She should have.

Pica takes a long swig of his wine and sinks further into his brooding. In the legion, he used his magic every day. He'd taken it for granted. He'd always taken it for granted. It's been nearly three weeks since he lost it, and the void inside of him only seems to get larger.

He knows he shouldn't feel sorry for himself. Everyone else around him does fine with less than the scraps that remain to him. He has his paladin powers—shouldn't that be enough? The fact that it isn't, the truth that he feels so incomplete—so *lost*—without his bloodline magic, shames him.

The cushion next to him shifts and Sparax sits with a sigh. "Eat," he says, shoving a bowl into Pica's hands.

Pica stares at it. "I'm not hungry—"

"I don't care. Eat it and listen."

Sparax has never talked to him like that before. He drinks the broth and stays silent.

"Dying isn't going to bring those people back, Lucius," he says. "So stop trying to kill yourself."

Pica gags on his mouthful of soup.

"Sane men don't try to feed their life force to a dragon they've never met—no offense, Levnys—or have their sister snag them out of midair and fight a dragon with a bleeding *dagger*. You're insane, Lucius, and not in a good way."

Pica wants to argue, but shame keeps his mouth shut. Sparax isn't wrong. Gods curse it, he's not wrong at all.

Levnys' eye is focused on him now. Davros transitions into a tune without vocals. Pica stares at his cooling bowl of broth, unable to look at any of them.

"I don't know why the legion broke you so badly, but I can't watch you destroy yourself." Sparax's voice breaks .He reaches over and touches Pica's chin, guiding his face up. Tears shine in his blue eyes, dark in the dim firelight. Pica's lips tremble when he sees the pain there. White mist curls over the ground like a creeping fog. "So next time you're about to throw yourself like a blood-mad gladiator at the next danger, remember none of us want to lose you."

Pica wants to close his eyes so he can't see the pain in Sparax's expression. He keeps them open, facing the shame head-on. Mist curls along his body. Davros' magic seeps into him, light and soothing. Pica's shame deepens when he feels the emotions there. The memory of the bard's racking sobs causes him to choke. Sparax pulls his head to his shoulder and then embraces him, entwining long fingers into his hair.

"There are people who love you, Lucius. I'm not going to let you forget that."

Pica lets the tears spill down his cheeks unchecked. How could he have been such a fool? Put into words like this, it's all so clear. He can see now how far he's fallen, how much he let the guilt drive him. The fact that he lived when so many others died has been his torture, his private torment.

He used to take pride in his power and relished the feeling it gave him. He was strong in a way his father was not. The legions twisted that pride into self-loathing, turning him into a weapon for the empire's bloody glory. Ever since he kindled that first flame, his fire fundamentally defined him, down to his core.

The unease that's haunted him since that power disappeared crystallizes, its facets finally coming clear. Without his powers, he felt like a rudderless ship, adrift. Yet some part of him was relieved—the beast was defanged. It was the least he deserved for the destruction he caused.

That lack of direction is the reason he threw himself into the thick of the planning these last weeks, reveling in all of the tiny details and moving pieces of a hundred different facets of information. That kind of work kept him sane in the legion. This time, he can save people and use what power remains to him for good.

He may not have his fire, but he's still a prince. Still a leader. The royal bloodline magic never manifested in Monedula, yet his uncle's legions are fanatically loyal to him. Despite Pica's disdain for Monedula's methods, he has to admit he learned a lot from him.

No matter what, he must keep fighting back against those birds and the entity behind them. He owes it to Andereth and the people of the Coast to try.

He owes it to those who haven't given up hope in him to try.

"I've decided something," Sparax says quietly. "Wherever you go, I'm going too. I have you back, and I won't lose you again."

"Sparax, I—" Pica tries to gather his thoughts, but they're a whirlwind, a tempest. "I want you by my side. I love you so much."

He said it. He finally said it. Sparax tips his head, resting his cheek on Pica's hair. "I love you too, Lucius. I never stopped. I don't intend to stop."

The white mist surrounding them thickens. Levnys' pleased rumble carries through the ground, vibrating the sand. Pica lifts his head to look at Sparax. "Normally, these kinds of conversations don't have an audience."

"Nothing about you is normal," Sparax retorts. "That's why I like you so much." His smile is a tender thing, full of relief and affection. "I'm not ready to be together, but—I wanted you to know."

"Alright." Pica leans forward and puts their foreheads together.

"You're still a reckless idiot, though. One who needs to rest."

"And not do anything for several days," Davros chimes in.

"And eat meat," Levnys adds.

Krakli chirps and pecks Pica on the arm.

"Alright, alright, fine," Pica says. "It's unfair you're all united against me."

"You're fine," Sparax says. "Come. I'll help you to your cabin."

The morning sun blazes bright over the beach. Pica squints, yawning, trying to focus on Ralex's update.

"—and some saddles," Ralex finishes. "Don't know why, but Seto told me you'd want them. They're on the ship."

"I do want them. Thanks, Ralex," Pica says.

The captain salutes him, then turns on his heel and walks away. Pica leans back against the tree trunk, watching the activity around *Raven's Flight*. Before they burned the town, the crew foraged a veritable market's worth of items: torches, cloth, sacks of grain and flour, amphorae of salted meat and fish. Sehuti stands nearby, leaves turned to the morning sun, and the roots around his feet dug into the rich volcanic soil. Pica watched him drink deeply of the stream earlier, blood and all.

Sehuti continues to distance himself from the other dragons, especially Okalth. Pica can't blame him—the orange dragon continues to watch him with suspicion, too, albeit less intensely than before.

More news about the birds reached them early that morning. Scouting reports from the dragons, the fate of the town, and word from passing ships all point to a single conclusion. The birds converge, and *Raven's Flight* is hot on their tails. Soon, they will need to fight.

Pica takes a bite of the dried meat Davros left for him. The preparations for departure are almost complete. The sailcloth anchored to her railings obscures the black timbers of the ship's deck. Now laden with the new supplies, *Raven's Flight* is much too heavy for her rowers to lift. Fortunately, they've come up with a different solution.

The rowers are in their seats, with oars pulled inside the ship. Sehuti yawns and shakes himself, settling his leaves against his bark-like hide. The roots retract and wind themselves around his legs. Pica stands slowly. He's not in pain this time, but the loss of blood makes him woozy.

Sehuti glances over. Pica gestures at the ship. "Time to go."

"Indeed." Sehuti holds out his hand. "I'll take you to the ship if you wish."

"That's very nice of you."

The nightshade dragon snorts. "I do not wish to incur the ire of your little bard again."

His little bard. Pica's heart swells at that inclusion. He climbs into Sehuti's palm, and the dragon carries him to the ship. Davros hurries to his side as soon as his feet touch the deck. Sehuti moves to the stern as Pica and Davros duck under one of the coverings. Pica stays near the entrance, eager to watch it all unfold.

When the crew is aboard and situated under the sailcloth, Levnys calls out from somewhere near the bow, "Ready?"

Sehuti's hands close around the upturned curl of the stern, and he unfurls his wings. "Ready," he responds.

"Ready," chime Okalth and Gythu.

"Lift!"

An enormous rush of wind buffets *Raven's Flight* as four dragons take flight. They rise upwards. Sehuti's wings beat hard to get him airborne—the ship tilts, first one way, then another. Rowers call out as they are tossed sideways into the bulkheads. Ralex bellows something from the stern, but his words are lost in the cacophony of wings.

"Forward!" Levnys calls, and they surge out over the water. An amphora slams against the railing, leaking olive oil onto the sleek black timbers. Pica pulls Davros close to him and loops one arm around the railing. The ship tilts again, then back. Thank the gods they secured the heavier cargo to the rails, or they'd be crushed.

"Lower!"

Pica's stomach lurches as they drop. The bow hits the water first. Then, the stern crashes down with an enormous splash. Sehuti releases his hold and rises out of Pica's vision.

Ralex's voice booms in the decreased noise. "—and get that water out! You! Secure that rope." Crewmen scramble at his orders. Shouts from the rowers' compartment become an industrial buzz of working conversation as they ready *Raven's Flight* for departure.

"Drop oars!"

One hundred and seventy oars hit the water with rapid splashes. The drums thunder beneath them, and singing fills the crisp morning air. Pica releases the railing and settles his back against it as the ship moves forward.

Davros smiles brightly. "Well. That's not something you see every day, is it?"

XXII
RELEASE

Davros

The spring air bursts through the cabin's window when Lucius opens it. Davros buries his face under the blankets, hoping Lucius thinks he's asleep. He makes small noises of displeasure when Lucius tries to coax him out, pulling the covers full over his head.

"Everything alright?" Lucius asks.

"No," he says into the pillow.

"Want to talk about it?"

The question hangs in the air. Lucius lies stretched out beside him, rubbing his hand over Davros' shoulder. Davros waits another minute, then peeks above the covers. "You're not going to leave it alone, are you?"

Lucius' lips twitch. "No."

"You have too much to do to worry about me."

"Not true," Lucius counters. He runs his fingers through Davros' hair, looking so beautiful and nice and trustworthy. "Tell me? Please?"

Shit. "Promise you won't make a big deal out of it?"

"Promise."

Davros sighs and pushes the covers away. "It's my birthday," he mumbles.

"Oh!" Lucius' face brightens. "Isn't that a good thing?"

"Well, um." Davros can't stand to look at Lucius' earnest expression. "No. It's not the day I was born because I don't know exactly when, so..." The tears threaten to overwhelm him. "It's the day I was abandoned in a tent."

"Oh." Lucius' fingers in his hair stop moving.

Davros' throat tightens. "Also, no one ever—I mean, there was Romero, but we didn't do much." He knows he's babbling, but the words tumble out of him unencumbered. "It got ignored most of the time. No one ever wanted to *celebrate* me being born."

"*I* want to." He says it so simply, so assuredly. "We don't have to do a lot."

Davros wonders what he did to deserve this wonderful man's affection. "It feels wrong to celebrate when so many people—" Davros' voice, already tight with emotion, catches. "When we're so close to having to fight."

Every dragon scouts now, even Levnys. In the two days since they left that horrid island, reports of the birds have poured in. Ralex has been reluctantly pushing his crew hard, only stopping after darkness has fell. The captain and Lucius argued about it last night. Eventually, Lucius conceded—today, they will only go as far as Gesi, an island four days away from Caltava. From there, Ralex said, they can scour the approaches to the city while letting the rowers rest.

"We can't let it keep us from living," Lucius says gently. "Trust me."

Davros believes him. "If we were to celebrate my birthday, how would we...what would we do?"

"What do you want to do?"

"I get a choice?"

"*Yes,*" Lucius says. "Of course, you get a choice." He hooks his finger under Davros' chin and leans closer. "Anything you want."

Davros melts when he feels the complex layers of emotion accompanying that statement. *I want you,* he thinks—*all of you.* The kiss that follows leaves them both breathless. Davros pulls back reluctantly. "I want to spend time with you," he says.

Levnys nearly knocks him off his feet that afternoon in human form. She's taller than him and deceptively strong, and he swears his heels leave the ground as she hauls him into a hug. "What is this I hear about your birthday? Why did you not tell me?" she demands.

"Uh, sorry," is all he manages to say.

Lucius puts his arms around them both. "Don't be too hard on him, Lev."

The double embrace is too warm in the afternoon sun, but Davros doesn't complain. He leans his forehead against Levnys' cheek. Activity swirls around them as he savors this moment. Ava was right. His life *has* changed, and he can say he's enjoyed his birthday for the first time.

Not that they've done anything special. Lucius was as busy as he predicted with preparation and meetings. Calvus made them spar for two hours in the late morning sun. Davros picked up a sword for the first time in months. Sure, he lost every bout, but he held his own, and Lucius' proud smile made him feel like he won every time.

Levnys takes his face between her hands. Davros looks into her turquoise eyes with his heart in his throat. Levnys is always beautiful, but like this, she's radiant.

"Very well," she says, her full lips quirking into a smile. "I will say it this way, then."

She presses her mouth against his. Davros' surprise is quickly replaced by elation as he savors her soft lips, her warm breath. Levnys' affection for him washes in like a wave, making his head float. Never in a thousand years would he think she'd want to be more than friends. Yet, her affection buzzes like lightning, filling the chasm of loneliness a bit more.

They only move back a little when they break the kiss, keeping their noses together. "Happy birthday," she says.

"Thank you," he replies, flushing.

"Ahh!" Lucius exclaims, then crushes them both into a hug.

"*Ow,*" Davros protests, wiggling to try and loosen Lucius' embrace. He may as well be trying to move a boulder. "Don't squish us, you big *yenok.*"

"This is why Sparax calls him 'aurochs,'" Levnys says. "I know you are happy, Lucius, but this is uncomfortable."

Lucius lets them go, still grinning. "What will we do now, then?"

"There is a market on this island and two resident dragons,"

Levnys replies. "Tisu will be pleased to hear it is a special day."

Davros wants to withdraw like a turtle into its shell. He wants to ask why they care so much about him, but he knows the question is dumb. Haven't they proven it by now? Why does his head refuse to accept it?

"Alright," he says, overwhelmed. Isn't this what he always wanted during those lonely nights in the troupe? Even after he joined Romero and Alatar and fled Soutori, he felt distant and apart. Alatar, the old master wizard, never showed a hint of warmth, and Romero, well, he was broken in a different way. Here is the treatment he's craved for so long, and he wants to shy away from it as if it's as poisonous as Sehuti's thorns. "The market sounds fun."

Lucius and Davros roam the town center an hour later, browsing the market stalls. Levnys parts from them upon their arrival, promising to meet them back at camp. The market bustles, people flowing down the cobblestone lanes between the tightly packed stalls. Everyone who brushes against him is cheery, happily going about their day. He tries not to read their emotions too deeply. Lucius always keeps a hand on his back or shoulder, a solid rock in the churning sea.

Do these people not know about the danger that lurks nearby? Surely, word has spread by now. You wouldn't know it, from what Davros can sense. Then again, here they are celebrating his birthday with a shopping trip.

The melange of scents—perfumes and fresh herbs, cedar smoke, and incense fill Davros' nose, fighting for attention. It's enough to make his head spin. Lucius pauses at a shaded stall selling reed pens and ornate ink pots. He buys one topped with a swan's feather, smiling as if enjoying a private joke.

When they step into a clothier's tent, Davros' heart soars. So many fine garments crowd every inch of the space. He wanders, drinking in every detail. His eyes finally settle on a finely made chiton dyed soft pink. The gradient in the fabric and the subtle patterning along the hem and sleeves—it's *perfect*.

Lucius' arms go around his shoulders. "Do you want it?" he asks.

No, he couldn't possibly ask for it. It's too much. "Isn't it expensive?" Davros whispers.

"That wasn't my question," Lucius says.

Davros flushes. "It's my favorite color," he says sheepishly.

Later, as they return to the ship, Davros slips his hand into Lucius', hugging the wrapped chiton against his chest. Someday, he will tell Lucius the truth—while he's bought plenty of clothes for his personas, this is the first thing he ever wanted for his true self.

The camp is lively when they emerge from the trees. Davros and Lucius stop for a moment, observing. The ship's crew haul razorbacks from the shallows, pulling the enormous fish onto the beach. Another group butchers them as birds, including a lone magpie, scream and squabble for the guts. Island dogs, dirty and lean, circle the perimeter, hoping for scraps. Zaitun is in the water, her silver head rising behind a thrashing mass of herded fish. An unfamiliar dragon helps her— another water dragon, golden in color, built like Zaitun but larger. Two tall fins arch from his brows and run along his long body in twin rows.

Okalth and Gythu stoke an enormous bonfire in a long trench dug into the sand. Sehuti is missing, Davros realizes. He's late back from patrol. The twinge of anxiety surprises Davros—he's not overly fond of the plant dragon, but no one deserves the kind of pain those birds inflict.

"Oh, there's Levnys," Lucius says. Davros turns and spots their bronze dragon amid a group of brightly-dressed locals. Another dragon stands beside her, metal scales copper in the waning sun. She is shorter than Levnys, perhaps as short as Zaitun, but stocky in build, with curved brown horns, bright green eyes, and an enormous grin.

"Ah, you return," Levnys says as they approach. "Lucius, Davros, this is Tisu."

The copper dragon giggles—actually *giggles*—and bows her head in greeting. "I heard there was a party!" she says, bouncing from foot to foot. "I love parties! I brought lots of desserts for everyone."

Davros doesn't know what to say. All this, for *him*. "Th-that sounds fun," he manages.

"Great!" She dips her head again and bounds off. The locals hurry to follow. A performing troupe, Davros notes from their dress. He sighs in relief—it looks like he has the evening off.

A bellow causes Levnys to jerk her head toward the sea. She calls back, and Davros sees Sehuti winging swiftly over the waves. He lands on a bare patch of beach and then pushes his way toward them.

"Gather. Everyone," he says, his breath coming out in great bellows. His eye is wide, the sclera rimmed with bright green. "I found the birds."

The sun is setting by the time the meeting breaks. "Eat and rest tonight," Calvus says. "Report to Pica before retiring this evening. We gather at dawn."

Davros sits on Levnys' back as each warrior approaches Lucius in turn. Each instruction differs slightly, a piece of a larger puzzle that Davros can't put together.

Sehuti approaches. The nightshade dragon eyes him, then settles into a crouch, putting his head uncomfortably close to Lucius. Levnys lifts her head. Davros doesn't miss the thread of annoyance that winds through her. Lucius, however, salutes the plant dragon. "Good evening, Sehuti."

"The same, mage." The branches over his brows twitch. "So. I cannot breathe destruction on our enemies tomorrow, and I cannot swim in the poison water. Knowing that—what will you have me do?"

Lucius is silent for a long moment. "Watch our backs," he finally says. "If we die, warn the residents of Caltava. There's a legion there. Warships. Mages. They can fight. Rally them and save the island."

Sehuti snorts. "What makes you think they'd believe me?"

"I'll give you a royal missive marked with my seal. Deliver it to the legate of III Caltavia. If we win, give it back."

"You trust me so much?"

"Yes," Lucius says bluntly. "Despite your initial hostility. I'm a man who believes in second chances. Enemies are circumstantial, Sehuti. You saved my life despite your words about being 'even.'"

The surprise in Levnys' aura is mirrored by Davros' own, along with a deepening sense of pride. Lucius has a way of making friends that Davros envies. How many times has Lucius looked a former enemy in the eye and forgiven them?

Sehuti's gaze drops to the sand. For the first time, the dragon's haughty pride falters. The leaves covering his hide flatten, covering his thorns.

"Oh." Sehuti stretches out his neck. Lucius puts his hand on the dragon's nose. Davros can't help himself. He lets his mist spill down Levnys' side, curious about Sehuti's emotions. At first, he doesn't sense anything. Sehuti has a labyrinth of defenses raised to protect his heart. Davros delves deeper. Beneath the stone walls is a creature craving acceptance through any means necessary. Davros reels back from the desperation in the dragon's emotions. He feels like a voyeur. But, isn't he the same—a lost creature seeking love?

Sehuti closes his eye and pulls his massive head back. He stands and turns, then pauses. "I will do as you ask, mage," he says, staring out over the sea. "Thank you."

Lucius remains silent as Sehuti walks away. He slumps back against Levnys' chest. Levnys lowers her nose to him, nudging his side. He pats her muzzle.

Several minutes later, the last dragon approaches—the one who helped Zaitun herd the razorbacks ashore. He bows deeply, first to Levnys, then to Lucius, introducing himself as Xemun.

"Regillus, it is an honor to meet you," he says. Davros hides his smile. The dragon's sophisticated tone reminds him of an old wizard. "Already tales of your exploits spread across our great sea."

"Wonderful," Lucius says.

The conversation soon turns to history, and Davros' attention wanders. He watches Tisu dance circles around the great fire. He observes Sehuti settle at the outskirts of the group, lowering his head to the sand.

After Xemun departs, Lucius leans back and takes a long drink of his wine.

"Are you satisfied with your plan?" Levnys asks.

"Oh. Yeah." Lucius looks up at her. "It's all coming together."

How can he be so calm? "What's next?" Davros asks, scaling down Levnys' side.

"What Calvus said. Eat and rest."

It feels wrong. They should be doing *something*. But what can they do? Davros can't imagine trying to fight them in the dark. "How do we know the birds won't attack us tonight?" he asks.

"They wouldn't reach us before dawn." Lucius' jaw tightens. "I asked Seto to send out some of his summons. If they move, we'll know.

I'm as worried as you, but there's no sense in letting it ruin your night. Eat and rest. It's best for morale."

"You can eat your fill of honey cakes, Dav," Levnys says, hauling herself to her feet. "Tisu makes the best sweet things."

Davros' chest clenches. He'd love to stuff himself with desserts, but it's not worth the risk. He opens his mouth to say something, anything, but the words don't come.

"He can't," Lucius says. "Right, Dav?"

Shit. "R-right." He finds Lucius' hand and grips it. It shouldn't surprise him that Lucius noticed—the signs are clear if you know where to look.

"What is the reason?" Levnys inquires, putting her head level with them.

Davros tries. "I, before Notri, I, um…" His voice fails him, and he stares at his boots.

Lucius saves him again. "I'll explain it to her," he says. "Can you get us some fish?"

Davros dips his head and hurries away, his cheeks flaming.

After dinner, humans and dragons come and go around their fire —Sparax, with his friendly ribbing and knowing glances; Kisara, seeking Lucius' help braiding her hair into neat rows against her scalp; Calvus, his grave face and solemn words a sharp contrast to the revelry. Though Lucius receives far more attention than he does, the prince's warm hand and constant presence are all Davros needs. He settles against Lucius' side.

After a while, Levnys joins the dragons' feast, gorging herself on razorbacks, bread, and honey cakes. Tisu brought a veritable shop's worth of desserts. Davros takes tiny bites, as much as he dares. He has to stop himself from shoving the entire thing in his mouth. The bubbly copper dragon knows her craft; that much is certain.

The dragon in question bounces from group to group, her wide grin ever present. Even Sehuti smiles when she presents him with an enormous fruit pie.

At sundown, Gethki priests make their way to the water's edge. Several slaves lead bawling oxen by their brass nose rings behind the opulent priests. Davros gives Lucius an inquisitive look.

"I requested a sacrifice," he says quietly.

"I didn't think you were religious," Davros says.

"I'm..." Lucius pauses. "I'm willing to bet on a few rituals on the bare chance it helps."

"Who do they represent?" Davros asks. "I don't know all the Gethki gods."

"Ah. You know Olomilo and Naltia?"

"Yeah. The gray robes are Olomilo, and the turquoise ones are Naltia, right?"

Lucius gives him a smile that makes Davros' heart skip. "Correct."

"Who are the other two?"

"Solis and Cetuna." Lucius nibbles on his honey cake. "The enemy doesn't seem to like them."

The enemy, the one behind the birds. Lucius told him about the serpent, the bat, and his visions. Davros accepted it in stride with everything else—wasn't his own existence plagued by strange phenomena? Besides, his magic permeated every muscle of Lucius' body at the time. Even the most skilled liar would struggle to deceive him under those conditions.

Lucius rises. Davros follows. They stop shy of the huddled group of priests, and Lucius raises his chin.

The priests chant. They implore their gods, one after another, to bless the trials to come. Lucius watches, implacable. They sacrifice the oxen until the blood spills into the sand to be lapped by the ocean tide. On the western horizon, the sun sinks. On the eastern, the nearly full moon rises. Davros' heart stirs at her pale face, beautiful and ethereal.

The few Gethki in the crew gather around, bowing their heads. Lucius steps forward and drops to his knees, facing the setting sun. The slaves carve the carcasses with ruthless efficiency, separating the meat from the bones.

Lucius stays bowed until the meat is roasted. Through his hand on his prince's back, Davros feels him tremble. It's not piety, merely fatigue. The priests present Lucius with the choicest cut of the beef, drenched in sauce, on an ornate brass platter. Lucius stands, bows deeply to them, and returns to his cushioned refuge. Davros settles beside him, a silent witness to a ceremony he doesn't completely understand.

The watching priests intensely scrutinize the first bite of the beef.

Lucius slowly chews it, then nods. As one, the spectators turn away, their duty done.

Lucius cuts off a piece of the meat, spears it with his knife, then holds it out for Davros. "Try it," he says. "It's good."

Davros takes a tentative bite. It's tender despite its quick roasting, the center a juicy pink. The taste of the white wine sauce floods his senses, sweetened with honey and dates. He hands the knife back to Lucius. They finish the meat together, and the few bites Davros dares to take linger on his tongue like a pleasant summer day.

The party winds down. Dragons, gorged until their stomachs bulge, sleep on the sand, ringing the coals of the smoldering fire pit. Levnys stretches out nearby and is asleep within minutes. Krakli, stuffed with fish guts, is an orb of black and white feathers perched on Levnys' curved horn.

Davros' worry about the birds fades to the background, replaced by a more immediate anxiety. Lucius' calloused fingertips run lightly along his forearm to trace his palm and fingers. His golden eyes reflect the orange and red of the waning flames. There's affection in the emotions pressing against his senses, but there's something else, too, something barely suppressed. Lucius leans forward and brushes his lips against Davros' cheek, letting his warm breath linger. Davros shivers.

"Are you tired?" Davros asks.

"No," Lucius replies. "But we can go to our cabin if you want."

Our cabin. Alone.

He fights the stab of anxiety, stuffing it away before Lucius can sense it. His body's panicked response is disconnected from what he desires. He *wants* to be alone with Lucius and overcome this fear. It may well be their last night alive. He can think of no better way to spend it than with him.

"Yes, please," he says.

The candles flare to life at Davros' urging as he follows Lucius into the room. His heart already pounds. Lucius strips himself of his tunic before the door is closed—something normal. He does this every night. Never mind how the light plays on his back and shoulders, glinting off the patch of scales peeking around his neck. Davros' fingers are on his belt, but he's imagining those muscles flexing under his hands.

Lucius catches him staring. A slow smile spreads across his face, and Davros doesn't need his magic to know what he's thinking. Lucius crawls into bed, propping his back against the wall. Davros wavers. His fingers fumble with his tunic belt. After an eternity, he pulls his *exomis* over his head. His skin heats when Lucius' eyes travel over him. Oh gods, the way Lucius looks at him makes him weak.

Breathe, he tells himself. *You're going to be fine.*

"Come here," Lucius says.

The gentle authority in his tone makes Davros' heart skip. He crawls across the bed to Lucius' side. Lucius' arm goes around his waist, his hand warm and soft against bare skin. Davros looks into those beautiful golden eyes, runs his fingers along his cheekbone, and brushes back the errant curls of hair that always escape past his ears.

Davros knows what comes next. It's been building in him with every touch and kiss he shares with this man. Their lips come together, and he has no more doubt. Lucius' hand on his skin, his soft lips, the eagerness in his kiss—he can't get enough. The kiss deepens, and finally—*finally*—Davros' need for this man overtakes the fear.

He swings his leg over Lucius' lap, straddling him. Lucius makes a soft noise of surprise and runs his hands over the naked skin of Davros' chest, his big hands gentle as always, his touch soft despite the rough calluses. Davros explores the lines of Lucius' body, down his shoulders and over his arms and chest, brushing the fine draconic scales and thick muscle. Those muscles flex as Davros runs his fingertips down his stomach. Lucius lets out a long groan that vibrates against his mouth and tongue. Lucius' hands move to his thighs, pressing their bodies together. Lucius' hips twitch—involuntary movements that send Davros' lust soaring.

His heart beats faster, and for a moment, he thinks he's about to panic. It threatens to rise in him, but it's something quiet now. The desire is louder, deafening him with the *thud-thud-thud* of his heart. He's breathless, floating in their shared auras. Even now, as the need within Lucius rises, there's no stink of greed, no swell of selfish lust.

"Lucius," he moans.

"Is it alright?" Lucius asks. When Davros nods, he smiles. "Remember, it's never too late to stop."

"Don't want to." Davros runs his fingers along Lucius' neck, causing him to shiver. "I'll tell you when I'm ready."

"Please do. I'll give you a night you won't forget."

"Mm. You're pretty confident about that, aren't you?" Davros teases.

"Why hide my strengths? I know how to please a man."

They come together again. The quivering tension between them blooms into something exquisite. Davros' arousal is almost painful. He takes Lucius' hand and moves it, pressing it against the front of his loincloth.

"Touch me," he says.

Lucius' lips curve in a smile. "Gladly."

He grips Lucius' arm as he slips his hand inside the loincloth. His other hand tangles in Davros' hair, tilting his head back as he runs his lips along a sensitive ear. Lucius' hand and lips are almost too much. Davros arches his back under his touch, pushing into his hand, begging for more. He grinds his hips against Lucius' erection, rolling them rhythmically as if dancing to a sensual tune.

Lucius moans in his ear, long and low. "Davros," he whispers, his voice rough with lust. "Gods, that feels so good."

Though the name isn't truly his, its sound is sweet music. He wonders what his real name will sound like on his lips. The thought doesn't scare him as he expected. No fear remains—only absolute certainty of what he wants. He wants nothing left between them. He wants Lucius to let go and be passionate without restraint.

"I'm ready," he manages to say.

Lucius' breath catches. He pulls his head back to study Davros' expression, irises shimmering like molten gold. "How do you want me, my sweet?" he asks, leaning forward so their lips brush together. His hand has slowed but not stopped. Those eyes, those lips, that hand and what it's doing, the way he asks permission—it all drives Davros mad.

"On top. Inside me. Gods, please, Lucius, I need you so badly."

Lucius withdraws his hand, then lifts Davros and flips him onto his back. Davros stares as he removes the rest of their clothes. Lucius looks like he's carved from granite. His chestnut skin gleams as the candlelight highlights his powerful thighs, the curve of his hips, and the erect length of him. Lucius' gaze travels to Davros' face, lingering, questioning, before he lowers himself down carefully. "I want you," he whispers, his voice almost pleading. "Let me make love to you."

Davros' heart lurches, overwhelmed by the twin pangs of desire and tenderness. He touches his cheek, relishing the love and lust in his prince's eyes. "I'm yours, Lucius," he replies.

Lucius' suppressed passion bursts forth at those simple words, raging through Davros' magic like a typhoon. Lucius kisses him hard, pinning him to the bed. The rest of the walls inside Davros crumble at that kiss, at the friction of their naked bodies rubbing together, at the sweet honey scent and weight of the man above him.

"*Suya*," he begs when Lucius' mouth moves to his neck. "Gods, *please*."

"Mmm, so eager," Lucius whispers in his ear, his baritone like sweetened wine. "I'm going to savor you. Find out what you like."

"But—" He gasps when Lucius gently bites the lobe. "What about you?"

"Don't worry about me. This is about you." Lucius' lips trace along his jaw and neck. "You deserve this, you know."

There, the heart of it revealed so casually. It's not enough that this man is so frustratingly attractive; he has to be introspective, too. Davros feels exposed, emotionally naked, his deepest insecurities laid bare. At the same time, he feels seen in a way that he didn't believe possible. This man, this perfect prince, understands his pain and doesn't shy away from it. No wonder he's fallen so hard. He doesn't trust himself to speak, so instead, he nods.

Lucius' mouth and hands move lower, along Davros' collarbone and down his chest. He tries to relax into it, into the pleased little breaths Lucius makes each time he expresses his pleasure. As Lucius' lips travel along his stomach and he realizes the direction of their attention, Davros' anxiety flares anew. Someone like Lucius shouldn't stoop to this. His thoughts stutter as the prince takes him into his mouth. A loud moan rips from him, and his hips rock. Davros wants to tell him he's not worth it. He should stop. But he doesn't want him to stop—not now, not ever.

Slowly, an oiled finger sinks inside him, preparing him, teasing him. When did Lucius get the oil? How can his hands be so sure, so steady? How does he know the right place to—?

Another finger. His hips rock harder. He can't think. He doesn't *want* to think.

Please. Oh, gods, please.

Right when he can't take it anymore, Lucius moves to kneel between his legs. His shimmering black hair hangs over his face. Davros entwines his hands in it, smoothing it back, letting the loose waves flow through his fingers. Lucius leans against his touch, one side of his mouth curved in a small smile. Like this, he's almost vulnerable, filled to his core with a deep love. Even in his most vivid imaginings, Davros never thought he would be so perfect.

Lucius slowly joins their bodies together. A brief twinge of pain makes Davros close his eyes, but Lucius is patient, letting him relax, and the pain morphs into something far more pleasurable.

"Still alright?" Lucius asks.

"*Yes.*"

His first thrust makes Davros gasp, the second, moan. Lucius finds his rhythm, and Davros' world narrows. The passion builds in a sensual crescendo, the faint threads of it blooming and branching deep within. His entire universe becomes this man's touch, the fullness of him inside—whispered sweet nothings and gasps of pleasure. Lucius repeatedly brings Davros to the brink. Each time Davros approaches it, he backs off. Lucius keeps it from him for a long time, and his satisfaction with Davros' reactions is evident through the magic that mingles between them. Davros approaches the precipice again, his entire body bowed under the intensity of the lovemaking. It builds in Lucius, too, and Davros wraps his legs around his hips, pleading, begging with wordless cries.

They ride the crest over the edge. The wave of their lust washes over them, making it impossible to tell their passion apart. Davros climaxes hard, gasping, his magic flinging around the cabin. He's so lost he almost misses the moment Lucius reaches release—then again, the big man seems to treat it like an afterthought. Davros entwines fingers in Lucius' hair, pressing his forehead against his shoulder.

Their breaths and hearts slow. Lucius kisses his hair, his cheeks, his brow. Davros opens his eyes to stare at the wooden ceiling. They did it. *He* did it. He can't stop the tears. Lucius gently brushes them away.

"I'm proud of you," he says.

"I'm proud of me, too."

Lucius withdraws and stretches beside him, running his fingers over Davros' cheek and hair with an affectionate smile. Davros casts the housekeeping spell, cleaning with a quick thought.

"Happy birthday, my sweet," Lucius says. "Did you have a good day?"

"It was wonderful," Davros whispers. "It was everything I could have dreamed."

"Good." Lucius rests his forehead on Davros' shoulder. "You deserve everything we can give you."

Davros bites his lip over the urge to argue. Instead, he places his hand on Lucius' chest, letting his magic flow into him. He wraps it around his heart, cherishing the steady beat before sending it into his limbs, following his arteries to the tips of his fingers. He moves from the physical to the emotional, finding the strings of his moods, reading them as he's done every day since he sang the lullaby. He lingers on his vast affection, blushes at the satisfaction from their lovemaking, and then pauses at the deep-seated tension that winds itself tight in his shoulders. There's something else there, too, something he'd never thought he'd find.

Self-doubt.

It feels dirty, like a wine stain marring an elaborate tapestry. He floods his magic into him, brushing the tension and sweeping it away. Lucius relaxes against him. "You're peeking again," he says.

"Guilty. What's wrong?"

Lucius sighs. "I'm worried about tomorrow."

"You think you're making a mistake."

The tension returns to Lucius' shoulders. "Yes."

"Are you going to blame yourself if anyone dies?"

The upswell in anguish makes Davros wince. "Yes," Lucius says in a rough voice.

"You shouldn't. We all know the danger. It's our choice to fight."

"You're not wrong, but..." His voice trails off. "I don't know if I can take losing anyone."

"I'm surprised you haven't tried to send me away to safety," Davros says. "Keep me out of harm's way."

"What makes you think I'd do that?"

"Seems like a heroic prince thing to do."

"You've been listening to too many stories," Lucius says. A smile creeps into his voice. "No, you're far too valuable to be sidelined. You possess a rare mix of damage and healing that any commander would kill to have. You act decisively when people's lives are on the line, and you're tough and resourceful. Also, I'd never disrespect you like that."

"Thanks," Davros says. "You wouldn't be able to stop me from helping you."

"That too." Lucius yawns loudly. "We should sleep. You'll need all the energy you can wring out of that little body of yours tomorrow."

"I'll make myself as big as you. Then you can't call me small anymore."

"You have clothes that fit?"

"Shit, you got me."

Lucius laughs. "Come on. *I'm* tired."

"No wonder. You did all the work."

Lucius barks a laugh and runs his lips along Davros's ear. "You should take charge next time," he says.

Next time. Lucius wants a next time. The thought thrills and terrifies him in equal measure. "You want that?"

"Oh yes."

Davros flushes. "I'll try."

"Mm, good enough."

Lucius rolls onto his back. Davros joins him, nestling into those big, warm arms. He snuffs the candles. A deep sense of calm settles into him. Despite the danger they face in the morning, two words stick in his head, their presence a great weight off his aching chest.

I'm safe.

XXIII

SUN

Pica

They make love again, deep in the night, after the shapeshifter pulls Pica from a dream. This time, his lover is more sure of themselves in the darkness. Under Pica's hands, they shift form, morphing from one body to another in sensual expression. Pica eagerly explores each one. Neither of them has trouble falling back to sleep afterward.

Krakli chirps outside the port hole before dawn, brushing Pica's senses with a soft inquiry. The familiar's mood is dark, and Pica doesn't blame him. The little magpie is about to face his worst fear. He portrays his wakefulness to the bird. Krakli rasps and takes wing again. Pica expresses his gratitude and pride for his brave little friend.

Rousing the shapeshifter proves difficult. She's in the form she fell asleep in, sprawled across his chest and snoring softly. After gentle pokes and nudges don't elicit a reaction, Pica resorts to magical means, sending a jolt of vigor through her veins. She twitches and covers her face with her arm. He waits a few more seconds before rolling her off him and rising out of bed.

She mutters and grumbles as he dresses, pulling on thick breeches. The stiff leather feels strange, but it's a necessary discomfort. All the human warriors will wear it to help block sharp beaks.

He is nearly dressed by the time the shapeshifter crawls out of bed, yawning as she shifts form. He watches with a mix of fascination and amusement. Her eyes are barely open, and her red-brown hair is a tangled mess. The shapeshifter crosses the tiny cabin to the awaiting leather, completing the transformation into Davros.

Pica helps him with the leather and armor. The breastplate they found for him is dark blue, marred by nicks and scratches, but otherwise well-maintained. Once dressed, he helps Pica with his banded metal *lorica*, his fingers deft despite the deep yawns that punctuate the otherwise silent ritual of preparation.

Finally, they are both ready. Sleepy blue eyes watch him with a mix of apprehension and affection. Pica pulls Davros close, and they share a long kiss before silently exiting through the door.

The sun peaks over the horizon when they emerge into the cold morning air. Pica eats his morning bread as they go along the beach. Davros pulls a chunk of the dark rye and eats with tiny bites.

The dragons are already awake. Levnys huge eyes travel over them, widening as they get closer. Her nostrils flare.

"I see," she says with satisfaction in her tone.

"Hey," Davros says.

She lowers her head, and Davros hugs her nose. A deep note of happiness rumbles in her chest as Davros lays his cheek against her forehead. After several moments, he kisses the dragon between her brows before releasing her and turning to face Pica.

"I need to go," he says.

"Yeah." Pica steps forward and kisses him. "Fight well, my sweet. Come back to us alive."

"I'll do my best." He turns back to Levnys. He grabs her horns and swings himself onto her neck. "I'll tell you about last night if you take me to Gythu," Davros says to her.

Pica watches his lovers depart with his heart in his throat. If things go wrong, he may never see his little bard again. He pushes the thought away with desperate ferocity.

Pica turns to the rest of the beach. Tisu is nearby, crouching as deckhands secure two saddles to the base of her neck, one behind the other. Ropes hang from each one.

Around her front leg is a thick leather band embedded with an enchanted glass orb. It swirls with pale blue smoke. Seto spent most of last week crafting them. The orb, when broken, will protect from most attacks, albeit for a brief time.

Tisu's green eyes are distorted by the enormous pair of goggles she wears. Pica hadn't known they made them for dragons, let alone in enough variety to be collectible. He gives her a wave of acknowledgment. She replies with a wide grin.

Kisara and Lucia approach her. Lucia's armor gleams in the morning sun, the shine distorted by countless scratches. She has a dagger at her hip. Kisara's armor is a padded vest. It was the only thing big enough to fit her. The rest of her body is covered in leather, and even her draconic feet are wrapped in broad strips. The three make a team: dragon, mage, and support. Each has its role. Pica has to hope it's enough.

Levnys returns and nuzzles him. He leans against her head. She settles into a crouch as the deckhands move to her, making the last preparations.

"I hope we did enough," he says. "I'm worried I can't protect you with my magic...missing."

"If anyone will manage, it is you, Lucius," she says.

He presses his lips against her nose. "We fight and die together, in any case."

"Yes. It is all we can do."

A throat clears behind him. Sparax. Pica turns around, letting his eyes wander over his former lover. The other paladin is clad in leather and steel from head to heel. His hair sticks out of his hood, and his goggles are pushed off his face.

"Hey. Sorry to interrupt. Everyone's ready."

"You're never interrupting," Pica says. "Let's do it."

Sparax pulls their foreheads together. "Hey, one thing. I know you're about to do your leader thing, where you say something motivational. So let me say something first. Whatever happens today, I know that you're doing your best. Try to internalize that. *You're doing your best,* and I'm with you all the way."

Pica's eyes blur with tears. "I don't want to be so scared. *Gods.* It's not—"

"You're about to say, 'It's not something a leader would be' or 'how a prince should act' or something asinine. Save it. I know you don't believe it."

"*Shit.* How am I supposed to be a mysterious leader if you keep calling me out?"

Sparax scoffs. "You're as mysterious as a pile of horse shit. Everyone can see what you're made of."

Wind blows over them as Levnys breathes out a startled laugh. Pica swears he sees sparks flicker over Sparax's armor.

Sparax tucks his hair into his hood. "Shall we?"

Pica pulls his hood over his head, flattening his hair, then puts on his goggles. The thick glass makes the edges of his vision blurry.

"Yes. Let's get going."

Pica doesn't feel brave or heroic as he looks over the leather and steel-clad warriors.

He only feels sweaty.

It runs down the sides of his face under his thick hood, pooling at the base of his neck. His hair is unpleasantly soaked. His breeches make squishing noises as he shifts weight in the saddle he's strapped to.

Krakli perches on his shoulder, trembling. A clear picture emerged between Sehuti's observations and his familiar's distress—hundreds of thousands of birds perched on barren trees, a swirling mass of death on deafening wings, aimed straight at the heart of Caltava. This will be their only chance to head off the swarm.

They've prepared the best they can. The warriors before him are all united in their goal and resolve. Pica takes heart in it, fortifying his determination to see this through. He has to fight despite his magic remaining out of reach. They're depending on him, and he on them. A legion is stronger than the sum of its soldiers, and so they must be, too.

You must never stop.

And he won't, not until his last breath.

All eyes are on him. He wonders what they see. Is it a broken man? A hardened warrior? A lunatic? Perhaps a combination of all three. He takes a swig of water and addresses them, his voice raw but steady.

"My friends. These foul creatures will drain every last living thing on the Coast. We will not let them. We will fly, and we will fight. We will destroy every single one of these miserable things. You have your orders. You know what we must do. Let's go do it."

Okalth snorts, smoke billowing from his nostrils. His laugh is deep and mirthful, rumbling the air.

"Regillus. What a speech. Short, sweet, vindictive. Like a paladin would." He turns to the other dragons. "Bear witness, dragons of the Coast. Today, these paladins fight for us. *With* us." He turns his head back to Pica. "Prove you're not like those white-clad bastards, Regillus."

Pica raises his chin. Those words cost the dragon something. "Fight with me," he says. "Let's go protect *our* home."

The horizon is dark with a storm of birds, the island a smear of black painting the sea. Four dragons and their passengers approach it with the morning sun at their backs. The light ripples off metallic scales and steel armor. At this moment, it's beautiful.

Pica pulls a smooth stone from his pocket. It hums in his gloved hand. He touches the enchantment inside and concentrates, forming an image in his mind, and plucks the thin strand of magic like a lyre string. A streak of fire rises from his palm into the sky, shifting in hue between white, blue, red, and yellow. Levnys bellows a challenge beneath him. The other dragons answer as they speed toward the undulating swarm.

Levnys banks to the right, then dives. Gythu rises, the sun catching the dark red of her wings. Pica takes one last look at Davros before Gythu leaves his vision. He'll be fine. Pica has to believe that.

Tisu and Okalth are already out of sight, moving into position on the left side of the swarm. Each dragon will take a quadrant. They aim to herd the birds together, making them easier to take out. Pica is betting on the tiny creatures reacting as any swarming mass does when a predator is near. Never mind that he's wagering with their lives.

A thick mist, silver-blue like morning fog, hangs over the water's surface. It rises through the swarm, engulfing the lower third, heavily obscuring the birds within. A silver head breaks the surface. Thick mist billows from Zaitun's jaws. Beneath, thousands of razorbacks thrash. The two water dragons herd them into a tight mass of panicked fish. Some razorbacks leap from the water, grabbing birds out of the air.

The sky blazes orange as fire rains from above. The mass of birds dives into the mist to escape the flames. When half of the birds are inside it, Pica releases his next signal—a blue-white orb that crackles and pops in the cool morning air. Levnys turns and heads straight for the swarm. Pica sets his jaw.

Levnys angles hard to the right, flying parallel to the edge of the swarm. She speeds past the breakaway groups that chase her, moving too fast for them to catch. Pica reaches into the pouch strapped to his left leg and draws out a handful of bark, handing half to Sparax behind him. They break them, sending arcs of pale blue magic deep into the cloud. When the magic contacts the mist, the droplets freeze, trapping birds mid-flight. They drop like stones into the water—first hundreds, then thousands. The water dragons release more mist to fill the gaps. The razorbacks thrash in a feeding frenzy. Hundreds of them leap out of the water. Trapped between the predators and the fire, the birds panic, swirling in mad circles.

They send magic into the swarm until the pouch is empty. Sparax rests his hand on Pica's shoulder. The blessing envelops all three of them as Levnys unleashes lightning at a pack of birds. The mist thins. The enemy's foul energy winds through the swarm. The mass of birds flattens, spreading out below the circling dragons before rising to engulf them.

"There you are," Pica murmurs.

Another signal—blue and yellow fire forming tendrils like lightning. Levnys turns into the swarm, unleashing her lightning in a wide arc. Pica lays his hand on the edge of his saddle, concentrating on the word "protect." Orbs of silver fire—Davros' fire—surround Levnys' hide. The orbs burn birds on contact, keeping them from finding purchase in the dragon's skin.

They clear the cloud and turn for another pass. Pica looks around, trying to take stock of the other dragons and their passengers. Tisu's lightning turns birds to blackened ruin. A halo of crackling lightning obscures her copper scales—Kisara's storm magic, forming an elemental shield.

Fire rains from above. The flame obscures Gythu and Okalth. Pica tries to locate Sehuti above the fray but doesn't spot the nightshade dragon. He glances below. The feeding frenzy is over. The mist dissipates as the birds spread out. Zaitun and Xemun break away from the school of fish and streak toward the east.

Pica releases the next signal. A crimson fireball ignites above him with a thunderous explosion. All four circling dragons dart and weave, spraying fire and lightning into the swarm. Gythu opens her jaws and spits an enormous cloud of flickering shards of black glass, with edges glowing red. Pica can barely see the obsidian dragon through Davros' silver fire protecting her. It flashes as birds impact it, the ashes drifting and swirling in the winds.

Now, it will be a slog. The test of endurance is when warriors fall. He tracks the flow of battle, wary of surprises. The island's trees are mostly bare now. Okalth's fire blasts from close by, making him twitch. The enormous gout of flame destroys a swath of the birds, sending ash into the sea. A flickering layer of fire courses over his skin, turning his gem hide into a sparkling gradient of orange, pink, and red. Petrus has his hand on Seto's shoulder as the wizard releases bursts of lightning, each spiraling after small packs of the swarm. Close behind Okalth, several of Seto's lightning summons pick off the stragglers.

Time for the next step. The signal is a pair of blazing orbs rotating around a central point to rise swiftly through the air.

Levnys flies out of the swarm and turns hard. Gythu and Tisu make a similar maneuver, circling in the same direction, tightening their spiral as they drive the birds to a central point with blasts of elemental destruction. In the middle, Okalth flies a tightly looping pattern, a ball of flame appearing at each apex. Soon, a dozen orbs are rotating around him. Birds explode in thousands of tiny puffs against his fire shield. Pica stares at the dragon in awe. At his full power, he'd struggle to keep up with Okalth and his magic.

The swarm compresses as the dragons circle. The enemy's foul power rakes against Pica's senses again. Groups of birds attempt to break away. Mages and dragons take each one out.

They're holding—for now.

Tisu flies across his vision with blinding speed, blasting another group of birds with a triumphant roar. She bursts through it—straight into a cloud of Gythu's obsidian blades. Pica's heart sinks as the sharp glass tears into the dragon's hide and punches through the membrane of her green-tipped wings. Tisu screams and slams her hand on Seto's shield stone, activating it. It sputters to life with a flash of blue light. It's too late. Birds surround her, trying to break through the magical barrier. She flaps in desperate panic, spinning out of control. Kisara and Lucia fall with her, strapped to the saddles on her neck. Lightning fills the air in ragged bursts.

The scene is wrenched from his vision as Levnys speeds to cover the gap. Pica screams and slams his fist on the saddle. He has to keep going. It doesn't matter that it's his family in grave peril. If he doesn't keep fighting, *everyone's* family will be threatened. Ava's words echo in his head, as clear as the day he heard them.

You must never stop.

It was folly to believe that everything would go smoothly. Even the best plans don't survive contact with the enemy. He knows that, and yet—and *yet*—he allowed himself to hope. He curls forward, clenching his head to keep himself from plunging into the darkness. Sparax embraces him, resting his head against Pica's shoulder. The gesture only lasts a second, but it is everything. Pica reaches back and squeezes Sparax's knee.

This time, he's not fighting alone.

Levnys and Gythu herd the swarm with the two of them. Okalth's magic continues to chew the cloud apart from the inside. Drums pound in a distant rhythm as *Raven's Flight* heads southwest, her oars turning the choppy water to roiling white peaks. The sleek ship leaps forward at full speed, flanked by the water dragons, almost in position.

Tisu, Lucia, and Kisara come into view again, surrounded by birds. At Lucia's sharp cry, frost surrounds the trio in a white blizzard. Birds drop away, frozen, revealing Lucia slumped against Kisara's back. The cloud reforms and closes in, chasing the plummeting Tisu.

Sehuti streaks from the clouds and snatches her above the water's surface, juking from side to side as he carries the much smaller dragon away from the fray. Tisu slumps in his grip.

Sparax's magic ripples over them again, re-energizing tired muscles and fatigued minds. The drums cease. A war horn sounds, cutting through the cool morning air like a scythe. A touch on the signal stone sends a streak of yellow fire into the sky. The tail of it lingers as a thick cloud of smoke.

Gythu and Levnys stop circling. They interpose their bodies

between the island and the swarm. Okalth rises from the dark cloud like a phoenix, dripping blood and fire, his eyes bright with angry flame. His wounds close, thanks to the glowing magic pulsing from Petrus' hands. Okalth flips in the air, joining the other dragons in their defensive line.

The sound of the dragons' collective inhalation cuts through the roaring wind. All three unleash their fury in a blinding wave of fire and lightning, causing the swarm to jerk away from the sudden onslaught. Davros and Seto raise their hands in the air, palms out. A wall of blue lightning and silver fire blazes to life high above the dragons' heads. The dragons advance, pushing the swarm away from their island, their stolen refuge—and *Raven's Flight* on the other side.

If Ralex and his crew were able to play their part, then the results should be visible right about...now. Pica turns in the saddle to watch. The remaining birds burst into the air as the branches catch fire beneath them, swirling above the island like turbulent water. The swarm jerks one way, then another. The birds coalesce around a central point. Pica braces himself. The drums roll again, and the birds descend upon the ship.

Pica swallows. This was always the risk. The crew took precautions, but will it be enough?

Twin roars split the air as two dragons rise above the trees—one copper smeared with crimson and one silver-white. Lightning rips through the swarm as Kisara and Tisu join the battle above the burning island. Relief and concern war for supremacy in Pica's heart. How long will they be able to fight?

Streaks of fire—hundreds of them—explode inside of the swarm. The ship's crew, using enchanted bark. Pica forces himself to turn back around. As he does, the magic in the saddle gutters out in flashes of white light. Now, Levnys is exposed. Pica grits his teeth. Right now, the birds are blocked, dying in their thousands, but if they manage to break through, Seto's shield stone will only last a minute. Should he signal? Should he wait?

The questions like this, the decisions on his shoulders, kept him awake at night in the legion. If they use the barrier too early, she will be unprotected later. Pica stares at the signal stone, then drops his hand. No. It's not time yet.

The swarm circles. Crimson feathers flash as thousands of birds open their beaks and regurgitate blood into the air. The blood gathers and grows, beating like a dark heart as it coalesces. Pica's heart beats in time with it. There's a tug inside him, a pull toward that crimson tempest as if his blood is begging to escape. Sparax gasps. The dragons bellow in pain. Through it all, a sense of dread, of shivering fear, grips his head. *Enemy*, he can almost hear the serpent hiss. *Foul adversary.*

Great dark wings spread to block the morning sun. The entity's bat-like form looms above them all, a bloody mountain with its dark cloud attending. Glowing red eyes open in the misshapen head, dripping with something visceral. They fix upon him.

"Vessel," the enemy snarls. "You are as persistent as a biting fly. Irritating."

Pica glares at the enormous bat, trembling. Levnys shivers beneath him, keening in distress. Sparax chokes and slumps against his back. The presence of the entity is unlike anything Pica has felt before. What can he do against such power? He tries to conjure his magic, to bring the tiniest flame to his hand. Blood pounds in his head, his muscles burn, but no fire comes to his desperate call. What can he do? What can any of them do?

The entity's lips peel back. Gleaming white fangs shine like daggers. Pica lays a shaking hand on Levnys' neck. He runs his fingers gently along her scales, trying to soothe her, to convey his vast affection. *We fight together,* he wants to tell her. *None of us die alone today.*

Pica pulls his dagger. He channels magic into it, illuminating the short blade like a beacon. It shines with golden light—Andereth's light. He screams in defiance, pouring his fear and anger into his centurion's voice. Levnys' roar joins his. Then the other dragons take up the call—flame and lightning stream forth as Pica's voice gives out.

The bat's eyes lock onto Gythu. Magic lashes at the obsidian dragon, a black lance faster than Pica can blink. It rakes her side, parting the ropes and harnesses, carving an enormous gash down her flank. The wound glows as her molten blood gushes over her black scales. Her bellow turns into a scream of pain. The saddles tip sideways, sliding from her neck. Birds surge for the helpless occupants. The wall of silver fire stutters and dies.

"Davros!" Pica tries to scream. The sound comes out as a weak rasp. *No. No no no please no.*

Davros' head jerks. A pulse of pink light passes over his body. He throws something, a tiny glittering ball—his prism. It shoots toward the doomed dragon like an arrow. Shards of glass twinkle in the air as the entity's jaws close around Gythu's throat, driving her into the sea.

Davros jerks at the knots holding him to the saddle, his deft hands moving almost too fast for Pica to see. Davros comes free, flips himself around, and grabs the saddle with his legs. He unties Calvus within seconds. Before they hit the water, Davros pulls the Grandmaster to him, cradling the older man's head against his chest. He releases the saddle. Tendrils of silver light coil around them as they impact, plunging into the school of razor-sharp fish below.

No, Davros, you can't die. Please, gods, don't take him from me!

Tears blur Pica's vision. He chokes back the sobs that wrack his chest and pushes away the dark despair. He can never stop. Not even if his precious bard is dead can he stop. He clenches his fist around the signal stone and plucks the thread of magic so hard it snaps. A sphere of blue fire blooms in front of Okalth's and Levnys' noses, its center hollow. It's a command that's come from his lips more times than he can count, a phrase that could define a man's time in a legion.

Raise your shield.

The two dragons slam their hands on their stones in unison. The bat bursts from the sea in a streak of crimson, catching Okalth in its claws. Okalth's head whips around, black teeth bared, fire flickering deep within his throat. The blast of fire rakes the entity's body, sending tendrils of crimson mist steaming into the air. Okalth's jaws sink into the bat's leg. Claws rake Okalth, scraping the side of the shield. Pica pulls enchanted bark from the pouch on his right hip and snaps the dry wood, one after another, sending streams of flame at the swarm. It's not enough. What can he do? *What can he do?* Helplessness consumes him and clouds his vision. The tears are unstoppable now. Visions of blood and death crowd into his head, jumbled together into a mass. Pica doubles over, clutching his stomach.

Okalth burns the entity again, and it releases him, snarling. The bat screeches, high and long, a piercing sound that drives daggers into Pica's head. His confused thoughts fracture further. *Do something,* he tells himself. *Do something, you idiot, do something.*

Another roar splits the air. Sehuti descends from the clouds. The nightshade dragon mutters to himself, switching between Gethki and an unknown language. Sehuti's sides heave. He raises his head and snarls, his eye a crimson orb set into dark wood.

"Behold," the entity crows. "Your friend. All mine."

Okalth snarls. "Vile traitor!" he spits.

Wait, Pica wants to shout. He tries to gesture at Okalth but can barely keep his eyes open.

"Kill them," the entity says.

Sehuti's head jerks. The leaves covering his hide tremble as he lashes his tail back and forth. "Stop," he says. "*Mela.*" His body shakes like a dog straining against a chain. Sehuti surges forward without a further word, arrowing at Levnys as if shot from a bow. Okalth intercepts him. His flame misses Sehuti's leaves by inches. They strike at each other, and the chase begins. The nightshade dragon is a much nimbler flier. Okalth's flame barely touches him, while Sehuti's thorns glance off Seto's shield. Sehuti whips his tail as the glowing barrier drops, and the thorns sink home. Flame courses over Okalth's skin, and both dragons scream in pain.

No. Please no. Gods, I beg you.

Sehuti retreats. Okalth pursues. Birds break off and give chase. The light in Levnys' shield orb winks out. They're alone against the entity, with no protection. The entity sneers and comes for them.

Levnys dodges its strikes, keeping her distance, unleashing lightning with every breath. Her breathing becomes labored, her wings flapping slower with each beat. Pica sends as much energy into her as he can. A great gash opens on her side. Pica and Sparax close it. His dragon is growing weaker. Soon, she will fall.

Not enough. What can I do?

"Pathetic," the entity sneers. "A weakling vessel for a weakling parasite."

Pica closes his eyes. *Think.* The entity still calls him a vessel. The serpent has to remain inside him. It's the only hope they have left.

He does the only thing he can. Turning inward, he pictures that lost place, layering the jungle around the pyramid, the sounds of the birds, the press of humidity.

He plunges into it.

"Serpent," he calls into the thick air. "Serpent!"

Pica pulls his sword and slashes through the thick jungle. Heat presses around him. Dark clouds obscure the sun. He pushes through the last vine and emerges into a bloody courtyard. The serpent is chained there. Their great coils are lashed to the pyramid by pulsing crimson steel. Pica runs to their side. The serpent's eyes fall on him. Their jaws are pinned to the cobblestones by a cruel spike, driven so hard into the stone that cracks branch like cobwebs. The clouds above them darken, turning the sky an angry gray. A crimson glow creeps into the clouds. Somewhere distant, pain.

Pica stares at his sword. The *gladius* rests easily in his hand, an extension of his arm. Everything else has been stripped away from him—except his blade. Except for his oath.

Until the sun falls and the moon crumbles to dust, I will be vigilant.

The sword trembles in his hand. The blade pulses with light—first golden, then azure. The colors of his bloodline, of his empire. Of Andereth. Of all that he is.

Until the stars dim and my sword turns to rust, I will be strong.

He strides forward. The chains seethe with vile crimson. Pica raises the sword above his head. His left hand flexes, curling around the handle of a phantom shield.

Until the earth heaves and the seas rise, I will be a shield.

He brings the sword down on the chain. The steel links scream as they part. Angry red mist swirls around his arms, burning his skin. Magic ripples over him. Sparax.

Until my last breath and death closes my eyes, I will be a protector.

One by one, he cuts the chains until the serpent's body sags free. He climbs onto their head, wraps his arms around the spike, and heaves upward with all his strength. The serpent's coils writhe behind him. His muscles scream with the exertion, but slowly, painfully, the spike comes free. Pica extracts it, tosses it aside, and kneels to put his hand on the serpent's bleeding head.

While I live, I am Andereth's shield.

"It's good to see you," Pica says.

"You came for me."

"Of course. The enemy is here. Can you fight?"

"I must," they reply. They raise their head, gathering their body beneath them. Under Pica's hand, scales and feathers knit together as they rise into the air. Above them, the clouds thin, pulling away from the sun. They rise into the brightening sky.

"What do we do?" the serpent asks.

Pica's mind races. There has to be something to even the field. The bat wasn't so big in the serpent's memories. What if—

That bat manifested out of the blood birds, Pica realizes. If Pica can call the serpent forth the same way, they may have a chance.

"You're a spirit," Pica says. "Can I summon you?"

The serpent's jaws open. "That could work. We must try."

Pica comes to with a raspy scream. The bat entity looms above them. His leg blazes with the pain of a hundred tiny pinpricks. Birds sink into his skin through a gash in his leather.

Fire kindles to life in his hand, and he burns them to ash. The serpent's presence fills his every limb, every muscle. He sheathes his dagger and raises his hands to the sky.

"Serpent, heed!"

Golden fire rages from his palms in a column as wide as he is tall. The serpent coils into the morning sky. The skin on his forearms and hands blisters under that heat, but he drives more power into it, gritting his teeth against the pain. Sparax's arms go around him. His heart quickens.

The serpent strikes at the bat, driving it back. They bring their enormous fiery coils between Levnys and their enemy.

"Ah-Xoc-Xin," the bat sneers. The sound of it is strange to Pica's ears, like the whisper of wind through reeds.

"Oh. That must be my name." The serpent displays their fearsome fangs. The red and orange feathers on their head crest fan out. "I am not done for yet, Itzel."

"It's 'Ah-Teya-Itzel,'" the bat growls. "You still disrespect me, worm."

Ah-Xoc-Xin's neck pulls back to form an S. "You deserve it."

Itzel snarls and lunges for the serpent. Ah-Xoc-Xin strikes, sinking fiery fangs into the crimson mist. Pica continues the stream of magic, channeling his restored flame into the serpent. Flaming butterflies rise from Ah-Xoc-Xin's feathers. They dart forward, engaging the swarming birds with puffs of smoke and explosions of ash.

"I killed you before. I'll do it again." Itzel's claws sink home, opening a fiery gash.

"I remember what you did." Ah-Xoc-Xin's feathered tail lashes, burning swaths of birds with one mighty swipe. "You tricked me. You tricked my sister, Ah-Uaya-Nih." The serpent's emerald eyes start to glow. Their voice swells with anguish and old pain. "You chased Ah-Deh-Det to this land and tried to kill her. I do not know why you are doing this, but I will stop you, Itzel. I swear it."

Two sets of ghostly limbs manifest from the serpent's back, spreading wide into magnificent wings. They blaze with color, like the mosaic in Dalos' bathhouse. With a great roar, Ah-Xoc-Xin surges forward, driving Itzel back.

Levnys circles higher into the air, above the swarm and battling giants. Her body trembles, her chest heaving with great laboring breaths. Pica wants to tell her to retreat, that she's done enough. His voice will never reach her over the wind. Neither Sehuti nor Okalth are in sight. Sehuti. He betrayed them, but why? Where is he? Pica feels exposed. Something doesn't add up.

He senses the nightshade dragon as Levnys does. Sehuti rises from below, thorns bristling. Levnys spins to face him, her growl rumbling through Pica's saddle. Something's wrong. A cloud of red mist surrounds Sehuti's head, thick and cloying. In his ruined eye socket, a bud pulses with that mist like a heartbeat.

"Where's Okalth?" Levnys demands.

"Lost," Sehuti says. His voice sounds strange, underpinned with a deep, thrumming note. He speaks in fits and starts. "I will. Take care of you. First."

The nightshade dragon jerks like a puppet on strings. His lips peel from his teeth, drop, and pull back again. The thorns bristle and lower. Green foam drips from his jaws.

"Kill. Kill them." Sehuti jerks his head from side to side, causing the branches on his brow to rattle. "No. *No! Sila!*"

The bud blooms. A chartreuse eye spreads to fill the socket before the iris floods with angry crimson.

XXIV
BETRAYAL

Levnys

Sehuti lunges. Pain and betrayal war for supremacy in Levnys' heart. Hot anger narrows her vision, a dark tunnel lit only by the fires of revenge. After all they did for Sehuti, he turned on them. She should have never let Lucius save him. Now, he will overpower her failing body and kill them all. Battle lust floods into her through Sparax's magic, sending her into a rage so keen every muscle screams for a fight.

Ah-Xoc-Xin and Itzel continue their battle in flashes of light. Sehuti twitches, his crimson eyes watching her as a predator watches prey. "Worth-less," he says. His voice is halting, strange. "Kill." Sehuti shudders. He wings forward with a burst of speed. He dodges the lightning Levnys aims at him and closes in with claws outstretched. Levnys meets him with her own weapons. The paladins heal her wounds, and Lucius' fire blasts above the nightshade dragon's head.

His fire. His fire is back. Perhaps they can win this, after all. Another blast misses Sehuti completely.

"Why?" she demands. "Why do this?"

"Why," Sehuti sneers. His voice changes pitch, becoming higher and more panicked. "Why? Whystopwhy?"

Levnys sinks her teeth into the wood of the nightshade dragon's shoulder. Sehuti struggles, his claws trying to find purchase in her flanks. Another fireball explodes in his face. The light from it is blinding, causing her to release the dragon and reel back from it. What is Lucius doing? Sehuti circles away from her, thrashing his head like a dog worrying a bone, growling incoherently. He resembles an animal with those baleful red eyes. Levnys goes for him. Sehuti spins in the air and brings his claws to bear, catching her with jagged teeth, even more like a beast. Levnys' rage grows. Does he think she is not worthy of a proper fight? Her lightning tears through the branches on Sehuti's wings. His talons rend her flesh. Magic makes her blood sing.

An explosion causes both of them to falter. Itzel and Ah-Xoc-Xin fill the morning sky with their enormous power. Levnys would have never believed such things could exist. The serpent scores a deep bite to Itzel's shoulder. The mist around Sehuti's head dissipates. The crimson retreats, revealing his chartreuse irises. He jerks out of Levnys' reach.

"Stop!" he cries. "*Drakaina*, please, I don't want to—"

Itzel's birds surround Ah-Xoc-Xin. The serpent cries out, releasing their grip on the bat. Lucius' ragged scream accompanies the return of the mist. Sehuti's eyes regain their bloody hue. Finally, Levnys understands. She has been a fool, letting her rage cloud the signs before her nose.

"Fight it!" she screams. She flaps and rises, putting distance between her and the stricken dragon. Her body trembles with exhaustion, her muscles burning as hot as Okalth's fire. Sehuti charges. She focuses on dodging, pleading with every breath. "You are strong," she says, pulling her wing away from a tail swipe. "Sehuti! You must not let it win!"

Sehuti falters at her use of his name. Behind him, Itzel snarls. Sehuti strikes. The serpent strikes.

Levnys screams as his claws sink into her flesh. She struggles, opening her mouth to breathe lightning, but he wraps one hand around her muzzle, closing her mouth over the sparks. He wrenches her head to the side, exposing her throat. Lucius' fire hits him squarely, turning leaves to ash and wood to smoking ruin, but the nightshade dragon does not flinch. The red mist pulses like a living thing, nearly obscuring the dragon's crimson eyes. Sehuti's jaws open and descend for the fatal blow.

The serpent's teeth sink home first. Their fiery coils wrap around

Itzel, setting the bloody body aflame. The blood birds dart in panicked flight, chased by the butterflies in rivers of light. Sehuti's grip loosens as the fiery insects surround him. Levnys jerks her head out of his fingers. His jaws close on air. He shrieks—a keening note, as the butterflies cover him from nose to tail. Itzel's scream is equally as desperate. The bat's body disintegrates, running in smoking rivers over Ah-Xoc-Xin's coils.

The remaining birds gather in a mass and flee for their burning island. A dragon rises to greet them, covered in raging flame. Okalth, he lives. He joins Kisara and Tisu in the sky above the inferno, white-hot flame jetting from his throat.

The butterflies disperse as Levnys slumps but does not fall. Sehuti's claws and thorns withdraw from her skin, but he does not drop her. His chartreuse eyes scan the sky, widening as the serpent approaches. The enormous entity circles around them. They roar to the sky in triumph. Their body bursts into butterflies in a rippling wave from nose to tail, then blink from existence in thousands of tiny explosions of light. On her back, Lucius gasps. Sparax shouts something, but it is lost in the wind.

The world blurs. Sehuti is moving, carrying her toward the island. Flame fills her vision, then the blue-green of the sea. A sand beach streaked brown and white. The last thing she sees is a great black shape sprawled on the sand before her eyes close.

XXV
HEALING

Davros

The shapeshifter thrashes her tail, beaching herself and Calvus on the burning island. She drags him onto the sand and rolls him onto his side. Pressing clawed hands to the old paladin's back, she tries to ignore the raging fire burning all around their tiny patch of beach.

She pours her magic into the Grandmaster's body—around his lungs, his heart, through his neck and head. Assessing his condition, falling into an old routine of healing, keeps her clinging to sanity. No neck or head injuries, aside from a slight concussion. Heartbeat steady, strong for a man his age. Seawater in his lungs.

With a quick push of will, she forces his body to expel the water onto the beach. She lets him draw a ragged breath, then repeats the treatment. Soon, he is coughing and spitting mucus and salty water. After a few more breaths, she cuts the contact and rolls onto her back.

She's so exhausted she nearly forgets to change form. Sleek green scales transform into olive skin. Hair sprouts from her scalp, tangled and soaked. A reptilian snout flattens, forming lips and a nose, and pointed ears grow. Her spine shortens as her tail disappears. The shapeshifter pants heavily as their vision shifts, and they complete the transformation back into Davros.

Calvus' breathing steadies. He sits up. Davros idly watches. Calvus' eyes fix on him, sunken and bloodshot but full of life. Calvus is safe, but Gythu...

Davros' heart sinks. He saw the shield orb break when he threw his prism. Was it soon enough? His right hand tingles. Something is about to happen. If only his *pater* would tell him what. He's too exhausted for games.

A burst of light makes him sit upright. He and Calvus stare across the water as an enormous serpent rises and engages with the bat. Was this the serpent Lucius mentioned? Does this mean that—

Calvus clears his throat, and Davros turns his head to see the Grandmaster regarding him. "Do you know what that is?" he asks, with the cadence of someone repeating themselves.

"It's—" Davros doesn't know what Lucius told others. "No."

"Mhm." He knows Calvus doesn't believe him. "What do you know about the gods, young Soutorian?"

"Why do you think I'm Soutorian?"

Calvus sighs. "We don't have time for the act, bard. I've had plenty of time to determine where you came from." The Grandmaster leans forward, resting his arms on his knees. "Answer the question, please."

Now hardly seems the time for a theological conversation. "Uh, I don't know a lot. We don't have gods like Geth does," he answers. "Fox spirits live in our forests and sky, not in some weird other place you must conduct rituals to reach. Why ask? Why *now*?"

Calvus is silent for a long second. "I grew up in Selucia, as you can easily guess." He raises a dark brown hand. "My parents are part of the Negasi diaspora there."

Davros tries to go with the conversation. "I've been there. It's where my ship from Soutori landed."

"Then you know that it is a diverse city. The native Fetocians. The people of Eugaria, like yourself. The Negasi refugees. The Gethki, of course. I've spoken with many people, and I've realized something strange over the years." Calvus drops his hand. "The gods in every culture will speak with their followers somehow, with two exceptions: the sun and the moon."

Davros knows he should grasp some truth within those words, but he can't connect the dots. Lucius would know. But Lucius isn't here. He's fighting while they rot on this beach, talking about theology. The dissonance makes his head hurt.

Five minutes, Nylocke says in his head. Davros' fingers become a painful mass of pins and needles. *Listen to the old man until then.*

It's the most words the demigod has ever spoken. Davros forces himself to focus, to consider the implications of Calvus' words. "I don't understand," he admits.

"It's alright. I have an interest in how deities interact with mortals," Calvus says. "Gods communicate with their followers in many different ways. At times, they manifest as separate beings. Other times, it is merely a voice. The gods of the sun and moon used to speak to their followers, but at some point, they went silent. Their celestial representations shine, of course, but their voices died."

The serpent's roar echoes across the water, wrathful and defiant. Near it, Levnys is fighting her own battle. Sehuti. Why is she fighting Sehuti? Davros feels helpless. He can't save any of them out there across the water. He struggles to focus on the conversation, but he's so tired. All he wants to do is take a deep nap. But—Calvus started this conversation for a reason.

"Have you told Lucius any of this?" Davros asks.

Calvus sighs. "He's never been interested in the gods, only the dragons. I never saw my observations as more than curiosity." He eyes the serpent. The entity is surrounded by thousands of tiny points of light, like the sun glittering through droplets of water. "It seems more relevant now."

He comes. Be ready.

Davros stands on shaking legs. Calvus turns his head to stare at him. "How much magic do you have left?" Davros asks.

"Enough. What is going on?"

"Can you stand?"

"Yes, but I will need your help. What is—"

Davros offers the Grandmaster his arm. He winces as Calvus puts weight on it. As Calvus stands, Davros moves for the water's edge, tugging the Grandmaster. Calvus follows with a bewildered expression.

Fire. Blood. Good luck.

Dull gold flashes in the surf before Xemun beaches himself. "Aea, thank all of the gods I found you." The water dragon's nostrils flare.

"Gythu is alive but will die if we do not help her. We cannot delay."

"Take us to her," Davros says.

Davros sprints up the beach as soon as his feet hit the sand. Fire blazes in the trees across the sandy shoreline. The hungry inferno consumes the dry wood and grasses of the island, licking the sky in a rippling orange wall. Zaitun stands near an enormous dark shape lying on the heat-blasted sand, shifting her weight from foot to foot in helpless worry. Davros chokes at the sight of the prone dragon. A wicked gash runs from her foreleg to her rump, half crusted with lumpy rock and ringed with shards of obsidian. The heat of Gythu's labored breath turns the sand in front of her nose to glass.

Davros reaches her and presses his hands to her side under the gash. He reels at the unfamiliar physiology. She can't be that different. He must find the thread and follow it to a conclusion. She's alive. Find the mechanisms and assess them.

Her blood is like molten rock, hot and viscous. Massive clots of it are hardened around the wound, branching through her veins into her left wing. Her foreleg is solid, with no circulation—no chance of saving it. He moves on. If he hurries, he can save the wing. Organs—yes, she has them—no lasting damage. Yet.

Calvus reaches him. "Report, healer," he says, putting his palms on Gythu's side.

"The clots, or she dies," Davros says. "Support me."

"Can you control her bloodstream?"

"About to find out."

Davros puts his hand on the clots and channels fire into the hardened rock. The stone softens but doesn't melt. Shit. Shit, shit, *shit*. It's not enough. He needs it to be hotter, but he's a *water* mage, for godssake. Okalth could do it, but he's out of reach. Lucius, if his power returned, could do it. But *he* can't.

"Zaitun!" he shouts, projecting his voice across the beach. "I need fire!"

She bounds toward the inferno. Davros clenches his teeth and pours as much magic as possible into his flame. The stone melts a little more, revealing the orange glow beneath it. Not fast enough. He can't do this. He's not strong enough. Useless. He clamps hard on the growing panic. No, he has to find a way. What did Nylocke say?

Fire. Blood. Good luck.

A shadow falls over the beach, followed by a rush of wings. Sehuti lands awkwardly, holding Levnys in his arms. She slumps onto the sand like an empty sack when Sehuti sets her down. Weren't they fighting? Davros watches with his heart in his throat. Levnys' passengers are strapped to her, but only Sparax stirs, tearing the ropes from his body before setting to work on Lucius' restraints. Lucius lies limp in the saddle. Davros wants to run to their side, embrace them, and ensure they're alright. No. Gythu needs him more.

Sparax joins him and Calvus a few seconds later. Davros opens his mouth to speak, but Sparax says, "They'll be alright. How can I help?"

"Support me."

Zaitun appears with a flaming branch clenched in her jaws. "Put it against her wound," Davros instructs her. Zaitun does so, jamming the lit end against the gash.

"Davros, what are you—"

Davros wheels on Sparax. "We are out of time!" He turns his back to the paladins. He is going to *do* something about this. Instead of the wound, he directs his magic at the burning branch, causing the flame to flare white-hot. Gloved hands settle onto his shoulders as both paladins channel magic through him. His senses blaze into overload as he struggles to block the emotions of both men. It nearly overwhelms him. He spins their magic together and directs it all— magic, fire, emotions—deep into Gythu's body. It's not enough. The panic gnaws at him. There has to be something else. Something he's missing.

Fire. Blood. Good luck.

His right hand tingles painfully, flaring with his *pater's* magic. Davros grits his teeth as he realizes there's one thing left to do. Something only an insane person would try.

Davros pulls his glove from his right hand with his teeth. He spits it out, turns one of his canines razor-sharp, and bites into the webbing between his thumb and forefinger. Before he can change his mind, he jams his bloody hand against the welling magma that is Gythu's blood. He screams as his flesh sears, blackening around the silver radiance of Nylocke's sigil. Strong fingers clamp on his shoulders. Healing magic ripples over his hand, repairing the skin in waves as it burns over and over. The agony is a living thing, burrowing into his palm, his fingers, up his arm. He channels it into the fire, cursing and sobbing, willing himself to see it through.

The rock melts, dribbling down the dragon's skin in viscous globs of glowing orange. The clots in Gythu's bloodstream break free, flowing through the tubes that are her arteries and veins, and then melt. His heart pounds in his chest and his ears until he thinks he will burst. Pain blurs his vision. He wants to retch, to empty his stomach until he's expelled his guts.

He shifts the last scraps of his attention to Gythu's wing, to the great blockage preventing the lava's flow. The rest of his will goes into his magic, that sparkling river of white fire pouring forth from his hand. Slowly, the blockage relents. Circulation returns to Gythu's wing, filling the blood-starved tissue with life.

Davros' legs buckle. An arm grabs him around the waist, pressing him back against banded metal armor. Davros leans against Sparax. No. Not done. He reaches for Gythu, the molten gash a searing line in his darkening vision.

"That's enough, Davros," Sparax says. "We can handle the rest."

Blue and yellow magic flares as the wound knits together, sending glittering obsidian tumbling to the ground. The glowing blood disappears, turning Gythu's flank into solid stone. The blackness edges in. Calvus is speaking. Both of Sparax's arms are around him now. He's being carried. Soft sand shifts as he's placed on the ground. A face appears in his blurred vision—red curls, blue eyes. The pain in his hand subsides in a warm burst of magic.

"Rest," Sparax says before disappearing from view.

Davros dozes for a while, basking in the heat of the sun. Someone's hand touches his cheek, waking him before their aura presses on his like a hot landslide. Gythu. Her slate-gray eyes meet his when he opens them. She's smiling, her rocky features creased and folded like distressed land. Below her shoulder, her left arm is missing, the stump capped with jagged chunks of obsidian.

"Hello, Davros," she says. "I am told you are the one to thank for saving my life."

"I suppose I had something to do with it," he replies.

"The way Sparax tells the tale, it was an ordeal." A cloak around her shoulders falls to cover her missing limb. "Calvus agrees, though he is less enthusiastic."

Sparax, why? "Well, I better take credit. How are you feeling? Do you need more healing?"

"Do not spend more of your energy on me." She shifts her shoulders. "Thank you. I am glad to have met you, warrior."

"It was an honor to fight alongside you, Gythu," Davros says. "I hope we never have to do it again."

The dragon's eyes track their surroundings. "It is not over. Okalth will continue to fight. So will I. Will you join us?"

"I can't," he says. "I'm needed elsewhere."

"I see. That is unfortunate." She pats his cheek and stands. "If I do not see you again, I will be upset. Visit me. Levnys knows how to reach my island." She winks, then walks out of his vision.

Oh.

Davros' lips quirk upwards. He feels warm and light, restored by his short nap and the sun's heat. Strange that it's this strong in the shade. Oh. *Oh.* He jerks his head to his left. Lucius lies on his back, several feet away. He's tucked into the curve of Levnys' body, who's also sleeping, her great head sideways on the sand. Behind her, a vast wall of leaves and thorns blocks the morning sun. Sehuti has his wings outstretched, basking as he always does. He lowers his head, putting his nose less than a foot away.

"Hi," Davros says, cringing away from the hot breath.

"Greetings, bard," Sehuti says. The dragon's voice is weary, heavy with resigned emotion.

Davros drags himself across the sand toward Lucius, willing his aching limbs into motion. Sehuti watches before nudging him the rest of the way. The dragon withdraws his head and pulls his wing in tighter, shading them.

Davros puts his hands on Lucius' cheeks. Lucius' magic is back at full force—no, *stronger*. Lucius stirs when their auras connect. When those golden eyes open, Davros breaks. Tears flood his cheeks. He throws himself forward, pressing his lips against Lucius' mouth in desperate relief. It's mirrored in Lucius, and when he pulls back from the kiss, the prince's eyes are as wet as his.

"Thank the gods," Lucius says in a ragged whisper. "I thought I lost you." His voice falters. "Gythu? Calvus? Are they—?"

"Alive." Davros relaxes onto Lucius' chest. "Is Levnys alright?"

"She is asleep," Sehuti says. "I am assured she will be fine with rest. It seems she has developed immunity to my poison."

There's anxiety in the dragon's voice. "What happened?"

Sehuti's wing shifts, and the dragon's head appears, silhouetted dark against the blue sky. The branches ringing his neck droop. "I was weak," he says. He clenches his eyes closed, causing the wood of his brows to creak. "I should have trusted you, mage. Regillus."

"Pica is fine," Lucius rasps.

Sehuti bears his teeth. "No explanation should earn your forgiveness, but you must know the truth."

"It better be good," Levnys murmurs. "You caused me much stress."

Sehuti flinches. He looks at the bronze dragon wide-eyed as Levnys raises her head. Davros is learning dragon body language, but Sehuti's embarrassment is apparent.

"How long have you been awake?" he demands.

"Long enough. Explain." Levnys' chin settles back on the sand.

Sehuti sighs. "After the birds attacked me, I began to have visions. They made no sense—images of death and destruction. After your ship was attacked, the urges began. I thought I could handle them, and for a while, I did—until that *thing* arrived. The voices became deafening, and I found myself doing things I did not want to do. After Okalth chased me off, I regained control long enough to plead with him. He hesitated, and I lost him. Were I him, I would have roasted me on the spot."

"Okalth is slow to resort to violence," Levnys says.

"Could have fooled me," Lucius mutters.

Levnys sighs. "Continue your story, if you please."

Sehuti's leaves lie flat against his skin. "I intended to fly away, but I was overwhelmed again. You must believe that I fought with all my strength. I did not want to hurt any of you."

"Why should we trust you after this?" Levnys asks. Her words don't have any heat to them, merely curiosity.

"You shouldn't," Sehuti says flatly. "I would not, were the roles reversed. I'm not asking for forgiveness, nor your trust. All I want to do is apologize and request a favor." He turns away, looking at something Davros can't see. "If that happens again, kill me. Don't hesitate."

Davros doesn't remember falling asleep, but when he wakes, he's lying on a mattress harder than the ground. Above him is a painted canopy. His body reports his injuries with annoying intensity. He tries to lift his arm, causing daggers to shoot through his shoulder. Someone in the tent moves to his side.

"One awake," Lucia calls from above him. Her warm hand presses against his forehead. "Can you talk?" At his nod, she smiles. "How are you feeling?"

"Like shit," he replies. Davros tries to turn his head.

Lucia clucks her tongue. "Don't move yet. Lucius is in the bed next to you. He's sleeping. Both of you are going to be alright. It was a stroke of good fortune that no one died."

Fire. Blood. Good luck. Thanks, Nylocke.

"We're two days from Caltava," Lucia continues. "So all you need to do is rest and not move around. Understand?"

"Yes, madam Draconia."

"Good. Now, if only my stubborn oaf of a nephew was so cooperative."

After she leaves, Davros dares to peek at the bed to his right. Lucius lies on it, his feet hanging off the edge. Krakli is a feathered ball perched on his chest. Davros wants to reach out to him but refrains, folding his hands over his stomach. The tent is dripping with paladin magic, the pleasant mixture of auras he's grown fond of. He slips into sleep, wakes to eat some vegetable broth, and sleeps again. Darkness falls, light rises, he eats, and he rests. Magic becomes his world as the paladins dutifully work to restore him and Lucius to something resembling whole.

The next time he's coherent, he's in their cabin on *Raven's Flight,* curled on Lucius' lap. His prince's arm tightens around him when he stirs. Lucius puts his scroll aside and buries his face in Davros' hair. Davros traces his fingers over the scales on Lucius' neck. There are more of them than before, traveling further up his neck in shimmering gold.

"Hi," Davros says.

"Hey." Lucius' deep voice is like gravel.

"How long since the battle?" Davros asks.

"Three days," Lucius replies.

"Is it over?"

"For now. The birds are nowhere near Caltava, at least." Lucius cups his chin and lifts it, meeting Davros' lips with his. Davros sinks into the sensation—no fear remains, no hesitation, no regrets.

"Okalth will send word when he finds new birds," Levnys says from the chair. "Until then, we will heal and prepare."

She's right. Surely, the birds spread over a large portion of the Sparkling Coast. They will have to keep fighting.

"We will arrive in Caltava this evening," Levnys continues. "If you are both able, would you join me on deck? I wish for you to see my home."

A tree stands at the rail when they emerge into the late afternoon air. Its gnarled shape resembles a human figure. When it moves, turning its head in their direction, Davros wonders if he's hallucinating. Only when the chartreuse eyes settle on him does he realize he knows this tree.

Lucius laughs. "You were right. Human is a stretch."

Sehuti watches them approach. Branches twist to form spindly arms and legs, with root-like feet spread wide on the black deck. An ethereal green glow pulses deep inside Sehuti's chest, its light radiating between the tangled branches. His face resembles a human's only superficially—a mouth, a nose, and interwoven branches that could be graciously considered hair.

"It is close enough for Ulene," Sehuti says. "But the Arundo no longer exist. How ironic that their likeness only persists through me."

Davros' heart aches for the exiled dragon. At least Davros can blend in if he wants to, hiding his true self with none the wiser. Sehuti has no such luxury.

They settle next to him at the rail. "What will you do now?" Lucius asks.

"Survive," Sehuti replies. "As always." He hands Lucius a scroll of parchment. "I didn't need it after all."

Painting the horizon is a low stretch of land. On the sea between, hundreds of ships swarm across the turquoise water. Many of them are Gethki warships with two rows of oars. "Quadriremes," Lucius supplies. Their painted golden eyes keep diligent watch over the others—Fresian and Caltavian passenger ships, Soutorian trading vessels, and hundreds of others of a kind that Davros has never seen before. *Raven's' Flight* slips among them, making her way toward the hunched cliff faces coming into view.

The ships follow a dredged canal toward the shore, falling into rough lanes and traveling in both directions from the bustling harbor. Sand bars lurk below the surface. Enchanted lights mark each one, glinting white like polished pearls.

Levnys points at a black speck across the water. "That is my lair," she says.

"Will we get to see it?" Lucius asks.

"In time. I must prepare. It must be perfect."

The city of Caltava rises above the cliffs, its buildings placed like toys stacked on the steep hill and crowned by a walled citadel. Looming in front of them, the harbor's entrance is a great maw, swallowing ships like grains of rice. The cliffs merge into seawalls, wrapped around the long rectangular harbor in a protective embrace. *Raven's Flight* slips between the concrete teeth of the entrance—low structures with rusted chains coiled like serpents at rest. Several barriers have towers, simple wooden structures operated by two guards in chain mail and crimson cloaks. Red banners hang from every tower and line the inner walls. Davros peers at the closest one. Two double-headed axes are crossed at their hilts, wrought in black. Ralex calls out to the guards. They greet him with an enthusiastic wave.

It's warmer here than out on the water. The magic of the place thrums strong against Davros' senses, as it did in Notri and Geth. Notri was undoubtedly Ava's presence, and Geth was so strong it overwhelmed him. Caltava is like a dream in comparison—bright and cheery, like the sun when spring turns to summer.

The ships around them peel off one by one, nestling into docks and niches set into a thick concrete quay. Wood and stone buildings are crowded into the narrow space along the waterfront. Vast warehouses loom behind them. A lumbering barge loaded with enormous trees ponderously turns into a section piled with wood so high, it nearly rises above the stone walls. *Raven's Flight* sails deeper into the harbor.

"That is the navy's port," Levnys says.

Davros leans out over the rail. At the end of the long expanse of water is a narrow entrance. Walls as thick as a building rise to protect it. Flanking the entrance are two statues—the Gethki six-winged dragon. Andereth, Lucius previously told him. She is wrought in marble, while everything around her is drab concrete. A more formidable set of watchtowers looms above the water.

Ralex shouts an order. The drums change. *Raven's Flight* slows to a snail's pace. Lucius eyes the statues, then glances over his shoulder at the trumpeter moving up the deck towards them, accompanied by Lucia. Lucius sighs. "I suppose," he says.

The trumpeter plays the Gethki imperial hymn. Both of the royals raise their hands to the sky. From Lucius' hands rise golden flame, from Lucia's, azure water. The magic spirals together in the air, and the counter-horns sound from the tower. *Raven's Flight* surges forward at Ralex's bellowed call, slipping through the entrance.

At Davros' puzzled expression, Lucius sighs again. "I don't like it, but we must speak to the *praefectus urbi* and *proconsul* as soon as possible. This way, we skip the line."

The casual way the titles of the most powerful people in the region roll off Lucius' tongue makes Davros' heart skip. Of course. This is the other side of his lover's life. Davros feels like he's been transported to the peak of a mountain when he was at its base a moment ago.

They emerge through the narrow opening, and Davros gasps. The naval harbor is a vast circular construction—an enormous concrete bowl filled with dark water. In the center rises a cylindrical tower painted gleaming white, decorated with banners of azure and gold. Nestled into the base of the building and ringing the periphery of the bowl are sheltered niches—dry docks, each large enough for a ship and her crew. Gethki warships bob like colorful toys on the water. *Raven's Flight* slips among them like a wraith, heading for the largest niche in the tower. Lucius stands tall with a raised chin, holding his back rigid. He cuts such a regal figure, with his rich cloak draped over an immaculate blue tunic.

The dock is much too large for their ship. As *Raven's Flight* is settled in the cavernous space, a group approaches the gangplank. One man, gray-haired and overweight, wears a senatorial toga with a crimson stripe. The other, tall and imposing, is clad in an immaculate golden breastplate wrought with snarling wyverns. Flanking them are a mix of city guards and legionnaires, clad head to heel in shining steel. Davros tries to slip away. This is so far above his social rank that he couldn't possibly be welcome.

Lucius puts a hand on his arm. "Please don't leave," he says. "I want you by my side."

Davros tries not to bite his lip. His chest swells with Lucius' words. Davros resigned himself to be kept in the background, separate from the inevitable public life the prince must navigate. Who would want to be seen with a no-name bard from a foreign land? Surely not the heir of the entire empire.

Once again, Lucius proves him wrong.

The regal mask settles on the prince's face as the welcoming party reaches the base of the gangplank. They all kneel with both knees on the ground, heads bowed. Lucius' fingers twitch. After several agonizing seconds, he says, "Rise. Approach."

The *praefectus* struggles to stand. Two of the guards haul him to his feet. Lucius' fingers twitch again. The *praefectus* and *proconsul* greet the royals coolly, but Levnys warmly. No one greets Davros at all. He's invisible, like the guards who barely acknowledge him. *Perfect.*

Davros lets the veneer of polite conversation wash over him. Instead, he observes, noting body language, appearance, shifting glances, and fake smiles.

Since that night with Lucius, he's developed a plan, turning it over and refining it. Although he has no status or wealth, there are things he does have—his voice, his shapeshifting, his magic.

You are the wind, the promise of spring, and you will lift the greatest of this land. Was this what Ava meant? It doesn't matter. It's everything he wanted.

"Excellent, Regillus," the *praefectus* says. "We will prepare for your arrival posthaste. It sounds like we have much to discuss."

They depart. As soon as they are out of sight, Lucius slumps. Lucia rolls her shoulder. Davros presses himself against Lucius' side, and the prince puts his arm around his waist.

"What now?" Davros asks.

"Let's get our things," Lucius says with tired resignation. "It's going to be a long evening."

XXVI
DEPARTURE

Pica

By the time the meeting ends, night's dark embrace grips the city. Pica stands on the stone balcony overlooking the harbor. Despite the late hour, ships come and go, dark shapes moving along dark water. The docks blaze with light. Oil lamps burn on anchored ships in the bay, turning it into a shimmering constellation, like the river of stars in the night sky. Pica savors the cool night air on his bare skin.

The *praefectus* insisted that they stay in Caltava's most prestigious inn—a fact he proclaimed as loudly as possible to the nobility crowded into the city's forum. They'd been taken instead to a modest but lovely house in the merchant district. Pica is grateful for the deception—no one is around to grovel and scrape for his attention, showering him with empty flattery and vapid words in exchange for royal favor. Bah. Gods curse the whole lot of those simpering leeches. Perhaps it would work with his father, but Pica has no tolerance for it.

Pica takes one last look at the harbor and turns away. Ah-Xoc-Xin rests quietly, as the entity does in the evening. The return of the serpent's presence has been strange, but they've settled into an acceptable coexistence. The serpent's emotions are clearer than ever, and Pica finds himself slipping into the peculiar spaces within their memories with ease. He tries not to dwell on Davros' revelation of more scales on his neck and chest. No matter what, he can only move forward along the path laid out before them.

Pica joins his lovers in the spacious bedchamber—a suite, in reality, though anything feels large compared to the ship's cramped cabin. The house has three rooms—a small sitting area, a sleeping chamber, and a private bath. It is tastefully furnished, with rich embroidered rugs and artful frescoes.

That night, he sleeps soundly, in a bed where his feet don't hang off the end and the wind doesn't rattle the shutters. There are no murmured voices of two hundred men, only the distant sound of the sea. This quiet calm sets his heart at peace in a way he never thought possible. Also present in his chest is a deep ache, a throbbing pain, because he knows, ultimately, what will happen. Soon, they will depart for Charris. Until then, he'll pretend, for a little while.

The next day, Pica finds Levnys and Davros entangled in a post-coital embrace. He can't hide his joy when he pulls both of them into a crushing hug, to the protests of Davros and the laughter of Levnys.

It's too easy to settle into life in Caltava. Pica feels at home in the warm city, with its white cobblestone streets and tall buildings, colorfully painted with frescoes. Levnys leaves before dawn each morning, rising into the cool morning air. Pica and Davros linger in bed, waking each other slowly with wandering hands and eager mouths. They take it slowly—sometimes, Davros' fear resurfaces, rising like a monster from the sea's depths. Pica wipes his tears, kisses his hair, lets him cry on his chest until the tremors fade. Each time, his heart breaks for his lover, as he tries and fails to understand how anyone could be so cruel.

At midmorning, Pica takes Davros on horseback down the winding streets to the wizard's tower. The slender building is more than it seems at first glance, as is the mage who resides there. The master wizard is a wrinkled Gethki man named Eligius, with wispy white hair, a stooped back, and eyes that miss nothing. Davros settles into his new job without much complaint, aside from a few pointed grumblings about the wizard's obsession with enchanting.

While he works, Pica visits the library, immersing himself in Caltava's vast collection. In the afternoons, after Davros' work is finished, Levnys joins them in exploring the new city. She takes them to the best places: the fish market, the vineyard, the *Circus* for the chariot races, the opulent bathhouse, and lively taverns. Each evening ends the same—enjoying each other's company with wine, stories, and lovemaking until the sun disappears below the horizon.

Today, it's early, right after dawn. The sweat dries on Pica's skin as the aftershocks of pleasure ebb out of his muscles. His lover yawns and rises out of the bed, stretching as she crosses the space to the wash basin.

The shapeshifter seems distant this morning, lost in thought as she cleans her face and hands. She pats her face dry and turns to him as he sits on the edge of the bed. Her green eyes catch the morning light filtering through the window, contrasting the black hair she chose for today.

"Good morning," Pica says. "You look lovely."

She blushes. "Thank you. Lucius, I..." She takes a few steps closer. "I think that..." Another two steps. "I want to show you my true form."

Pica opens his arms, and she settles sideways onto his lap. "I'd like that," he says.

She closes her eyes. "Don't speak too soon."

He rests his hands lightly on her back. The shapeshifter transforms. Her heart-shaped face narrows and stretches, shifting to a noble visage with high, delicate cheekbones. Hair shortens, seeming to retract into her scalp, then lightens to silvery-white, brushing ears that lengthen in long, tapered elegance.

Next comes the shapeshifter's body—hips narrow, shoulders widen as the female body shifts to male. Pica frowns when their smooth stomach falls inward, retracting rapidly as the skin tightens over prominent hip bones and ribs. Olive skin lightens in a ripple to pure white like freshly fallen snow. The paleness highlights the sharp bones of their arms and legs. Beneath Pica's hands, rough lines of scars rise, gray against the alabaster skin. Pica's heart sinks. Whipping scars.

Pica doesn't look at them, examining the other details of his lover. He wants to understand the reasons behind their apprehension and self-loathing. Here and there, light gray veins are visible beneath their skin. There's no pigment, no pink or brown underlying their tone. His lover's lips are light gray, as is the tongue that flicks out nervously between them.

The shapeshifter opens eyes rimmed with white lashes, their

irises bright silver against a black sclera. Pica strokes an alabaster cheek, waiting for his lover's trembling to lessen. He channels every scrap of affection he has for them into his thoughts, ensuring their auras mingle together.

"Hi," the shapeshifter says with a voice as thin as blown glass. "My name is Jin."

"Jin," Pica repeats. "Jin, what?"

"Just Jin. I only have one name."

"I like it," he says. At his lover's tiny twitch of a smile, he adds, "Let me tell you, you're—"

"Frightening? Hideous?" Jin supplies.

"Skinny," Pica says, running a finger over their collarbone. "I was right. You were starving."

"Uh, oh. Yeah." Jin glances down. "I was."

"You've been through some terrible things, haven't you?"

"I had a bad year. It's better now. Ava saved me, and so did you."

"I didn't do anything special."

Jin snorts. "You're wrong, but I won't argue about it. I have to leave eventually."

"Mmm, wise." Pica strokes Jin's cheek and runs his fingers along their tapered ear. His lover shivers and raises a snow-white hand to Pica's mouth, tracing his bottom lip with elegant fingers. Pica studies their shimmering silver eyes. "You're beautiful, Jin."

"No, I'm cursed," Jin protests.

"Cursed with what? Being cute?"

Jin's cheeks turn light gray. It takes Pica a second to realize his lover is blushing. "Did your grandmother ever tell you about the *sipu*?"

"It's a song, isn't it? Something about the end of days." He stares at his lover with sudden understanding. "Skin of winter's snow, eyes of spun moonlight. Oh, you think *you're* the *sipu*."

Jin cringes at the word. "It makes sense, doesn't it? Tiny, shriveled, milk-skinned shapeshifter who deceives people and brings forth the apocalypse. I'd say things are getting pretty apocalyptic with the appearance of those birds." Jin's voice becomes breathy. "Also, there's —"

Pica cups his lover's face, gently holding it fast. "No. I won't let you follow a thread of thought that's destroying you. Can I help you stop?" At Jin's nod, he says, "First of all, you're not 'tiny,' you're barely shorter than Petrus. I've known smaller legionnaires than you."

"B-but compared to you, I'm short and weak."

"Compared to me, everyone is weak. Strength *is* my strength." Pica smiles as Jin's nose wrinkles. "There are lots of things you're better at than me. You're so nimble and graceful. I'm a lumbering ox next to you. Also, I've seen what you can do with those hands. You're *very* good with them." He grins as Jin blushes harder. "Anyway, next point. *Shriveled*? You've been starved, and that's not your fault. *Next* point. 'Milk-skinned' is not how I'd describe you. You're like a blank fresco panel; your forms are the paint. You've made some gorgeous portraits so far—I'm smitten." Jin's silver eyes widen. "Well, I think the analogy is great. No, let me finish. Jin, my sweet lover, why don't you see you could also be the *suroribi?*"

"I can't convince myself it's true."

"I don't see a twisted, evil creature when I look at you. I see a sensitive soul with a big heart and bigger magic. You risked your life to save others, fought alongside us, and shared your wonderful voice. You say I saved you, but you also saved me." He kisses Jin on each cheek. "I don't care if you're the *sipu* or the *suroribi* or anything like that. I want you to be happy." Jin kisses him hard. Pica holds them close, stroking their hair and their cheek. "Thank you for trusting me," Pica says after their lips part. "I know this is hard for you. I'll never take it for granted."

"You mean it, gods. I can't believe it. You like my real form even though I'm skin and bones and paler than parchment?"

"It's you. I like *you*. Everything about you is so fascinating and wonderful, and I will remind you as much as you need me to."

"It's starting to sink in," Jin says.

"Good." Pica stares into those big silver eyes. "I want to ask you about something, but you don't have to answer if it's too much, alright?"

"Alright."

"Can I get a better look at your scars?"

Jin's breath catches, but they climb from Pica's lap and face away. Pica runs his palms over the gray welts. Most concentrate on the left side, with short and vicious cuts crisscrossing from shoulder to hips.

Pica wishes the pattern wasn't so familiar to him.

"Were you a slave?" Pica asks.

"Not officially," their tiny voice responds. "No one ever owned me, only confined me. Chains, fear, isolation."

"No papers I have to find and make go away?"

"No. People tried to hang onto me, but I always got away. The last one locked me in the hold whenever they got close to shore."

"You're so brave." Pica draws his lover back into his arms, turning Jin to face him. "I'm glad you made it out. How do you have scars? You're the best healer I know."

"Simple. I had to hide my magic lest I be abused worse. You know sailors are superstitious—I figured they'd kill me if they knew I'm a mage, let alone a shapeshifter. My wounds couldn't disappear. I kept myself from getting sick, at least."

"Who whipped you?" Pica asks flatly.

"Someone dead."

"Did you kill him?"

"*Yes.*" Jin spits the word. "He deserved it. I did it and got out the first chance I got."

"Good."

Jin settles back into his lap. "You don't care that I killed him?"

"No. Good riddance. If anyone else tries, kick their ass. I'm sure Levnys knows the best arbiter in this city."

"Can I get that in writing? Royal Decree from Regillus Pica: Kick their ass."

Pica chuckles. "I'll do whatever is needed to keep you safe. I want you to thrive, sweet lover. You'll never go back to that again." He runs his lips along their ear, eliciting a shiver. "*Live*, Jin, and heal so I can give you the life you deserve."

Jin grips his forearm. "You don't ask for much, do you?"

"Only everything you are."

"Is that all? Trade accepted. One little bard for one handsome prince."

"I'm coming out the richer," Pica says. "Are you hungry? We have time before I take you to Eligius' tower."

Jin's form rapidly shifts, and after a few seconds, Davros grins at him from his lap. "That sounds wonderful. Will you buy me some bread?"

Ah-Teya-Itzel must be stopped, Ah-Xoc-Xin says, pressing against Pica's senses. *He will only increase in strength.*

I wish we could find Andereth, Pica says. *She would be a big help.*

We do not have the time, they reply. *We must be patient, my friend.*

Friend. Pica supposes the serpent is, by now. They'd spent hours discussing theories about the celestial dragons, comparing histories, and combing through Ah-Xoc-Xin's fractured memories.

If we do something about Itzel, then the threat to Andereth will be neutralized, Pica admits reluctantly. Lately, he feels like he's on the verge of a breakthrough. Something in his memories nags at him like a splinter. Combing through his notes hasn't helped. Discussing it with Ah-Xoc-Xin hasn't either.

The serpent is correct, however. Itzel must be stopped. How, Pica doesn't know—they barely won with half a dozen dragons and two weeks of preparation. Now, they seek to challenge the entity directly —on Charris.

With Davros' help, Pica ensured coin landed in the pockets of a few dock workers. Every day, the rumors and stories pour in. Most are fabrications and exaggerations, but combing through the chaff reveals the seeds of truth: the Sparkling Coast is in crisis. Whole islands have been stripped of their populations. Pair that with the daily letters from Xemun, and the somber picture becomes clear. They must do something or the entire region will be left barren.

Their evening conversations take a darker turn. The shapeshifter stays silent, but their set jaw also tells Pica everything he needs to know.

The illusion of peace shatters. Every day, the paladins meet, and every day, they plan. Supplies. Old maps. Rumors. Finally, the day of departure is set, and Pica's heart is torn.

"I'm staying here," Jin says one morning. "I want to protect Caltava."

"I know, love."

Though Pica received the *proconsul's* reassurances of action, he knows all too well the empty promises generals make. Pica ensured Jin also met the leader of the auxiliary mages, just in case. Between them and the shapeshifter's link to the wizards, they may be able to hold out until the *proconsul* is forced to fight, whether through public pressure or Jin's machinations.

Jin has their own path. Over the last two weeks, the shapeshifter shared pieces of their work for Eligius, small indications of a much grander design. Pica barely understands the most basic explanation. One day, Eligius invites him inside, leading him through a richly decorated greeting room upstairs to his impressive personal library. In the tall room stacked floor-to-ceiling with scrolls and manuscripts, Pica finds the usual scholarly fare—a sturdy cedar desk piled with magical implements, quills, ink pots, and glimmering stones of all sizes. A series of concentric golden rings glowing with runes is set into the floor. Jagged pillars of stone three feet high are placed at the cardinal directions.

"This is what you wanted to show me?" Pica asks Davros.

"Yes. It's what we've been working on." Davros glances at Eligius. The wizard nods. "This is one of two points establishing an empire-wide network. Carbay is the other point, but we'll eventually add all seven cities. If we do it right, going between them will be like stepping through a doorway."

The implications crash against Pica like a wave. Oh gods, being able to travel from one end of the empire to another in moments rather than weeks. They could spread information quickly. He could comb the libraries. He could visit his son in Curia. His sister in Fresa. His grandparents in Selucia. His mother and siblings in Geth.

"Oh," he says, dumbfounded.

"You understand, Regillus, that this information doesn't leave this room," Eligius says. "Not yet."

"Right," Pica says numbly. "Why tell *me?*"

Eligius places his hand on the crimson stone next to him. It hums under his touch, pulsing with power. "If half of the things Davros tells me about you are true, Regillus, I'd be a fool not to." Eligius traces a finger over the ridge of stone. Motes of light chase it, swirling like a swarm of illuminated insects.

Pica glances at his lover, quirking his eyebrow. Davros flushes and smiles at him sheepishly. "I see," Pica says. "I look forward to seeing it."

* * *

The morning before Pica must leave, Levnys invites them to her lair for the evening. That afternoon, Pica finishes belting his tunic and walks from the bath. Jin stands from lacing their boots as he enters and gives him an uncertain smile.

"How do I look?" they ask, with gray spots high on their cheeks.

"Amazing," Pica says, studying them. "That's not how you wear a chiton, though."

Instead of tied and bunched at the shoulders, Jin has the chiton folded over the front of their body like a Soutorian kimono. The garment is belted with a wide sash of floral patterned turquoise cloth, emphasizing their too-thin waist. The soft pink of the chiton pairs wonderfully with their alabaster skin and bright silver eyes. An intricate cuff made of pink gemstones and delicate silver chain hugs one of their long ears—a gift from Levnys.

"I like it better this way," they reply wryly. "Only you and Levnys will see it, anyway."

"You're being very brave, my sweet," Pica says. "I'm proud of you."

Jin puts their arms around his waist and lays their head on his chest. "It's all because of you."

They meet Levnys in the courtyard. She nuzzles them both with her soft nose. Her eyes sweep over them before her jaws open in a grin. "Both of you look very nice. Come. I am eager to show you my home."

"Why did it take two weeks?" Pica teases. Levnys almost knocks him off his feet when she nudges him.

She holds out a hand, and Pica climbs into it, pulling Jin into his lap. "Don't drop us," Jin says.

"I would not dream of it," Levnys replies.

They rise rapidly into the air. Jin clings to Pica, trembling. Through their shared auras, Pica discovers it is not from fear but the cold spring wind. Pica pulls his cloak around them, cradling Jin against his chest. Neither of them take their eyes from the dragon's-eye view of Caltava.

The citadel's walls are hexagonal, enclosing the government buildings and temples with thick stone. Two more rings echo from the center like ripples on a pond, surrounding more and more of the city. Houses cling to the walls, with dirt paths crisscrossing like shattered pottery. The outskirts of the city sprawl to the water—a mishmash of villas, insulas, taverns, workshops, and brothels. Pica notes with bitterness that this is where most of the native Caltavians now live, outside the protection of the city walls that used to be theirs.

Several large roads lead west and southwest, crawling with insect-sized travelers. Vineyards and olive groves stretch to the north, gradually blending with the forest clinging to the sides of a looming volcano.

To the south is a cemetery. Some crypts are large enough to be seen from their height. A legion is stationed next to the somber expanse of concrete, nestled within their fortifications. Supply carts stream into it from the harbor, drawn in a long train by oxen and donkeys. The *proconsul* is keeping his word—so far. Hopefully, the legion will soon join the war for their Coast's survival.

They circle above the harbor. Pica can smell it. All big harbors have the same stench—fish, brine, and unwashed humanity. The slave market is there, too, its wooden platforms holding the sapient beings to be bought and sold like every other commodity. His stomach roils. The foul trade always disgusted him. Once he learned the filthy reality, he vowed to banish the entire practice. Though no attempt so far has succeeded, it doesn't mean he isn't going to try. His younger sister, Tiberia, currently lays the groundwork in Fresa, and he plans to join the fight when he returns.

Levnys takes them out over the bay. The view makes him breathless. Jin finds his hand and grips it, tucking their head under his chin. Levnys banks to the left, heading to the largest island in the bay. It's a vertical rock formation, rising above the water dramatically in contrast to the low specks of land surrounding it. The cliff face is constructed of large stones piled to mimic the sides of a natural formation. Trees and shrubs cling to its sides, brown and green against the black volcanic rock.

Jin nudges him, and they peer together into the water. Beneath the rolling waves is a dragon's skeleton, missing its head. Schools of fish weave between the enormous ribs. The seaweed clinging to the bones dances in the water—so much life, surrounded by death. Poor Levnys. She's reminded of her mother's death each time she comes home.

Levnys fans her wings, coasting to an opening set high into the side of the cliff. Marble pillars frame the entrance, thicker than any

Pica has ever seen. A grand lintel, gleaming white against the black stone, greets them with draconic glyphs glowing with blue light. Levnys lands, her claws barely ticking on the smooth blocks beneath her feet. Pica's legs tremble when he steps out of her hand. Jin clings to him, looking around with huge eyes.

"*Ata*, Levnys," they say. "This is fancy."

"My mother had good taste," Levnys replies wryly. "Wait here. You do not want to trigger the traps."

"Traps. Gods." Pica studies the marble beneath his feet. The blocks are threaded with color—branching pigments of blue and gold embedded into the stone itself. A forgotten art, Pica notes, lost during Anserus' purge. The throne in Geth is made of nearly identical materials. How powerful was Levnys' mother? Pica remembers the skeleton and shivers. It was enormous, much larger than Gythu. He didn't know dragons could get that big.

Levnys touches the walls of the grand arch, pressing her claws into indentations in the stone. Sparks leap from her fingers into the rock. Light flows down grooves, twisting and turning the length of an enormous corridor into the island. Pica whistles. "Come," Levnys says, starting down the corridor. Jin's fingers intertwine with his, following her along the glowing hallway.

Their feet squeak on the polished marble as Levnys leads them deeper into the cavern. She stops at the edge of a black expanse and lowers her head to their height. Her turquoise eyes gleam in the fey light radiating from the walls.

"Welcome to my home, my loves," she says. "I hope you like it."

Turquoise light filters from pools ringing the perimeter of a gargantuan cavern. In the center of each pool, a statue is placed on a plinth. Both dragons and humans are depicted in more of the same marble as the entrance. In the middle of it all is a vast pool, with lily pads twice as wide as Pica is tall. More light emerges beneath the rippling surface from rocks shaped like seashells. Plush dragon-sized couches sit to the side, flanked by low tables.

They're not what Pica stares at. As the light shifts from turquoise to yellow, the cavern comes into full view and, with it, the focus of Pica's attention. For there, placed like a toy on display, is a Gethki warship. Pica tries to drag two thoughts together. How? *Why?*

Are you alright? Ah-Xoc-Xin asks, alarmed by his shock.

I'm. Uh. Wow. Even in his thoughts, he's speechless. His feet move before he knows it, dragging a protesting Jin behind him. Levnys' laugh echoes through the bowl-shaped chamber.

Pica reaches the ship, staring at it with his heart in his throat. Three files of reinforced oars bristle from the ship's sides, like *Raven's Flight*, but much larger. The bronze ram is polished to a mirror shine. This ship's eye is azure, shot through with lighter blues. On the sail is a painted dragon—not Andereth, as would be the norm, but Levnys, turquoise-tipped wings spread wide in flight.

Jin prods Pica in the side. "Explain, please."

"It's a quinquereme—the newest type." Pica points at the figurehead. "Ram class, for Solis. We started producing these ten years ago." Pica runs his hand over the sleek wood, then turns to Levnys. "How do you have one?"

"This ship was constructed in Caltava's shipyard. It was a gift from the *proconsul* before this one. He wanted to thank me for helping him through the first years of his deployment." Levnys touches the railing. "We meet for drinks, sometimes." She walks past the ship toward the sloping edge of the cavern. "Come. There is more to see."

"What? You have more?"

"Indeed."

They follow her. Pica spares a glance at Jin, who smirks up at him. "What?" he asks.

"Nothing, enjoying seeing you flustered. Come on, I want to see what else she has."

They pass through an arched opening. As the lights rise and the contents become visible, Pica laughs. "Dragons. Gods, this is not what comes to mind when I think of a 'hoard.'"

"Did you think I would sleep on an enormous pile of gold?" Levnys inquires.

"You haven't?" Jin asks.

"It does not sound comfortable." She tilts her head at the room. "Go on. Inspect them. I wish to hear your thoughts."

This room is square, much smaller than the cavern behind them. It could still fit an entire legionnaire camp inside of it—an ironic thought, considering the contents. On the left side of the chamber, in sword-straight rows, are 20 complete sets of centurion's *lorica*, each enameled a different color. The banded breastplates are overlaid by round disks of silver, gleaming on their leather straps like polished coins. A plumed helmet, shield, two *pila*, and *gladius* accompany each set, along with a banner on a crossbar. A row of horse statues runs along the wall, armored in chain and leather. Ringing this half of the room are dozens of colorful shields of blue and gold, each painted with Andereth's sigil.

Pica stops in front of a set, running his fingers along the polished blue steel. He carefully studies the straps, the weapons, settling on the roaring dragon depicted in teal and blue on the hanging standard.

"I wore these colors," Pica says softly. "The eighth, out of the mother city herself." He touches the hilt of the *gladius*. "These have never been worn. It's an older style, from 60 years or so ago. The leather is different, as is the enamel." Pica looks over the other sets. "They're all from different time periods. This is the newest." Pica touches the shoulder of the red armor next to him. "The ninth was re-founded twenty years ago."

He turns to face the other side of the room. In contrast with the neat rows of Gethki equipment, these pieces appear disorganized, although Pica doubts that. Mounted on a stand in the middle of the motley mix of gear is a pair of double-headed axes, crossed at their hilts—the symbol of Caltava and their signature weapon. More mannequins, adorned in leather and chain mail, surround it, varying wildly in styles. Here is a horse statue, clad in light leather barding, with a short bow mounted on a rack next to it. There is a war chariot, outdated by one hundred years. Pica walks between them, touching the shoulder of each. "Lutecia. Nidia. Curia. Fresa. Caltava. Fetocia. Isca. All never worn."

He turns to Levnys. She watches him expectantly. He gathers his thoughts and indicates the Fetocian armor. "This one is also 60 years old, like the eighth." Pica swallows. "Each piece is from when the Gethki took over each culture, right?"

"Yes, Lucius." Levnys lowers her head. "I was curious if you would notice."

"I didn't know you had this," Pica says. "Why?"

"It fascinates me how humans fight and conquer, especially your people." She turns and heads for the archway. "We have one more room. Come."

Jin touches Pica's arm. Pica feels their magic permeate his skin. The shapeshifter is reading his mood. "Are you alright? I imagine this isn't easy for you."

"I'll manage. It's a wonderfully complete collection. A scholar's dream." He gives Jin a reassuring smile but knows they aren't fooled. The collection unsettles him—so much war distilled into a clean display. "Come, let's not keep her waiting."

The last room isn't what Pica expected. It's stacked floor-to-ceiling with scrolls and stone tablets. Hanging from the ceiling is a set of bronze armor made to fit a dragon much larger than Levnys. Unlike the pristine equipment of the other display, the armor is covered with scratches and dents, marring the thick plates. Glowing runes, like the ones above the entrance, are etched into it, pulsing with blue light.

Pica stares at it for a long time. He's heard of the dragon war that transpired in this region centuries ago, but to see something like this—his stomach churns at the thought of a battle where this equipment was needed.

Eventually, he drags his gaze away and scans the rest of the room. Nestled between shelves are myriad other items: runic axes, gladiator armor, and old weapons he doesn't recognize, made of bronze and stone. Jin touches the sheath of a thin Soutorian blade. Everything here is made for war, Pica realizes—like him.

Levnys moves to the center of the room. An enormous circular bed piled high with cushions is nestled into a recess in the marble floor. Tables laden with food and wine are set next to them—cheese, bread, olives, dates, dried fish, and several cooked birds stuffed with something fragrant and mouth-watering. Some of Tisu's desserts are there, too—honey cakes and fruit pies set onto enchanted warming stones.

Levnys settles onto a cushion and transforms, reclining in her human form against a plush pillow. Power pulses through the room, thick and alluring, and Pica swallows. Jin turns from the sword to stare at Levnys.

"Join me," the dragon says, crooking her finger.

The wine flows like a river between them. Pica pushes away all thoughts of tomorrow and all worries for the future. It's easy to forget everything, with his head swimming and hot mouths on his body. He immerses himself in the magic of the place, drawing his lovers' ecstasy into him. The melange is sweeter than honey cakes, more intoxicating than mead. He drinks of it like a man parched, savoring every drop.

Levnys draws Jin down, guiding them inside her. Pica runs his hands over their undulating bodies, sensing the magic building, pressing against his skin like a heat haze. He positions himself between Jin's legs, slipping oiled fingers inside, teasing them. Jin's moans turn desperate, and Pica can't hold it back anymore. He presses himself inside the shapeshifter, pushing both Jin and Levnys beneath him into the soft bed. He slides his hand under Levnys' hips. Their bodies move in rhythm, Pica's thrusts driving Jin deeper into Levnys' body. The shapeshifter's legs shake with uncontrolled pleasure. The press of bodies, the sweat, the sounds of their lovemaking—they drive him to the brink.

Glowing lines appear in the walls, pulsing with dim blue light. As the three of them move, the pulsing speeds as their heart rates do, colors shifting from deep blue to green to yellow, increasing in brightness. Finally, they blaze white, bathing the cavern in blinding brilliance as Levnys gasps and shudders beneath them. The magic hits him like a wave, and he is lost. The dragon's presence is overpowering here, in *her* domain, at the peak of her strength. He and Jin climax at the same time, overwhelmed by the melange of magic and power.

The lights fade as they stretch out next to her. Pica puts his arm over Jin and Levnys, resting his cheek on a pillow above their heads. Levnys plays with Jin's silken hair as the shapeshifter buries their face under her chin. "I am happy to be home," Levnys says. "I am also glad both of you are here."

"I noticed," Pica says. "Is that going to happen every time?"

"No. I wanted to give you both a show."

"It worked," Jin says.

"Do you have control over everything here?" Pica asks.

"Yes. My power is in the very stones. Nothing happens here that I am not aware of, should I be in attendance."

"I like it," Jin says.

Levnys touches each of their cheeks. "I know we will all be apart for a while, but after that..." She kisses each of them. "I will build you both a home here if you wish."

A home. Pica's heart longs for such a thing. Jin buries their face against Levnys' shoulder, embracing her. Pica says, "I'd love that, Lev."

"Let us not worry about it further," she continues. "I do not wish to speak of tomorrow; I will only enjoy your company tonight."

The sky is too beautiful for such a somber day. The sun is warm, stirring Pica's magic pleasantly. Ah-Xoc-Xin basks in the glow, but Pica broods through the extended ritual of political send-offs. He plasters a polite smile on his face for the nobles and legionnaires, but all he wants to do is bury his face in his hands and cry.

Finally, they leave with empty promises and emptier words, back to their comfortable lives while Pica wallows in pain and turmoil.

Only Levnys and Davros remain near. The crew and his companions give them space. At this moment, words fail him. What can he say? Every part of him longs to remain, to return to the warmth of his lovers' arms and the peace they represent. They've given him a taste of a life without violence and pain, a stable and happy place where he can live the life he yearns for. Leaving them is like tearing the scab from a healing wound.

Davros throws himself into his arms, burying his face into Pica's tunic, his body wracked with sobs. The anguish coming from his aura is too much to bear. Pica can't leave like this. What if he never sees them again? What if he dies on a forsaken island with regret in his heart?

Levnys lays her hand on Davros' shoulder, wrapping an arm around the sobbing bard. Pica embraces them both, pulling their bodies close to his. He can't control the tears. They tumble down his cheeks freely. He doesn't want to go. Gods curse him. All he wants in his life is right here.

"I'll come back to you," he says. "I swear it."

"Don't you dare die," Davros says. "I'll never forgive you."

Levnys remains tearless, but Pica knows she's in turmoil. He can tell by her downcast eyes and slumped shoulders. He rubs his hand across her back, trying to soothe her in a way he can't soothe himself.

"Neither of you better die," Davros repeats. "I can't live without you."

"You can," Levnys says. "I'll be back, too."

Levnys made the decision Pica knew she would—to join the fight raging out there on her precious Coast. The comforting illusion he let himself be absorbed in breaks for good, leaving him empty. He must return. There's so much left undone, so much love for him, here in a city that feels like home.

The horn sounds. Crewmen stream around them, giving them a wide berth and only the barest of glances, and Pica knows his time grows short.

He bends and kisses each of his lovers with trembling lips. "Be strong," he whispers to them. "We'll see each other again."

"Be strong," Davros echoes. "Fly high, magpie, and don't you dare die."

Pica holds them until the second horn sounds. Each step away from them feels like it will drag him down and make him stay. He can't remain. Too many lives depend on him and on the ship he now boards. Levnys and Davros stand together, watching him with their arms around each other. Sparax's hand settles on his back when Pica stands at the rail. It's not too late. He can still go to them. Calvus would understand.

He doesn't move. The drums pound beneath his feet. *Raven's Flight* is shoved down the rails into the churning blue water. He's a strong swimmer—if he jumped over now, he could make it back. Lucia would forgive him.

He doesn't jump. Kisara joins him at the rail, putting her arms around his shoulders. Pica leans against his sister, the tears blurring his vision. The oars splash as they deploy. The ship surges forward, leaving the dock behind. Kisara could transform, take him back. Surely, he could convince her.

He doesn't speak. *Raven's Flight* leaps ahead, threading her way through the navy ships and into the trade harbor. Pica doesn't tear his eyes away until they are into the bay itself. He slumps to his knees, burying his face in his hands. He doesn't bother to hold back his sobs. He brushes the enchantment in his cloak with trembling fingers, letting Jin's sweet voice fill his head—a quiet lament.

Kisara and Sparax remain at his side. He leans on them, grateful for their silent strength. Although his heart feels as if it's been torn from his chest, somewhere deep inside of him, a voice reminds him he's not alone. None of them are alone.

And now, more than ever, he has a reason to fight.

EPILOGUE

Paladin

The wax bulges from under Pica's ring as he seals the last letter. His eyes burn with fatigue and oft-shed tears. He rubs them and yawns, stowing the letters in his bag for that night's landing. Most are official missives—orders to the groups moving on his behalf. Two of them are more personal. Soon, they will move out of Gethki waters, and the certainty of the letters' delivery will be in question.

Do you wish to speak about it? Ah-Xoc-Xin inquires. *You seem upset.*

Later, he replies to the serpent. After a pause, he adds, *Thanks for checking on me.*

It is not a problem. I wish you to be well, my friend.

Pica pulls out his research scroll and pours over it, attempting to concentrate. The cabin feels enormous with only him in it, and he tries to distract himself, to no avail. He lifts the winged goblet Levnys gave him and takes a sip of *posca*, rubbing his eyes.

Sparax walks in without knocking. Pica looks up and tries to smile. "Hi," he says.

"Heya." Sparax rests his hand on Pica's shoulder, squeezing it. "Come with me. It's time to train."

Pica nods numbly. Some action will do him good. Hasn't he always trained to keep himself occupied? Isn't this merely one more kind of pain?

He joins his companions on deck as *Raven's Flight* slips westward into the unknown.

Bard

Davros lets the sound of stomping feet wash over him as he plucks the last chords to his new song. His fingers tingle as he mutes the vibrating strings.

He finished the song yesterday—a complex, upbeat tune, building with each verse to a raucous climax. It's meant to invoke escalating determination in the face of never-ending adversity. Judging from the reaction of the tavern's patrons, they like the beat, at least.

He pauses a few seconds before starting a Caltavian drinking song. High-spirited chaos erupts as he sings the song's guttural words. He doesn't worry about his performance—the crowd will drown him out with their drunken rendition anyway. He can let his mind wander.

It's been days since Lucius and Levnys left him. It took all of his willpower to remain behind, safe while they go off to fight. He's poured his energy into his music and enchanting, determined to make something of himself.

The new song is a start. He's immeasurably proud of it, certain he's captured the essence of Lucius' strength in his music. The entire affair makes his head spin. He feels like a tiny fly caught in a maelstrom, struggling to keep his wings.

He finishes the song and starts another, his fingers flying through the familiar chords, his voice floating over the top of the din. He pours magic into it, making it resonate through the room. His light foot taps become a booming drum. He adds layers of illusory sound to the music: a trilling flute, a melodic lyre, and additional vocals in complicated harmony.

This is what he will do. He will play his new song, and others, every night. The tale of the prince's determination will spread, and soon, the words will be on everyone's lips, the dramatic opening chords easily recognizable. His voice will lift them all. He wonders what the view is like from the top.

Dragon

Levnys' wings flex to catch an updraft, and she soars higher, rising through the wispy clouds. She has been on the wing all day, the endless water stretching beneath her. It is dotted with ships and islands as far as she can see. Migrating birds join her in the sky, heading north to their spring nesting grounds on the Gethki mainland. The cries of gulls are an ever-present accompaniment.

She has been traveling for days now. Her nights are lonely without the company of her lovers, and she wonders how they fare. The sound of Jin's sobs and Lucius' anguish, when they parted, tore her heart to shreds.

Her winged goblet, twin to the one she gave Lucius, is nestled deep inside one of her new bags. There are several of them strapped over her back legs, rump, and between her wings. The new leather straps creak as she moves. They are durable and waterproof, protecting her cargo as she flies headlong into danger. The bags are not all she carries. She suspected it for a few days, but now she is sure.

She is pregnant.

At first, she could not believe it. She mated only with Lucius during her fertility. It should not be possible—human males can not impregnate a female dragon. It only works the other way around.

Perhaps the serpent made it possible. It is the only plausible explanation. It adds a desperate note to the entire mission. She can only fight for a few months before laying her eggs. She clenches her jaws together. If she does not fight, there will be no safe place for anyone on the Sparkling Coast. She will join the others and protect her home.

She wrote a letter as soon as possible, hoping it would catch Lucius before he left Gethki waters. It was all she could do.

Levnys cannot allow herself to wallow in despair. She pumps her wings harder, speeding toward an island visible on the horizon. She will rest there, then fly onward. She must keep going. She must never stop.

About the Author

V.L Lanius, also known as Vee, is a queer author and artist from the Midwest United States with an unhealthy obsession with ancient history. In their free time, they enjoy drawing, video games, board games, and miniature painting.

Acknowledgments

To my partner, who has steadfastly remained by my side through all of life's trials, including writing this book.

To my parents, who got me hooked on books as soon as humanly possible.

To the Ussies. It takes a village to raise a child, and the same is true for books.

To glizzy, for the advice, the community, and the wake-up call.

To Honey, for your enthusiasm and wild theories.

To Story Spellcraft, my developmental editor, for helping me give RMO the emotional punch it needed.

To Liv Betz, my copy editor, for adding the final, essential polish.

To all my beta and alpha readers, without whom this story would still be a meandering mess.

To my tabletop RPG party, past and present, who wanted to play in this humble little world of mine.

To you, reader, for taking a chance on a queer little indie series.

Pronunciation Guide

Geth - Get

Andereth - Ahn-der-et

Lucius - Loo-ki-us

Draconius - Drah-cone-ee-oos

Regillus - Reh-geel-loos

Pica - Pee-kah

Levnys - Lev-nees

Ah-Xoc-Xin - Ah-Shok-Shin

Ah-Uaya-Nih - Ah-oo-ah-ya-nee

Ah-Teya-Itzel - Ah-te-yah-eet-sel

suroribi - soo-roh-ree-bee

GLOSSARY OF TERMS

An asterisk denotes a conlang or fictional term

Disclaimer: Many terms were taken from ancient Rome and its contemporaries, but due to artistic license, may not be used in the same context or have the same meanings. This book is a work of fiction and should not be used as reference material.

agnomen — An additional component to the ancient Roman naming conventions, usually related to a person's achievements.

*Agymah — A semi-arid region in the northeast portion of Tekan.

amphitheater — An oval- or circular-shaped open-air stadium, with tiered seating, generally used for gladiatorial games and executions.

amphora — *pl. amphorae.* A tall ancient Greek or Roman jar with two handles and a narrow neck.

*Aquillus — An agnomen derived from the Latin word for "eagle," *aquila*, representing a former or current Emperor.

*Arundo, the — An extinct race of tree-like sapient bipeds native to the Agymah region in Tekan.

*ata — Soutorian exclamation or curse, roughly equivalent to "damn."

aurochs — A large bovine with enormous horns.

ballista — *pl. ballistae.* An ancient missile weapon that launched bolts or stones at a target.

cacao — The dried seed of the cacao tree, from which chocolate can be derived, used commonly as currency in Mesoamerican cultures.

calamus — A hollow reed used as a pen in ancient Rome.

*Caltava — A southern island city known for its shipyards.

*Carbay — A northern fortress city nestled at the foot of the Skypiercer mountain range.

centurion — An elected officer in command of a century, or one hundred men, in an ancient Roman legion: 80 combat legionaries and 20 support staff.

*Charris — A western island at the furthest reaches of the Gethki Empire's trade network.

chiton — A form of tunic that fastens at the shoulder, worn in ancient Greece and Rome.

Circus — A large, open-air venue used mainly for chariot racing.

cleric — A magic user with healing magic, usually from a divine source.

cognomen — The third name in the Roman naming convention, usually a nickname.

cohort — A military unit in an ancient Roman legion, generally composed of 480 soldiers (six centuries). Ten cohorts would constitute a legion.

conditum — A spiced wine flavored with honey, pepper, mastic, laurel, saffron, and dates.

*Contradraco — Derived from Latin and meaning "against dragons," this paladin order led an extermination of the Sparkling Coast's dragon population.

*Curia — A large city nestled into a vast bay on the southern coast of the Gethki mainland, known for its many canals and rich trade.

*Dalos — A large island off the coast of the Gethki mainland, in the Sparkling Coast. Home of the last dragon enclave.

dango — A Japanese dumpling made with rice flour, eaten with sugar, syrup, red bean paste, and other sweeteners, generally made into round shapes and served on a skewer.

dominus — A Latin term for "Lord" or "Owner," commonly used by slaves to address their masters.

*Draconius — The nomen of the royal family, derived from the Latin word for "dragon."

drakaina — A Greek word for "female dragon," sometimes depicted with human-like features.

*Eugaria — The western continent with a long history. The region known as Soutori is the primary contact for the Gethki empire.

exomis — A Greek sleeveless tunic, generally worn over one shoulder for freedom of movement.

*felina — A global race of sapient bipeds resembling various species of felines, including lions, jaguars, and wildcats.

*Fetocia — The greater northern region at the edges of the Gethki empire, encompassing the cities of Carbay and Selucia.

Forum — The central public space in an ancient Roman city, serving as a political, religious, and social hub.

*Fresa — A large coastal city on the north side of the big southern island, known for its stunning architecture.

fresco — A painting technique where pigment is applied to fresh plaster.

*Fulminus/Fulmina — The title given to a mage specializing in lightning magic, generally associated with a legion.

*Geth — The mother city and namesake of the Gethki Empire and the seat of its power.

gladiator — An armed combatant who entertained audiences via violent confrontations with animals or other gladiators.

gladius — A short thrusting sword used by Roman soldiers.

garum — A fermented fish sauce used widely in antiquity.

harpax — An iron grappling hook designed to capture enemy ships.

insula — An apartment building found in urban centers.

*Isca — A small city situated at the straits between the Gethki Empire and Sardiora, known for its impressive lighthouse.

kimono — A traditional Japanese garment wrapped in the front and secured with a wide sash.

lantriculi — Also known as *Ludus latrunculorm*. A two player strategy game resembling chess.

legion — The largest military unit in the ancient Roman army, comprised of approximately 4,800 men (10 cohorts).

lorica — Latin term for "body armor." Though the lorica segmentata (banded plate armor) is the most commonly depicted style, there was a wide variation throughout Roman history.

*Lutecia — The first territory conquered by the Gethki empire, granting it access to sea trade.

mage — A spell caster blessed with elemental bloodline magic.

mosaic — A pattern or image made of small pieces of colored stone, glass, or ceramic held in place by mortar.

*Negasi, the — A group of human refugees from the western region of Tekan, forced to flee north due to persecution. The main diaspora resides in Selucia.

*Nidia — A region conquered by the Gethki Empire early in its imperial history.

nomen — The family or clan name in ancient Roman naming conventions.

*Notri — A large island on the trade route between Curia and Caltava, known for its expansive brothel district.

*notuda — Soutorian for "noble one" or "nobility."

*o-sanribi — A nine-tailed divine fox worshiped in Soutori. The prefix "o-" denotes a concept of "above all" or "greatest," and is used for the queen of the divine foxes.

paladin — A warrior imbued with power from a deity or divine entity who specializes in battle magic.

passum — A wine derived from semi-dried grapes developed in ancient Carthage.

pater — Latin for "father," used as a term for a demi-god who has granted a mortal divine powers.

pilum — *pl. pila.* A javelin/missile weapon used by the ancient Roman army, with a pyramid-shaped head.

posca — An ancient Roman drink made by mixing water and wine vinegar, generally consumed by soldiers and slaves.

praefectus urbi — A ceremonial magistrate position in the city of Rome. Used as a term for a regional urban leader in-universe.

praenomen — The first, or personal, name in the Roman naming convention. Only around a dozen were common by the first century BCE.

proconsul — An official of ancient Rome who acted on behalf of a consul, generally during military campaigns. Used in-universe as a military commander under the authority of the Emperor.

prosit — A word used to wish luck and good health before drinking.

quadrireme — An ancient war galley with two banks or levels of oars, with two rowers per oar, sometimes referred to as "fours."

quinquereme — An ancient war galley with three banks or levels of oars, with a 2-2-1 rower arrangement, sometimes referred to as "fives."

*Regillus — An agnomen derived from the Roman cognomen meaning "prince." Used in-universe as an honorific for those born with the royal bloodline magic.

*Sardiora — A continent to the far east. Not much is known about its inhabitants due to distance. Most migrants are the draconic wyverni.

*Selucia — A northern coastal city with a rich history of trade with Eugaria, the western continent.

*sipu — A malicious shapeshifter from Soutorian folklore, known best for its duplicitous and manipulative nature. One of two entities in the Soutorian apocalypse myth. *See also: suroribi.*

*sita — A Soutorian word used in a dedication or toast, like "cheers."

*Soutori — A culture inhabiting the coast of Eugaria facing Geth. Though the sea crossing is perilous, there is a healthy trade and ideas network between the two empires, though they remain culturally distinct.

stola — A type of dress worn by married Roman women as a counterpart to the toga. Used a bit more loosely in-universe.

*suroribi — A five-tailed shapeshifting divine fox spirit from Soutorian folklore. One of two entities in the Soutorian apocalypse myth. *See also: sipu.*

*suya — Soutorian for "please."

tabi — A type of split-toed boot, later becoming a type of sock worn with thonged sandals.

Tali — A type of chance game played by rolling knuckle bones.

Tekan — A vast continent to the south of the Gethki empire. Trade with the northern and northwestern coasts is frequent, although the remainder of the land is unknown to the Gethki.

*The Sparkling Coast — A sea between the Gethki mainland and the two southern islands, known for its abundance of food and rich trade.

toga — A semicircular cloth between 12 and 20 feet in length, draped over the shoulders and around the body. Restricted to Roman citizens, it was seen as a type of formal wear, much like a suit.

triclinium — A formal dining room with three lounging couches surrounding a low table.

trireme — An ancient war galley with three banks of oars, with one rower per oar.

tunic — A simple garment covering the torso, reaching from the shoulders to somewhere between the hips and ankles. Many variations exist. *See chiton; exomis.*

*Utuka — An old draconic word meaning "sunrise," or, more rarely, "born in the sun."

wizard — A type of magic user who specializes in enchantments.

*wyverni — A race of draconic, sapient bipeds from the continent of Sardiora.

*yenok — A large, hairy bovine native to Soutori.

*zata — A Soutorian word meaning "affirmative," generally used when receiving orders.

*zygius — A variation on the Greek word *zygitai*, denoting a rower from the middle row of a trireme.

The Gethki Pantheon

Olomilo
God of the Sky
God of the heavens, father who sired the earth.
Depicted as a dragon surrounded by thunderclouds.

Naltia
Goddess of the Sea
Mother who birthed the earth.
Depicted as a sea serpent in a school of colorful fish.

Solis
God of the Sun
God of warmth and daylight.
Depicted as a ram.

Cetuna
Goddess of the Moon
Goddess of the starry sky and cool darkness.
Depicted as a blue wolf.

Zalaris
Goddess of War
Goddess of the legions, valor and glory.
Depicted as a blood-red mare.

Zeties
God of Peace.
God of diplomacy, oration, & democracy.
Depicted as a white stag.

Oros
God of the forge
God of metalworking, armor and shields.
Depicted as a bull.

VIHNA
Goddess of the bow
Goddess of woodworking & hunting.
Depicted as a hunting hound.

OGTRIS
Goddess of art
Goddess of poetry, music, and sex.
Depicted as a fox.

EBRIS
God of magic
Depicted as a black cat.

DYDIA
Goddess of Spring.
Represents rebirth, flowers, & fertility.
Depicted as a sparrow with red feathers.
Aspect of the East.

ULIOS
God of Summer.
Represents explosive growth, olives, wine, and celebration.
Depicted as an eagle.
Aspect of the South

DOHMOS
God of Autumn.
Represents the harvest, the home & family.
Depicted as a golden pheasant.
Aspect of the West.

UKTON
Goddess of Winter.
Represents death, decay, and the underworld.
Depicted by a raven with white-tipped wings.
Aspect of the North.